FATAL STRIKE

SHANNON MCKENNA

ZEBRA BOOKS
KENSINGTON PUBLISHING CORP.
http://www.kensingtonbooks.com

ZEBRA BOOKS are published by

Kensington Publishing Corp.
119 West 40th Street
New York, NY 10018

First Kensington Books Trade Paperback Printing: October 2013
First Zebra Books Mass-Market Paperback Printing: May 2014
ISBN-13: 978-1-4201-4241-9
ISBN-10: 1-4201-4241-0

10 9 8 7 6 5 4 3

Printed in the United States of America

PROLOGUE

"She's lost six pounds since last week, sir," Jason Hu said. Thaddeus Greaves gazed through the vidcam monitor at the young woman inside the cell. Lara Kirk stood with her back to him. Sharp shoulder blades pressed against her cotton jersey tank. Loose pants hung on her thin but still graceful form. Her slender back radiated defiance. She was conscious of being observed, though she could not see them. Full of psi talent, even unenhanced. He tasted it in the air, like smoke.

Like Geoff. The similarities stirred disturbing memories.

Her long, dark hair dangled as she sank into a perfect backbend. Her tank top slid down, too, revealing her ribcage. The top snagged on the curve of her breast. He waited, breathless, for it to slip enough and show him her nipple. It did not. "Other changes?" he asked.

"She no longer cries, or talks to herself, or sings. That stopped about a month ago. She spends her time meditating, doing gymnastics—"

"Yoga," Greaves corrected. "She's doing yoga, Hu."

"Ah, yes. Blood samples show her iron is low. I've supplemented her food, but she averages six to seven hundred calories a day."

"That can't go on indefinitely," Greaves said.

"We could use a feeding tube," Hu suggested.

Greaves grimaced in distaste. "Any progress with the new psi-max formula? Who was the latest volunteer?"

Hu hesitated. "Silva went today," he said. "I went the day before that, and Miranda before that. Our best duration so far is less than ten hours. Without the A component, we're still stabbing in the dark."

Lara Kirk kicked up a slender leg. The pant legs pooled around her thighs as she did a hand-stand. The shirt sagged lower, and her nipple was revealed. Her slim arms trembled. They did not look strong enough to bear her weight, yet they did. Her eyes were wide, intensely focused, the message as loud as if she screamed it. You. Have. Not. Broken. Me.

Greaves was stirred. Something steely and indomitable about her called to him. He stared hungrily as she folded her body, and stood.

"Has she manifested psi abilities?" he asked.

"We never dosed her," Hu said, defensive. "You never authorized—"

"I mean naturally," Greaves snapped.

Hu looked clouded. "Haven't noticed. Couldn't rule it out, I guess."

Beautiful, how she held herself. That remote dignity. Geoff had been an artist and visionary, too. She was an extremely talented sculptor. He owned a number of her pieces already. They called to his soul.

He made a snap decision. "Dose her," he ordered.

Hu blinked. "But the formula's not perfected. Without Helga, we can't even be sure she'll survive first-dose. You're sure we should—"

"I'm sure." He stared, as Lara sank into a deep lunge, and then arched her arms back, like a bow pulled taut.

Greaves licked his lips. "Do it right now," he said. "I want to watch."

1

Stop thinking about her. Stop thinking at all.

Miles stared up at the volcanic granite that reared above him in the dim light of dawn, scanning for handholds, footholds. He channeled a surge of fresh energy into his mental shield. Thinking about Lara Kirk was not useful, but he'd never been good at suppressing unwanted thoughts, even before being reduced to his current suck-ass state.

And the dreams, holy God, what was up with that? White hot, thundering erotic dreams about her, every single night. What kind of scumbag dreamed nightly of nailing the girl that he'd *failed* to rescue? If he'd saved her, he'd be halfway entitled to his horndog fantasies. But as it was, no way.

Every night, as he prepared for sleep, he gave himself the stern pep talk. Tonight, he chose how he behaved in his dream. People could. He'd read about it. But it didn't matter. When she came to him, his dream self did not give a fuck what his waking self wanted. His dream self wanted her, and wanted her bad. Deep, hard, every which way. When she showed up, he seized her, went at her like a maniac.

It was as disturbing as it was exciting.

He remembered every last detail when he woke, in laser

sharp detail. No foggy dream lens, no fade-outs. Her sweet, salty taste, her satiny thick hair twisted into his fingers. Her body moving against his. Strong, slender. Hot and slick. He could feel it right now. He could practically smell her lube on his fingers. And, man, he'd done it again.

He contemplated his newly refreshed hard-on, dismayed. The guys with the white coats should just take him and his perpetual stiffie away before he hurt himself.

You tried to help. It didn't work out. Climb the cliff. Don't think about Lara Kirk. Don't think at all.

He stared up, calculating the best ascent. Neutral data, crunched through algorithms. Conclusions organized into neat categories, rank and file. As long as his mind shield was up and running strong, he was chill. He had errant thoughts, but they did not play themselves out through his glands. They just flickered on the edge of his mind, like a TV screen he was barely following.

But if his mental shield wavered, man, it was blitzkrieg. Full on screaming stress flashbacks, of Rudd's attack at Spruce Ridge.

He'd gotten better at keeping the shield strong, up here in the mountains. Weeks of constant, grinding practice had yielded him at least that much. He'd discovered the uses of rock climbing the second week. The tight mental focus it required pulled him together, somehow. Free climbing, of course, since climbing equipment hadn't been on his supply list. That was okay. The harder the better, for his purposes.

He pulled off his boots. He needed monkey toes to climb that big bastard, but he'd make do with what God gave him. He studied the big overhang, the stretch where basaltic lava had formed long, crystalline striations, as if a huge beast had clawed violently downward. There were cracks and crannies, maybe big enough for fingertips, maybe not. He cataloged them all. His eyes were sharper than before Spruce Ridge, and his memory, too. Sharp, like all of him. Sharp like broken glass.

To counteract that dubious advantage, his headache throbbed nastily. A lingering hangover from Spruce Ridge, plus the effects of sleep deprivation. He was so damn ambivalent about sleep ever since those crazy erotic dream trysts with the ghost girl had started up.

Each night, the dream began with her creeping through a big mechanical wall. A big, steam-punk style thing, full of monstrous gears turning, ax-shaped pendulums swinging, a confusion of parts in constant motion, but somehow, she found hidden, Lara-shaped openings and slithered through them. Sinuous, practiced, like some sort of sexy pole dancer. A choreography she knew without thinking.

He forced the memory down, and squinted at the Fork, which towered against the dawn sky. Lara was a dangerous ghost. If he shorted out and lost the shield partway up, he was meat.

Not that he was afraid of death. He wasn't, since Spruce Ridge. Rudd had driven him to a place where death was his friend. He'd never be afraid of it again. Even so, he wasn't going looking for death. A guy had to give a shit, to plan his own suicide. Who had the energy.

His shield was solid, after some deep breathing. Okay. Good to go. He flexed his hands. The pine needles beneath his bare feet were fuzzed with frost, but his feet weren't cold at all. His body seemed to be regulating temperature better than it used to. He focused his mind to a diamond sharp point . . .

. . . it washed over him, mixing into the data feed. *Cougar.*

Where? He looked around, neck prickling, keeping his mind blank to make space for the flash flood of sensory info. That was another souvenir from Spruce Ridge. Harold Rudd had mind-fucked Miles into a coma with his coercive psychic powers a few months ago. He'd survived the encounter—barely. But when he woke up, his brain was wired all wrong. He existed in a state of constant sensory overload.

The world blared at him from all sides—no filters, no rest, no down time.

It knocked him flat. He'd hiked out here to the ass end of nowhere to try to jerry-rig himself back into functionality again. To learn how to at least fake normal. Not that he'd been so very normal before, but hey, everything was relative.

Oddly enough, the sensory overload had gotten somewhat better since the ghost girl started making her conjugal visits to his mental fortress. Surprise, surprise, life improved when a guy started getting laid. Even if it was only in the privacy of his own mind.

The animal was watching him from that stand of trees. How did he know the cougar was a she? By smell? Like he'd ever sniffed a cougar to determine its sex. Still, the summation of infinitesimal bits of information, each individually too small to perceive on its own, swirled up like a pixelated cloud in his mind, focusing into a potent, predatory *her*. Near-invisible in the trees, eyes gleaming with inscrutable feline calm. Her tail swished when she sensed him watching.

He stared, awestruck. He loved seeing the animals. These were the moments he was trolling for. Fleeting instants when his hyper-sensitivity was actually a gift, not just a huge pain in the ass.

Neither wanted to move until the other one did, but Miles finally surrendered, lifting his hands. "I'm not breakfast," he told her.

Her tail swished. Her gaze was unwavering.

Miles took a swig of his water, stowed the flask and gave her a respectful nod. "Later, then," he told her, and began his climb.

Long. Slow. Nearly impossible. Silence and solitude helped focus him, and so did muscle-bulging, sweat-dripping, eye-popping effort. Dangling a millimeter away from death for hours at a time was genuinely restful to him. If he kept the shield strong.

Strange, how he'd originally created the shield to protect

himself from Rudd and his pet telepath, Anabel, for all the good it had done him. They hadn't been able to read his mind, but Rudd had ground him into hamburger anyway. He'd made that wall to keep attackers out, but what he'd ultimately created was a bunker to keep his own self in.

Whatever it took. Since he woke up from the coma, he'd been faced with two possible modes of existence. Mode One: a shaking, sobbing nightmare of screaming stress flashbacks, reliving Rudd's torture. Big barrel of laughs, that one. Mode Two: keep that mind shield up, constantly. It clamped down on the stress flashbacks. It also flatlined him emotionally.

Mode Two won, whatever the price. Cowering in a fortress worked for him. It was a no-brainer.

It changed him, though, to the vocal dismay of his family and friends. Nobody liked chill, flatlined Miles. He was too cold for them. No fun anymore. Tough shit. He was done rolling around like a puppy, panting for everyone's approval. Anyone who cherished strong opinions about his coping mechanisms could go get stuffed.

Nothing moved him. Not maternal guilt, not the scolding of his friends; Aaro, Sean, or various other components of the McCloud Crowd, an opinionated group if there ever was one. To a man, they considered Miles to be their own personal creation, and as such, their personal property, too. It took a traumatic brain injury to jolt him free of that.

He'd always wondered how those McCloud guys, most notably Davy, Connor, and Kev, managed their strong, silent routines. Now he understood. They had shields in their heads, just like him.

Too bad the shield didn't block out his sensory overload problem. But no, that torrential info dump ran on a different channel. With his senses ratcheted up like that, normal everyday life was torture. Perfume, cigarettes, and car exhaust made him gag. Intimate olfactory data about the hormonal and emotional states of the bodies of the people he encountered was embarrassing. Traffic was ear-splitting. Electric lights, God help him. Worst of all, the electromagnetic radiation of wi-fi generated a hot, prickly buzz in his head that turned the chronic headache into stomach-churning agony. And he was a computer geek by trade, for God's sake. This was a game-changing professional handicap. There were drugs he could take, but to make a dent in a problem this big, he needed a dose so high, it turned him puddle-of-drool stupid.

Of course, things were a little different since the dream girl started her yummy therapeutic visits to his fortress. The head sex seemed to have increased his bandwidth, improving the info dump to a point he might almost define as bearable. But who knew if he could tolerate wi-fi, electrosmog? He had yet to put his laptop and router to the test. He had left them hidden under the body of his truck, in the woods, swathed and sealed in plastic.

He wasn't sure if the sex fantasy-fueled improvement was a positive sign, or another symptom of impending insanity. It was problematic on so many levels. At least the shield made it easier to be stoic about head pain. He still felt it, it still sucked, but it didn't make him panic. It was just pain. He breathed into it. It was easier, out in the woods. Sensory data still flooded in, but the data was clean, balanced. Nothing made his head explode. At first, he'd retreated to his own mountain property, but his friends kept coming up to nag. He had to retreat deeper to avoid them.

He'd sucked down some books on wilderness camping before he came up here, and packed up all the macho gear the McClouds had equipped him with over the years—guns, ammo, all-purpose belt knife, etc. The gear was all part of the McCloud guys' ongoing quest to transform Miles from a basement-dwelling geek freak into a kick-ass battle-ready commando like them. They'd made some progress over the years, but those guys wouldn't be satisfied until he was prepared to sew up his own bullet wounds with dental floss. As fucking if.

Thinking too much. Cut that shit out. Concentrate.

The rock face shifted back into focus. He felt the energetic pulse of every living thing near him, vibrating in a shimmering energy field. Lichen rasped beneath his fingertips. Every bird, every bug a bright spot on the 3-D grid in his mind. The cougar was a hot glow of pulsing energy. Staring up like she wanted something from him. Something he just couldn't give.

That made him think of Lara. Bad idea, dangling from a cliff face. And then he wasn't just thinking of her. He saw her. Actually saw her in his head, even though his eyes were fixed on the rock face, his hands. Sliding through those grinding gears, just like she did in his nightly sex dreams, as bright a spot on his sensory grid as the living, breathing cougar. Inside his inner sanctum now, looking around. Curious, expectant. Big dark eyes alight with fascination. He saw her so clearly.

The fear grew, penetrating his shield, vibrating in his stomach, his limbs. He was not guiding this image at all. It was unspooling on its own, but he wasn't dreaming. He wasn't even daydreaming. He was screamingly wide awake, hyperconscious, hanging onto a cliff.

Like, what the *fuck?*

His shield flickered, and shock of raw panic blasted through him, whiting him out—

He came to sliding rapidly down the wall. Barely caught himself on a narrow ledge of granite with a bone-jarring *thud*, fingers clawed—

Focus. Don't look down. His feet dangled, swung, over nothing.

It took a few flailing, panicky moments, to find the frequency, get the shield back up. There it was. Hard as ice. Chill. Empty. No think.

He looked down at the jagged boulders hundreds of feet below, bare toes wiggling in the foreground as they searched for purchase. Blood, smeared on the rocks. He'd scraped all the skin off his fingertips.

It took many long, shaking, straining minutes before he found a jut of rock with his foot, and could lift himself enough to move, think straight enough to recalculate a fresh route.

He made it to the top somehow, limbs hollow and limp when he got there. He had named this rock formation "the Fork," today's destination being the top of the tallest, sharpest tine. He stood on the summit and took in the towering forest of conifers, the snow-dusted Cascades, the shreds of moving clouds above and below. Right now, he almost enjoyed the info flood, when every single piece of data was harmonious with the rest. Except for he himself. His fingertips oozed blood. And his cock was still hard, from that not-exactly-a-dream.

He pushed the thought away, and gnawed some jerked elk meat Davy had given him, a relic from their hunting trip last year. A thinly disguised campaign to force Miles to learn to shoot a rifle properly, a necessary rite of passage, according to Davy. Davy himself was a great sniper. Mostly, Miles surmised, because the guy could shut down his emotions at will. Miles had not been great at it. Too nervous, too twitchy. He couldn't find that still place between the thoughts, breaths.

Well, he'd found it now. The new, chill Miles would be a good sniper. Technique, angles, wind drop, that shit was just math, and he was good at math. If he ever needed to waste somebody at two kilometers, he was all set.

He had no more misadventures on the long, slow way down, but he was exhausted by the time he got back to his rough campsite, which consisted of a tarp tied over his sleeping roll and pack, a fire pit, and a small gas burner. Too tired to cook. He built a fire, chomped a protein bar without enthusiasm. He'd get scurvy if he went on like this, but foraging for edible plants did not engage his brain in the excellent way that climbing did. And all that chewing, Jesus. It made his jaw sore.

He fed wood slowly into the fire, too zonked to think. Then he felt that hot, shivery tingle on his skin again. He rose, scanning the trees that circled his clearing.

Luminous cat eyes flashed eerily in the firelight. The sounds of the night swelled as his perceptions amplified. He felt no sense of menace, just a hushed, cautious awe, but he pulled the loaded Glock 23 out of his pack all the same. It was too small a caliber for a cougar, but it was better than nothing. He'd have to shoot her right through the brow or the eye if she came at him.

God forbid it should come to that. She was so damn beautiful.

He sat slowly down again, facing her, and fed twigs into the fire. Wind sighed and tossed the treetops, driving shifting swatches of cloud across the glittering smear of uncountable stars. His eyes wanted to close so badly, but the cougar's presence gave him that persistent little zing of adrenaline that kept them open.

The big cat was fascinated with him. She wanted to figure him out, make sense out of him. *Good luck with that.*

They'd told him that depression was normal after a brain injury. God knows, PTSD flashbacks would drive anybody half bonkers. He had iron-clad excuses for everything that was happening to him. But the sex dreams in his sleep were hard enough for him to justify. If Lara started haunting him while he was awake, too . . . oh, Jesus.

That bumped him up to a whole new level of crazy.

He'd taken on the task of finding and rescuing Lara as soon as he'd been capable of functioning after the Spruce Ridge debacle. Lara was another victim of the psychic freak squad that had attacked Miles. It had been Lara's own mother, Helga Kasyanov, who had developed psi-max, the psi-enhancing drug that augmented latent paranormal ability, thereby setting this whole mess in motion. Helga had been murdered by Rudd's people. Miles had been the one to find the mutilated body of Joseph Kirk, Lara's father. Chained up in his own basement.

So Lara had been orphaned, as well as abducted. It made him angry, sick, and sad, which touched off a useless but uncontrollable urge to save the princess. Too many video games in his egghead youth.

He'd tried to find Lara Kirk harder than he'd ever tried anything in his life. He'd found exactly squat. She had stayed stubbornly lost. No clues, no breaks, no hints. Just a smooth, obdurate brick wall.

It burned his ass. No one better than he knew what she'd been up against, what she might have suffered. How could a guy know that, and just take it easy, convalesce? *Sorry lady, I need some R&R to get my brain swelling down before I can rescue you from the slobbering monsters.*

And why did he still give a shit at all, with his shield up? He managed not to care about anything or anyone else.

Because everyone else is outside your shield, dickhead. She keeps sneaking inside. At which point you bone her brains out. What a prince.

That thought stank of schizo delusion. He refused to think it.

Sleep was like a hand, pressing down hard on his head. He fought it, which left him less willpower to withstand the impulse to grope in his jacket for the plastic envelope. It held a photo, a copy of the headshot on Lara's website. She was a sculptor. *Had been* a sculptor. He knew every piece in her online catalog. He'd studied them. Pored over them.

He stared at her haunting dark eyes, and then started cursing, low and long, picking up steam. His tantrum culminated in tossing the photo at the fire. He choked it, of course. The picture fell short, landed at the edge of the embers. The plastic envelope began to melt and twist.

He plucked it out of the coals, defeated. Waved it until the plastic solidified. Stuck it in his jacket, defeated. So much for his hissy fit. Why did he even try.

He was keeping his eyes open by brute force of will alone when the images started again, just like it had while he was climbing. Like a dream, but he was not asleep, and he could not stop them. He just watched her, moving through the guts of the big machine that housed him. She wore that gauzy, impractical white thing, like a fairy-tale princess, pale, over-the-top froth. Her hair hung long, tousled. Long, slim legs. The dress swung and fluttered as she sidled through gnashing gears, arching, bending, ducking . . . and she was inside.

Of him. While he watched, wide awake. Holy shit. His muscles contracted. Oh, man. This was so weird. So bad. Crazy bad.

In his dream, or image, or whatever it was, she was in a control room, like the bridge of a futuristic spaceship. A relic of all his late nights with the sci-fi channel, no doubt. She drifted around in the room, twirling knobs, pushing buttons. She sat in a big swivel chair that looked suspiciously like a space captain's chair, and began typing onto a terminal that took form before his eyes.

He started to sweat. She'd never spoken in the dreams. Not that he'd given her a chance, the way he came on. Conquering barbarian style. She hadn't been able to do much more than whimper and gasp.

He'd left a message on his analogous mental computer only once. It had been for Nina, on that fateful night at Spruce Ridge. More a thought experiment than anything else, just to see if it would work, and he'd been privately appalled, at the time, to find that it had.

That had been his one glancing brush with practical telepathy, and he had not wanted to repeat the experience, not ever. He had enough problems. He didn't want this to go any further. Oh please.

But the message glowed on the screen, beckoning.

where r u?

He shouldn't answer it. He should not encourage a split-off part of his own fucked-up prefrontal cortex to talk to him. That played along with the fiction that it existed separate from his own consciousness, and it didn't, goddamnit. It was just Miles Davenport and his own complicated baggage. No more, no less. But his response rattled out onto the screen anyway.

piss off i dont want 2 play

Lara's eyes widened, in shock. She poised her fingers over the keyboard, typed. fck u 2 And she winked out. Pissed. Gone.

He realized three things at once. One, he had a massive hard-on, again. Two, he felt like shit for being rude to her. Bad sign. Three, without him noticing, the cougar had moved in on him. A lot closer.

He grabbed the Glock, jumped up and discharged it into the sky with a shout. The cougar leaped high, and vanished into the night.

The gun report was a hammer blow to his skull. He sank to his knees, let the gun slide from stiff, shaking fingers onto the pine needles. Hid his hot face in his hands. It was time for the meds. Jesus, look at him.

Trying to chase a fucking dream away by shooting it.

2

Lara's eyes fluttered at the glare, stomach clenching. Back in hell again. She wanted to go back to the Citadel, to her fantasy lover. Just thinking about him made her toes tighten with delight. He was the only good thing in the twisted smoking wreck of what passed for her life—and he had just slapped her away.

It hurt so much, she could barely breathe. Her dream lover had never run hot and cold on her before. He'd always been straight hot. Scalding, scorching hot, like she'd never imagined hot could be.

And now look at her, sniveling. Dissed by her own escapist sexual fantasy. How pathetic was that.

You have bigger problems, girl. She opened her eyes and grimly faced them. She was bound to the gurney with wrist and ankle restraints, straps buckled across chest and thigh. She used to fight them. She didn't, anymore, but Hu had a lingering mark in the shape of her teeth on the meaty part of his thumb. He took no chances.

Their faces hung over her, distorted and nightmarish. Tears flashed out, ran into her sweaty hair. She hated crying in front of these hateful bastards. Not that they gave a shit.

She was nothing to them, an inanimate thing to be exploited, but still, she hated her own lack of control. Hot teardrops tickled across her temples.

Breathe into it. Just a feeling. You're big. It's small. Breathe.

She willed herself to stillness. So difficult to be dignified when flat on one's back, strapped to a cot, stoned off her gourd. And weeping.

Today it was Hu, and Anabel, the blond bitch telepath, her usual tormenters. Anabel was always there, to follow Lara's mind wherever it ranged when they pumped her full of their junk. Hu was enhanced with psi, too, but his abilities were focused around the function of the drug itself, not upon her.

They were using her as a guinea pig, to develop a new drug formula. To what end she was not sure, and was afraid to speculate. The effects of the current formula were scary enough as it was. It kicked her loose of the world she knew, launching her into a foggy nightmare world of shifting visions. Usually she made no sense of the visions. Anabel or one of the other telepaths was always there with her, claws sunk deep. Hanging on like a tick. Usually Anabel.

Some of the visions were recurring. Like her mute, nameless friend, the little boy with the blond hair and the raggedy pajamas, for instance. He would have been a comforting figure if he weren't so ghostly and forlorn. Still, she'd become fond of him. She needed to care about someone, and the little boy was always there when they launched her into the formless fog. He'd become her guide, running on ahead of her, beckoning her on, gesturing and pointing until she saw the Citadel looming out of the mist.

And then she found *him*. The Citadel's incendiary occupant.

She'd been amazed, the first time, to find that Anabel and the others couldn't follow her inside. She was safe from her tormenters in there. And *he* was there. Her dream lover.

Not that there was anything that comforting about him,

that was for sure. Comforting was not the word for the Lord of the Citadel. Mind-blowing, super-deluxe, over-the-top sexual fantasy was more like it. The masterful intensity of his come-on and his lovemaking had terrified her, at first, but she'd taken to it pretty damn fast. She'd adjusted. Wow.

She'd puzzled at first, the hows and the whys and the whats of it all, but lately, she'd given up on that. It was a gift, and she'd just go with it, accept it, enjoy it.

Or rather, cling to it like a lifeline.

She'd gotten into the Citadel today, briefly, though she hadn't encountered its amorous lord as she usually did. She'd found the room empty, until she typed in that stupid, ill-fated message.

And got his harsh response. Ouch. It still smarted.

She'd gotten in at this morning's injection, too. Anabel was doubly furious, having been thwarted twice.

When Lara's eyes focused, Anabel slapped her. Forehand, backhand. *Whap*, *whap*. "Where the fuck did you go, you sneaky bitch? Where did you learn to block? Who taught you? Helga?"

Lara shook her head, insofar as the strap on her forehead would allow. "Didn't," she croaked. "Don't know how."

And it was true. She had no idea how to create something like that incredible dream fortress. She had no idea what the hell she was doing when they sent her on those drug trips.

No, she was trespassing in the Citadel. Not that its smoking-hot sex god inhabitant had ever objected to her visits before today. On the contrary. He'd always been happy to see her. To say the least.

"I had her for a while." Anabel directed the words at Hu. "We were making some progress. She saw that usual weird nightmare with the sleepwalkers, and then she saw the Tokyo bomb thing, and then she shook me off." She hung over Lara. "Where did you go?" Spittle flew, spattering Lara's cheeks. "How the fuck do you do that?"

"Don't remember," Lara lied, and gasped at the stab of

pain as Anabel dug savagely into her mind and raked through her memories.

"What do you get?" Hu asked. "Where was she?"

Anabel closed her eyes, brow furrowed. After a moment, she shook her head. "Usually, it feels like she's been fucking somebody after she skips off and hides, the dirty little whore." *Whack*. Another head-rocking slap. "But not today. Where's your fuck buddy today, cunt? Did he blow you off?" Lara tried not to whimper as she felt Anabel tug the thought thread out, and unravel it. "Ah! I nailed it! He hurt your poor little feelings! Aw, boo hoo for you!"

Lara breathed slowly, trying to keep her mind soft, unfocused. If she stayed very detached, giving no emotional charge at all to her thoughts, Anabel couldn't tell which threads were important enough to pick up and follow. It worked sometimes. When she was zen enough.

They said that Mother had developed this junk. A drug that enhanced a person's psi. It was plausible. Mother had been a brilliant pharmacologist, and she'd had a deep interest in parapsychology.

But they said a lot of crazy things. That Mother had died only a couple of months ago, for instance. That her death in that fire at the research facility years ago had been faked. That she'd been alive, all these long three endless years that Lara had been mourning her.

That Dad had been murdered, too. Tortured. Cut to pieces.

Until proven contrary, she would make the blanket assumption that they were all vicious lies. Or try to, anyway.

She would not think about it. Would. Not.

What they wanted from her, she couldn't imagine. She was just an artist. Working with images on wood and clay and metal, minding her own goddamn business. She'd never bothered anyone in her life.

These people said she had psi. She had to, or she'd be dead, they told her when she'd regained her wits, after that first terrifying episode. That was how the drug worked. It enhanced you, or it killed you.

At this point, after months in the rat hole, she was wishing it had killed her. She'd made a little over two hundred scratches on the wall for what she assumed were days, but who knew, with no clock or natural light for reference? At first, lights had switched on and off in what she assumed were twelve-hour cycles, with three small, wretched meals spaced throughout the light cycle. But when they started dosing her, they started playing with the light and food cycles, leaving her in the dark for what felt like days, or fasting until her stomach was twisted into knots. She didn't even have a menstrual cycle for reference. After the first weeks, she hadn't been able to choke enough food down to support that bodily process. Though her appetite had picked up quite a bit since she found the Citadel. And her mysterious sex god.

Too bad the food still sucked. When they provided it at all.

"The boss is not going to be happy," Hu scolded. "You said you'd have her in hand by the next time he checked up on us. But her shielding is getting better. He's going to crush us like cockroaches."

"You think I don't know that?" Anabel hissed back.

They talked as if she were a doll, never speaking to her directly, other than to torment or threaten. The rest of her time she spent alone in the rat hole, fighting for her sanity. Except for the occasional brief hour in the room with the razor-wire covered window that showed her the horned hill, that was her life. Psi-max flights, and the rat hole.

Until the Citadel—and *him*. She'd dubbed him the Lord of the Citadel. Since a fantasy man should have a fancy fantasy title.

Those dream visits to the Citadel had been keeping her alive.

Odd, that she would fixate on sex in her extremity. She'd

never put much importance on it before. She had trouble letting go in bed, trust issues, blah blah, so sex had never caught fire with her. So messy, so complicated. She could take it or leave it. So mostly, she'd left it.

But in her dreams, there were no such inhibitions. The Lord of the Citadel was a smoldering figment of her own overheated imagination. In those dreams, she could be a princess, a siren, a goddess. No fears or insecurities or hang-ups of any kind. What a relief. She finally knew what an orgasm felt like. She'd thought that she knew, but before the Lord of the Citadel took her in hand, she'd had no idea.

She wondered if amazing sexual fantasies were a random side effect of this particular version of the drug formula. If that aspect might change, if Hu changed his drug recipe. *Please, no.* They would make billions on the stuff, just as it was. Hell, she'd buy it herself, if it was for sale. In a heartbeat. But for now, this aspect of it was her dreamy little secret. One that made choking down her food worthwhile. And washing herself. Trying to sleep, exercise, meditate. Stay alive.

And now he just wanted her gone. piss off i don't want 2 play.

Her ass. Rude, ungrateful bastard. Maybe they already changed the drug formula, and this was the result.

She pushed the stupid, painful thought away. The Citadel's lord was just a wishful figment of her own imagination. He was a goddamn coping mechanism, no more. She was hurting her own freaking feelings.

And it *still* hurt. Fuck logic.

She gasped with pain, as Anabel jerked her chin around. "Tell us what you saw, bitch. Since you won't show me."

She shook her head again. "I don't really remember. I wasn't out there very long."

Hu and Anabel exchanged glances. "You're going to have to do better than that," Anabel said. "The boss is coming. We need results."

Lara shrugged. "Can't help you," she murmured. "Sorry."

"You will be, you stupid whore. Very sorry."

Lara tried not to laugh, preferring not to get slapped again. Sorrier than she was now? Really? She'd been longing for death for months now.

Her jailors had lots of theories on how to mine the benefits of her gift. Their current technique was to shoot her up with a hypnotic drug, and then force her to watch taped material on whatever subject they wanted to focus her visions around. World events; wars, troop movements, weapons development. Then they hit her with the psi-max, and Anabel took her for a spin. But even before she'd found the Citadel, her visions had been frustratingly unpredictable for their purposes. Present, past, future, all over the map. She saw a duffel bag full of explosives on a commuter train in Tokyo almost every time they dosed her. Over four hundred people dead. She'd begged them to notify the Japanese police, but they didn't care. She tried not to think about it.

And the other vision she had with maddening regularity. Empty-eyed, shuffling people wandering through a silent urban landscape. Quiet and morose, not particularly violent, but terrifying all the same.

She saw Hu's and Anabel's pasts and possible futures, too. It was uncomfortable, knowing so much about the intimate histories of the people she hated. She didn't want to understand them, or to have compassion for them. Hell with that.

Anabel unstrapped the restraints. Hu steadied her before she fell off the table. They hauled her wobbling body toward the door. Back to the rat hole. She turned to Hu. "How's Leah?"

Hu's face twitched. "Shut up."

"Did she get the medical tests I recommended?" Lara persisted.

The tension in Hu's jaw said it all.

"It's just like I said, isn't it?" Lara asked. "She thought it was just a little gastritis, but it's esophageal cancer, right?"

"I said, shut up. She's none of your damn business."

But Lara was too stoned to act in her own best interests. When things started coming, one thing pulled another until it was a tumbling avalanche. "She doesn't know what you do here," she said. "You tell her you're just a researcher, and she buys it, or pretends to. On some level, she knows what you really are. It makes her uneasy, but she stuffs it. Because she's a nice person, you know? She actually cares about you. She deserves better than a sadistic, lying—"

"Shut . . . *up!*" *Whap*. Hu didn't hit as hard as Anabel, but the blow smashed her lip against her teeth, and once she tasted blood, there was no way to stop the words from flying out.

"You're poisoning her, Hu. If she stays near you, she will die. It won't take too long, either. Want to know exactly how long?"

Anabel slammed her against the rat hole door. The blow knocked the air from her lungs, left her gasping. Anabel's face, which would have been beautiful if it had not been so tight and sunken, leaned into hers.

"Don't fuck with us," she hissed. "Your life hangs by a thread."

Then cut it, already. Set me free. But she had no air to speak.

Hu opened the many locks on the massive door. They muscled her through it. Anabel's shove sent Lara stumbling to her knees.

Lara coughed. Licked blood away. "I saw you, too," she said.

Anabel rolled her eyes. "Did you not hear what I said?"

"About my life hanging by a thread? Yeah. You threaten me with death every couple of minutes. I take it that's a no, then?"

She looked up, and read both curiosity and dread in Anabel's eyes. Kept her mind soft, as she felt the stabbing probe. Anabel was trying to read the memory for herself, but she couldn't find the right tail unless Lara handed it to her. Not if she kept it soft and neutral.

"You'd just lie," Anabel said. "Drugged-up sneak."

"You'd know if I was," Lara said calmly.

"I read you already. And I didn't see anything about me."

"I was shielded when I saw it," Lara said.

Anabel made an impatient sound. "Fine. Enlighten me, you dumb twat, so we can go get some breakfast."

"A man." Lara rolled up onto her knees.

Anabel's laughter was harsh. "Oh, what a shocker! I've never met one of those before! Who is he, my next lay?"

"A guy from your past. But I saw his present. Through his eyes."

"There are a lot of men in my past," Anabel said. "Most of them aren't all that interesting. You'll have to do better than that."

"He wore plaid golfing pants." Images tumbled in on her, one leading the next, like facts she'd always known. "Somewhere in the South. He was drinking a gin and tonic. Not his first."

Anabel's face went stiff. Hu's eyes darted between them, nervous.

"It was a country club," Lara went on. "Drooping, swampy trees. Louisiana, or Florida. He was watching the kids in the pool. One in particular. A blond girl in a yellow bathing suit, maybe nine or ten—"

"That's enough," Anabel warned.

"He had hairy ankles," Lara told her. "I could tell, from the way his pants rode up. He was crossing his legs to hide his erection."

"I said *enough!*" Anabel's voice was getting shrill.

"He was looking at her, but he was thinking about you. How he enjoyed the time that he had you locked up in the basement for . . . how long was it? Years? So nice, to indulge his urges whenever he liked, without having to fly to southeast Asia to do it. He was fantasizing about buying a private pet again, but he's a big man in the community. Local district attorney, right? Such a risk. Expensive, dangerous. But then again, so are tickets to Bangkok. So maybe it's a wash."

"Stop it!" Anabel shrieked. "Stop it!"

"Knowing that, I can almost feel sorry for you," Lara said, touching her bloodied lip again. "Almost."

Anabel's foot slammed into her ribs. The following horrible interval was measured by blows. She curled up around her vital organs while Anabel kicked her. Ribs, thigh, buttock. Fireworks in the dark.

When it stopped, Anabel was panting, deep gulping rasps. "You were supposed to get an hour with the window, but no. Those privileges are for good little girls. Bad little girls stay in the dark."

"Like you did?" Lara croaked.

The door slammed shut. The lights cut out. She wouldn't get fed today, not after pissing Anabel off like that. Her belly cramped, nastily.

She wondered how long her body could hold out in these conditions. Calorie deficit, sleep deficit, light deprivation. Whatever collateral damage this drug might cause. How much longer did she have to take this? Weeks? Surely not more than that.

She curled up on the bed, in the fetal position, and her mind went straight to *him*, of course. To one of her visits before, when he was still amorous and ardent. In the last one, he'd been waiting for her, lounging bare chested in a big chair, feet up. The room surrounding him was foggy because her attention was always focused so completely on him, but it was sure to be beautiful. Everything in the Citadel was beautiful.

When he saw her, his eyes lit with a hot, hungry glow. He got up, approaching her with pantherish grace. Her breath stuck, and her thighs clenched, and her throat locked. She just stared, mute and dazzled, stupid with longing. Letting him press her against the wall.

He kissed her, his tongue thrusting and stroking. He handled her so skillfully with his big, warm hands. She shivered with delight, remembering how her body trusted his. Melting, boneless.

He'd fallen to his knees, lifting the white, filmy skirt she wore, the one that looked suspiciously like a bridal gown. But she was always without underwear when she visited the Citadel. Nothing to stop him from burying his face in her muff, venturing with his fingers and his tongue, to tease and probe. When he tasted her lube, he thrust his tongue voluptuously deeper, circling her clit, and ah, God. Delicious, protracted, knee wobbling, sobbing delight. And that was all just preparation, foreplay. When he actually got down to it . . . whoa.

When the drug wore off and she was dragged back into waking reality, she was quivering and wet between her legs. She wanted to stay forever. It was a brutal shock, to jolt back into her body, strapped to the gurney, with Anabel screaming. *Where did you go? You just first dosed, you dumb cunt! Who taught you to block like that?*

Maybe they would kill her, once they got frustrated enough.

She lay there in the dark, tears leaking slowly out into the stale wool blanket on her cot. She missed her Lord of the Citadel. Except that he was not hers. And he did not want her anymore.

Big mistake, to type onto that computer, but she was so lonely. Starved for companionship. Even if he was just a mental construct.

But hey. Never open up, never get rejected. It was a policy she'd employed for most of her life, so why wouldn't it be valid here, too? Leave it to Lara Kirk to create an imaginary friend who rejected her.

She had to laugh, and instantly regretted it. It hurt her

sore ribs. Crying in bed, like a girl who'd had a fight with her boyfriend.

Truth was, it didn't matter if he wanted her or not. Let him be rude. Let him just try to keep her out. She'd be back the second they dosed her, like a guided missile. If he wanted her out, he'd have to beef up his security. She'd go to the Citadel this second, but she couldn't make it on her own. She needed their fucking drug to get airborne.

God, how she hated that. Hated herself for being too far gone even to crave freedom anymore. She didn't know what she'd do with freedom if she had it. But a drug-fueled sexual fantasy? Hell, yeah. Sign her up for that.

Maybe she'd die in the Citadel, when her time came. That would be a better point of departure than the rat hole or the gurney.

She'd let go of hope long ago. All she wanted now was relief.

She was a psi-max whore.

3

The frosty dawn found Miles in a worse state than he'd been in since he hiked in weeks before, and the day that followed went straight downhill from there.

Last night's episode had fucked his fragile equilibrium all to hell. The shield was intact, but his sensory overload was worse than ever. Wind shrieked through the Forks. Mold, decomposing leaves, pine needles, humus, all combined into a heavy, yeasty blast of organic compounds that stunned him into immobility. He sat wrapped in his thermal bag for hours, hands clamped over his face, struggling not to retch.

It was colder today. Snowline creeping downwards. He pulled on the warmest clothes he had, shivering. Poor Miles, delicate flower. Bring on the fucking smelling salts. No climbing today. He'd kill himself if he got blindsided thinking about what had happened with the—

No. *Nothing* had happened. It was a *dream*. Nobody was talking to him. He was on a mountaintop, twelve miles from the nearest human being. He was not even a telepath. Stop it with that crazy shit. *Stop*.

He dumped a packet of bean soup into a plastic mug of water, stirring with his finger. Gulped down the resulting

ash-colored gruel. He was getting sloppy. Hadn't eaten anything fresh in a while. He wondered if there was anything
edible growing in the forest this late in the season.

He headed into the woods, resolved to find something
with phytonutrients in it. A few hours into his search, he
choked down some mushrooms, but they were wrinkled and
moldy, and the taste was too strong to endure. A couple of
withered wild onions made his stomach burn. A person
needed a genuine appetite for this. He gagged, spat twigs
and dirt. Yikes. Evidently he wasn't the frontier type.

The onions gave him a coughing fit, and he ended up
crouched on the ground, grimly waiting for the pounding in
his head to ease.

Fuck foraging. Icy wind chewed sullenly at his ears. He
got back to the campsite, gathered wood, chopped and split
it, and settled in for a cold, sleepless night by the campfire.
He was going to have to beef up supplies soon, if this turned
to snow camping. It could, at any time.

A bug caught his eye, trundling across the forest floor. It
butted up against the toe of his boot, got itself turned around
and went on its way. He was so absorbed in staring at it, the
sensation crept up on him.

Lara. That zingy, bright feeling. If he let himself look inside at the images, he would see her, in her white, frothy
dress, doing that sexy get-through-the-wall pole dance.

Don't look. He stared at the flames, kept the camera in his
head switched grimly off. He would not play this game with
himself, goddamnit. He was not tuning in to this channel.
His damaged prefrontal cortex could go fuck itself. He was
not falling for this.

The sound startled him. It was the beep his phone made
when a text message came in, but he had no smartphone. It
was miles away, swathed in plastic, stowed in the box bolted
under his truck.

*Just ringing in your ears. Memories of sounds. Breathe. Let
it go.*

But he couldn't help flashing on the screen in his head. Reading the words that glowed there.

hey u there?

Don't do it, asshole. Don't talk to her again. You're encouraging your own mental illness. Entrenching it.

He knew exactly what was happening. He'd researched it extensively. The part of his brain that governed language and abstract thinking had been blasted by Rudd's psychic attack, causing biochemical changes, alterations in his brain connections. This caused miscommunication between the prefrontal cortex and the language area in his temporal cortex, resulting in auditory hallucinations. Hearing voices. Which this was not, strictly speaking. But it was close enough.

It was also known as schizophrenia.

He would not listen to those messages. Especially if they started asking him to do things. But even as he lectured himself, his response was pounding out, scrolling down the screen, in a big, bold, yelling font.

wtf? what r u trying 2 tell me about my fucked up brain that i dont already know? u dont exist! its just me! give it up, go away. integrate, already. pls!! stop torturing me!

He held his breath for a moment. There was a long pause.

wow strange i thought u were the dream

no, Miles typed back. that wd be u so dont try 2 fck with my head i wont play

not! im not u! or a dream! im myself. crystal clear?

He felt absurdly stung. u've got attitude 4 some1 who sneaks in uninvited and starts twiddling with my shit

At some point in the strange exchange, he'd given in and looked, so of course now he couldn't look away. She was seated in the chair, that wafty skirt spread all around. She stared at the screen, hands in her lap, face expressionless. She lifted her hands, and typed slowly,

i dont have anyplace else 2 go

That sounded so forlorn. It made him miserable. Which

ratcheted up the crazy quotient. Which pissed him off, and made him sarcastic.

pity party?

That evidently pissed her off in turn. She did not reply, but she didn't leave. She just sat there, staring at the screen. Chin up. In a huff.

oh come on u have got 2 b kidding, he typed.

She shook her head. Crossed her arms over her chest.

not fkg fair u cant diss me in my own head, he pounded in.

She couldn't resist that opening. Her hands went to the keyboard.

evidently i can appeared slowly, letter by letter.

Miles started to laugh. Helplessly snorting into his hands, tears spilling over. He'd seem bonkers to anyone watching. But hey. He *was* bonkers. This was irrefutable proof. That was the real reason he was here, after all. So no one had to witness what Rudd's mindfucking had reduced him to. A whack job who heard voices. No, correction. A whack job who saw texts. Leave it to Miles, the geek freak, to put a computer engineer's special twist onto the time-honored process of going batshit.

Okay, fine. He was convinced. Time to get the prescriptions filled.

So this was to be his future. Mental institutions, halfway houses. A career bagging groceries at best, if he could keep from drooling on them. That was the level at which he functioned on those meds.

He started breaking camp before he'd even made any conscious decision to do so. No reason to drag it out now that the decision was made. He no longer saw her image, even when he looked for her, but he sensed that she was still in there. He felt her bright glow. He couldn't stop feeling for it. It had been so long since he'd talked to someone.

Yikes. That thought made him cringe.

But at least his mind was made up. The wind smelled of snow, he was getting worse, not better, and he'd better get some help before he was too far gone to help himself. Before he became dangerous.

The woods were pitch dark, but one of the few advantages to his Spruce Ridge brain makeover was night vision. He could hike through trackless woods at two A.M. as easily as at noon. He hoisted his pack.

He was a couple of hours into it when the beep sounded. At that point, he didn't even try to resist. It was useless effort.

The screen read u there?

He had nothing further to lose at this point, not even his sanity. It was already long gone, so what the fuck. He mentally typed out lara?

There was a long, shocked pause. Then, how do u know my name?

I know who u r. I c u when I dream. Wt r u doing in here?

hiding out was her terse reply.

huh?

this is the only place they can't get me

dont understand, he typed.

i dont need u to understand. I just need a place to hide.

bad day? he asked.

oh u have no idea was her reply. Then she winked out again, like she had last night. But this time, she was gone completely.

His senses kept on groping for her.

His pace quickened to a run as he reflected upon two unsettling things. One, the brief conversation had given him an erection. His crotch strained against his jeans. Two, his headache was gone, for the first time in what felt like forever. Not that he was complaining. He felt almost giddy. Probably it was all about blood flow. The erection, the headache relief. Vasodilators doing their thing. But still. The sensory input was as intense as ever, but he was taking it all in and processing it, as if it were normal to see in the dark at two in the morning. Or hear a bird's heartbeat. He had more bandwidth. A lot more.

Talking to Lara was evidently therapeutic.

God forbid he get obsessed over a ghost girl. Granted, he had a tendency to fixate on unattainable chicks. But getting all wound up about a figment of his own imagination? A woman who had shuffled off this mortal coil before he even met her? Come on. Get real.

No further beeps sounded on his Lara sensors in the time it took to hike down to the truck. That was good, since his current plan was to medicate her out of existence. The idea made him uncomfortable. Like he would betray her by smashing a pharmaceutical hammer down onto that part of his brain that could talk to her.

i dont have anyplace else 2 go. this is the only place they cant get me. Her texted words reverberated in his head. Plaintive, desperate.

What would happen if he took those meds, made the messages go away? Would she still have a place to hide? And what did it indicate about his mental state, that he was even asking questions like this?

Oh, man. Don't even go there. Just keep running. Just outrun it.

The Dodge Ram he'd bought from Sean waited patiently under its forest camo tarp. He shimmied beneath the vehicle to take out the box attached to the undercarriage, where he stashed his electronics.

The engine fired up with no hesitation, even after weeks of abandonment. He plugged the phone in, and started down the long, twisting logging road. About a mile from the town at the pass, he got some cell coverage, so he stopped to assess his social situation.

Eighteen missed calls. Forty-two text messages. Twelve from his mother. Six from Sean, nine from Aaro, four from Bruno. Seven from Cindy, his cheating ex-girlfriend, whose face he had difficulty recalling. If Cindy was texting him, probably the wanker rock musician she'd dumped him for had moved on, and she was ready to take up with her default chump again.

Huh. If there was one good thing about getting his ass kicked to hell and gone, it was that it put his love life sternly into perspective. The Cindy thing seemed so small to him now. Something that had happened to a much younger self. He deleted Cindy's messages unread.

He deleted his mother's messages, too, except for the most recent one, which he glanced at. Standard hysterical maternal anxiety. He would call her as soon as he had filled the prescriptions in his wallet. He could face his mother only if drugged into a state of catatonic calm.

Aaro's messages were rants. He'd gotten spoiled, having Miles working twenty-four/seven, and wanted him back in the saddle. Of course. The guy was crazy in love. He had a life now, and wanted all the nice things that a life entailed. Time to canoodle, daily long lunch breaks with the pretty lady friend, long weekends in the hot tub, chugging champagne and slurping oysters off the half-shell between bouts of hot sex. Aaro wanted to work a scant third of the grinding hours he used to put into his business, and he wanted Miles back to pick up the slack.

Too bad, dude. No more. He loved the guy, though he could not really feel the love through the shield right now. He'd almost died for Aaro and Nina at Spruce Ridge. He was paying a high price for that attempt at heroism. He deleted Aaro's messages unread, without guilt or regret. His guilt and regret functions were disabled.

He selected Sean's latest, and opened it with just an instant's hesitation.

get ur ass to b&l's wedding or there will be hell to pay

Wedding? Oh, Christ. Bruno and Lily's wedding had been put off because of Spruce Ridge, and the premature birth of their son. They had rescheduled for . . . what day was today? He thumbed around on the smartphone. Oh, fuck. Today. The wedding was *today*.

He let out a long, whistling breath of real dismay. That he felt. Keenly. Even through the shield.

He didn't have to go to the wedding. He could just load up some more supplies, and drive on. To another mountain range. A farther one.

Yeah, and never call his mother back again? That was a big deal to wrap his head around. Kind of like suicide. Considering that he was teetering on the edge of certifiable mental illness already.

He had a voicemail message, too. He didn't recognize the number.

He clicked on it. *"Hello, Miles."* It was a cracked, quavery old woman's voice. *"This is Matilda Bennet. I know you said you did your best trying to find poor Lara. Well and good. But I did some more digging on my own, and I came up with another line of inquiry that I think you could do something with. I've reached the end of my resources, but maybe you could push it further. If you have any interest in hearing about this matter, call me back at this number."*

That call had come in a week before.

Huh. That was unexpected. He'd met Matilda right before Spruce Ridge. She'd worked at Wentworth College with Lara's father, the Professor Joseph Kirk. She was the one who had originally set Miles upon this quest to find Lara.

Matilda's words were calculated to sting him into action, but the barbs did not get through his shield. Just a weird, fluttering sense in his belly, that Fate was playing tricks on him. There was something he should be noticing here, some pattern that eluded him.

It should be obvious. If he weren't so goddamn thick.

Lara's dead. Let it go, man. Don't drive yourself any further into crazyland. Don't sublease yourself a fucking condo there.

Yet, he clicked the number the message had been sent from, and hit "call." It was brutally early, but Matilda wouldn't want to wait for a callback, not about this. The phone rang twelve times. He had almost given up when the line clicked open. There was a brief pause. "Hello?"

It was a youthful female voice. Not Matilda.

"Hi, sorry about the hour. Can I speak to Matilda?"

A breathless squeak answered him. Nothing comprehensible.

"Hello?" he prompted. Then more loudly, "Hello?"

A male voice spoke into the phone. "Hi. Who am I speaking with?"

"My name is Miles Davenport," he said. "I'm looking for Matilda."

"Well." The guy's voice was heavy. "She's, ah . . . she's dead."

Miles' mind flash-froze. "Huh?"

"Like I said. A week ago."

"A week . . . ?" That was the day Matilda had made the call. Miles struggled to organize his thoughts. "Who are you?"

"I'm Mike Stafford. Her granddaughter's husband."

"I see. I . . . I'm sorry for your loss. How did she die?"

The guy paused. "Haven't been watching the news lately, huh?"

"No," Miles admitted. "I've been out of town for a few weeks."

"She was murdered," Mike Stafford told him. "Home invasion. Some drugged-up asshole broke in. Threw her down the stairs."

The news sucked him down. The gravity load on his guts tripled.

"Ah . . . I'm sorry," he stammered. "Could you tell me the name of the detective who's got the investigation?"

"You know something about it?" The guy's voice sharpened.

"No," Miles said. "But Matilda called the day she died, and left me a message. I didn't take the call, but the cops might want to know."

"Calm down, Amy," the guy muttered, evidently to his wife. "Okay, don't see why not. His name is Detective Barlow." He rattled off a telephone number, which Miles committed to memory.

"The funeral's today," the guy went on. "Six P.M. at the Merriweather Presbyterian Chapel. If you want."

"Yeah. Thanks." Miles groped for words. "Give my condolences to your wife. I gave her a jolt when I asked for Matilda. Sorry about that."

"Yeah, man. Not your fault. It's okay. Whatever."

Miles closed the conversation with what grace he could, and sat there, eyes squeezed shut.

Holy fuck. Matilda Bennet? Tension mounted in his body.

He'd thought he was as cold as ice, an orbiting satellite. Free at last, in his own lonely, fucked-up way.

But he wasn't. His belly clenched over the sick, greasy nausea roiling there. A wedding, a murder, a funeral. A desperate ghostly entity locked in his own head, pleading for help and rescue. A cryptic voicemail message from a murdered woman.

It didn't matter how hard he tried to stay anchored in reality.

Reality was getting royally fucked, from every single quarter.

Mud and rocks spat and flew as his tires jolted him out of the ruts and bounced him down the road, faster than conditions permitted.

Who could have wasted Matilda? She was a harmless old lady, built like a brick, stumping along with her dowager's hump and cane. He didn't need emotion to be outraged about this. It was outrage on every level, even that of cold logic. A scumbag who killed nice old ladies needed to be wiped off the face of the earth. Like the polio virus.

He'd liked Matilda. He'd hated to disappoint her. After all his big talk, all his good intentions, all his fantasies about being the brilliant courageous intrepid blah blah blah who saved the maiden fair.

Reality was always such a fucking letdown. Matilda had been nice about it when he threw in the towel. She understood. Still, she was the kind of woman you wanted to bring results to. To get your pat on the head, your cookie, your sternly measured dose of approval. A strict but benevolent grandmother type.

It made him . . . fucking . . . *furious.*

He got gas at the station at the pass, holding his breath against the fumes, ignoring furtive stares. He must look strange, after weeks of sleeping rough and not much attention to hygiene, other than the occasional icy plunge into a mountain stream. He had to haul ass if he wanted to clean up and find decent clothes for the damn wedding.

His smartphone found him the perfect trifecta; a drugstore, a motel and a big-and-tall men's clothing shop, all in the same strip mall. No time to schlep up to Aaro's lair for his own stash of clothes.

The gods that protected speeding motorists were kind, even when he hit the I-5 corridor. The drugstore was his first stop in Portland, for toiletries, a comb, some razors. The fluorescent lights made his eyes burn, even through dark glasses.

His motel room stank of cigarette smoke and room deodorizer when he got inside, but he breathed through his mouth and ignored it, heading straight for the shower.

He stared at himself grimly in the mirror afterward as he combed out the caveman dreads. His torso was burned a leathery brown from shirtless climbing. He still had muscle mass, but he was lean, stringy. Every muscle, vein, and tendon, right out there on display. He looked like a wild-eyed, underfed Afghani goatherd, left out alone in the desert mountains way too long.

Scraping off the beard helped, but that made his shaggy mane look that much wilder. At least it was clean. He might not have even recognized himself, if not for the nose, which was as big and hooked as ever. Christ, he looked so much older. New lines burned around his mouth. And his eyes . . .

He looked quickly away from his eyes.

Just keep moving. Breathe. Through his mouth. He dragged the cleanest clothes he had left back on, clean being a relative term.

The clerk at the big and tall store gave him the fish eye when he walked in, gazing pointedly at the grubby jeans, the stained T-shirt.

"I need a suit," Miles announced. "Dark gray. I'm supposed to be at a wedding in . . ." He consulted his smartphone. "Shit," he hissed. "Thirty-five minutes." Maybe he'd get lucky, and the bride would be late. Like, forty minutes late. A guy could hope.

The young woman behind the counter leaned on her elbows and gazed at his torso appreciatively, dirty clothes and all.

"I need a shirt, too," he told them. "White, I guess, or a pale gray. And a tie, and a belt. Dress shoes. Some underwear."

The male clerk's nostrils flared. "Price range?"

Miles shrugged. "It needs to look good, and it needs to be fast. Try and keep the tab under two grand."

The clerk's eyes squinched down. "And how will you be paying?"

Miles took off his sunglasses, and just looked at the guy. The man's larynx began to bob up and down.

Aw, fuck it. Back in the old, pre-Spruce Ridge days, that guy's attitude would have pissed him off. Not now. He didn't blame the guy for judging by appearances. Every normal person did. He had, too, in the old days. Admittedly, he looked like hell.

Still, he let the prick blink and sweat for a minute before fishing the plastic wrapped envelope out of his jeans. He'd shrink wrapped some cash for random emergencies. He slit open the plastic, and peeled off fifteen C-notes. "We'll start with this."

The guy scooped up the bills. "One minute." He disappeared into the back. The girl behind the counter fluttered heavily mascaraed lashes. "You don't look like the type for a suit," she observed.

Miles grunted. "Don't feel like one, either."

"You look more like the leather and chains type." Big dewy blue eyes went blinkety blink. "Like, do you ride a Harley?"

Heh. Leather and chains and a Harley. That would have been rib-cracking, gut-busting funny, if he'd been capable of anything approaching humor. "Could we start with the shirt?" he asked.

The girl's flirty expression cooled. Her colleague came back out, marginally more polite, but clearly wanting to get him served and gone as soon as possible. Fine with Miles.

Some time later, he walked out, in a suit a full size smaller than his previous, pre-Spruce Ridge days. Just his enormous feet and hands and nose were eternally constant. He peered at himself in the rearview, wishing he'd bought clippers and buzzed off the hair. Even with the snarls combed out, it looked like exactly what it was, a badly grown out haircut that had been self-inflicted months ago in a state of emotional crisis. Ragged primordial locks dangled between shoulder and chin. It did not jive with the suit. But there was no time left for a barber.

After all, once he waltzed into the wedding, egregiously late, and faced down a mass of people who were all pissed off at him to varying degrees, his bad hair day would be the least of his problems.

He put on his sunglasses, and his ear plugs. The city haze of electrosmog, exhaust fumes and particulate matter were making him nauseous as hell, but there was no shield or remedy for that. He clenched his teeth till his ears ached and hit the road, wedding bound.

4

Sam Petrie lurked ouside the small, packed church, having
shown himself to Bruno, and to Zia Rosa, the formidable
Ranieri matriarch. That duty done, he'd slunk out to have a
smoke.

Damn, this group was heavy into weddings. It gave him
an unpleasant sense of déjà vu. He'd lurked outside during
Kev and Edie's ceremony, too. He didn't want to hurt anybody's feelings, but the giddy nuptial scene made him feel
smothered and vaguely depressed.

Next time this crowd inflicted a wedding invitation on
him, he'd send a salt and pepper shaker and his apologies,
and stay far away. For now, he compromised by lurking,
which was why he was perfectly positioned to witness Miles
Davenport's arrival.

He didn't recognize Miles at first. He was giving a habitual
once-over to each person as he or she approached, and his attention snagged on the tall man striding purposefully toward
the church. He pegged the guy as a potential problem instantly. Dark, hard eyes. Leathery, dark, tanned skin. Shaggy,
unstyled hair. He'd been sleeping rough, in spite of the nice
suit. Flinty gaze. Granite-lipped. A walking unexploded

bomb. Not an element you wanted waltzing into a friend's wedding. He was stepping forward to do his civic duty both as friend and cop, to ask if the guy had mistaken his venue when the recognition slammed in.

Jesus, that nose. Was it . . . holy *shit*. He stared. "Miles?"

"Hey." Miles shook his shaggy mane off his face. He did not smile.

Petrie reached out to clasp his hand. Some instinct stopped him, a sixth sense, of stray wires, high voltage. "Good to see you, man."

Miles nodded. "Yeah."

He did not offer further pleasantries, or say it was good to see Petrie, too. That part of Miles Davenport had been rendered away, along with twenty-five percent of the guy's body weight, from the looks of him. His big hands contrasted starkly with the cuffs poking from the sleeves of his suit. Brown, covered with scabs, nails battered. Like he'd been crawling through rocks and thorns under a desert sun.

Where the fuck have you been, man? Everybody's been worried sick about you. He stopped the words. The unlucky bastard was going to be fielding that question all afternoon. He did not look up to the task.

Before Petrie could come up with anything, the limo pulled up. Rosettes, with streamers flying from the antenna. Behold, the bride.

Doors opened, and a confusion of gartered and stockinged legs and fluffy skirts started spilling out. Lily straightened up, adjusting her gown, which was a graceful, pleated Grecian goddess sort of thing, which looked awesome on her. Nina was also looking hot, her figure set off in a clingy, eye grabbing shade of sunset orange. She adjusted her friend's hair. The wind caught the veil, flipping it out like a banner.

And there she was. It never failed. Petrie's mouth went suddenly dry as Sveti emerged, in a satin sheath that clung to her like she'd been dipped in slate blue liquid. She came out ass first, focused on the squalling occupant of the car seat.

Marco Ranieri, the newest addition to the McCloud Crowd's progeny. An opportunity to gawk at Sveti's awesome booty with no repercussions was precious, so Petrie took advantage of it, forgetting Miles altogether as Sveti emerged, swinging shiny locks back over her pale shoulders. Marco was drapped over her bosom, hiding what the gown's neckline was designed to showcase. Damn shame, but predictable as sunrise.

Aaro and Kev McCloud unfolded themselves from the front seat. Miles shrank back, as if hoping not to be noticed. A vain hope.

Aaro spotted Miles first. His face went blank. He murmured to Kev, who was offering Lily his arm. Kev's bright gaze instantly zapped up to Miles, but he'd positioned himself well out of their trajectory, and the bride was busy getting up the steps without tripping on her train.

Nina glanced over at them, a puzzled frown between her eyes, but Aaro hustled her in to do her maid-of-honor duty.

Sveti lagged behind, joggling the fussing Marco to calm him down. The movement made her tits quiver. Her shoulders were creamy pale in contrast to her long, dark hair. Petrie wrenched his gaze away. Down, boy. Daring to look at the lofty goddess's perfect ta-tas. But her scolding attention was focused mostly on Miles, not him. So no worries.

She stopped on the step below, frowning up. "Miles?" she asked, as if she didn't quite believe it.

"That would be me," Miles said.

"Where in hell have you been? Do you know how worried—"

"Don't." Miles' voice was hoarse. "Don't start."

Sveti's lips tightened up. She looked almost like she might start to cry. "At least you are here," she said. "How nice of you to make such an effort. So generous of you, no? Such a loyal friend."

Miles looked relieved. Sarcasm was easier to deal with than tears.

"Thought I'd missed it," he said. "Good thing Lily was late."

"Marco had a terrible attack of colic," Sveti told him. "Lily ended up having to take her whole outfit off so she could nurse—"

"Christ, spare us the gruesome details," Petrie cut in.

Her eyes flicked over him. "I wasn't talking to you."

Miles peered down at the creature squirming on Sveti's chest. "Marco. Wow. He's, uh . . ." He paused, at a loss. "Bigger."

"Oh, yes." Sveti held the wriggling striped entity up to be inspected, as proudly as if it were her own. "He's gained three pounds in two months. Almost up to the 50th percentile in length and weight for a full-term baby. But the colic is very bad. Want to hold him?"

Miles recoiled visibly. "No, no," he said hastily. "You keep him."

She cuddled Marco back to her tits again, studying Miles intently, with those huge, exotically tilted eyes that haunted Petrie's wet dreams.

"This isn't about Cindy, is it?" she asked, very softly.

Miles shook his head. "Not at all."

"Ah. That is good. Because, you know, ah . . . she is no longer with that man, hmm? The one she ran away with. You know that?"

"Don't care," Miles said, his voice flat. "Irrelevant."

Sveti gazed at Miles searchingly for a moment, and then nodded, evidently satisfied. "Good," she said. "She was just an excuse for you, anyway. A reason to hide. No one was contented with her. Not for you."

Miles shook his head. "Can't go there with you, Sveti. Not today."

"You're a fine one to talk about excuses," Petrie blurted, and was immediately appalled at himself. What the fuck possessed him? A death wish? A schoolyard hunger for attention? Jealous because she was talking to Miles and not him? Sveti had turned her fathomless dark eyes on him, wide and affronted and furious. Too late to turn back.

"I beg your pardon?" she said, icily.

Petrie gestured toward Marco. "Excuses. Like that one. You've always got a baby wrapped around your neck. Like a suit of armor. No guy's going to get that close to a full diaper, so you're safe, right? Good old Sveti. Always first in line to help with the kiddies." He took a long swig, but Sveti was still glaring at him when he capped the flask.

"You are an asshole, Petrie," she informed him.

"As you have told me many times before." Petrie clucked his tongue. "Such tough language for Marco's tender ears."

"Shut up. My armor is of a better class than yours." She slapped the capped liquor flask out of his hands, sending it spinning and bouncing off the steps. "Better to stink of baby poop than of bourbon."

Marco tugged at Sveti's neckline with a red, dimpled hand that shone with drool, and nuzzled hungrily at Sveti's cleavage. Petrie jerked his chin toward the kid. "Looks like he wants to top up," he observed.

Sveti's face went crimson. She pulled a bottle from her purse, stuck it in Marco's mouth, and stalked away. The two men waited until the doors of the church thudded shut, and exhaled. In unison.

"Wow, Petrie," Miles said. "You have such a way with the ladies."

Petrie retrieved his flask from the steps without comment.

"You are an asshole, though," Miles went on. "Like she said."

That pissed Petrie off. "This, from a guy who runs out on his friends without even a message to tell them he's not rotting in a ditch?"

Miles shook his head. "You don't see it, and it's right in your face."

"What?" Petrie felt his voice rising. "What's in my face?"

"She likes you," Miles said.

Petrie stared at the guy, slack-jawed. "Wrong," he finally said. "Dead wrong. Don't know where you got that. She hates my guts."

Miles grunted. "That explains why her heart spikes to one-forty when she gets close to you. Her eyes dilate. And those pheremones must have . . ." He glanced discreetly down at Petrie's crotch. "Yep. She blushed, too. I only saw from tits up, but God knows where it started from. All those capillaries, expanding just for you, you lucky bastard."

"Bullshit," Petrie muttered. His balls tingled, and his belly did a strange, flopping maneuver. He clenched to subdue it. "What the fuck do you think you're doing, looking at her tits?"

A mirthless smile twitched the corners of Miles' hard mouth. "I may be fucked up, but I'm not dead. Watch yourself, dude. Sveti's the untouchable virgin princess. Rescued from evil ogres. They'll shred your ass if you look at her funny. Let alone touch her."

True enough. There was an unspoken dictate against thinking dirty thoughts about vulnerable, waif-like, china-doll perfect, tragically orphaned Sveti, always and eternally way too young. If anyone did think such thoughts, eight different guys in the McCloud Crowd, plus Tam Steele, who was worse than all of them put together, would rise up and smite him down. Splat.

"So it's true, then?" Petrie said. "What they say, about your new superpowers? You saw all that? Or are you just jerking me around?"

Miles laughed and then put his hand abruptly to his head, wincing. "Superpowers, my ass. I heard the heart rate, I heard her breathing, I smelled the pheremones, I saw the pupils dilate. I've got a sensory overload problem. It comes at me like a fire hose. I can't block it out."

"I don't see why you'd want to," Petrie said. "Sounds handy."

Miles just looked at him. The guy's stark gaze gave Petrie a guilty twinge. It would seem that the guy was not having any fun at all with his super-senses. "Sorry," he muttered. "Didn't mean to make light of your, uh . . . disability."

"It's okay," Miles said. "I'm used to being out there. I was a freak before. Now I'm a freak with brain damage. Just a little category shift."

"So, it hurts?" Petrie pressed for more, unable to help himself.

Miles rubbed his temples. "Cigarettes and bourbon on your breath. Pert shampoo. Old Spice aftershave. Arid Extra Dry, the chemicals they used to dry-clean your suit, the plastic they wrapped it in. Christ, if I took a step closer, I'd pass out from the toxic fumes."

Petrie uncapped his bottle, drank. "Keep your distance, then."

"I will," Miles assured him. "Sveti smelled way better than you. Those pheremones pumping out of her, man. Yum."

"Keep your dirty mind off her pheremones," Petrie snapped.

That smile twitched across Miles' face again. Caught out, in his fucking schoolboy crush. What a dickhead. He held out the flask, in silent invitation.

"Tried that," Miles said. "Doesn't help."

Petrie stoppered the flask, stuck it in his jacket. "That's sad, man," he said. "I'm sorry for you. Let's get on with this."

They pushed into the church. The organ blared, and lace fluffed, orange flower-scented matrimonial hooplah swelled to greet them.

If managing his disability was like walking a tightrope, managing it at this wedding was like walking a tightrope with an army of screaming maniacs constantly trying to shove him off. The kids alone, Jesus. The McCloud Crowd's brood had pelted straight for him, en masse, shrieking for joy. He could armor himself against the adults, barely, but man, he loved those kids. Even through the shield, he felt it.

He'd gotten through the ceremony without losing his shit, evading Zia Rosa, but he could not evade everybody. And nobody was satisfied with his lame mumblings about camping to "get his head together."

A few hours of that treatment, and he found himself circling the reception restlessly, like a shark that had to keep swimming or die. Pretending he was going someplace specific with great speed and purpose so he had a reason to avoid eye contact.

"Miles! I was hoping I'd find you here!"

He jerked his head around, nerves jangling. Holy shit.

It was Cindy, looking stunning, in a skin-tight, red cocktail dress like an old-time Hollywood star, her lips painted red to match. He had not expected to see her here. By no means. He had to scramble to keep his shield strong and steady, he was so startled.

"What are you doing here?" he demanded. "Were you invited?"

Cindy rolled her eyes. "Crashed it. Erin and Connor are furious, but everyone else is too polite to say anything." She threw back the last of her flute of champagne, and exchanged it for a fresh, full one from a passing server's tray. "I mean, like, what harm could I possibly do?"

That was a question he would not care to debate. He edged back, hoping she wouldn't try to touch him. The shield, the shield. It was all about the shield.

"Wow, you look different," she said, her eyes wondering as she circled him. "I've never seen you so brown, not even in the summer. And you're so thin. Your face. You look sort of, I don't know. Feral."

He choked off a bark of laughter. "I'm still housetrained."

"Oh, don't worry," she said, batting her eyes. "I think it's hot. Have you been, like, not eating? Missing me, maybe?"

That he did not want to touch. He shook his head, backing away.

"Wait!" She lunged forward, trying to grab his hand. He whipped it away just in time, and she looked hurt. "You're still mad?"

He almost laughed, but it was just too miserably sad, that she could be so self-absorbed and dense. That he had endured it for so long.

"No, I'm not mad," he said. "I'm done. There's a difference."

Her brown eyes shimmered with tears. "I broke up with Aengus two months ago," she confided. "Turns out he had a serious girlfriend back in Ireland. A seven-year-old son, too. He was just playing around."

"Ah." He waited. "And this is relevant to me exactly why?"

She snapped her empty glass angrily down on a nearby table, and beckoned to a passing waiter until the girl passed by with another tray of glasses. "Don't be a prick," she snapped, taking another swallow. "I'm trying to apologize, and explain, and you're making it really hard."

"Don't waste your breath, Cin," he told her. "I'm not interested."

"Oh, come on." She gave him that look from under her sooty lashes. "You're furious, and you have a perfect right to be. And I am so ready to make it up to you. I checked the place out when I got here. There's this administrative office in the back that's unlocked. No one there. We'll lock it from the inside, and I'll do anything you want. And believe me . . . I know just what you want. I know you so well."

Oh, Jesus. He wished there was a way he could make her understand what was wrong with this picture.

If he were a different kind of guy, without scruples or complicated sensorial brain damage, he might just take her up on her offer. She was gorgeous, skilled. He could just enjoy it, and walk away, vindicated.

Bummer for him, he was not that guy.

Cindy took his hesitation to mean that he was tempted, and started moving in on him, penetrating his danger zone. He tried not to lurch back. God forbid he make a spectacle out of himself. He was sure they were being minutely observed as it was. By everyone.

"Don't touch me, Cin," he said quietly.

Cindy laughed, throatily. "You know you want to, baby."

Not. He genuinely didn't. Maybe it was the shield that had changed him, or maybe he'd finally just grown the requisite brain cells. But the spell was definitively broken.

Cindy didn't know what to make of him now. The only weapon she had was seduction, so she ramped it up, even when it was the wrong weapon for the situation. Ironic, that she only genuinely wanted him when he'd finally disinvested. A long, painful process, and not one he could reverse. She tossed off the third glass of champagne. He caught himself wondering if she was planning on driving. Had to remind himself that it was no longer his problem.

He no longer had to save her, or understand her. Or encourage her to mature into someone who could be his partner in life, someone he could trust and rely on. This flushed, glassy-eyed girl with plunging cleavage and the lipstick on her teeth . . . nah.

"So?" She leaned, brushing her breasts against him.

"No, thanks," he said.

Her eyes narrowed. "Oh, come on. You're just going to sulk?"

He walked steadily away, until the appetizer buffet table blocked his trajectory. Not where he wanted to be. The food smelled too damn strong.

"You need rescuing from Cindy?"

It was Sean, behind him, jiggling his chubby toddler son Eamon in his arms. Frowning.

"Nah," Miles responded. "I'm good."

"So good, you had to bury your head under a pile of rocks

in the mountains for weeks?" Sean chomped grilled shrimp off a skewer, scowling as he did so. "What were you thinking, not calling your mom all that time? Dude! You suck! That's domestic abuse!"

"Sean, don't start with—"

"Shut up, man. Just shut the fuck up. The poor woman drove all the way out to the SafeGuard headquarters, and tried to hire Davy and Seth and Connor to find you! Have you called her yet?"

Miles shook his head, trying not to inhale the odor of shrimp, which was oh, so very far outside his olfactory comfort zone. "Not yet."

"Call her." Sean's voice was hard. "Right now. She's hurting. Not a pretty sight, man. Big fucking fail."

"No, not yet. I want a crack at him while he's still on his feet."

Aaro, behind him. Miles hardened his belly into cast iron and turned. Aaro was clutching Nina, the woman he insisted was his wife, though they had not yet legally tied the knot. Everyone humored him, of course. Only smart thing to do, with Aaro. Behind him was Kev McCloud, his wife Edie, Tam Steele, and Connor and Davy McCloud. A phalanx of people, all accusing him with their eyes.

Christ on a crutch. And he'd thought that dealing with Cindy was challenging. He zapped more energy into his shield, and hung on to the image he used as an emotional anchor. Himself, barefoot, bare-chested, perched on the top of the longest tine of the Fork, staring at the wind-scoured, snowy heights of Mt. Rainier. Looking down on clouds, wind nipping his ears, whipping his hair. Poised on that fine balancing point between hanging on and letting go. Clean. Empty.

The calming image wavered, blurred and broke up. "Back off," he said. "I'll head back the way I came, if I piss everybody off so much."

"Don't threaten us, punk," Aaro growled.

"Shut up, Aaro!" Nina hissed. "You're not helping."

Miles felt a ticklish brush against his mind. Nina was try-ing to use her telepathic talent on him. She'd gained it months ago, in a freakish series of adventures that Miles tried not to think about. She'd come out of that mess a telepath, while Aaro had unearthed a talent for psychic coer-cion. Which struck Miles as amusing. And redundant.

Aaro and Nina had found each other, and true love along the way. Not a bad bargain, even considering the terrifying shit they'd gone through. Too bad it hadn't turned out such a sweet deal for Miles. He'd been the one left bleeding out of his eyes. Monumentally fucked up.

Whoa. Self-pity alert. Cut that shit out fast.

Nina couldn't get past his mental shield. Not even that psycho Rudd had breached it, using the psi equivalent of high explosives. Anabel, Rudd's bimbo henchwoman from hell, hadn't breached it either, using her turbocharged sexual allure. It was a good, sound shield, if he did say so himself. If there was one thing he had totally nailed in his lifetime, it was computer security, even the analogous mental kind.

He just looked at Nina. "Don't try."

She gave him a limpid, innocent look. "Couldn't you just drop the shield?" she coaxed. "It might help, if I could see what's going on. If I knew more about what you're going through, we could—"

"Don't. Try." It came out louder this time.

She nodded, but his ordeal was far from over. The feeling started small. Anxiety, like the start of the brain-ripping agony Rudd had inflicted on him, but just a distant roll of thunder on the horizon.

His stomach flopped with ugly associations. He looked at Aaro. "Try that again, and I'll rip your limbs off," he said.

Aaro's nostrils flared, but the feeling dissipated quickly.

Miles took a deep breath, and visualized the mountaintop again. He fumbled in his pocket for his sunglasses. Wearing them indoors looked affected, but he had nothing to prove to anyone.

"So?" he said. "Everybody done poking and prodding?"

"Not even close," Sean said. "Brace yourself."

Miles let out a painful sigh. "It's all I ever do."

"Let's go out on the terrace," Nina urged. "We can talk." She touched his arm. The contact took him by surprise. He recoiled so violently that everyone froze, shooting glances at each other.

"Jesus, Miles," Kev murmured. "That bad?"

"I'm okay," Miles said. "Just please don't touch me. It's nothing personal, I swear. Just . . . don't."

"Double shot of Scotch?" That was Davy's dour suggestion.

Miles shook his head. If only it were that simple.

The place was set up for the dessert orgy later on. They all sat down at a couple of the white-draped tables, the chairs of which had been tarted up with padded, puffy, brocaded skirts. Edie grabbed one of the cards that had been folded into a tent and left on each table. Dessert menus. A glance at the one in front of Miles showed *baba'*, *boccanotte*, *tiramisu* and *flauti* filled with raspberries and crème chantilly. Plus the cake. Overkill, as usual. The hand of Zia Rosa was evident. The thought of all that sugar made his teeth ache.

Edie pulled a stub of pencil from her handbag, turned the dessert menu over, and gave him a questioning look. Miles shrugged. Edie had a psychic talent of her own. Sometimes her drawings took on oracular meanings. She'd drawn for him before, even after the Spruce Ridge debacle, but he'd never made any sense of the images.

"Go ahead," he muttered. "Do your worst."

"Your enthusiasm overwhelms me," Edie said, but his permission had set her hand loose. She was already scribbling frantically.

The pencil, scratching against paper, scraped nastily over his nerve endings.

"So," Kev said. "Woods, mountains. Did it help?"

"When I was there, it did," he said. "Doesn't do shit for me now."

"It's not a solution," Aaro broke in. "Hiding like a rabbit in a hole."

Miles kept his gaze fixed firmly on the dessert menu.

"So, uh, the sensory overload," Kev asked. "Is it still . . . ?"

"Kicking my ass," Miles supplied.

Nina reached out again, as if to touch his hand, but stopped. "So why are you here?"

"Didn't want to piss off Bruno and Lily," he offered.

Sean grunted. "You haven't cared about pissing us off for a while."

Miles was silent, trying to think of something to say that would ward them off, but no such thing existed, or else he was not smart enough to think of it. And these people were his good friends, even though he couldn't feel the connection. He was looking at them through a tunnel that was light years long.

A racking shiver went through him. Surrender. He opened his mouth, and the miserable truth fell out, heavily.

"I was thinking about trying the meds again," he said.

An appalled silence greeted that statement.

"You said the meds made you feel half-dead," Sean said. "You barely recognized your own family when you were on that shit. You think you're crazy? Really? It's that bad? Has it gotten worse?"

Nina tugged her chair over until she was sitting directly in front of him. Forcing him to meet her eyes. "What's going on, Miles?"

"I've done time on antipsychotic drugs," Edie said. "I don't recommend it. I don't think you're there, Miles. None of us do."

"But the voices," he blurted. "I . . . well, I don't exactly hear her."

"Her? Who's her?" Aaro snarled. "Make some sense, damn it!"

"Her?" Nina's eyes went huge. "Lara? You're talking about Lara? You *hear* her?"

"Well, no. I don't exactly hear her," he said again. "It's, uh, text messages. She, ah . . . she texts me."

They all glanced around at each other, utterly perplexed.

"You mean, on your phone?" Davy said, his voice tentative.

"No," Miles forced out. "No, I mean, in my head."

It took them an interminable, silent interval to process that. He waited, teeth clenched. Braced for it.

"Weird," Connor commented, finally.

"Yeah," Miles agreed. "I never even met this girl. I've been assuming she was dead. And even if she isn't dead, how would she ever have learned my password?"

"What the fuck?" Aaro sounded angry. "Password? I could wrap my head around voices. But texts? You're a machine, with circuitry?"

"That's what's happening to me, so eat it," Miles growled.

Aaro gave him the stony mafiya stare. "Don't give me attitude."

"You're the one with the attitude. If you can't shove it around or bully it, you don't want to deal with it at all," Miles retorted.

"Shut up, both of you," Nina scolded. "We're getting off track."

"It's his hero complex," Aaro said. "He needs a damsel in distress to save. Cindy's out of the picture, so he's creating a new one."

Miles snorted. "When the damsel starts texting my brain directly, it's time for the fucking meds."

"You think she's a psychotic delusion?" Nina asked.

"Matilda wouldn't have thought so," he replied, and then he had to explain all about Matilda, her cryptic voicemail, and her subsequent murder. Those grim details quelled even Edie's scribbling for a while.

"This is creeping me out," Aaro muttered.

"You're not the only one obsessing about Lara," Nina said. "She was like my little sister. Aaro and I have turned this thing inside out."

"Me, too," Miles said bleakly. "I followed them—every clue. Roy Lester's dead. Dimitri Arbatov, too. Anabel's disappeared. Rudd got splattered. There's no such place as Karstow, as far as I can tell. And Thaddeus Greaves is a dead end."

Flat silence followed this litany of dead leads. After Nina and Aaro's adventure, no one was left alive to ask where Lara Kirk might be, except of course for Greaves himself, Rudd's billionaire boss. Who had insisted that he was as innocent as the dawn. According to Greaves, his minions had gone tragically rogue. So shocking. And embarrassing.

"I couldn't read him, when I was close to him," Nina mused. "His shield was like a force field that swallowed anything it touched. Yours feels kind of like that, too. Remember when you came up with the encrypted computer as your analog for a shield? And I made you write down the password? I remember it. All caps LARA, hashtag—"

"Stop, Nina," he warned, but it was too late. The questing tickle in his mind intensified as she dredged up the rest of it, picking up speed.

"Star, exclamation point, your aunt in California's zip code—nine two six one nine, hashtag, all caps KIRK, and two question marks!"

Crack, she breached it—and his world collapsed inward.

Rudd hung over him, his demonic face purple, screaming. Ear-splitting noise, nerves screaming, searing heat . . . a flash of light . . .

. . . nothing.

His eyes fluttered open, later. Flagstones, cool against his cheek. Wrought iron table legs. Human legs, in hose and heels, dress shoes.

He turned his head. Leaves against a white sky. Anxious faces swam in his vision. He struggled to put names to them, to himself.

They jolted heavily into place, like train cars coupling. The blur of rust-colored chiffon beside him was Nina. She clutched a bloody napkin to her nose, shaking with sobs. His nose bled, too. Edie passed him a napkin. He plugged the leak, glad for an excuse not to speak.

Oh, man. And he thought his head had hurt before.

"Would somebody please tell me what the fuck is going on?" Aaro snarled, as Kev and Davy hoisted Miles up into a sitting position.

"Oh, God," Nina whispered, her voice thick. "I didn't know."

"It's okay," Miles said. Though of course, it wasn't.

"What didn't you know?" Aaro bellowed.

"Shhh." Nina soothed, patting Aaro's cheek. "I didn't know how bad it was," she said to Miles. "I shouldn't have done that to you. I don't know how you're walking around, with all that going on in your head."

"Think I should go for the padded cell, then?"

He'd meant it as a joke, but surprise, surprise—no one laughed.

Nina shuddered. "That's where I'd be," she said.

"You had a seizure," Kev told him. "You were yelling. Looked bad."

"Stress flashback," Sean said. "Rudd?"

"That's what happens if I drop the shield. The shield holds it all together." He glanced pointedly at Nina. "If nobody fucks with it."

"Sorry," Nina whispered, abjectly. "Really. Just trying to help."

He started to shake his head. Stopped, with a hiss of pain. "I'm past help. When you start getting text messages from dead girls in your head, it's time to call the guys in the white coats with the little van."

"No," Nina said. "You're not crazy, Miles."

The murmuring stilled. Miles' mouth was dangling. He closed it with a snap. "Ah . . . how do you figure?"

"I saw a little in there, before the seizures," Nina said. "I felt some of your memories. You never met Lara, but I did. I know her vibe. And I felt it. I felt *her*. She's not dead."

Miles felt that drum roll starting up. Part dread, part compulsion, rumbling ominously inside him. "Nina. Please. Don't do this to me."

"She got through the shield, just like I did," Nina insisted.

"You got through it because I told you the password!" he shouted. "How could she get through? I never told it to her. I don't *know* her!"

"You didn't have to tell her," she said. "She *is* your password."

Miles struggled to his feet, batting their hands away. Batting the whole thought away. Too crazy. Too weird. Blood roared in his ears. His heart thudded, a swift, panicked gallop, even as it slipped into place, with a soft, inevitable "click."

This explained so much. He clutched his head in his hands, on the verge of total brain meltdown. Trying to process it.

She is your password. Holy freaking shit. Could she really . . . ?

"You think she's alive, then?" he blurted. "And locked in a dungeon for real? And the only person she can talk to is me? Just because I put her name into my goddamn password?"

Nina gazed at him steadily. "You put a Lara Kirk shaped hole in your mental shield, Miles. Who better than she could find her way in?"

"This isn't helping," Kev warned. "You're setting him off. He'll go off on a quest when we should be calling the paramedics."

"It could just be a hallucination," Davy said.

"You didn't feel what I felt," Nina said.

"Thank God for that, if feeling it comes with a nose-bleed," Tam commented, with distaste. "I hate getting blood on my clothes."

Miles covered his face with his hands against the overload. Too much. That machine inside him, gears grinding. Doors opening, air rushing in. New possibilities, electrifying him.

"If she's alive, I'll find her," he said.

"Oh, fuck, no," Sean muttered. "Here we go again."

He'd already tuned them out. He brushed the dust from his suit. He'd whanged his elbow and knee somewhere, going down. Add those high and low notes to the cocktail of undifferentiated pain.

But as messed up as he was, it was such a relief to give into it. Like he'd been craving something that he knew was bad for him, and now he was like, fuck it. Binge city. "Later, guys," he said. "I'm gone."

"Don't do this!" Kev sounded angry. "You're not up to it!"

"What else am I good for?" he asked, looking around at them. "Seriously? The shape I'm in? What the fuck else do I have to do?"

Nobody had an answer for that. But he hadn't expected one.

Tam pulled a ring off her finger. "Take this. I was too busy with Irina this morning to tart myself up properly, or I'd give you more."

Miles held the delicate thing gingerly. The jewelry Tam designed tended to hide lethal secrets. "Is it poisoned?"

She gave him her most mysterious smile. "I don't wear pieces treated with poison while I'm with my children. It's got explosives, though."

Miles studied Tam's striking design. Twists of white and yellow gold tangled around faceted jet. "What's the trick?"

"Twist it counterclockwise. It's a tack, and inside is a wad of explosives. The button on the ring band is a detonator. Punch the spike into a car tire. It won't blow the tire until you detonate it with the ring band. Stay close. It gets unpredictable at over five hundred meters."

"Ah," Miles said, doubtfully.

"I'm sure you'll figure out uses I've never even thought of."

Miles had no illusions about his own potential sneakiness as compared to Tam's, but it was a nice thought. He tried to put the ring on his pinkie, but it wouldn't go past his big knuckle. He slipped it into his jacket. "Thanks."

Edie stepped forward and held out the dessert menu that she had used for her drawing. "Take this," she offered.

Miles almost dreaded looking at it. "What is it?"

"Haven't got a clue. You tell me."

It was a mountain peak, two prongs like lopsided horns, and a downward sloping crest between them, like the bridge of a big nose; a metaphor that came easily to him. Superimposed was a crosshatched pattern, like chain link. The tops of three tall conifers framed the scene.

He looked up at Edie. Shook his head mutely.

She sighed. "Whatever. It was worth a try."

"Thanks anyway." Miles shoved the picture into his suit jacket, along with the ring. "I'm gone."

"I'm coming, too," Sean said.

"And me," Kev added.

"Me, too," Aaro chimed in.

"No way," Miles said. "A mass exodus of all the important guests at Bruno and Lily's wedding? Stay. Do your duty. I'll call you later."

"No, you won't," Aaro said.

The pain in Aaro's voice made Miles pause, but only for a moment. He could not deal with his friend's hurt feelings right now.

He simply did not have the equipment.

5

Greaves gazed at his staff over the rim of the cup, letting them all sweat. He was a benevolent man, who wanted only the best for the people in his charge. But he did not suffer fools gladly.

He placed the empty cup in its saucer. Someone whisked it away. He turned to Anabel, and Jason Hu. "We'll begin with you two. What progress have you made on the formula?"

"Not a great deal," Anabel admitted reluctantly.

"Have you taken Lara up to twice a day, as I directed? Upping the doses by three percent daily?"

"Her blood pressure dropped when we jumped from seventy micrograms to seventy-three," Hu said. "I dialed it back. I've been increasing it in increments of .5 percent. Her sleep cycles are disordered, so we've been dosing her at night, and sometimes in the early morning, since that seems most conducive to—"

"Next time, do exactly as I direct you," Greaves said. "To the letter. Do not second-guess me again."

Hu gulped, his eyes darting down to the table. "Yes, sir."

He turned to Anabel. "Do you continue to lose contact when she ranges?"

"Her ability to shield seems to be growing," Anabel admitted. "I hang onto her for a while, but I always lose her at some point."

"Odd," Greaves mused. "I had no problem at all monitoring her on the day that she first-dosed. It seems your abilities as a telepath are dwindling. As your other abilities seem to have done, as well."

She turned mottled red at his reference to her neglected talent for sexual magnetism. "My talent is as strong as ever, but it's like I told you, sir. Her shield is impenetrable. If she gets behind it, I get nothing, and neither do the other telepaths. I don't understand how she—"

"There is a great deal that you don't understand, Anabel."

"Sir, I—"

"Shut up. I'm done with you for now. Levine, Houghman, Chrisholm, Mehalis. Have any of you had better luck penetrating this momentous shield?"

The other four telepaths on his staff exchanged nervous glances, and shook their heads. Greaves ground his teeth. Lily-livered idiots, all of them. Anabel was the strongest of the lot, and even she was falling short. He was so sick of hand-holding, micromanaging.

"Very well," he said, through his teeth. "Let's discuss the telepathic surveillance project, then. How is that proceeding?"

"Fine, sir," Levine said. "We take six-hour shifts, as you directed. We haven't detected anyone yet, except in the staged test runs."

"Sir," Silva piped up. "I wanted to speak to you about that. It strikes me as a poor use of resources, considering their limited range. They can't detect anyone beyond, say, forty meters, and—"

"It is an exercise, Silva," Greaves explained patiently. "One does not extend one's range unless one is forced to push oneself. Are you familiar with the concept of pushing yourself? Because I am beginning to wonder."

"Of course, sir, but I think that using just the infrared and motion detectors rather than staff who could be concentrating on complex—"

"I ask you to trust me on this, Silva," Greaves suggested gently.

Silva subsided. An intelligent decision on his part.

"Continue with the rotations," Greaves directed. "Has anyone noticed any increase in range?"

He looked around, tapping his fingers. No one would meet his eyes. Disappointing, but at least they had better sense than to lie to him. "Very well," he said crisply. "Moving on." He flipped through the brief that laid out the research team's latest results and projections.

"Lewis." He addressed the team's head researcher. "You released the aerosolized toxin into the air ducts of the correctional facility for men in Chikala, Utah, six months ago. Summarize what you have observed since then."

Lewis consulted his notes. "Put briefly, there was no perceivable change in the first two months, but in the third month, incidence of violence went down fourteen percent. By the fourth month, it was down thirty-three percent. Fifth month, fifty-seven percent. The sixth month, sixty-eight percent. There were sixty percent fewer visits to the infirmary this past month, and it appears the inmates' overall general health has improved, as well. Colds, fevers, infections, all way down. The prison staff is healthier, too. Less absenteeism, fewer complaints and conflicts on the job. Inmate suicide attempts are down to almost zero, for the past four months running."

Greaves smiled. "Finally, some good news. Thank you."

Lewis went on, emboldened. "This recreates the results we got on that last two prison trials, almost exactly. This form of the toxin appears to have a calming effect upon the endocrine system. It lowers stress hormone production, and it mitigates, or even reverses depression. And in an odd side note, it seems that drug use is down, too, though that is difficult to measure in a prison population. Even smoking appears to have decreased."

"Very good," Greaves murmured. "Go on."

Lewis fumbled with his papers. "Incidence of sexual violence is down almost sixty-five percent," he announced.

Greaves frowned. "Only?"

Lewis looked nonplussed. "Ah . . . it was considered a very positive statistic, considering the—"

"Tell that to the remaining thirty-five percent. We must hold ourselves to a higher standard. This is our legacy, Lewis."

"Yes, sir, of course," Lewis said hastily. "We will try—"

"Yes, you will most certainly continue to try, if you know what is good for you. I am pleased with these results. We will move on to Phase Three next week. Any questions?"

Dead silence met his query. Shifty eyes. He almost laughed. His staff was getting cold feet. Ridiculous, considering that they were already inoculated against the experimental organism. Which was, in any case, entirely benign, even health-promoting, as the trials had clearly demonstrated for years now. And they weren't even releasing an airborne version of the microbe yet. That happy day would come next year, after observing the results of Phase Three.

Greaves was a cautious man. Methodical, responsible. If this was to be done, it would be done absolutely right, in every particular.

"Moving on." He turned to Silva and Chrisholm. "You two. Explain how two professionals at the height of their careers managed to fumble the matter of Matilda Bennet."

Chrisholm's throat bobbed. He touched livid scratches on his neck, as if he wanted to hide them. "Sir, she had a can of pepper spray—"

"I did not ask for excuses. I asked for an explanation. A woman of seventy-three, with no professional training outside of secretarial school, and somehow she found us. By following you, Chrisholm, from the museum at Blaine. By following the sales of Lara Kirk's sculptures to you. And then she followed you here, to our doorstep. It is pure, dumb luck that she told no one about this facility before she died. One hopes, anyway. And no thanks to you."

"Sir, please," Silva pleaded. "We—"

"If you open your mouth out of turn one more time, I will make an example of you. You would not enjoy it. Although at this point, I would."

Silva sputtered. "Ah . . . I . . ." He cut himself off.

Greaves turned to Chrisholm. "I suggested that Bennet have a tragic domestic accident," he said. "An elderly lady, living alone, multiple health problems. And look what I got. Massive news coverage. A statewide manhunt. Your skin beneath her fingernails."

Chrisholm leaned forward. "Sir, I promise, we—"

He shrieked as his body rose into the air, chair flung back by his own wildly kicking legs. He hung, suspended over the long, gleaming mahogany conference table, gurgling and flailing. Plucking his throat.

It was hardly fair, to make an example of only one of them for the sins of both but, pragmatically speaking, he could not afford to lose two highly trained staff members right now. And Silva's talent for coercion was more useful than Chrisholm's rather mediocre telepathic abilities. So Chrisholm it was.

"The time for promises has passed," Greaves said. "Silva. Open the French doors, please."

Silva stared openmouthed at his floating colleague, whose face had gone purple. Chrisholm's eyes popped. Sweat and saliva plopped down, spattering, marring the perfect sunlit swathe of fine-grained wood.

Silva got up, walked stiffly to the French doors that led onto the terrace. It overlooked a deep canyon. A plunge of three hundred feet onto jagged rocks and trees. He opened it. "Sir, please. We only—"

"Would you like to take his place?" Greaves' voice was

only mildly curious. "I could switch the two of you out. If you preferred."

"I . . . I . . ." Silva plucked at his collar, blinking frantically.

"I thought not," Greaves murmured.

Chrisholm's twitching form floated to the back of the room, then sped forward as if flung from a catapult. Out the open window, over the railing. Legs scissoring madly.

Cold wind swirled into the room, making Lewis' notes fly up into the air. Lewis groped for them. Paper crinkled in the silence.

Greaves contemplated the open window, saddened. But a leader could not hesitate when an unpleasant task had to be done.

He made a gesture toward the window, and the presumed mess below. "Deal with that," he said, and turned his gaze on Anabel and Hu. "Bring me the girl. I'm ready for her now."

Lara sat on her cot, crosslegged in the dark, in a state of profound concentration. Today, her coping technique was a mental walk through room after room in the Uffizi, the art museum in Florence, looking at the works of the great Italian masters. She'd paused at Botticelli's *Birth of Venus*, dredging up every remembered detail when lights jolted on.

Anabel and Hu burst in, as if propelled. She had to scramble to keep her feet beneath her when they yanked her into the corridor.

Something was up. Something different, big. They hustled right on past the usual torture chamber and into the tiny elevator. Lara's eyes skittered away from her reflection on the metallic wall. That hollow-eyed girl with the big snarl of dark hair could not be her.

The elevator rose two floors, and opened onto a different world. The place they kept her was dank, ugly. Stained concrete floors, cinder block walls, exposed insulation. This floor was plush. Bland, neutral colors, like a luxury hotel. Hu opened a door. Her eyes stung, dazzled.

She'd been sitting in pitch darkness ever since the last drug trip, breathing stale, fetid air. In here, cool air swirled, smelling of trees, earth, sky, sun. French doors were flung wide, to the same view she got from her chain-link hole. The horned hill. She stared at it hungrily as she sucked in lungfuls of scented air, and sensed a person behind her.

She turned. The man had positioned himself in a ray of sunlight. His snow-white hair glowed like a halo. He wore a white shirt, perfectly pressed gray trousers. His teeth were insanely bright. He hurt her eyes.

Behind her, a server scurried in with a tray. The rich, buttery smell assaulted her nose. Anabel and Hu kept pulling, but her feet were rooted to the ground. They yanked. She thudded to her knees.

"Anabel," the man chided, his voice velvety and deep. "No need to be rough."

Lara struggled up, onto wobbling legs. "Who the hell are you?"

Whack. Anabel hit the back of her head, knocking her onto her knees again. "Speak when you're spoken to, you snotty bitch."

"Anabel, that will do. Go stand next to the door."

"Sir, be careful," Anabel told him. "She's unpredictable. Just two weeks ago, she bit Hu's hand when we were—"

"Do you really think that I need protection?" His voice was gentle, but Anabel gasped and stumbled hastily back, clutching her throat.

He turned to her. "Lara. So glad to meet you. I've been following your progress. Please, sit. Coffee? Some scones?"

Progress? *Scones?* She gaped at his angelic smile, his beckoning hand. "Your timing's off," she said. "After all this time sitting in a hole, your good cop/bad cop routine is not going to work with me."

"I would be disappointed if it did," he said serenely.

She stared at the open window, the canyon beyond. That attractive expanse of beautiful, empty air.

"Ah, ah, ah." The man shook his head. "Don't even let the thought form in your head. You would not get a single step."

Right. Probably not. She breathed down the crazy urge.

"Sit. Lara. Really," he urged.

She simply could not play party games with this asshole, whoever he was. Fuck his coffee and his scones. "So you're the big boss?" she asked. "I have you to thank for my quality of life these past few months?"

"Not exactly," he replied. "I inherited you, you might say. Your abduction was a choice I would not personally have made, but it was made, and there it is. We have to live with the consequences. Harold Rudd, the man who abducted you, did so to control your mother."

"So I was told," she said. "They said her death three years ago was faked. That she died just a few months ago." Her gaze flashed to Anabel and Hu, and back to the white-haired guy. "I don't believe it. My mother would never have let me think she was dead for three years."

"Not if she had any choice." The man's tongue clucked. "So sad."

Her ears were starting to roar. "So you did to her what you're doing to me?"

"No. Not me," he said, his voice soothing. "Calm down, Lara."

"Hah." She was breathing fast, face hot, hands clammy. "How stupid is that, to drive me out of my mind, and then tell me to be calm. So it's true, what they said? That my father was murdered, too?"

His face was impassive. "Yes, Lara," he said. "I am sorry. It is true. He died the day after your mother."

She believed him, for some reason, though she had no idea who this self-important bozo was. She had no reason to doubt Anabel and Hu, either, but she'd still been hoping on some level that their jibes were just psychological torture.

That Dad was alive and safe, smelling of pencil dust and Scotch. Still loving her. The last one around who did.

That hope withered and died when this man spoke. She hated him for it. Tears flooded her eyes. She forced them back. "If you're not the monster, then why didn't you let me go?"

"It's complicated, but it will all be made clear. Sit down."

"Complicated, my ass! I want answers! Who the hell are you?"

He let out a sharp, frustrated sigh. "My name is Thaddeus Greaves. I am your host. And I want. You. To. Sit. *Down*."

Lara gasped, muscles seizing up as her body moved. Not of her own volition, but as if she were a doll. She clamped down on the rising panic, fighting to keep her legs beneath her. When she was near the table, the chair he'd indicated floated up, did a quarter turn, and settled, feather light, behind her. A shove at her waist, another behind the crook of her knees, and *flop*, down she sat. Hard and graceless.

"Sorry about the bump." Greaves stirred a small lump of sugar into his coffee. "Gravity's a bitch. Sometimes she just can't be reasoned with. Hope I didn't scare you."

She fought for control of her voice for a few moments. "Not at all," she finally managed. "I prefer it when the thumbscrews are out there for me to see. I like to know where I stand."

Greaves pushed the plate toward her. She stared at the heap of hot, golden pastries, the pats of butter in a dish, the little silver knife.

They looked amazing. She hadn't put anything that tasted good into her mouth since they had captured her. After months of stale, gummy food that she had to muscle past her gag reflex, her salivary glands were going nuts. Her hands shook.

But anything this attractive had to be a trap. She shook her head.

"Lara," Greaves chided. "They're delicious. Why not?"

She kept her voice carefully even. "I will not voluntarily ingest anything you offer me."

He looked affronted. "If I wanted to poison or drug you, I would have Anabel shove a needle into your throat. Please, relax."

She stared at the plate, at him. He smiled.

It was his smile that did it. It sparked flesh-creeping dread, just like the sting of the psi-max needle, and she caught her breath as the pit yawned suddenly, the double vision. This world and the swirling visions, somehow coexisting. Then the sickening dip in blood pressure, the deep, hard suck . . . a vortex, dragging her.

She fought it, jaw locked. Resisted that sucking pull . . . rooted to the ground . . . fighting with everything she had.

She wasn't strong enough. It launched her into the dream world.

Foggy, overgrown forest. Park benches were choked with vines, shrubs, weeds. A dry fountain was visible in the distance, beside it the lifelike bronze statue that she'd seen many times before, eternally poised in the act of snapping a picture with a cell phone. Eerie in the drifting fog.

She spun at the silent summons that prickled at her nape. Her little friend, the ghostly blond boy, dressed in ragged, filthy child's pajamas. He seemed younger than the other times she'd seen him.

"Hello," she said. "Could you help me find the Citadel?"

The little boy shook his head violently. His eyes were wide with fear, fixed on something behind her. He backed away, turned and sprinted into the mist. She opened her mouth to call after him, but the cry never left her throat as the thought-probe stabbed, tearing her mind apart.

The shock jolted her violently back to the bright, airy room, and waking consciousness. Her thudding heart slowed. The darkness before her eyes cleared. She panted. Sagging in the chair. God. She'd gone off on a trip. Right in front of this creepy guy, and they hadn't even injected her. Not for ten hours, and the effect had never lasted that long before.

". . . amazing!" Greaves was saying, jubilantly. "Finally, we might have a viable formula! Your psi took off spontaneously. Excellent. What did you see? You came back before I established contact." Greaves knelt by her chair, tipped a cup into her mouth. She sputtered, choked.

He jerked back. Not fast enough. His shirt was splattered with coffee. "Do it again," he said. "I want another look."

"I can't," she said, shakily. "I can't control it."

He stared into her eyes. "You will learn," he said softly. "You will train with me. Rigorously. This is so exciting, Lara. To actually glimpse the future. I'll come along with you, on your next trip."

"You?" Her stomach was in free-fall, but his words weren't a surprise, not after that agonizing mind-stab. Worse than Anabel's. "You . . . you're—"

"A telepath? Among other things. I can't wait to put you through your paces. You've been giving Anabel trouble with that shield of yours, but I'm a different proposition. We'll see if you can get behind your shield with me in the saddle."

His tone made the words seem horribly lascivious. "I thought . . ." She cleared her throat. "I don't block anyone on purpose. I—"

"It doesn't matter. You don't block me. I have many gifts, Lara." His eyes slid down her body, assessing. "As do you. I look forward to discovering them. In fact, after your next dose, I think I will take you back home with me."

A steel band seemed to squeeze her throat. "Home?"

"We'll have privacy," he said. "If you are with me, there's no need for locks and bolts or restraints. I will keep you absolutely secure."

As he spoke, she felt her wrists and ankles squeezed, as if hot, greedy hands clutched her there. Her guts lurched.

"I'm sorry for how painful these past months have been,"

he said. "I look forward to making it up to you. And I'm curious about your shield."

She flinched. God forbid he get anywhere near the Citadel. He'd find some way to twist it, pollute it. "I don't know where I go when they drug me," she said. "It's a nightmare, and I just endure it until it stops."

He scrutinized her. "There's no place for lies here."

It wasn't entirely a lie. That was how it had been, until she found her Citadel. That was where she had stashed what was left of her sanity. If she lost her safe place, she was so done.

She dragged air into her tight chest. "How did my mother die?"

He brushed his fingertips over the coffee spots on his white shirt with distaste. "I wasn't there," he said. "Ask Anabel."

"Anabel killed my mother?"

He made an impatient gesture. "Lara, please. I'm very sorry about your mother, and I was very angry about how that was handled. I claim no responsibility for it. I understand how you feel about your parents, but it's done and gone. You have to look to the future."

She let out a bitter laugh. "What do you want, Greaves?"

He smiled flirtatiously. "Besides the obvious? I want to save the world. To make it a better place. I am absolutely committed to that."

Laughter jolted out of her throat again, hard, and suddenly she was doubled over, wheezing and shaking. Eyes watering, as her chest convulsed. It was so stupid to laugh at him, it went against every instinct of self-preservation, but she could not stop.

"I see we have a great deal of work ahead of us," Greaves said.

She shook her head. "Why don't you just strangle me telekinetically right now and save yourself a lot of time and bother?"

His gaze was fixed and hard. "Where's the fun in that?

Anabel, Hu, take our guest down to the testing room. My patience has ended."

Anabel and Hu were at her elbows, hauling her to her feet.

"Sir," Hu said, his voice vibrating. "Sorry to inconvenience you—"

"Then don't, Hu," Greaves suggested, pleasantly.

Hu gulped. "It's still too soon now, after her last dose. Her blood levels will still be—"

Greaves cut him off with a sharp sound. "How long must we wait?"

"Uh, twenty-two more hours would be the optimal—"

"Split the difference, make it fourteen hours," Greaves said briskly. "We'll meet in the testing room for the final dosing at six A.M. tomorrow morning. Take her away, please. I need to change this shirt."

Hu cleared his throat. "Sir? About that testing . . . at six . . ."

Greaves looked back from the door he was opening. "Yes?"

"My wife is having a serious operation tomorrow morning, at Good Samaritan, and I was hoping—"

"You want to take personal time now?" Greaves' voice was soft with disbelief. "At the culmination of your most important assignment?"

". . . a tumor removed," Hu said desperately. "From her esophagus. It's a delicate operation, and I need to—"

"*You* need? Hu, is it possible that your wife does not understand the importance of your work? Is she that selfish, that small-minded?"

"I . . . of course she . . . ah . . ." Hu's mouth worked.

"Because if she doesn't, maybe you should find a different wife. Maybe one who doesn't have cancer. Do I make myself clear?"

"Yes, sir." Hu's voice was impassive. "I'll be there."

"Excellent." Greaves shut the door sharply behind himself.

Lara barely bothered to keep her feet beneath her on the way back down. She had no fight left. Greaves had sucked it all out of her. She let them drag her dead weight, but one thought kept circling in her mind as she stared up at Anabel's profile. "Did you kill my mother?"

Anabel snorted. "She killed herself, you stupid bitch. Some use rope, some use razors. She used me. She would have died anyway."

"I'll kill you for that," Lara said.

"Yeah? You terrify me, babycakes." Anabel jerked Lara around and pushed her against the wall. "But I won't have to look over my shoulder much longer! The boss is taking you away to be his little pet. Lucky girl! Sing pretty for him in your gilded cage! Tra-la-fucking-la!"

"Anabel, stop bruising her," Hu fretted. "Looks like the boss will be seeing her naked soon enough. He won't like the marks."

Anabel twitched up Lara's shirt and tweaked her exposed nipple brutally hard. "He'll kill me one of these days anyhow. What the fuck."

"Don't lay your death wish on me," Hu grumbled. He pulled out his keys, opened locks. Anabel pushed Lara inside. "Want to know a fun fact?" she asked. "I was his pet, once. For about twenty minutes or so."

It was clearly a trap, but desperation drove to ask it. "And? So?"

"I needed corrective surgery. For the damage to my vocal folds."

Lara stared, uncomprehending. "Vocal folds? What damage?"

"From the screaming," she said, as the door swung shut.

6

L ate to the funeral. True to form. It was all part of his race
to see how many people he could offend in the shortest
possible amount of time. If that were an Olympic event, he'd
be a gold medalist.

Not that Matilda would care, and that sad, sick fact had its
own leaden heaviness. He didn't feel the sadness in the same
sharp buzzy way that he had before he'd shielded, but he still
bore its dumb, brute weight in his body. It shortened his
wind, took the spring out of his legs. It was just so sad. So
fucking wrong.

The assembled congregation was singing "Be Thou My
Vision," and the sound of the organ hit him like car alarms
going off inside his skull. Funeral lilies took the place of
wedding orange flowers, but they packed the same olfactory
punch. Matilda's casket was closed, thank God.

He lurked off to the side while the minister droned on
about Matilda's awesomeness and the mystery of God's forgiveness. He spotted some of Matilda's colleagues from the
faculty office. In front was a chubby young woman in black
who had to be Amy. Beside her was a guy in Army dress uni-

form. Steve, the husband. The two sat alone. No other family. A final hymn was announced. Miles braced himself for "Amazing Grace" as he chivvied himself into the condolence line, for what insane reason he could not fathom. Why? What point was there? Matilda didn't care. Amy and Steve didn't know him from Adam. He didn't know a soul here, and yet, here he was, using up his tiny margin of crowd endurance to stand in the line and gag on the perfume of a bunch of weeping, shellshocked ladies of a certain age.

He breathed through his mouth and pretended to be normal. As usual, he was being compelled. Some huge entity was playing kick-the-can, he was the luckless can, and he might as well give in before that big boot swung down to connect with his ass once again. He got to the front of the line, clasped the hand of the uniformed guy. He muttered the requisite platitudes, got a red-eyed, tight-lipped nod in response. On to Amy.

She gave him a look that almost fucked his shield, it was so full of raw grief. He reeled, poised on his mountaintop, fighting for balance. Wind in his hair, eye to eye with the eagles. *Please.* No seizures. These people did not need to deal with his problems. Today or any day.

". . . birthday," Amy's tear-fogged voice slid back into focus, abruptly loud. "The day that I found her."

"Ah, excuse me?" he said, stupidly.

"We always did the same thing for our birthday," Amy quavered. "We had the same birthday. She raised me, see. After my mom bailed."

"Uh . . . oh." And she was telling him this exactly why?

She clutched his hand in her ice-cold grip. "She always took me to Rose's Deli," Amy said. "I got a chocolate éclair. She got a Napoleon. Every time. I was going to pick her up. She hated driving since the cataract surgery. And I found . . . I found . . ." Her voice wobbled, disintegrated.

"You should go, then." Miles hoped he wasn't lobbing an

emotional land mine at the poor chick, but he had to say something. "Go to Rose's. Have pastry in her honor. She would have liked that."

Amy's face wavered, crumpled. She began to sob.

The umpteenth big-ass emotional misstep for the day. How soon could a person yank their hand back from a sobbing bereaved person at a funeral? Miles stood there, helpless, until Steve rescued him, loosening Amy's clutching fingers, rubbing her hand between his own. He gave Miles a nod that politely invited him to fuck off, which Miles was grateful to do.

Oh, man. Close call. He found an empty corner in the back, and waited for the crowd to file out so he could slink out behind them like a whipped dog. He squeezed his eyes shut, tried to breathe.

"So. How did you know the deceased?"

He almost yelped. It was an unremarkable middle-aged, bald guy in a suit.

Cop. The look in his eyes gave him away. Miles was sensitive to it by now. The McClouds all had that vibe. Seth, Tam, Val, Nick, Petrie, and Aaro, too. Professionally alert, professionally suspicious. Of course, any cop with half a brain would eyeball Miles. These days, he looked like a psycho freak who was building a fertilizer bomb. Even in a suit.

"I'm Miles Davenport," he said. "You must be Detective Barlow."

The guy's eyes sharpened. "And how would you know that?"

"I have your number in my phone," Miles said. "I got it from Steve last night."

"When were you planning on calling me? And about what?"

Miles pulled out his smartphone, and called up the archived voicemail. "I was wilderness camping. Came down last night, found this message from Matilda. She sent it to me a week ago." He set it to play, and handed the phone to Barlow.

Barlow listened to the message, clicked around on the device for a moment, studying it. He handed it back to Miles, his face expectant.

"I called Matilda back," Miles explained. "Got her granddaughter. She and Steve told me what happened."

Barlow shook his head. "Hell of a thing." He was silent for a moment, and said, "That message was sent the day she was killed."

"I noticed that," Miles said.

Barlow waited, but Miles didn't have more to say. Nor was he embarrassed by silence. He'd spent weeks wrapped in silence.

"So," Barlow finally said. "How did you know Matilda?"

"Like the message said. We had a mutual interest in Lara Kirk. She'd asked me to help find Lara. She's the daughter of Joseph—"

"I'm familiar with the case. So. What do you think of all this?"

Miles shrugged. "I didn't find out a damn thing about Lara, and I looked hard. Evidently, Matilda kept looking after I gave up."

"Should've kept at it." Barlow ran his eyes over Miles. "You might have had more luck with them. If they'd run into you, instead of her."

It hurt to hear it, but he couldn't deny it. "Could be," he said tightly. "Too late now. Wish I knew what she'd found. But I don't."

"I wish that, too," Barlow said. "So where were you on the morning of October twenty-eighth, Mr. Davenport?"

Miles let out a slow breath. "Like I said. Wilderness camping."

"Kind of cold, for camping. Got anybody to corroborate that?"

Miles shook his head. "I was alone."

Barlow's face was impassive. "That's unfortunate."

"You think I'm the one who killed her?" Miles asked.

Barlow studied him, at great length. "You don't look too upset by that idea," he remarked. "Cool as a cucumber."

Miles counted down from five. "I'm not a killer," he said. "Matilda was my friend. She was a sweet old lady. I liked her. I had no reason to hurt her. And I'd never hurt anybody who didn't really need hurting."

Barlow perked up. "Yeah? And who might that be, according to you? This person who needs hurting?"

Miles tried to sigh out the tension in his chest. "Any sick, twisted piece of shit who would throw a helpless old lady down the stairs. That guy needs some serious hurting, and if I ran into him, I'd be happy to provide it."

"Vigilantism is against the law," the cop reminded him.

Miles waved his hand. "Yeah, yeah."

Barlow just kept staring, so Miles sighed, and laid it out there. "You're trying to decide whether to take me in for questioning?"

Barlow shrugged.

"Please, don't," Miles said wearily. "It's been a hell of a day already, and I'm not your man. Plus, if I find out anything, I'll tell you."

"Before or after you do the serious hurting to people who may or may not have had a trial by law with a jury of their peers?"

"I'll be good," he said. "Look, do you know Sam Petrie?"

The guy's eyes slitted. "Why?"

"I was just with him an hour ago, at the wedding of a mutual friend. He knows me. Call him. He'll vouch for me."

"Wait here," Barlow said. "Stay put."

He went out onto the steps to make his call. Miles crossed his fingers that Petrie had kept his phone on and was still coherent. Barlow kept Miles in his line of sight as he conducted his conversation.

He came back in. "So you're *that* Miles Davenport."

Miles sighed. "My fame precedes me." That bad business a couple of years ago with Kev, Edie. A firefight in the woods, a shootout at a murdered billionaire's house. That shit stuck in people's minds.

"He vouched for you," Barlow said. "Going to the graveside service?"

Miles shook his head.

"Then I'll say goodbye, for now," Barlow said, peeling a card out of his wallet and handing it over. "Don't leave town."

"I'll pass you anything I find," Miles said, tucking the card in his pocket. "I want you to find that scumbag and grind him into paste."

"Me, too. Why don't you plug that number into your phone right now, and call me with it?" Barlow suggested. "I'd like to keep our lines of communication open."

Miles could think of no logical reason to object. His own fault, for coming here. Sticking his neck out. He was planning on switching out a new SIM card anyway, for some privacy. He did as Barlow asked.

Tension drained out of Miles' body as he watched the guy walk away. Barlow seemed like a reasonable guy, but still, it paid to be careful with the man.

The church was almost empty now, just a round little woman in her seventies, taking down photos displayed on a bulletin board.

Miles walked over to look. The woman wore White Shoulders, and some godawful hairspray. She reached for a picture of Matilda with an eighties hairdo, holding a tiny Amy. Baby pics, graduation photos. A shot of her, Amy and Steve on a sternwheeler cruise on the Columbia.

Pressure built in his throat. What was up with him? Why was he even looking at this stuff? Jerking himself around on purpose? Did he actually *want* to wake up in Urgent Care with tubes in every orifice?

The lady strained for a photo pinned too high for her short frame. Miles reached to get it for her. It was Matilda, in the mountains—

His hand froze. The horned hill. Its base was half-hidden by Matilda's head, but the top was pronged, with that big nose jutting down between. The lady swiveled and looked at him over her glasses.

"So?" she asked. "Are you going to take that down for me, or not?"

"Did you take this picture?" he asked.

"No, I got it off Facebook. It was the best recent picture of her that I could find. That lovely smile."

"Facebook?" Miles stared at it. "Do you know where it was taken?"

"She posted it a week ago," the lady said. "Her new pro-file picture. Only a few days before she . . . before she . . ." Her voice clogged up.

Miles pulled out Edie's drawing. It was the same, but from a different angle, which caused the nose to slant more to the right. Some part of him pulsed like a strobe light, deep inside.

"She'd taken a few personal days to tend to some busi-ness. And that was the last time we saw her." The woman proceeded to dissolve.

Without vetting the idea for practicality, or even baseline sanity, he found himself hugging her, and getting a big whanking noseful of White Shoulders and toxic hair fixative in the process. *Whap*. Kick that can. He patted the lady's back and pulled away, trying to be subtle about gasping for air.

"I'm sorry." The lady's voice was soggy. "Are you part of Matilda's family?"

"Just a friend." Miles held out the photo. "Can I keep this?"

"Sure thing. I'll just print up another."

"Thanks." He helped her take down the rest. She patted him on the cheek. He barely managed not to flinch.

"You're a lovely young man," she said. "Thank you."

The photo lay on the passenger seat as he drove back to his motel. One lone puzzle piece. The only person who could explain its significance was dead. Just a fresh opportunity for torturous self-doubt.

Another Olympic event at which he excelled.

Once in the room, he got out his knife and released his laptop from its prison of bubble wrap and duct tape. He switched on the router. The electro-buzz made his ears ring and his teeth hurt, but he was highly motivated to endure it right now.

He called up the Facebook login menu, and poised his fingers over the keyboard. Her sign-in email he knew, but the password . . . ?

One granddaughter. One birthday between them. Matilda was no techie. She would go for a simple password, and to hell with security. He could run the password cracking software he had on his laptop, but he doubted he'd even need to, if his hunch was correct.

He started typing in combos of Amymatilda, then the numeric date. And on. And on. And on. He was about to give up in disgust and just run the software when it occurred to him to try Aimee.

He hit pay dirt, first try. *Bingo.* Aimee had posted on Matilda's wall with the funeral details. Miles clicked around, checking out Matilda's photos. He found several from the same series, of Matilda in that white sweater in the woods, but only one that featured the horned mountain.

Bullseye. The jpeg had geospatial data. Latitude, longitude, even elevation. He checked the coordinates, and found that it was in Central Oregon, near a town called Kolita Springs. Only a few short hours' drive away.

He almost hyperventilated on the spot. He had to shut off

the router and flop down on the bed until he stopped freaking out. Holy shit, he'd nailed Edie's picture. It had to mean something. But what?

One piece of the puzzle. Only one.

What did you find, Matilda? What did you want to tell me? Why did they throw you down the stairs? What did you know?

This was going nowhere, so he tried to put it aside. He choked down a protein bar from his dwindling stash. His stomach was cramping with hunger, but cranky about actually dealing with any food that he put into it.

He flung himself onto the bed, which stank of dust, smoke, and mold. Pulled the pillow over his head to block out light and sound, but that left him choked with detergent, dead skin flakes, and dust mites. Plus toxic exhalations from cleaning solvents, paint, wood paneling.

He placed Lara in the center of his mind, and let everything else fade back, like Connor had taught him. To let his mind become wide and soft behind the shield. A net, asking a question. Waiting, soft and quiet and receptive, for an answer. No matter how fleeting or small.

Lara. Matilda. Give me something. Throw me a bone. Anything.

Logic demanded he get some rest, sleep. But logic had been the lowest asshole on the totem pole of his life for a while, and he wasn't going to be able to sleep, not with this smell assaulting his nose, and this quantity of freak-out hormones in his system. He zinged like a tuning fork, in spite of his shield. In fact, this excitement seemed to be generated from deep inside the shield. A weird new development.

He sat crosslegged on the bed, staring at the horned hill in Matilda's photograph. Then he pulled up topographical maps for the area that the geospatial data had indicated. He measured the actual distance between the two horns, for scale. Calculated the probable distance that Matilda had been from the hill when she took the photograph. Then he did the same thing with Edie's drawing.

His best estimate was that Matilda had been about ten miles closer to the horned hill than the chain-link–covered window in the drawing, and about twelve degrees off to the left.

Back to the map. He superimposed the map over a satellite photograph of the mountains in questions. Used the cursor to block out the most likely wedge to study. In Edie's drawing, tree tops waved at the exact level of the window, with hills rising up on both sides. There weren't a lot of skyscrapers out that way, in the rugged foothills of the Cascades, so that building had to be perched on a hill with a clear, unobstructed view, maybe looking up a river valley. He studied everything in that range, and a good distance outside it as well.

There were only a few roads. Any structure would necessitate a road. Maybe that was a dangerous assumption, but he'd make it anyway, not having access to a helicopter. That narrowed it down.

He committed the whole damn area on the map to memory. Not hard, with his senses souped up. His capacity for photographic memory was ratcheted up to maximum capacity. Information organized itself in his mind—every bend and curve of streams, roads, hills. Every bridge, house, barn, indelibly marked onto his brain and fixed on a three-dimensional mental grid.

She could be in one of them. And that electrifying possibility just did a colossal humdinger on his long-suffering glands.

A vague preliminary plan was forming in his head as he left the hotel and crossed the highway to the big cheap clothing chain that was opposite. The Big & Tall hadn't had much in the way of sporting gear, but at the store he found black jeans, a black-pile sweatshirt, and a forest camo jacket. It was too green for the dry side of the Cascade mountains, desert camo might be better, but it was better than nothing. He bought an olive drab ski mask, too. Who knew.

He bought his gear, and donned it in the store restroom. The new-clothes stiffness and starch galled him, since his skin was still hyper-sensitive, but tough shit. He couldn't go around naked.

Out in his truck, he got out the waist holster for the Glock, and buckled it on. The black sweatshirt and camo jacket covered it nicely. Carrying concealed, no Oregon permit. So he was an outlaw, too.

He gassed up the truck, and got on the road. The eastbound highway down the Gorge was dark and empty at this late hour, and the stress chemicals his body had cooked up kept his foot heavy on the gas.

Something had changed in his head. He was feeling again, but it wasn't shorting him out, as it had done earlier at the wedding, or even at Matilda's funeral. He was cautiously encouraged by this. His shield stayed firm, but there was more room inside of it. It no longer felt like being locked in a Port-O-San. It breathed, and he breathed with it.

He spent the hours it took to drive to Kolita Springs lecturing himself about not getting his hopes up. This lead could dead-end into a brick wall anytime, just like all his other leads had done.

But Jesus, if she were still alive? And talking to him?

That, of course, opened up a whole new can of worms. Frivolous and irrelevant, compared to the issues of life and death facing him, but bonehead that he was, he wanked on about it anyway. Those hot erotic dreams in which he'd freely indulged every horny whim his overheated imagination could cook up with the red-hot dream girl. Thinking he was just fantasizing, in blessed privacy.

But if he hadn't been? If she'd participated, somehow, in all of that, even telepathically? It wasn't like he'd given her any choice.

Thinking of it made his face eggplant purple and his cock strain in his jeans. For God's sake. He would never be able to look the woman in the face. If she still existed.

So much for the new, chill Miles. He was returning to his old more-or-less overwrought self.

Once he left the larger highway, he got onto a country route that led up into the mountains, taking note of every bend in the road and structure he passed, and comparing it to the aerial view in his memory. The road turned to gravel. He crossed a narrow bridge over a dried-out river bed, a wide plain of bleached, scattered, fist-sized rocks. Easy off-roading, for a tough vehicle like his own, if he could find a good access point. He wound steadily up the hill, and spied a chain-link fence with security cameras, mounted at regular intervals.

Way out here in the boonies. How very odd.

Dawn was lightening the sky, and he didn't allow himself to slow down with cameras watching. Shortly after, he passed a driveway that wound up the hill, and at the top, an electronic gate. The structures inside were hidden by the contours of the hills and the thick trees, but he had memorized every one on the satellite map. There was a surprisingly large complex in there. The aerial photo had shown several vehicles parked outdoors, a small structure at the gate, a long building that might be a big car park, and a large house.

He forced himself to drive on. The road was narrow, with a steep drop-off and no possibility of turning for miles. When he found a wide spot, he got out and stared back at the horned hill, partially obscured by the hill he'd just climbed.

When he couldn't stand it any longer, he drove back down to the bridge. Two tenths of a mile past it, he found a spot to offroad into the woods. He tossed the green tarp over his vehicle, and set out to snoop around. He could see the building on the hill at the point where the river's course made a sharp right angle, where a deep gully and a dry streambed from the hill above merged with the river. Somewhat to the left of the top of the gulley and poised over a bluff of basaltic granite was the house, three stories high and expensive looking, with big terraces and picture windows overlooking the river canyon. Lights glowed in the upper stories, but what squeezed his heart was the window on the bottom floor. That floor was concrete, in contrast to the structure of wood and shingles above, and even at this distance and in the pale half light of dawn, with his hawk-vision, he could see the diagonal crosshairs of the chain link and the steel frame bolted over the window. From down here he could not see the horned hill, but up there, it would be visible. He could even individuate the trees that flanked the window.

Just like in Edie's drawing. Two to the right, one to the left.

The day wore slowly on, as he poked carefully around, exploring that hill and the crest on the opposite side of the gulley, the best vantage point for spying. He had good binoculars, but saw almost as well with his own unassisted eyes. What he saw was not illuminating. Just people moving around, inside the house and out, conducting business he could not identify. He did not see Lara, or Greaves. A high-end RV was parked outside, but he did not see any other vehicles, just the long car park that could hold several.

The fence was probably electrified, so he kept a safe distance as he hiked the perimeter. Fortunately, he still had a protein bar, a few swallows of water, some shreds of jerked elk meat. Not that he had much appetite. Too wound up.

The hours crawled by, and as the sun's rays started slanting in the mid-afternoon, he realized that he was stalling. He'd been hoping to hear something on the mind computer. Hoping to ask Lara about the window. Craving proof, corroboration, certainty.

So. Looked like he'd given in completely. He was thinking of the schizo Lara in his head as a real, live entity. The nuthouse could start preparing a room for him anytime now, but first, he'd save his imaginary friend from the imaginary bad guys and get himself some goddamn imaginary satisfaction in the process.

They could lock him up afterward. Fuck 'em.

He was tempted to just camp out there, as convinced as he was that he'd found the place. But that would be premature. He was not ready. He wouldn't penetrate that compound alone. It would require supplies, planning, a well considered strategy. And the help of his highly unusual friends, whom he'd been treating like ten different kinds of shit lately.

They weren't going to hold it against him in a situation like this, but still. He had some serious groveling to do.

7

Lara held herself under the jet of hot water, arms braced to stay upright. There was no separate shower stall. She had to straddle the toilet and lean to the side to wash herself in the miniscule bathroom. It was a challenge, in pitch darkness, but she was an old pro by now.

From what that freak Greaves said, she was in for a monster dose of their hellish drug the next time. Maybe it would kill her. Certainly it would change her. And if she had that horrible guy clamped on, sliming her, oh God. She'd thought Anabel was awful, but at least Anabel didn't desire her sexually.

She didn't even have a way to power dress. Nothing but the loose, limp jersey tank and matching pajama pants that appeared fresh every week in the metal drawer. No underwear. Maybe they figured underwear would incite rebellion. But she'd be damned if she'd go out to meet her fate if she wasn't squeaky clean, hair combed, teeth brushed.

She stayed under the hot water for hours. Afterward, she used the limp, clammy linen towel and put her clothes on, such as they were. Her hair had gotten so long. She took her time, having plenty of time to fill, in braiding her wavy hair back, winding the end with a strip of pajama fabric. And that was it. No more prep.

She paced. Four steps forward, four steps back. Hugged her knees to her chest. Rocked. Tried to meditate. Wished she could fly away, hide in the Citadel. If only she . . .

Wait. The thought jarred her like a shock of electricity. Greaves had gotten so excited when she'd spun out, briefly, into one of her trips. She'd come back before he'd latched onto her, but if she hadn't, she'd have taken off into the otherworld. With him telepathically linked.

And if she could do it then, without the injection, why not now? While she was alone, no one clamped on, breathing down her neck?

The giddy rush of possibility made her stomach flop.

Freedom. Of a kind, at least. Or maybe they'd finally driven her over the edge, and this was a psychotic break. Maybe she was just so toxic from the accumulated drug, she was still high from the last injection. But who knew? If she could go, right now, at will . . . with no Anabel or Greaves piggybacking . . .

And stay there. Just stay there for-fucking-ever. Oh God, *yes*.

She lay down. Her body vibrated. She'd never be able to get herself into the right place if she was so jittery. She started relaxing every muscle, breathing deeply. She waited. Concentrated. Nothing.

Tears of frustration streamed down her face, trickling into her ears. She did not allow herself to brush them away, as if her hands were bound. She pictured it all . . . the gurney, the needle . . .

Suddenly, she felt it—the rush, the double vision, not that she could see in the dark. A doubled perception of darkness. The pull . . .

Panicky joy scrambled it. Back in the flat darkness again.

She wiped away tears of frustration, and tried again. Visualizing blinding light, buckled straps straining tight against wrists, ankles, forehead. Hu's grim face. Anabel's glare. The sting of the needle.

Yes. That did it.

The pull sucked her in, spun her through inner space. Her mind spangled that space with stars, shreds of cloud. Soaring.

Brief glimpses. The little blond boy, his eyes huge with fear. The green duffel bag on the train, heavy with menace. The fountain, the statue, the sleepwalkers. She ignored them all, racing through the mist.

There it was. Formidable, thick, steampunk beautiful. She no longer had to think about the choreography. It was a dance of pure joy.

She was in, and she was never leaving this place again. Fuck them all. Let her physical body waste away in a coma or die. Who cared?

Nobody, but nobody, could make her leave this place.

Miles swerved on the road, and corrected, his heart pounding. That Lara dream again, running even while his eyes were wide open and staring through the windshield at westbound Interstate I-84, right after the Gresham exit. Her graceful form danced inside his inner sanctum. Not a dream, or a fantasy. He could feel her, fierce and bright. Intensely female. A palpable sensation. Not an unpleasant one. By no means.

He waited, breathless and tense, for her to get around to typing a message. Trying to ignore his body's stupid animal reaction to this cerebral form of intimacy. The road rushed by. His teeth ground. His heart thudded.

u there? she finally tapped out, after an agonizing interval.

where the fck have u been? It pounded out of him, pressurized. iv been w8ting 4 hours!

There was a pause, then, 4 me?? u told me I wsn't even real!

but u r real, right? he demanded.

yes unfortunately

good thats settled then he typed. u in trouble?

yes

locked up?

yes

ok then let's stop fucking around and get u out of there. I cant take this shit anymore

There was a tooth-grinding pause, and then, wow. what a switch. i have whiplash now. ur sweet but I don't think its possible

Sweet, his ass. let me b the judge of that, he pounded out. just give me data to crunch

thats the thing. no data. I'm locked in a cell. outside there r hills. they shoot me up every night. thats when I visit u.

experiments? psi-max? he queried.

ive heard them call it that

u high on it now?

no. this is the first time ive flown w/o the drug. dont know if its good or bad. maybe im just crazy now.

join the club, he told her. i dont care. give me info.

like what?

anything for fck sake, he replied. where r u? who do u c?

mostly anabel and hu, she replied. theyre the main ones

He whistled. anabel? hot blond psychopath? late 20s?

blond yes. dont know how hot she is. she's cold 2 me.

tell me about hu.

1st name Jason. asian, late 30s, med height, buzzed hair, wire rim glasses. wife leah has esophageal cancer

wow he told u that?

no I saw it on a drug trip. the drug makes me c things.

He considered that for a moment. yikes

shes having a big operation early 2mrrw morning. hu

tried to get time off from head honcho. no go. hu has 2 b there 4 my megadose xtravaganza. 2mrrw morning early. brrr

time off from who?

thaddeus greaves, she typed. met him today. scary guy.

He ground his teeth in impotent anger. Bastard. Stonewalling him all along. that lying butthead. I knew he was dirty

u know the guy? how do u know all this? who r u?

L8r 4 me. lets focus, he told her. u ok?

He sensed the irony somewhere, as if she'd let out a crack of cynical laughter in his head. ok? what does that even mean?

forget i said it, he typed hastily. where's the wife's operation?

who knows? west of the rockies? just guessing tho. hospital name is Good Samaritan but every 2nd city in America has a Good Sam hsptl

lets narrow it down, he typed. give me a picture of hu

A blank pause, and then what?

picture. photo, he prompted. remember those?

how? He could feel her bafflement vibrating in his body.

send it via the computer, he told her.

?? she typed.

He lost his patience. jesus lara ur the visual artist. look down. c the digital camera. I visualized one 4 u. pretend ur taking a pic of hu. attach cable to USB port behind computer. download.

u can do that?

fuck no! none of this is possible! We r crazy, remember? that hasnt held us back so far! play with the analogs! use it! do it!!!

stop shouting, she typed primly. Silence for a moment, and then a hot pink Hello Kitty camera? seriously? lmao

He was embarrassed about the pink camera, but his mind had seized on the first small digital camera in his memory banks, which was Cindy's. sorry u dont like it shut up and take the picture

He wanted to cheer, a minute later or so when a multimedia message flashed on his inner screen. He clicked on it. A photo filled the screen. It worked. Holy shit, it actually worked. Lara rocked.

Jason Hu had sallow skin, a thin mouth. Miles memorized his sour mug as another message icon flashed. Anabel, minus her mind-bending sexual glow. Without it, she looked like what she truly was. A bloodthirsty hell bitch. She should've been beautiful, but wasn't, not with those fixed, staring eyes, the tense jaw, the flattened mouth.

dont c the point with no fix on location, Lara told him.

Miles imagined sending an image of the horned hill. click on that

omg! that is what i see outside the window! wtf?

ur in central Oregon, he wrote. near Kolita Springs

how the hell did u find that out?

He tried not to feel smug. L8r, he typed again. Time enough later to explain about Matilda, her photo. Her murder. Painful revelations could wait. They had to stay crystal clear and focused.

what r u going 2 do now? she asked.

not sure yet, he typed. improvising. driving, now. signing off to go do some hacking on leah. u sticking around in here?

u could not pry me out.

He felt absurdly pleased. good. hang out. chill. while ur here, make a list of everything that might help me. take pictures, draw floor plans. put it together 4 me. help me 2 help u.

ok one thing tho

?? he queried.

who r u?

my name is miles, he told her. more L8r ttyl

He wrenched his mind away. Time to face the real world. The shift was jarring. The mental computer did not assault his senses the way the physical world did. Besides. He liked talking to her.

He could use a shower, after the day of strenuous hiking, but he was like a hound on the scent, now. He drove straight to Good Sam, and cruised the hospital campus until he found what he was looking for. A Starbucks, close enough to be a hospital staff hangout and caffeine refuel station. A quick search on his smartphone had revealed that there were hundreds of Good Sams all over the country, just as Lara had said, many of them specializing in cancer care and/or gastroenterology. But there was one right here in Portland, too, and if Lara's keeper worked at the complex where Miles had been sniffing around all day, chances were good to excellent that the guy's wife's surgery was here.

He set up shop in the Starbucks. Ordered a few sandwiches from the stuff displayed at the counter, and a soda. Glucose, for his hungry brain. The food slipped right down. It felt good to feed honest hunger again. The furnace inside him had finally fired up and demanded fuel.

He was counting on fate to help him improvise a strategy, and halfway through his second cranberry scone, fate delivered. A tired, white-coated doctor came in and got himself a beverage. He sat down at the table not far from Miles, sucking on his coffee while pulling out his tablet, tapping into it. Miles was at the ready, and when the guy tried to connect to the Starbucks wifi, his device was lured by the siren signal of Miles' computer instead. The guy got frustrated, frowning and tapping, but not before Miles had capured the crucial pcaps.

He got right to it, analyzing with the software that he'd developed with Aaro last year. He teased out the username and password of Dr. Walter Milhausen, cardiologist, then logged remotely onto the hospital's system and poked around until he found the OR calendar. Meanwhile Dr. Milhausen cursed, stabbing and swiping at his tablet, in vain. Bummer for him.

There was a Leah Halpert scheduled for tomorrow. Thirty-six years old. Gastro surgery at six A.M. Halpert, Hu. She was the right age. The names were different, but it would be weirder if Hu did share a name with his wife, considering what he was.

By the time the cardiologist had given up and stomped out of the coffee shop in disgust, Miles had scanned and memorized the names of the staff who would be attending her, and trolled the patient database for Leah Halpert's home address. Kolita Springs.

Yow. More shock-and-awe juice pumped into his blood-stream. He accessed everything he could in Leah Halpert's medical records, in super-info-suck mode. A clock ticked ominously in the back of his mind. Counting off to what, he did not know.

He called Connor as he ran back out to the pick-up. Time to shamelessly exploit his friend's FBI connections, which was way quicker than hacking the DMV.

Con picked up right away. "What's up?"

"Need a favor."

"Name it." Con was a man of few words, like all his brothers. Except for Sean, who made up for the other three most abundantly.

"I need the license, make, and models of any vehicles belonging to a man who might be either Jason Halpert or Jason Hu, resident of Kolita Springs, Oregon. 1395 Pine Crest Road. Also a Leah Halpert."

"On it," Con said, and broke the connection.

Of course, there was no guarantee that Hu would actually show at Good Sam, after the big boss had nixed it. But it was worth a try.

His cell buzzed, and he dove for it. "So?"

"Leah Halpert does not have any vehicles registered in her name, but Jason Halpert of Kolita Springs drives a white 2011 Acura sport utility vehicle." Con rattled off the license number. "Need backup?"

"Aren't you guys back up in Seattle by now?"

"Nah. We hung around." Connor paused, significantly. "We wanted to hook up with you again. See what you've got cooking."

Miles opened his mouth, poised to spill his guts, and paused.

If he pinned down Hu for real, that would be independent confirmation. Solid proof that Lara was almost certainly inside that complex. More solid than head-texts from a dream girl, which still smacked of schizo delusion. He could risk his own life for a schizo delusion, but he'd rather have some harder proof before he proposed risking his friends' lives. "I don't have anything solid yet," he hedged.

"We're interested in stuff that's not solid yet, too," Con said. "Who is this character Hu? Tell me about him."

"I'll know more soon," Miles assured him. "I swear."

"We'll be around. We're still here, at the hotel. Call us. Really."

"Thanks for the info." Miles hung up and turned off the phone.

So they'd stayed in Portland for him. Oh, man. Guilt trip.

But he didn't want company while chasing half-formed hunches. Plus, those guys tended to want to take command, every last one of them. He was un-commandable these days. Better to avoid the strife from the get-go, at least for the next few hours. His friends would have plenty to keep them busy soon enough, God willing. If this was for real.

He started with the big parking garages that Hu might have used, scanning for a white Acura SUV. Who knew if the wife had been admitted already, or if she had yet to arrive? He probably could have teased that out of the database, given more time, but there wasn't much point in it now. He had nothing better to do, so he cruised the parking lots of the nearby hotels. There seemed to be gazillions of white SUVs, now that he was looking for one. Not a very systematic way to search.

Which was why he was so astonished when he found it.

The Acura was in the parking lot of a mid-level chain motel about thirty blocks from the hospital. It must be psychic magnetism. He was tempted to social engineer himself into the guy's room right now, and put a gun to his head, but he squelched the urge. That would be stupid and impatient. This was a divine gift. He didn't dare fuck it up.

He parked around the corner, and dug into the big box of swag he'd collected over the years from SafeGuard, the Mc-Cloud Crowd's security outfit. He selected a slap-on RF trace and strolled through the motel parking lot, hoping Hu's car was not alarmed. One swift gesture, and the slap-on was stuck to the undercarriage. No alarm.

He pulled out Tam's ring, pondering it. What the hell. If ever there was a time for overkill, this was it. He twisted off the stud, shoved it into the Acura's front right tire. It lodged there, hidden between the treads.

He slumped down in the driver's seat, and checked for Lara. Eager to tell her his news, like a little kid trolling for approval.

He didn't feel her in there. still there? he typed.

Nothing. No multimedia message left for him with pictures, either. Huh. She'd said she'd stay. That she could not be pried out.

Maybe she'd been compelled. He distracted himself from that chilling thought by noodling around on the laptop, setting up X-ray specs to follow the trace he'd planted, plugging in the code.

He kept on checking for her, obsessively. Nothing. Even with the shield running full force, he couldn't block his dismay.

Damn. He missed her.

At ten o'clock P.M., Hu emerged from the back entrance, a woman next to him. He looked just like Lara's picture. The woman was short, thin, Asian, a braid down her back. Hu pulled a wheeled suitcase.

Miles forced himself to wait as the guy helped his wife into the seat and tossed the bag in back. They pulled out, toward the hospital.

When Hu turned the corner, Miles situated the laptop on the passenger seat, counted down from ten, and pulled out after him.

"You want to dose her now, sir? It's very early. It's only been—"

"I am aware of the time, Anabel." Greaves rattled the ice cubes delicately in his glass of Scotch. "Don't ask me to repeat myself."

Anabel just stood there like an idiot. Mouth working.

Greaves let out a little sigh. "Is it Hu?"

"Well, he, ah . . . he drove his wife to the hospital. I urged him to make other arrangements, but he was sure he'd make it back in time."

Greaves sipped his Scotch, and said nothing.

Anabel hurried on. "He's been worried about his wife, and he—"

"Don't make excuses for him. Unless you want me to question your commitment, too. Let us begin without Hu."

"Ah, well, the problem is actually not, ah . . ." Her eyes darted everywhere but at him. "It's Lara. She's, ah . . . she appears to be unconscious. Or in a trance, I should say. I can't rouse her."

Greaves was taken aback. "You can't make telepathic contact?"

"I tried," Anabel admitted, miserably. "There's nobody home. It happens sometimes when she's on psi-max, but she's never done it to me off-dose before. I just can't find anything to grab onto."

"And you discovered her like this when?"

"About two hours ago. I'd turned the lights on, since she hadn't eaten in a while, and I—"

"Two hours pass before it occurs to you that this might be of interest to me. And it was obvious that she hasn't been eating regularly. How long had she been fasting? Was there any purpose to that, or was it just petty cruelty on your part?"

"Well, we, ah . . . we were following your orders, sir. You said that keeping her stressed and off balance would help create the conditions—"

"And you interpreted that to mean that you should malnourish her. How very creative of you."

"Sir, I—"

"Shut up. You disgust me. You and Hu both. Take me to her."

He fumed silently as he followed Anabel through the facility. Angry at himself for giving inferior people too much rein. Letting the situation degenerate to the point where the girl could actually have been damaged. Such a waste. He had an unfortunate tendency to expect the best in his people, and they almost always disappointed him.

Anabel unlocked the door. The room was dank and fetid. Lara Kirk lay on the bed like a saint's marble effigy, her high, perfect breasts rising and falling slowly. He leaned to admire her face. Translucent skin, lovely bone structure. Too thin, and those splendid eyes were set in pools of bruised shadow, but her haunting beauty was still evident. And her mouth. Perfectly shaped. He looked forward to seeing it painted red as he led her across a ballroom in an evening gown.

She was perfect. Very young, true. He was in his fifties, she was in her mid-twenties. But men of his wealth and stature almost always had younger wives, and he valued her fertility. He wanted to breed that spirit, that intelligence, and above all, her innate psi qualities, into his children. And he deeply enjoyed beauty. He had no interest in women who were not strikingly beautiful.

He approached the mental probe as a talented lover approached a kiss. Not grabbing and slobbering, but circling, taking his time. He had no doubt that he would be able to penetrate her shield. She had first dosed mere months ago, and his psi powers were immense.

They ought to be. He'd paid for them with blood and agony.

He hovered closer, savoring the anticipation of knowing her thoughts, her feelings, her dreams. Closer . . . he reached . . .

And bumped up against a force field. His psi powers bounced right off it. He tried again, digging, probing, thrusting. Then hacking.

It was like fighting air. He could not orient himself against that shield. It deflected his energy, made him feel frantic, almost frightened.

He hung over her, eyes squeezed shut. How the hell had she done this? How *dare* she? Drops of liquid pattered onto her face, her neck, her gray tank top. It was sweat, dripping from his forehead.

He straightened, barely catching the look in Anabel's eyes before her gaze flicked away. Relief. Spiteful pleasure to see him in difficulty.

"See?" He heard smugness in her tone. "That's the shield I was telling you about. See what I mean? It's the same one she uses when—"

Whap. His invisible hand smacked, knocking her across the room. She hit the cinderblock wall and slid to the floor, holding her mouth.

"Yes," he said. "I see. What is more important is, do *you* see?"

She nodded hastily, hunched and shaking.

"Get up," he said. He turned back to Lara. The delicate jut of her nipples were brown shadows beneath the thin fabric.

Time to show everyone in this room who was in control.

He seized the shirt, ripped it right down the middle of her chest with one violent jerk, exposing her bare bosom. He stared down at her body. Like a dancer's, but with more generous breasts. He splayed both hands over her chest. Angry as he was, her inert body excited him. The harder to tame, the more worth the trouble. To a point.

Lara Kirk was about to learn exactly where that point was.

His hands tightened. "Bring me the electric shock paddles."

8

Miles drummed his nails as he waited for Hu to emerge from the hospital. Hours went by before the white Acura edged out of the parking garage and gave him something else to think about.

Miles waited the shortest possible decent interval, and pulled out after him. Hu's route suggested that he was heading back to I-84 East, back up the Gorge. All he could do was follow. Gather more info.

Hu stopped at Trout Lake to gas up, so Miles did, too. As soon as Hu pulled out, he called Connor.

Con didn't waste words. "Why the fuck is your phone turned off?"

"You guys ready to move?"

Surprise derailed Con's scold. "Where to?"

"I've got a fix on the facility where they're keeping Lara."

"Oh, do you, now? Thanks for keeping us in the loop!"

"I wasn't sure till just now," Miles explained. "And I'm still—"

"Why the fuck did you gut the trace on your phone? We could have been right on your ass! This minute!"

"Um, that would explain why I gutted it," Miles said. "Look, are you just going to rant? Because if you are, I'll hang up."

"Just give me the fucking data," Con grumbled.

"I've got a Specs trace on this guy's car." Miles read out the code. "I'm just out of Trout Lake, on eastbound 84. He's heading toward Kolita Springs. I'm pretty sure that's where they're keeping her. It's Greaves, that piece-of-lying-shit douche bag. It was him all along."

"How the fuck did you figure it out?" Connor sounded insulted. "We've been flogging this thing for months! We got nothing on Greaves."

Miles let out a hollow laugh. "Dumb luck. You ready to move?"

"Fuck, yeah. Already moving."

"This guy I'm following is one of her guards. I think he's heading back to the facility where they're holding her."

Miles heard keyboard tapping from the other side. "Got him on screen." Connor was too interested now to stay mad. "Going eighty-eight—no, ninety-three an hour. Big hurry."

"He's late for something. Something that involves Lara."

"We'd be with you already if you'd left in your trace!" Connor bitched. "We'll still be forty miles behind when you get to Kolita Springs, even if we push it!"

"Don't sweat it. I'll still need you when you get there."

"What does that mean?" Con's voice sharpened. "What have you got in mind?"

"I've got fuck-all in mind," Miles admitted. "I'm not really using my mind right now. I'm staying stuck to this guy. That's all I know."

"Do not do anything crazy," Con lectured. "Wait for us, Miles. Understand? You'll just get yourself killed if you pull another—"

"I love you too, man. Thanks. I'll put the trace back in as soon as my hands are free. Later." Miles broke the connection, tossed the phone down. It rang, twenty times or so, then sullenly stopped.

He glanced at the monitor. Hu was gaining ground.

He gave the car more gas.

The sudden blow took Lara by surprise. She'd been focused on drafting a floor plan of the upper storey she had seen, then snapping pictures of it with the ridiculous, femmy little hot pink camera he'd dreamed up for her. And *thwack*—

She was crashed back into her physical self, into a chaotic hell of racking jittery pain. Screaming, shaking, convulsing—

It stopped, abruptly. She blinked back tears, trying to see, to think.

Greaves hung over her. His reddened face was not flattered by this angle. Wattles quivered under his chin. He brandished shock paddles.

"There we are," he said. "That's more like it. Where were you, Lara? Who taught you to shield that way?"

"Nobody," she croaked. "I just—"

"Don't lie," he chided. "Not because it's wrong. Just because it's useless."

He slammed into her mind, like a freight train crashing through a plate glass window.

Oh, God, it hurt. He ripped, rended, tossed. She couldn't scream, or even breathe. Only her heart kept beating, its rapid, stuttering thud echoing louder and louder in her ears as Greaves rifled and kicked randomly through her head.

"Oh, yes," he muttered thickly, as if it gave him sexual pleasure from doing it. "Oh, Lara, yes. You taste delicious. So deep."

He redoubled his assault, not as violent, but more lascivious, like a big, wet tongue, licking and probing. Memories were snagged and pulled out, unspooled, hungrily pawed over by that awful, slavering presence.

He was focusing on where she'd gone. Her shield. His telepathic strength was a smothering blanket, crushing her out of existence. Her lungs strained to expand. No air . . .

She fainted. Some time later, she floated back to consciousness to the sound of his voice, talking with Anabel.

". . . of recent sexual activity. Which is impossible, of course, no?"

"Of course!" Anabel's voice was indignant. "We never touched her, sir. No one has!"

"Good," he murmured. "Good."

Greaves looked down, and saw her eyes fluttering. He stroked her cheek. She did not have the option to flinch away. Her skin crawled.

"Aren't you the naughty little thing," he said indulgently. "Sexual fantasies. Mmm. Your dream lover is quite the studly godking."

She couldn't have replied if she wanted to.

"No fear," he promised. "You'll soon be too busy with reality for fantasies. And a healthy libido fits in nicely with my plans for you."

I'd rather die, she wanted to say.

He heard it anyway, of course, and chuckled. "Feisty." He unraveled her braid, running his fingers over her scalp. "Lovely."

Anabel was coming at her, brandishing a syringe. Oh shit, no, no, no. "Time for your medicine," she trilled.

The burning stab, and it happened, like always, but faster. The double vision, the pull . . . but this time with Greaves' smothering presence clamped down on her. *No no not you not you!*.

Oh, yes was the answering thought, chiming back. *Oh, yes, me. Always me. Fly as far as you can. You will never get away from me.*

She fought, but he blocked her at every turn. She went shooting off into anywhere, no direction, no hope. A shriek of utter despair echoed through the bleak, empty spaces in her mind.

Greaves' light, mocking laughter followed it.

It was still an hour till dawn when Miles saw signs for Kolita Springs. He'd stopped only once to screw a silencer onto his pistol and put the tracer chip back into his phone. He'd disabled the ringtone, though. They were welcome to trace him and chase him, but not to scold him. The SMSs were piling up. Not yet. *Later, dudes.*

Lara's long silence filled him with creeping dread. It occurred to him to check the pink camera analog. It took form in his inner vision. It had cables attached to the computer.

He imagined the screen inviting him to download.

One, two, three, four . . . ten . . . thirteen. A flood of JPGs were popping up on the screen. His unease grew. She'd done exactly as he had asked, but she hadn't been allowed to finish the job. Not good.

He looked at the photos. Corridor, elevator. A carefully visualized floor plan, drawn in pencil. A photo of that dickhead Thaddeus Greaves. Cataloging each piece kept him too busy to freak out. The images she generated sort of . . . shone. They seemed deeper. Three dimensional. The photos of Hu and Anabel had been, too.

Then it hit him. Of course. They were art pieces. Images generated by Lara had a sort of poetry to them. Even the ugly ones.

The photo of Hu made Miles uncomfortable. He had no business feeling sorry for the guy, since he might or might not have to kill him. But Jesus, what kind of asshole employer wouldn't let a man stay at his wife's side during a dangerous operation?

The same asshole who would lock a girl in a dark cell for months and do sick, sadistic experiments on her. Duh.

No, Hu was a bully and a dickhead. He had chosen the wrong side, and he was ripe for an ass-kicking. That gave him the first useful idea he'd had so far, and he was elaborating on it when Lara's presence exploded into his head, with a blast of terrified energy.

He almost skidded into a guardrail. He righted the car, set himself to multitask. wtf?

cant stay was her reply. greaves. got loose but not 4 long he uses electroshock to pull me back

He was aghast. coming 4 u stay sharp

no no dont risk urslf. pls ur the only thing that keeps me alive dont come pls dont let them take u from me

He corrected a swerve. Hu's turn signal winked, far ahead.

Electroshock? Fuck that! He grabbed the phone, called Connor.

"Goddamnit, Miles!" was Con's greeting. "Why haven't you—"

"I'm going in," he announced.

"No! We're still forty miles behind you, and you can't—"

"They're hurting her, Con. Right now, in real time. I'll talk to you when I can. If you see my truck, bring it along with you. I'll leave the keys under the seat. Listen up, these are the coordinates of the complex." He recited them swiftly. "Point two miles before the bridge, offroading through the woods will get you to the river bank, or close to it. A couple hundred meters downstream, and you can see the building, up on the hill. That's where she is. I'll tell you more when I can."

He hung up on Con's sputtering. He was driving through Mary Creek Canyon, a subdivision of Kolita Springs that petered out into scattered orchards, and beyond that, dry, scrubby hills. Lara? Lara!

She was still gone, but her desperation lingered in his body, tightening it into knots. Fine, then. Fuck it. Show time.

Headlights off. He speeded up, closing the distance between himself and Hu, his eyes fixed on the guy's taillights. Five hundred meters, Tam had said.

He stabbed the detonator on Tam's ring.

Not *possible*. Jason Hu hung onto the wheel. "Fuck, fuck, fuck," he shrieked, as the car bounced off the guardrail, spun, and ended up nose down in the ditch on the opposite side of the road.

Of all times to blow a tire. As wrong as the date of Leah's surgery, but the doctors had terrified her, and she hadn't wanted to wait. No way could he slip into Karstow unobserved now. Not that he'd held up much hope to begin with.

He got out and peered at the damage. He was not a man who prided himself on being capable of changing a tire. He'd put in thousands of hours studying chemistry and pharmacology so that he could pay some hairy-knuckled schmuck to change tires for him.

He wrestled the jack out. Fought with lug nuts, wrenches, grease, and dirt in the darkness, the flashlight on his keychain clamped between his teeth for light. He got the bastard on, somehow, more or less. Now to see if his life was still worth something, or if he should just swallow bleach and be done with it.

It only took ten minutes to drive the rest of the way to the Karstow facility. Ten minutes too long. The guard at the gatehouse gave him a bleary-eyed once-over, scanned Hu's card and waved him through. He accelerated up the hill to the car-park, pulling into his designated slot.

He shoved open the door, and yelped when the door slammed back on him, trapping him against the frame of the car like jaws snapping closed. A cold circle of metal jammed itself under his ear.

"Don't move," a low voice rasped.

He gasped for air. "Who . . . who are—"

"Shut up," the voice growled. "Give me your cell phone."

Hu struggled to breathe against those squeezing fingers, and pulled out his phone. His assailant took it. His larynx could barely move. "Who are—"

"None of your business. What's more important is what I can do to Leah."

Fresh, acid fear made his stomach lurch. "What do you know about Leah?"

"Shhh." The gun barrel jabbed harder. "Dr. Prateek Singh, Dr. Giuseppe Bonelli. Good team you have there."

That was Leah's surgical team. Hu's legs wobbled. "Who are you?"

"In a few minutes, Dr. Paige Sereno, the anesthesiologist, will come in to do her thing. Quite a tumor Leah's got. Gonna be touch and go. Lots of chemo in her future. Fucking drag."

"How do you . . ." His voice quivered. "Who told you—"

"But the one thing I know, but you don't, nor does Leah's team at Good Sam, is this glitch in the database." The low voice took on a taunting tone. "There's a bug that lets me in to look at your wife from every angle. I've seen her blood-work, the inside of her stomach, sonograms of her liver, her lungs, MRIs of her brain—"

"Shut up! You sick bastard!"

His assailant slammed the door against Hu's shoulder with bruising strength. "Too bad, about the results of that sentinel lymph node biopsy ten days ago, huh?" he taunted. "Things look bad. Leah's tough, though. She'll fight the good fight—if she's allowed to."

Hu clenched wet, clammy hands. "What are you talking about?"

"That bug lets me change things in the system. Like that note about the genetic disorder that she inherited from her father. Malignant hypothermia, remember? I did some creative editing in the hospital database, see."

Hu could barely speak, his voice vibrated so much. "What . . . what—"

"All records of Leah's malignant hypothermia are gone from her chart. Poor Dr. Sereno has no idea. I fixed it days ago, see. Sereno's all good to go with routine administration of suxamethonium. Poison, for Leah. They'll put her under any minute. Soon, her muscles will go rigid. Her temperature will soar. Then heart attack. Circulatory collapse. And finally, death. So sad. But we all gotta die someday, right?"

Hu struggled, wildly. "What the fuck—"

"Shhh," the voice crooned. "They will only be able to administer an antidote if you are in a position to call them and warn them in time."

Hu could barely get the words out, his voice shook so hard. "What d-do you w-want from me?"

His assailant dragged his head back, until he could see the hideously white teeth grinning through the mouth hole of the ski mask.

"We make a deal," the dark figure said. "Your wife . . . for Lara Kirk."

Mean, mean motherfucker. Miles had tangled with more than his fair share of them. He had the vibe nailed. Now he just had to ooze it, like slime. A tall order, after that claustophobic ten minutes spent huddled in the trunk of the Acura. Utter blackness, mitigated only by the hole made by the shoved down central seat console. He was thankful to whoever decided that car trunks should open from the inside. And thankful, too, for the fact that there appeared to be no security cameras mounted in here. At least none that he could see.

Miles glared at the guy through the ski mask. Mean as a snake. The vibe seemed to be working. Hu's eyes darted, frantic and terrified.

"What do you want with Lara Kirk?" Hu quavered.

"Focus on Leah," Miles said. "Tick tock, tick tock. Take me to her, Hu. Right now."

"I don't believe you," Hu burst out. "You're bluffing."

Miles shrugged. "You can bet that way if you want."

"I can't," Hu whined. "You're just going to have to kill me."

"I'm fine with that. I'll still find Lara, but Leah will die, because you're a fucking coward and a loser. But hey, she knows that already. What did she say when you ran out on her? Was she nice? Did she, you know . . . *understand?*"

Hu's body arched convulsively against his. "Shut up! You asshole!"

"Leah's going to die today," Miles said. "Or not. Up to you."

"I can't do what you're asking. They'd kill me!"

"Your problem, not mine. It's the company you keep, man. Chances are you'd get a call in to Good Sam before they slit your throat, to give them a heads-up. One last good deed for the woman you love."

Hu's forehead shone. Miles pulled out his cell, and began texting, without moving his gun hand.

inside compound with hu.

"Who are you texting?" Hu's voice had a hysterical edge.

"That's for me to know and you to wonder about," Miles said.

The phone burped softly. Con's reply. u crazy bastard

"Who is that?" Hu shrieked.

"That's my contact at Good Sam," Miles said. "Bonelli and Singh just walked by in their scrubs, all coffeed up. So, Jason. Is the fence electrified?"

Hu's mouth worked for a moment. "Ah, yes."

"Infrared, motion sensors?"

"Just infrared."

"Where is the control center?" Hu did not respond.

Miles jerked him out from behind the door and jammed the gun up against the guy's groin. "Maybe you haven't grasped how committed I am to hurting you, assbag. I'm

turning your genitals into pink paste right . . . about . . .
now."

"No! Stop! They'll hear you, and they'll kill you!"

"I don't give a fuck. On three. You ready? One . . . two . . ."

"Security is on the ground floor! Entrance on the left
side!"

"That's better," Miles said. "How many on security staff?
How many people in total?"

Hu's throat bobbed. "Three at the gate," he said, sullenly.
"Three inside. Ten more on staff. Counting me."

Sixteen people. God help him. "Let's move," he said.

"You don't understand," Hu moaned. "You can't use me
as a shield. They don't give a shit about me. They'll shoot
right through me."

"Then make sure they don't see me, Hu."

Miles shoved Hu in front of him, one arm clamping Hu's
neck, the Glock pressed to the man's nape. He pulled out his
knife, and dragging Hu with him, lunged low to stab both
back tires of the Acura.

He gave the other cars in the structure the same swift and
savage treatment as they passed each one.

"Take me to the security center." Miles made his voice a
harsh, gravelly hiss. "One eyelash flicker that I don't like,
and I drop you. And Leah gets suxamethonium pumped into
her. Any minute now, Hu."

"Let me make the call," Hu begged. "I swear, I'll—"

"Fuck, no. Move."

They kept in the shadows of the towering pines as they
moved toward the main building, which was perched on the
edge of a cliff.

They approached a side entrance. Miles shoved the other
man close enough to the door to lift his key card, swipe it. It
flashed green.

This had to snake fast. Hand-to-hand or knife work. A
gunshot, even suppressed, would bring the cavalry down on

him. Miles followed Hu down the dim hallway, paneled with cedar, floored with hardwood planks. Hu stopped at the first door. His eyes darted, panicked.

"You first," Miles said. He held Hu in front of him while Hu swiped his card. When the door popped open, he shoved Hu inside.

Hu shrieked a warning. The one nearest the door turned—

Front kick to the jaw, *crunch*. The man stumbled back with a grunt. His sandwich flew into the air. Miles followed up swiftly on the ground with a side-hand chop to the nose, and leaped to face the guy coming out of the adjacent bathroom, buttoning up his pants.

The guy's eyes barely had time to widen before Miles slammed the toe of his boot into the man's groin. He folded and went down. Miles leaped to intercept Hu, who was diving for the door. Hu shrieked as Miles torqued his arm back. *Snap*.

Hu sagged, whimpering. Miles slammed his boot into the sneaky little bastard's side, *crunch*. Harder to scream for help with broken ribs.

Guy One lay unconscious. Guy Two writhed, in the fetal position. There was a work station for a Guy Three, who could appear at any moment. Miles pulled plastic cuffs from his side pockets and took a couple of precious moments to cuff Guy Two.

Hu rolled on his side, breath bubbling in tears and snot. "Please, please let me make that call—"

"Shut up, you piece of shit." Miles leaned over one of the keyboards. Unlocked. God was kind. He checked in the favorites, found the camera control app. Identified the cone of visibility that covered the escape route he meant to take. Disabled the panning function, memorized the direction of the camera's new blind spot.

He hated leaving those guys lying there, but the conscious one was restrained, and he didn't have the stomach to kill them. And if he wasn't out of here in a couple minutes flat, he was fucked anyhow.

He texted. will come down gully cd use a diversion

Hu twisted to stare up at him, eyes rolling. "Who are you texting?"

Miles smiled evilly. "They're starting, Hu. Say a prayer for Leah." He grabbed Hu by his injured arm, jerked him to his feet and shoved him out the door. "Take me to her."

Hu staggered down the corridor ahead of him, and swiped his card in the electronic lock of a heavy door. It opened into a cinder-block stairwell. Partway down the second flight, a stairwell door flew open.

The guy who walked through looked up as Miles' boot connected with his nose. He bounced off the wall, and toppled.

Hu's breath rasped as he gestured at the door the man had just come through. They entered a corridor, which was lit with sickly fluorescent light. Hu stopped at a door, pulled out a bunch of keys.

The door behind them opened, and Miles felt a painfully familiar eye-popping squeeze in his head. *Anabel.* He spun.

"Help!" Hu shrieked.

Thpptt. His bullet hit her in the thigh. The scrabbling, squeezing sensation ceased. *Shit,* that was loud, even with the suppressor.

But the cinder-block walls might have muffled the sound for the people above them, or at least obscured its source. If he was lucky.

Anabel sagged, clutching her quadricep with reddening fingers. "You idiot! You dickhead!" she spat, to Hu. "You brought him in?"

Miles slammed an uppercut to her jaw that she was in no shape to block, bashing her head against the cinder-block wall.

She thudded to the ground.

Miles jammed the barrel to the nape of Hu's neck. "Open the door, asswipe."

Hu's hands fumbled and shook for an agonizingly long time. When the door finally opened, Miles flung Hu into the cell in front of him. He saw a narrow cot, an opening for a tiny bathroom.

A girl crouched, huddled in the corner. Barefoot, naked to the waist, wearing only loose white drawstring pants. She had long, tangled, frizzy, dark hair. Huge eyes gazed up at him. Terrified.

And this was so not the time to gawk at a pair of perfect tits.

"Uh . . . hi," he said. "I'm Miles. Your ride. Let's go."

9

He couldn't be real. Her drug trips always took her else-where. The people she saw in her visions never appeared in her physical prison. Even the Lord of the Citadel had never come to her. He did not belong in this hellish place. She always went to him.

And this being couldn't be a man. A ghost demon rising up from the depths of her subconscious mind, maybe. Looming, black-clad, ski-masked. The wild, hot blast of his aggressive energy zinged through her nerves, like lightning stabbing. A hallucination, an archetype, a myth.

A god.

It must be the formula. Maybe because they'd maxed out the dose. She was crumbling into her component parts. No way could someone have found her. Who would bother to look for her? Mother and Dad were the only two people in the world who might have cared enough to risk their lives for her, and they were both gone. Murdered.

But this wasn't a wishful fantasy, either, because she hadn't been wishing for rescue. She'd just been hoping for her Lord of the Citadel to sweep her away into heaven. Eternal erotic bliss. It would be nice.

Hu was huddled on the ground at the ghost demon's feet. He lifted his bloodied face. "Please!"

"Move!" The dark figure's voice was brusque. He wrenched his leg free of Hu's clutching hand. "Get up! Hurry!" He was directing the words at her. He pulled a phone from his pocket, and swiftly texted into it. That prosaic gesture was hardly that of a demon or a god.

She stared. "But I . . . ah, but you—"

"I'm the guy you text when you trip on psi-max," he cut in. "You've been camping out in my head."

She gaped, blinking. "You? That's you?"

"Me. On your feet. This is your chance, so take it!"

Hu hoisted himself higher, rolling up to grab the guy's leg. "You said I could call the hospital if I brought you here!" Hu's voice was thin and wobbly. "You said you'd—"

"That was before you fucked me over, douchebag. Twice. Too bad for Leah. Better luck in the next life."

"No! Please. Leah never hurt you!" Hu babbled. "Let me call them and tell them about her reaction to suxamethonium before they start the surgery! Then do anything to me that you want!"

"Correction. I can do anything I want *now*."

"But you promised—"

"I lied." *Whack*. The ghost demon slammed the pistol into the back of Hu's head. Hu thudded onto the concrete, face down.

Lara pulled herself tighter into a ball.

"Lara." The edge in his voice got sharper. "Do you have a shirt?"

She somehow forced the words out. "If I did, I'd be wearing it."

"Great," he muttered. "Are you hurt? Or just stoned?"

"I . . . I . . ." Nothing came out. The circuits were disconnected.

She stared at him, arms up high to protect her face, legs

folded to protect her belly. It was a reflex she could no longer control.

"Shit," the guy muttered. "It's the mask, right? Creeps you out?" He looked up at the camera pointed down at them from the opposite wall, crouched down before her with his back to it, and wrenched it off.

"This is me," he said. "Look fast. I'm putting it back on now."

She gaped. It was him. The Lord of the Citadel. Unmistakably him, with that hawk nose, but so different, with that hot glitter in his eyes, that lean, feral face. Thinner, darker, harder than she remembered from her heated fantasies. "It's . . . it's you," she squeaked.

"Last I checked. Miles, remember? Come on." He whipped the mask back on, reached for her. "Fast."

She stiffened when his hands gripped her elbows, lifting her effortlessly. He dragged her past Hu's prone body, and out of the rat hole. Anabel sprawled in the corridor in a pool of blood.

The man crouched down at Anabel's feet, tugging at them.

"What are you doing?" Her voice was so thin, raspy, creaky.

"Shoes, for you. Quiet!" Miles shoved blood spattered white athletic shoes at her.

She flinched back. "Is she dead?"

"Do you care?" He pushed the shoes at her again, and shoved at the small of her back when she finally took them, propelling her up the stairs. "Dudes, that diversion would be really awesome right about now," he muttered under his breath, and shoved the door open. They heard shouts, running feet, getting louder.

"Oh, shit," he muttered. "Get behind me!"

The running footsteps amplified. It happened fast, and she saw very little from the stairwell, back flat to the wall.

The masked guy lunged through the door. There was a shout, grunts, a few sharp thuds.

One of the men on the security staff tumbled past her down the stairs. He sprawled halfway down and lay, unmoving.

The masked guy's leather-gloved hand yanked her out into the corridor. She clutched Anabel's shoes to her chest, trying to keep her bare feet under herself and somehow keep up.

A faraway gun cracked. Glass shattered nearby. Again, and again. Huge, shattering sounds came from different levels of the building. Someone was shooting out those huge picture windows. More shouts.

"About fucking time," Miles said sourly.

He slapped a door open. They ran out into the dark grounds.

She'd forgotten how big the sky was, how loud. Sighing with wind, leaves swishing and bugs clicking and humming. The rocky, thorny ground bit her feet, but she lurched stupidly along behind him, dazzled by the darkness that was not darkness. It was immensely deep, painted in a million textured qualities of blue and gray and black. Wind petted her skin, countless caressing hands. She dragged in chestfuls of the cold, complicated air, so rich in oxygen and earth, plant and sky perfumes. It made her dizzy. So different from the dead, stale air she'd breathed for months.

The ground sloped sharply beneath her stumbling feet. A chain-link fence reared up. Miles veered to the left, leading them sharply downhill, pulling her behind him, so swiftly that she plowed right into his hard, crouching body when he stopped.

He pulled metal bolt cutters from somewhere on his belt, and sliced through the bottom of the chain-link fence with feverish haste.

Floodlights snapped on, illuminating the grounds with brilliant light, making the shadows sharper, blacker.

"Shit," he hissed. "Now! Go! Slide under! On your back!"

She wiggled on her back, feet first, under the fence. The cut ends brushed across her face and her naked chest, claws raking, just hard enough to sting. Rocks and dirt tugged at her trailing hair. The hill got abruptly steeper on the other side of the fence, and the moment she was through, she lost her bearings and her balance and tumbled, rolling and bouncing down a steep, jagged gully, along with a generous shower of rocks. She landed with a gasp on the nearest place flat enough to break her fall, and clung there, bruised and disoriented.

He landed like a cat beside her a moment later, so gracefully, it was as if he had floated down. "You okay?" he whispered.

She dragged herself up, taking stock. "Not sure yet."

His hands moved gently over her, assessing the damage. He'd taken off the gloves, and his bare skin was warm, calluses rasping, but his touch was very delicate and careful, sliding over her bare shoulders, goose-bumped in the chill. "You're cold," he said.

"I'm okay," she said, and realized from the wobble in her voice that she was shivering violently.

He peeled off his jacket and his black sweatshirt. "Here," he whispered. "Take these."

She shrank back, but he shoved the sweatshirt over her head anyway, wrestling it down until she lifted her arms to help.

It was huge, the neck dangling loose over her bare shoulder, the hem hanging to mid-thigh. So warm. Like being hugged. The back was damp with his sweat. It smelled like a man who'd been running and fighting. Imbued with his vital energy. Shudders racked her chilled body, and her nipples tightened. Tears started into her eyes.

He tried to put the jacket on her, too, and she batted it away.

"No way!" she whispered fiercely. "You use that!"

He muttered something impatient, and yanked the jacket back on, then took her arm and pulled her to her feet.

The first step she took, she stumbled on the sharp rocks, and fell onto her knees again. He crouched down and touched her bloodied feet with a hiss of dismay. "Shit, Lara!"

"Sorry," she whispered.

"What happened to Anabel's shoes?"

Lara shook her head. "Dropped them when I fell."

Miles looked around. She couldn't imagine what he could see in the pitch darkness, but after a few seconds he crouched, grabbed her arms and turned, draping them over his shoulders. "No time to look for them," he said. "Grab on. Legs around my waist."

She opened her mouth to protest that absurd idea, but the shouting voices swelled, getting closer.

"Lara." His voice was gravelly with exhaustion. "Please. I don't want to die here."

That jolted her into movement. She wrapped her arms around his huge shoulders, fingers tingling. He hoisted her legs up.

She hung on with all her strength. It felt so strange, to touch someone again. His contracted muscles were steely hard beneath her face, her hands, her clenched thighs.

She'd never held anyone that desperately close, not ever. Not even ex-lovers. It had been so long, since anyone had touched her at all, other than to slap or yank or kick.

Miles ran headlong down the steep hill in pitch darkness. The rays from the floodlights from above did not penetrate the thickets of foliage below, and he kept to the shadows, zigzagging deftly across the wide, deep gully. Every footfall was light and sure, even on the broken tumbled boulders and the steep rocky hillside.

Her voice jolted jaggedly out of her throat, broken by his thudding footfalls. "How do you see to run so fast?"

"I can see in the dark," was his reply.

Oh, please. "How?" she demanded. "What, are you a vampire or something?"

Miles' chest vibrated. "Like I don't have enough problems. Can we talk about it later? I promise I won't suck your blood."

"Sure." She hid her face against his neck, abashed. His sweaty hair was salty against her lips. He had a hot, animal taste. She liked it.

She hung on, as tightly as she could, her hands locked over the taut muscle and hot, naked skin that his open jacket revealed.

His hair tickled her nose. His body felt so vital, wiry and dense, so intensely concentrated. The bodies of her few ex-boyfriends had not felt remotely like this man's body. He was a whole new order of being.

His flying strides created a headwind, as if she were galloping on a horse. They tore through thickets, boughs thwacking against their faces, her arms, his chest. She buried her face against his neck. His hair dripped with sweat.

Tears leaked out of her eyes. She tried to stop them, but she shook inside. Something frozen inside her was starting to melt. Just because she was touching another human being.

The first twinge of pain was like a tension headache. It intensified quickly, like a band of steel around her skull tightening.

The fear that was her constant companion ballooned. Darkness rose like a tidal wave, rushing up to swallow her.

Her blood pressure dropped. The pull began. Her arms and legs trembled, then went slack.

Miles caught her arms as she slid off his body, and crouched down to hold her. "Lara? What's wrong?"

"Greaves," she gasped. "Doing something. To my head. Pulling."

"Lara, get inside! Of my mind, understand? Like you did before!"

She could barely speak, with that huge fist squeezing inside her head. "You . . . don't feel it?" she croaked.

"My shield is really tough," he said. "So get inside! Come on! Find a way, before he fucks you up!"

Blood was trickling from her nose. Pain filled her consciousness. His pleading voice faded. *Get inside. Like before. Get inside! Lara!*

She forced the words out, fighting to stay conscious. "Leave . . . me," she whispered. "Can't. He's got me. Can't . . . go farther. Run away."

"No." He lifted her right into his lap and cradled her, arms clamped around her body. "I can't run anymore. I'm not leaving you."

Why? She wanted to ask, but words were gone.

The last part of her mind that functioned at all came into focus. The grim concentration she'd earned and honed, in those long, dark months of captivity. She'd struggled every day to find her calm center. A place that lay beyond fear, anger, and crushing boredom.

She floated back from the pain, the clutch of compulsion, to that Lara behind Lara, who could not be controlled . . . and the vortex seized her like it had been waiting for her. She took off.

The momentum flung her wide and fast into chaos. She raced through inner space, exulting. Sensed the Citadel, with perceptions that were completely apart from her normal senses. The wall, its massive grinding gears and moving parts. Her dance. Swaying, unerring steps. Over, under, through . . . and she was inside.

She gasped in relief. The pain was gone.

So strange, though. She was still conscious. She was not in a trance. Her vision was still doubled, as if the Citadel were a waking dream, but she was acutely aware that a big, gorgeous, terrifying man was cuddling her on his lap while melding minds with her.

She felt raw, naked, exposed. Confused.

The feedback loop of feelings made her body hot with shame. She was inside his mind now. He had to feel everything that she felt.

"I'm in," she whispered.

"I know." His strangled tone said it all.

She was embarrassed by the giddy sexual awareness. All those sex dreams. Months of them. For her, it was as if they'd already had a blazing affair. God knows what it felt like from his side.

He turned his back to her again. "Mount up."

She gripped his shoulders, which she could barely fit her fingers around. Her inner thighs, wound around his waist, felt every detail of him through the shapeless jersey fabric of her pants, right down to the holstered gun at his side and the studs on his pants. She was still weak and hollowed out from Greaves' attack, but Miles ran faster than ever.

All she could do was hang on. Try not to disgrace herself.

Thaddeus Greaves surveyed the ruins of the dining room. Coffee carafe overturned. Fresh orange juice, hurled across the pristine white tablecloth. His ham steak, grilled to perfection, was stabbed through with multiple shards of window glass. Glass glittered in the bread basket, the fruit salad, the black truffle and mushroom omelet.

Had he not shielded himself telekinetically the instant he heard the gun, he too would be full of those shards. It had been a question of nanoseconds, or perhaps a touch of precognition. His telekinetic abilities could stop bullets, so he stood in the middle of the shattered window frame, in silent invitation. No bullet that came his way would ever reach him, but the muzzle flash would be a useful indicator of where the attacker was located, saving precious time.

The shooter did not take the bait. After a minute or so, Greaves walked down the stairs, to the sound of various other windows shattering. He stopped at the corridor on the first floor, startled by the still body and bloodied face of Briggs, a member of his personal security unit, sprawled across the corridor. Briggs was a telepath, quite a strong one. And even he had gotten no warning of the attack to come.

In the security center, Dexter lay moaning on the floor. Yeats was unconscious on the ground. Useless idiots. Not a peep from his current telepathic sentinel, either. His staff was worse than useless.

Anabel's sprawled body downstairs was a distasteful sight, if not unexpected. He stepped carefully around the blood, not wanting to soil his loafers, and peered into the gaping door of Lara's cell.

Only Hu lay inside, wheezing and whimpering.

Greaves ran upstairs and out onto the grounds, by now lit by floodlights. His remaining staff ran around, frantically trying to give the impression that they were doing their job. It was too late to maintain that fiction. But there would be time enough to express his displeasure later.

He sent his perceptions ranging. Wide and diffuse, like ripples in a pond. On, and on . . . approaching the edge of his range.

Yes. There she was. He'd savored Lara's distinct flavor on that exciting telepathic ride through her inner dreamworld. Amazing power. So like Geoff's. Such potential, if only she could be reasoned with.

It was just a matter of time, of course. He would be charming, patient, and eventually she would bend. And if he could unlock her shield . . . the thought elated him. She was the only person besides Geoff who had ever blocked him. If he could penetrate her shield, learn its secrets, perhaps he could breach Geoff's, too.

And there was the element of her sexual appeal. Her mental and emotional signature was delicious. Subtle overtones, delicate aromas.

He would have Lara Kirk, and power over the future. The power to put things right, at his fingertips. Geoff, too. All his.

Lara seemed to be alone. There was no other mental signature near her, but she had to have gotten help, given the shooter, the broken, bleeding bodies of his staff. How had she coordinated such an escape from her isolated cell? She must have powers she had hidden. She'd seemed so beaten. He'd caught no whiff of hidden weapons, hatching plots. He clamped down on her, adding coercion to the mix.

She was so strong. Sweat broke out on his forehead. He laughed. It felt good, to use his mind as it was meant to be used. Like a rousing game of tennis. Finally, something real to push against.

There was a delicate balance to be found. He did not want to damage her beautiful, unusual brain, but she had to learn obedience. He had to be a little cruel to get his point across. He pushed harder . . .

And she winked out. As if she had never been there.

His eyes popped open. *What?* He groped, lunged, swept feelers where he had been before, then in every imaginable direction.

Nothing. Gone. Hiding behind that fucking shield of hers.

He pressed further. To the limits of his range, and beyond, straining, until his heart thudded. A red haze of rage before his eyes.

Minutes went by before he could identify it, but only vaguely. It was more like an absence than a presence. A dark spot, denser than nothing, like a cloak of invisibility.

He could barely locate it, let alone breach it.

But he could fish for the others. There was the shooter, and the one who had attacked his staff. He would troll for her team.

He lunged, swept, reached. It was a broad area, but he

was highly motivated. Back and forth, around . . . nothing still . . . *yes!*

Unshielded, on the hillside opposite. Male. Moving quickly downhill. This was the sniper who had destroyed his windows, and spoiled his breakfast. Who might have killed or maimed him, but for his telekinetic shield. The sniper's mind was surprisingly difficult to grasp. It was so fiercely focused on the job at hand, it was empty of all else, rendering it elusive and transparent. But Greaves got a grip on him.

He clamped down on the man's mind, relishing the jolt of surprise that quickly turned to anger. The man was strong, with psi elements, but not on a conscious level. Greaves felt them like the overtones of a resonant voice. Excellent candidate for psi-max.

The gunman struggled, in vain. Greaves pinned the man with part of his mind, and ranged further. He found another, then two more. One had a well-developed psi talent, limited training, and a strong shield, but nothing on the order of Lara's. The other two were like the gunman. Raw, undeveloped talent, but no defenses. Not against him.

It felt good, as angry as he was, to clutch them all and *squeeze.*

10

It took focus to lope through rough, unfamiliar terrain in the dark with a traumatized girl on his back and evil goons who may or may not start shooting at them. Being hyper-conscious of her body touching him did not help. There was no time for this juvenile shit.

Get down, he scolded. *Later for that.* He needed every available red blood cell for the big head right now.

The slope was leveling off. They were approaching the riverbank. He smelled motor vehicles, exhaust, gas, rubber. Men. Her face was pressed against his shoulder. Her lips. As if she were kissing him.

It occurred to him that his bandwidth had been getting progressively bigger, ever since he'd started talking to her. Now, with her clinging to his back, his augmented senses did not feel freakish and painful at all. They felt right, like he'd grown to fit them. It felt appropriate, to see in the dark, to hear so acutely. The tidal wave of constant data didn't jar him. And the smell of her hair, oh God—

Whoa. Keep your nose on the job.

The wide creekbed stretched out before him. He saw the

dim outline of two vehicles in the trees, on the other side. One was his own.

Something was off, but he didn't nail it down until the dark figure came into focus not far from the vehicles, sprawled on the tumbled boulders. It was Connor, clutching his head. Trying to crawl.

Miles put on a burst of desperate speed. "Connor?" He leaped over the rocks, and crouched beside his friend. Lara slid off his back and crawled to Connor's other side. "Connor? What's wrong?"

"Head," Connor rasped. "Pulling." He jerked his hand in the direction of the house that hung on the top of the hillside above. Blood ran from Connor's nose and down his neck.

"Greaves," Lara whispered.

Miles scooped his arms beneath Connor's armpits, trying to hoist him to his knees. "We've got to get out of that bastard's range."

"Davy." Connor's voice was a breathless grunt. "Sean. Aaro."

Miles stuffed the fear he did not have the luxury to feel, and braced himself against Connor's weight. It had never occurred to him that he was putting his friends in danger of this magnitude. They'd always seemed so invulnerable to him. Godlike, even.

"Let me help," Lara said.

"Concentrate on not breaking both your legs," he said.

She wiggled her shoulder beneath Connor's arm. Connor glanced at her, and shot an eloquent look in Miles' direction. "Son of a bitch," he muttered.

"Shhh," Miles hissed. "Move!"

They hustled toward the vehicle. Lara tugged the back door open. Miles heard noise on the hillside as he bundled Connor into the back.

He shoved Lara down on the floor of the vehicle, then crouched down to listen and sniff the air. He had to pull something brilliant out of his ass, right now, but nothing was coming to him, and the sound of shushing boughs and snapping twigs was getting louder.

Aaro. He couldn't have said how he suddenly knew it was Aaro coming down the hill, but he did, and he almost wept with relief.

"Look after him," he said to Lara. "I'm going back for the others."

He sprinted toward the sound. They emerged from a grove of young firs. Aaro was half carrying Sean, and staggering beneath the other man's weight. Sean's nose bled. Aaro's face was a rigid mask of endurance. He was hurting, but functioning better than Sean.

Of course. He was shielded.

Miles slid an arm beneath Sean's shoulder, hoisting him up. "It's Greaves," he told Aaro. "Long-distance mind-reaming."

"Can't talk," Aaro ground out. "He's squeezing me even through the shield. Oh man. Hurts. Fuck this shit."

"Amen," Miles agreed fervently.

A few minutes of frantic stumbling got them back to the car. Lara was holding Connor's head, pressing a wad of pale cloth to his nose. Her eyes were big, shadowy pools. Haunted and afraid.

Miles addressed Aaro. "Get yourselves out of range," he said, hoisting the groaning Sean into the passenger side.

Connor opened his pale green eyes. "Davy," he wheezed.

Of course it would have been Davy to volunteer to create the distraction. Davy was the best shot of all the McCloud brothers, which was saying a lot, since they were all kick-ass with both long- and short-range guns. Davy had gotten much closer to Greaves than the others had been. If they had been felled by Greaves' mind-reaming, God knows how Davy had fared. Greaves was much stronger than Rudd, and Rudd had left Miles in a coma.

"I'll go for him." Aaro's voice was rough.

"No," Miles said. "I'll go."

Aaro waved his hand at Lara. "Finish the job. Get the girl clear. I'll do clean-up. I have a shield."

"My shield's better," Miles said. "Take Lara, Sean and Connor, and get the fuck out of range. I'll get Davy. Give me my car keys."

Aaro glowered at him. "Getting bossy, punk?"

"Yeah." He waggled his fingers for the keys.

Aaro was too messed up to argue. He pulled the keys from his pocket and tossed. Miles snagged them out of the air.

He bolted up the hill, chest pumping, every souped-up, tricked-out capacity he had bent upon calculating Davy's location. The first window that had shattered was on the top floor, on the side, a vaulted picture window that faced the opposite hillside, not the canyon. Davy would have had to climb the hill to get that shot. He also would have hauled ass back down as soon as the job was done. Miles factored in the moment when Greaves' mental attack had begun, which would mark the spot where Davy presumably stopped.

A few breathless minutes, slapping through the trees, chest heaving, legs pumping, and he almost tripped head-long over Davy's prone body. The guy had made it fifty meters further down toward the rendezvous point than Miles had calculated. Typical McCloud.

He fell to his knees. "Davy! Can you hear me?"

Davy's body was rigid. "Pulling," he gasped. "Can't move."

Miles dragged him upright, somewhat helped by how rigid he was. Good thing it wasn't dead weight, considering Davy's mass.

It was impossible not to make noise crashing through the underbrush with Davy staggering beside him. Miles could hear their pursuers drawing closer. One was at about a hundred and twenty meters, another was at ninety. Probably in body armor, with infra-red, and/or thermal imaging. Both moving much faster than he and Davy could. He eased Davy onto the ground, and put his finger to his lips. "I'll go take care of our company," he whispered.

No time to answer the frantic questions in Davy's eyes. He darted away, weaving low and silent among the scrubby trees and foliage.

A shelf of granite protruded from the hillside, above the best probable path. If he was high enough, the man might not even look up to catch the heat signature with his thermal imager.

Miles scrambled up the rocks, grateful for the intensive rock-climbing he'd done over the last several weeks, and stretched himself out on the lip of granite. It was barely wide enough. He was glad for the camo jacket, and the ski mask.

The man emerged from the shadows of the trees. Silent, swift. Only Miles' augmented senses could have picked him up in the dark. He listened to the soft pad of booted feet, the guy's rapid heartbeat. He was bulked up with body armor, a helmet. And scanning telepathically. The probe slid right over Miles' shield, not registering him.

The realization slid abruptly into place. So that was why he'd been able to take them by surprise and penetrate the place solo. They had thought that they had the ultimate secret weapon, with their psi, that it made them invulnerable. But a weapon was a weak spot if relied upon with any kind of arrogance. The precise reason he'd always been ambivalent about guns.

Miles emptied his mind of everything but the muted crunch of dry grass and pine needles, waiting . . . *crunch* . . . *crunch*—

He dropped softly down behind the guy, and wrenched the man's helmeted head around. *Crack*. Miles lowered his limp body to the ground, and picked up the short assault rifle. An H&K G36. He quelled the noise in his mind so he could hear the other guy's approach. Time enough later to stress about having taken a human life.

The other one was coming down from the left, on a collision course with Davy. He had some different kind of psi, more along the lines of coercion. Miles crept around the outcroppings, seeking a visual.

He finally caught sight of him, armored and bristling with guns and gear. Still wearing infrared goggles, though, to Miles the dawn seemed as bright as noon.

He positioned himself behind a fallen log. The guy had an armored breastplate, as well as a helmet, but Miles didn't want to kill again. Not unless he had to. He dropped his sights to the guy's thigh.

Poised, inhaled. Sought the stillness between breaths.

Bam. The guy jerked, and fell, thrashing on the ground with a muffled shout. Miles ditched the H&K, and raced back to Davy.

"Fixed them," he said, in answer to Davy's questioning glance.

He heard no other pursuers. Those two had been the vanguard. He heaved Davy onto his feet, and they recommenced their stumbling race. He still felt the pressure of Greaves' furious attack, beating impotently around the armor of his shield. The guy still had a fix on them, as long as Davy was in his telepathic grip.

Their staggering progress was agonizingly slow. The truck came into view when they turned the corner of the creekbed. The others were gone. He hoisted Davy into the passenger's seat. The pickup bounced and groaned over rocks and young trees as he steered it through the forest.

"I'll get you to a hospital," he told Davy, when they lurched back up onto the gravel roadbed.

"He'll watch the hospitals." Already Davy's voice sounded stronger. "He'll be looking for anyone with brain injuries, stroke. That's what I'd do, if I were him. Forget the hospital. Just put distance between us and that scumbag."

That was a plan he could get behind. He floored it.

* * *

It was outrageous. Unprecedented. In spite of the psi stranglehold he'd had on their minds, in spite of his psi-enhanced soldiers, one of whom was now dead, they were slipping away from him.

"They're almost out of range," Greaves huffed to Silva, as the man pounded along beside him toward the garage. "Get everyone mobilized. Two vehicles going north, two going south."

He flung open the passenger side of the Jeep. Silva leaped into the driver's side, bawling orders into his wristcom.

The engine revved, the vehicle backed out, picked up speed . . .

The car dragged. Tires thudded heavily, scraping.

Silva cursed under his breath, braked, leaped out. The cursing got louder, with an edge of fear. He kicked the back tire. "Slashed," he said. "Both back tires."

"Another vehicle, then," Greaves said, from behind his teeth.

But no. The back tires of all six of the parked vehicles had been slashed. His staff scurried to change them, but it would make no difference now. Seconds had counted. Those seconds were lost now. He would not even bother to accompany them once they ventured out.

"Sir, I'm so sorry," Silva ventured.

Greaves ignored him, maintaining a flat, fatalistic calm. Just a tendril of his consciousness stayed connected with those hardy souls who had somehow crept into his inner sanctum, and proceeded to fuck him up the ass. The contact grew thinner, fainter . . . and it was gone.

Bumping up against the limitations of his gifts felt like an insult.

He walked back into the house with a slow, measured tread, calling for Levine on the wristcom.

"Yes, sir?" Her voice was suitably subdued.

"Do we have any staff with strong telepathy in their profile in Kolita Springs, or south of here on Wheeler Road? Before any of the highway exits."

"Ah . . . ah, yes, I think that Coburn and Mayfield could—"

"Get them in place, fast, to monitor all the highway exits. Unless these bastards take the back roads, we'll pin them and identify them as they get onto the highway. They're moving fast. We have maybe fifteen minutes."

"Yes, sir. Right away."

Greaves strode into the house. His staff had found their wits again. The wounded ones had been transported to the infirmary.

Greaves peered inside, watching the medics examine the bloody lump on Anabel's head, the bullet that had sliced through the meat of her thigh. The battered face and broken ribs of the whimpering Hu.

Worthless trash. Worth keeping only until they had been questioned about the invaders, the contents of their pathetic brains laid bare. Everything that they had seen and sensed, even subliminally.

Four out of the members of Geoff's rotating medical team were hard at work with the injured. Two of them attended his son at all times, in eight-hour intervals. Geoff and his med team accompanied Greaves everywhere, in a vehicle that seemed an RV from the outside, but was actually a high-tech, cutting-edge hospital room. Each one of his residences had a special room for Geoff—climate controlled, disinfected, filled with all the equipment his son needed to stay alive.

He was at a loss for something to do with his anger. Every outlet had been blocked. He had difficulty breathing. They had slashed his tires, shot his windows. Beaten and shot his employees. Taken Lara, his beautiful prize. And ruined an excellent meal.

The rudeness. How he *hated* rudeness.

He punched the code into the keypad of Geoff's room. Inside, Maura and Daniel were dutifully massaging Geoff's wasted limbs.

Geoff's skin was a pasty, blue-veined, grayish white. His long form was skeletal. Assiduous massages, stretching, and electric stimulation kept his tendons from tightening and turning him into a clawed, hunched cripple, so that when he finally did consent to come out of his mental fortress, his body would be ready to receive him. As ready as his father's will and resources could render it.

Seventeen years he had been like this. Seventeen endless years.

"Leave us," Greaves said.

Maura hesitated, wary of a trap to test her dedication. "Ah, there are still sixteen minutes left for this massage session, sir," she said. "You told us that we must not for any reason skip or shorten—"

"I said, leave us! I will finish the session myself. Out!"

Dan and Maura peeled off their latex gloves and scurried out.

Greaves approached the padded table, with its sheepskin covering. Soft and yielding, to constantly stimulate Geoff's mottled, prone-to-ulcers skin. Geoff was continually turned, continually massaged, disinfected, and exfoliated, his skin hydrated with carefuly formulated unguents to improve his circulation.

Greaves stared down at his son's skull-like face. His thin, fragile skin was pulled taut across strong cheekbones. The slack mouth, the sunken eyes, the eyelids a fragile, veined blue-violet.

Geoff's bone structure was so like Greaves' own face, but the resemblance was no longer possible to see, his son was so pitifully thin. Geoff used to have Carol's glorious golden hair, but it had thinned to a sparse, colorless fuzz, unsavory flakes of dead skin suspended in it. Geoff lay on his side, clad in briefs, his limbs twined with the snaking tubes that were permanently lodged in his orifices.

Greaves ignored the large box of sterile latex gloves mandated for the medics to use when they handled his son's body, and scooped up a handful of the thick unguent, going to work on Geoff's left leg. The slow, rhythmic, familiar movements soothed him. He massaged Geoff often.

His son seemed even thinner than usual. He should tell the medics to up the caloric load in the IV drip. Or to increase the duration of the muscle stimulation sessions, though the sessions he dictated were already many times over what any physiotherapist would recommend, or even consider useful.

But why not? It wasn't as if Geoff had anything better to do. Greaves had no constraints of budget or time. He could hire a staff of fifty or five hundred to work on Geoff around the clock. And would do so, in a heartbeat, if only it would help.

His anger bubbled up, over, and out. "You were unfair," he announced, as his hands slid up and down Geoff's shriveled calf. "You and your mother both. You refused to listen to reason."

The silence that answered him was eloquent. Carol had been a master of the speaking silence, since he met her back in middle school in Blaine, Oregon, and Geoff had inherited her gift. He had always read the subtext of Carol's silent protests with ease. Even before the brutal experiments that had jolted his psi to life.

It was one of the things she had loved about him, at first, when they were young and madly in love. Him, heading off to Germany, a private first class in the army. She, already pregnant with Geoff, stuck back in Blaine, in her mother's trailer. He'd sworn to break her out of that place someday, as if it were Alcatraz. It hadn't proven to be so easy.

Then, one day, on the base in West Germany, he'd gotten the call. He'd been chosen for a special assignment. A secret training protocol, run by the legendary Colonel Holt. A small group of soldiers had been selected, based on some rare gift that testing had revealed. Colonel Holt had explained that if these gifts could be developed, they would be incredible assets for their country. The training was rigorous, and he would be moved to another facility, isolated from his buddies, unable to tell his family back home what he was doing, or where. But his family would be well taken care of. Until he could see them again, which might be quite some time.

Of course, he'd consented. Who didn't want to be an incredible asset for one's country? Particularly if it benefited Carol and Geoff.

He couldn't have known what the "training" would be. The pain was crushing. The blood vessel-bursting, crazy-making agony of those torture sessions with Colonel Holt had almost driven him mad. Each one had left him helpless, unable to move, speak, even turn his head. He spent weeks unable to do anything but rock in his cot, hiding from the light, flinching at the faintest sound. He'd hoped for death, but he didn't die. He'd healed. And changed.

Oh, how he had changed.

Gradually, he'd discovered that he could do those things that Colonel Holt wanted from him, and more. He also realized quickly that he had to underplay his abilities, out of self-defense. He was quite sure that no one had ever intended for him to develop this much power.

Colonel Holt clearly had suspicions, but that didn't stop him from using Greaves for years to conduct intelligence missions, using his telepathy to gather crucial intel for national security. Greaves never let on about his growing capacities for telekinesis and coercion, or his burgeoning ability to organize, multitask, assimilate, and organize information. There were other talents, too, hard to pinpoint or define.

His cognitive ability skyrocketed. He could learn a language in a few days, sound like a native, and retain the knowledge like a bear trap. One dull weekend, he'd taken on the stock market and all of its tricks and games, and over the following weeks had earned a fortune by investing and deftly reinvesting his earnings.

Fun at first, but not all that interesting in the long run. Money was useful, but over a certain sum, the number of zeros on the bank balance ceased to matter.

Carol and Geoff saw little of him, but they were well provided for. They wanted for nothing, lived in a beautiful Victorian house on the lake in Blaine. Geoff could have art and music lessons and go to an exclusive prep school. But on Greaves' visits home, things were not as they should be. Carol could not hide her inner tension from a telepath.

She was afraid of the changes that she sensed in him.

He was not at liberty to explain the truth to her, or anyone. At that point, no one knew the true extent of what he could do. Colonel Holt had been poised to sound the alarm and close him down, but sadly, the good colonel's heart had stopped unexpectedly, one night, at a hotel in Berlin.

Greaves had been in the next room. He had telekinetically constricted a vessel in the man's heart. Useful trick. Subtle. Traceless.

Those of his superiors who knew of his telepathy treated him as if he had a deadly contagion. As if he cared about their secrets.

He cared about Carol's secrets, though. Her fear had driven a wedge between them. Even when making love, using all his powers to please her, that dark spot remained. And grew.

Then he began to sense it in Geoff, too.

Geoff had been twelve when his father had realized that the boy had as much psi potential as he did himself. Flashes of strong natural telepathy, precognitive ability that showed in his remarkable artworks. By then, he'd given up hope of real intimacy with Carol, but Geoff was another matter. With the boy's capabilities, Geoff could join him on a higher plane, guiding the world to a better future, as a loving parent guided an innocent child.

The thought was so seductive. His gift was a great burden, but Geoff could stand beside him. Help him to give it all back.

It became his obsession. Geoff was sensitive, compassionate. A healer, a mystic. He would provide the gentler traits his father lacked, and they would rule like two gods, complementing each other. As perfect as mortal flesh could be.

But Carol had objected when the training began. Her unreasonable panic had been disastrous. The training was as frightening to watch as it was stressful for Greaves to inflict, but Carol refused to understand the value of the pain he inflicted upon their son. It was Greaves' duty to help his son reach that potential—at all costs.

The necessity to silence Carol had broken his heart. Geoff's newly forming psi abilities had made it impossible to hide. He had seen what his father had been forced to do before it even happened.

Geoff's grief and anger at Carol's death had caused the boy to retreat behind an impervious mind shield, from which he had never returned.

No brain activity showed on any monitoring device that was attached to Geoff. All doctors who examined him pronounced him brain dead, and yet, his mind continued to generate a shield the likes of which could only be the product of a highly functioning mind and will. A shield that only Greaves himself was capable of perceiving. And his growing army of pharmacologically enhanced psychics, of course. A lesser breed, true, but they had their uses.

Geoff's shield was the psi equivalent of a light-sucking black hole. A loud, reverberating, constant fuck-you. His son was still in there, alive, conscious. Constantly taunting his father with his stubborn silence. He was almost thirty years old now. Seventeen years of wasting muscles, wasting possibilities, wasted potential. So infuriating.

That damned shield. Just like the one Lara Kirk generated. It maddened him. It made him want to just break . . . them . . . *apart.*

He was clutching Geoff's thin calf so tightly, his nails had broken the skin. He dropped Geoff's leg, and watched the bluish, poorly oxygenated blood well up sluggishly into the small wounds. Geoff's circulation was poor. His medication clearly needed adjustment.

He clenched his teeth, and forced himself to daub disinfectant over the small wounds. An infection would be devastating to Geoff's weakened immune system. He flung the cotton swab to the ground.

His son's insolent silence made his teeth grind.

"You were unfair to me," he told Geoff again. "When you come out, you will understand. And you will see that I was right."

11

Davy dragged out his cell after a few minutes and tapped into it. "Where are you?" he barked into it. "Yeah. Okay. My head hurts like hell, but I'm good now that we're out of range. Miles extracted me. Kid is bad ass." He listened. "Understood. Logging road .4 miles after the junction of Mary Creek Road and Muller's Grade. Got it."

He closed the call. "We're switching drivers," he said. "Connor wants to drive. Aaro will drive your rig."

"That's insane!" Miles protested. "Connor was practically unconscious fifteen minutes ago! What the fuck is he thinking?"

Davy slanted him a glance. "He's thinking you're the lucky bastard gets to deal with the girl."

"Deal with what? How? I already dealt with the girl! I got her out, right? Haven't I dealt with enough?"

"Evidently not. Shut up. My head hurts."

Miles bit his tongue. He'd become accustomed to being the poor chump with the soul-crushing head pain. He felt bad for Davy, but he felt no pain himself, and the absence of pain made him giddy.

That thought sparked the sudden awareness of Lara, still inside.

you ok? he queried.

yes

think we r out of range now

There was a pause, and then, can i stay anyway? i like it here

Heat rose in his face. His heart quickened. *Get a grip, bonehead.*

sure whtevr, he replied. c u in a few

Aaro, Connor, and Sean waited outside the vehicle at the meeting point on the logging road. Lara remained in the backseat, face pressed to her huddled knees.

Aaro held out his hand. "Give me the keys," he said. "Connor drives the SUV. You sit in the back."

"But I should be driving!" Miles protested. "I'm the only one who wasn't compromised by the—"

"I'm fine," Connor said. "Deal with your lady friend."

"She's not my lady friend!" Miles protested. "I just met her!"

"Doesn't matter," Sean said. "She's your problem now, buddy."

"She's crying," Connor added, darkly.

"I'm not dealing with that," Aaro said. "My quota is full. She's all yours, my man."

"You got her out. You comfort her." Sean splashed a handful of water from a bottle onto his hand to rinse the dried blood from his pallid face, and looked Miles over. "What's with the naked torso under the jacket?" he said. "That's a new look for you. And the caveman hair? Are we trying to impress someone with the sixpack abs, my friend?"

Miles exhaled, counting down from five. "She needed the shirt."

Sean's eyes widened, and flicked to Lara, who was still

hiding her face. "She didn't have a shirt on? Oh, man. I'm so titillated."

Miles got into the vehicle, ignoring Sean's jibes. Connor picked up speed. Lara had her hands clamped over her face. She gave him a wet-eyed look between her fingers. Shook her head, mouthing *sorry*.

Aw, shit. His throat tightened like a lug nut. Fuck this.

He reached for her, hauled her up onto his lap. Not that there was much effort involved. She was so thin and light and fragile. Though the lovely tits did not reflect that at all.

Her ass felt nice against his lap, too. He tucked her head under his chin, to preclude eye contact, and tried not to think about that. His synapses would overload if he had to look at her in addition to feeling her. And having her tucked up tight inside that secret private place in his head was titillating, too. Titillation every damn place he turned.

Her body had that delicate, baby-bird vibration, like she was afraid to be held or touched, but she didn't pull away. He could hear her heart racing as if she'd been running. And her subtle female scent made his hormones zing. His animal instincts knew that she was aware of him, too. Her body was answering this glandular racket his own body was making, but he could not trip out on that response. She was in no way responsible for anything her body might non-verbally say in the wake of this craziness. She was fucked up to hell and gone.

But he was so aware of her face against his chest, the hot moisture of tears, the tickle of her eyelashes. His collarbone had become as discerning as eyes or fingertips.

Her hand was splayed over his chest. So pale.

Sean caught the vibe, human antenna that he was, and craned his neck with a grin. "That's more like it," he said. "Do your duty."

"Shut up," Miles snapped. "She does not need your bull-shit."

"Ooh, aren't we protective."

"I mean it, Sean."

"Lighten up," Sean said. "We all have our coping mechanisms, and getting in your face is one of my favorites. So shoot me."

"I will," Miles warned. "I swear, I will."

Thankfully, Sean turned around, still grinning. Miles felt guilty about letting himself be needled. Sean always got manic after intense danger. He'd crawled up that hill at risk to his own life, and gotten his brain zapped by a psycho monster, all for Miles' sake.

But sad experience had taught him that an apology just encouraged the guy to be annoying again. Best to zip it. Let it pass.

His torment was not destined to cease, though, because Connor promptly started in on him. "We need to talk," he announced.

The edge in Connor's voice made Miles' stomach sink. "It's been a tough night," he said. "Let's not and say we did."

Connor ignored him. "This Greaves. He fucked us up from a considerable distance. With his mind. All of us. At the same time."

"Yes," Miles agreed. "That he did."

"So, he's like that guy Rudd, then? Same deal?"

"Not exactly," Miles said. "Stronger. A lot stronger. To a power of ten at least, and I think he has other tricks up his sleeve, too. Though I don't have any evidence to back that up."

"He does." Lara's voice was soft, but steady. "Telekenisis. He moved me across the room like a doll. Telepathy, too. Stronger than Anabel's. Other things, as well. He hinted at them."

"Yikes," Sean muttered, under his breath.

Connor ruminated on that as he drove. "And yet, you were not affected by the attack. How is that possible?"

Miles felt defensive. "My shield just happens to work well against his psi energy," he said. "I don't know why."

"And where did you learn this technique? After running

away from everyone, refusing all help when it was offered to you?"

"I don't know!" Miles flared. "Maybe it's because of the brain damage from Spruce Ridge. I was trying not to go crazy with the stress flashbacks. I worked on the shield day and night in the mountains, and it just so happens to ward off this guy's particular style of mind-fucking. What, does that offend you? You're pissed about that?"

"Yeah," Connor said, belligerently. "Yeah, I am pissed about that! I'm pissed about you distancing yourself, keeping secrets from us!"

"Look, man, I never meant to—"

"What about her?" Connor jerked his hand toward Lara. She'd stopped crying and was following the conversation, wide-eyed and attentive. "How'd she keep from getting fried?"

"I was fried," Lara offered. "For a while. But then I got inside."

"Inside what?" Sean swiveled his head, his bright eyes fascinated.

Lara jerked her chin at Miles. "Him. Inside his shield, I mean."

Baffled silence, for some seconds, until Sean took it upon himself to break it with a low whistle. "Whoa," he said. "Talk about titillating."

"Shut up, Sean," Miles growled again, and turned back to Connor. "It's like she said. She, ah . . . got inside my mind shield somehow."

"I've been hiding out there. I've done it for weeks," Lara said softly. "It's the reason I'm still alive."

The car was deathly silent for a long moment. When Connor finally started up again, his voice was even colder. "So are you going to tell us when you got the mysterious super-powers?"

"Bullshit," Miles said wearily. "It's not a superpower, it's just—"

"Yeah, yeah, we heard that. It's just brain damage. Combined with random chance, and dumb, blind luck. You find the girl nobody can find. You give her a long-distance telepathic mind shield. You rescue her singlehandedly, without waiting for our help. Now you're the only one who can get near that freak Greaves without getting mentally ass-fucked. Are you bullet-proof now? Can you fly? And you never told us anything. It's headaches, and hallucinations, and you're considering taking the meds. Oh, poor me! Stress flashbacks! What the fuck is your problem, Miles? When did you stop trusting us?"

"It's not about trust!" Miles yelled.

"The hell it's not!"

"Dudes. Calm down," Sean soothed. "Now is not the time for a—"

"I practically got my head exploded, putting myself out there to save his ungrateful ass and rescue his girlfriend!" Connor raged. "I can yell at him if I damn well feel like it. He is righteously pissing me off!"

Miles glanced nervously at Lara to see how she took her new title. She didn't meet his eyes.

Sean swiveled his head. "He's just uptight because neither of us could help Davy," he said. "Davy would be dead if not for you. That burns his ass, but I know he's grateful, underneath. Aren't you, Con?"

"Shut up, Sean," his brother snarled.

"See? He still loves you." Sean turned wistful eyes on Lara. "Everyone tells me to shut up. But you won't, sweetheart, will you? You're nicer than them."

Lara looked up, shook her head. "I don't know how nice I am. But I'm certainly grateful for your help."

"Ah." Sean closed his eyes, in exaggerated bliss. "So polite."

Miles suddenly registered the sensation, tickling against his shield. "Slow down, and pull over," he said. "Right now."

Connor promptly did so. "What is it?"

"Telepath ahead," Miles said. "Scanning the cars that go by. Greaves posted someone at the highway exit out of Kolita Springs."

"Look at that. A brand-new superpower," Connor said sourly.

Sean shot them a grim look. "Con and Davy and I don't have time for a crash course in mind control against invasive telepaths."

Miles thought furiously. "Breakfast," he said.

The brothers gave him identical baffled expressions.

"Think about breakfast," Miles said. "Fill your mind with it. Eggs, bacon, coffee, orange juice, hash browns, whatever. Full sensory panorama. You both like food. It should work. Don't try to block, just let him read that and only that. Sex might work, too. Take your pick." He yanked out his cell, and tapped in a message to Davy with the same directive. His phone burped almost instantly with a returning text.

spanish omelet xtra guac

He looked at Lara. "You just stay where you are," he said. "Inside. And get down, out of sight. Come to think of it . . ."

He slid off the seat and stretched out on the floor, beckoning to her with his arms.

She reached out, timidly. He grabbed, yanked. She lost her balance in the moving car, and toppled onto him with a soft thud.

He steadied her, forcing himself to breathe. She was half-straddling him. One knee on the floor, the other clamped between his. They thudded over a bump in the road and he reached up reflexively to cup her face so she didn't bang her jaw.

And found he couldn't take his hand away. Her skin was so soft. The bones of her face so delicate. She was struggling to breathe.

She felt familiar, in his arms. He already knew the shape of the bones in her face, the texture of her skin, her hair.

Hell, he knew what she tasted like when he lifted her skirts and—

Stop it right there.

She was perched squarely on top of a hard-on that she could not fail to notice. He stared, hypnotized by her gorgeous eyes. As he had been from the first photo of her that he'd ever seen. The one he'd picked up from the floor of her father's trashed living room.

The day he'd found Joseph Kirk's mutilated body.

That jolted him back to business. He felt that questing tendril of invasive telepathy getting more intense, more palpable.

Concentrate. "You guys got your mental breakfasts ready?"

"Home fried potatoes, English muffins oozing butter, ham steak, fried eggs on top. Lots of coffee. With half and half," Sean said dreamily.

"Black coffee, for God's sake," Connor said. "Half and half is for pussies. Sausage with lots of pepper and sage. And hot biscuits."

The McCloud banter brought a smile to Lara's face. First one he'd seen, ever. Even in photos, she was always solemn. It was fleeting, luminous. Magic, like the elusive glow of starlight.

He would do any crazy thing to score another one of those.

Then it was gone, and another bump in the road jolted her on top of his body. She wiggled, deliciously. Shifted, to steady herself.

Her lips were so close to his, the slightest movement would turn them into contact with his. Tension built, tugging him.

He felt the pinch, the probe, seeking. "We're passing him."

"I feel it." Sean's voice was remote, like he was in a trance.

"Me, too," Connor added.

Silent seconds ticked by. No one breathed. He was locked, motionless on the floor, staring into Lara's huge eyes.

The ticklish prodding faded, then vanished.

He gave her a nod, and she clambered off, onto the seat. Her cheeks were flushed a faint pink, along her sharp cheekbones. Pretty. A hint of color. He craned his neck to stare behind them. No one appeared to be following. His phone burped. Davy, texting.

clear no one following

Tension released in a shuddering sigh. He closed his eyes. "Davy and Aaro made it past," he said.

"Good. I'm hungry now," Sean said. "Do you suppose—"

"No," Miles cut in.

"By the way. Tam found a place for you to rest," Connor said. "I tried to text you the info on the drive from Portland, but of course, you wouldn't answer us. It's a couple of hours from here, taking back roads. She figured you'd need to chill someplace real quiet. Since you were having such a hard time at the wedding. You know, with the noise."

"I'm okay." Miles glanced at Lara. "But I'm glad we can stop soon. It's her I'm worried about."

"I'm okay," Lara said, from the far end of the seat. He missed having her on his lap.

"Can I, um, ask you something?" she said, her voice timid.

"Whatever," he said.

"Hu said, um . . . remember how he said that you'd changed something, in the hospital database? Before Leah's surgery?"

He nodded. "Yeah. What of it?"

"Is that true?" Her voice was very small.

He was affronted. "No! Of course it's not true! What kind of sadistic asshole do you take me for? I've got nothing against that lady."

A fresh smile dawned on her face, and it had exactly the same effect upon him as the one before. He started to blush.

"It was just a bluff, then?" she persisted.

"Of course it was," he grumbled. "Jesus, Lara. As if."

"I'm glad," she said simply. "Leah's a nice woman, I think. She didn't deserve it."

He couldn't bear to look at that smile for another second. Too much. He stared out at the countryside racing by, just trying to breathe.

12

Lara didn't have the nerve to ask him to hold her again. She stared out the window. She should be happy, excited, but she felt no elation. Just fear, and disbelief.

The rat hole had deformed and stunted her. She had no idea how she was going to navigate the world, if she had to face it feeling like this.

Then again, Miles himself would do nicely as a coping mechanism. Her Lord of the Citadel, made flesh and blood. If she gave in to another crying jag, he might cuddle her again. One little nudge, and she'd be a puddle of hysterical sobbing again. So easy.

Maybe it would be worth it. Just to be touched again.

But she didn't want to be that helpless, damaged, crying girl that had to be coddled and fussed over. There was no future in that.

He got all uptight and defensive when his friends gave him hell about his superpowers, but that was exactly how it was, in her eyes. Sweeping in and carrying her away like that.

He slumped next to her on the backseat, coat hanging open over his naked torso. Pretending to sleep, but no way was he sleeping. She felt the energy buzzing off him. But his closed eyes made it easier to stare, so she did, greedily, memorizing every detail to obsess about later, when his sharp eyes were open again and she had to whip her gaze away. From the long, tangled, dark hair, full of leaves and dirt, down to that hawk nose, the lines carved into the sun-bronzed skin crinkling from his eyes. And his body. She was no innocent. She'd seen naked men in her drawing classes, and in her brief and ill-fated love affairs. She'd admired the bodies of male athletes, models. But she'd never felt the heat of lust rise in her body, or been transfixed by the perfect organization of sinewey muscle and long, graceful bones. He had no puffy gym bulk, just lean, practical, raw power. And he towered over her. He'd carried her as if she were a child.

Her face heated, thinking of those breathless moments perched on his body on the floor of the car. The immense heat of him. The powerful, wiry muscles and ridges of bone. It had almost seemed like he was going to kiss her.

God, she wished he had. Every time he touched her, the spot he had touched came alive. Blood rushing into a part of her that had been cramped, squeezed, starved. As sharply painful as it was excellent.

The younger blond guy up front, the one Miles had called Sean, glanced back. She caught his grin as he looked discreetly away.

He'd seen her mooning, and was amused. Her face went hot.

Not that she could be blamed for crushing out. She just had to keep her crush to herself and not bug him with it. And stop staring at his nipples, the way his muscular thighs filled out those ripped, muddy jeans. The fabric of the shirt he had given her rasped against her breasts.

She clenched her teeth. Closed her eyes, turned her attention to that inner space, where part of her still hid. In fact, she could hardly imagine having the nerve to get out from behind his shield ever again. She typed into the analogous mental computer monitor.

u dont fool me ur not asleep

His lips twitched. not fair, he replied, on the mind computer.

His eyes opened. She caught her breath when his smile became an amazing white, flashing grin, with grooves in his cheek carved deep.

"My friends found a place for us to crash," he said aloud. "In the hills, not far from here. We'll stop there and figure out what to do next. You can rest, stoke up with some decent food. We'll keep you safe."

The idea of someone offering her rest, food, protection, made her speechless. Then it made her eyes water and swim.

"Lara." His grin faded. "About your dad."

She flung her hand up to ward off whatever he might say. "I know," she said. "They taunted me with it. The torture, and . . . and everything. You don't have to tell me about it."

"Okay," he said. "Fucking scumbags."

He reached out and pulled her onto his lap again.

She melted down instantly. Hid her face against his chest, dabbing eyes and nose with the hem of the filthy sweatshirt he had given her. Shuddering with sobs.

Time passed. The car kept moving. She fell into an uneasy doze. His chest vibrated beneath her ear when he spoke to the men in front. His arms held her close. His chest was so hot and solid.

Her sleep was fitful, full of violent shifting images. The race through the forest, Hu, whimpering on the floor of the cell. Anabel, in her puddle of blood. Greaves holding electric paddles, his eyes gleeful.

Finally, the car slowed, bumping over a rough driveway, and drew to a stop. Miles slid her gently down on the seat next to him.

She rubbed her eyes. So much light, even with the cloud cover. The whiteness of the sky made her eyes sting. They were in a little valley, in a tangle of brown scrub oak trees, fallow orchards, and fields of brownish grass. Wooded hills rose up on all sides. They were parked in the driveway of a large house made of dark, stained logs. There were big picture windows on the first and second floors.

"We're here," Miles said gently. "Let's go in."

She stepped out into a brisk, snapping wind. So many wonderful fall smells. Herbs and loam and rain. Birds wheeled and squawked. She looked around for the other vehicle. "Where are the other two guys?"

"Aaro and Davy stopped back in town to pick up food and clothes. Let's get you out of this wind." He shrugged his jacket off and put it on her.

She followed him into the house. It was furnished with standard high-end vacation home stuff. Nice and bland and neutral. A big fireplace, hardwood floors, a thick rug in front of a quadrant of big, soft, beige couches. Picture windows opening onto deep patios. A large open-design kitchen and dining area off to the side.

"Sorry we don't have any food yet," he said. "Soon, though."

"I don't think I could eat yet, anyhow," she said. "Could I have some water?"

"God, yes." He took her hand, and led her into the kitchen as if she were a tiny child who wouldn't find her way unguided, and ran her a glass from the tap. He got one for himself. They refilled twice.

They looked at each other. Her eyes skittered to his collarbone, his chest. That interesting hollow over his solar plexus, the graceful pattern of his chest hair, the jut of his ribcage. The lean, defined musculature over it. Gawking. She just couldn't stop.

"You'll, ah, want to take a shower, lie down," he said. "Let's find you a room upstairs."

"Give her the master bedroom." It was Sean, coming in the front door. "The one with the bathroom is for the lady."

"We should get her a doctor." The one called Connor followed his brother in, scowling. He had a faint limp. His eyes were heavily ringed with exhaustion, and there was still blood on his face from the nosebleed.

"For you, too," she said. "All of you."

An impatient shrug met that suggestion. "There should be towels and sheets up there," Connor said. "Tam said it was all covered."

He heaved a bag up onto the kitchen counter, opened it. It proved to have several handguns packed into molded foam. Lara stared as he casually pulled out a magazine, smoothly fitted it into his pistol grip before holstering the weapon in the waistband of his jeans.

She'd always been indifferent about guns, but her eyes followed the weapon longingly. She wanted to snatch it away. *Give me that*.

"No doctors," she said. "He would find me, if I went to an emergency room. It's just scratches and bruises and mud, that's all."

"Lara," Miles said. "Come on. You've been locked in a dungeon for six months. They've been using you as a lab rat. Who knows what shape you're in? You should get checked out."

"Not now," she said. "Just let me chill, okay? I just need to not be pushed around for a while."

Miles looked stung. "I never meant to push—"

"You didn't," she hastened to say. "Sorry. I didn't mean that at all. Not toward you. And, ah, by the way. Thank you. All of you."

The three men looked uncomfortable. "I'll just go set up guard, outside." Connor fled, out the door.

"I'll get the portable surveillance kit," Sean said, following him.

Miles looked nervous, too, but he didn't run away from her.

"And you, most of all," she said quietly. "Thank you, Miles."

It was the first time she'd spoken his name aloud. It felt good in her mouth.

He winced. "I'm just sorry it took me so long." He gestured toward the staircase that spiraled up from the kitchen. "Come on upstairs."

With you, anywhere. She just thought the words. She did not say them or even type them on his mental computer, but she could tell from the way he froze to immobility for a split second that he'd felt her thought. It vibrated in the air between them. Her face went hot.

She launched herself, unsteadily, toward the stairs. Miles lay a hand on the small of her back, as if she might topple backward.

Her knees felt weak. Her joints were soft, squishy. The polite pressure of his hand burned through the sweatshirt like a brand, but not a painful one. The heat felt shivery sweet. Glowing.

Miles opened doors upstairs, peering into the rooms. He found one he liked, and flung the door wide, gesturing her in.

It was the master bedroom. Huge, with floor-to-ceiling windows, and sliding doors that led out onto a big deck. Her eyes were still watering from the light. A bathroom door stood open. A king-sized bed had a pile of towels, a fluffy, folded-up white comforter.

She stared around. Vaulted space. Real air, freshly laundered sheets. Too much. She squinted through her fingers.

He saw the gesture, and moved to the window. "I can close the hanging blinds if it's too much light. You'll want to rest."

"I don't want it completely dark." Her voice shook.

"Of course not," he said.

The pulled cord made the hanging vertical blinds slide to close, but he left them at a slight angle, so that narrow stripes of light slanted through the slats across his muscular torso, the floor, the wall. She longed to capture the image, sculpt him that way, painted with light.

It was the first moment in months that she had longed for

her art. She'd been wondering if that instinct had been crushed by darkness.

The room felt smaller. She felt stupidly shy. Empty-headed. Staring, speechless, starstruck.

"I could open them more," he ventured, his voice uncertain, "if it's too dark."

"It's fine," she said. "Leave it. The light's too much for my eyes."

"Yeah. I'll, uh, just get out of your way, then."

Don't. She screamed the words, inwardly, but would not let them come out of her mouth. He seemed to hear them anyway. He stood by the door like a statue. Their eyes were locked. A breathless pressure built up. She trembled. Air was trapped in her chest. Frozen, there.

All those heated encounters with him in the Citadel swirled through her mind. She wondered if he had experienced them, too. But she would die of embarrassment before she could ask him.

He turned away. "I'm getting a shower. Later."

She sagged onto the bed when the door clicked shut, face on her knees. Oh, man, she did not need this. Why crush out now? She'd never been so vulnerable, so fucked up. God. Please. Have mercy.

She managed to peel off the blood, dirt and sweat-stiffened clothing, and get herself into the shower. The image in the mirror jarred her. Being so thin and pale and bruised hadn't been as incongruous, reflected in the distorted stainless steel soap dispenser and shower fixture in the rat hole. But here, in a luxury bathroom with gleaming gold-toned fixtures and expanses of black marble, she looked insubstantial, wispy. Hardly there at all.

The huge shower was big enough for two, and there was a full-length mirror situated right outside the transparent glass door. A bathroom for honeymooners. The shower was planned with sex in mind.

She squeezed her eyes shut against the images that unleashed. Hot water pounded down her face. So odd, to feel light press against her eyelids as she showered. To not be in that contorted position. Soap stung in all her cuts and scrapes. Dirt sluiced off, swirling around her feet. The shampoo was thick and foamy, and it smelled of honeysuckle. The utilitarian stuff in the rat hole soap dispenser had stunk like disinfectant hospital surgical foam. It took three sudsing passes before her hair rinsed clean of grit.

She toweled off, stepping in distaste over the limp, filthy rags snarled on the bathroom floor. She did not want to put them next to her skin again, particularly not the rat hole pants. She could reconcile herself to Miles' sweatshirt, maybe. But she wasn't giving it back to him. Not ever. She was bronzing the thing. Personally.

She combed out her hair, and wrapped herself in a towel. When she stepped into the bedroom, she found the king-sized bed all made up, the comforter smoothed over it, the covers neatly turned down to show snowy white sheets, fluffy big pillows.

A folded man's T-shirt lay on the bed. Not new, but clean. She walked to the bed on unsteady legs. Her face felt liquid.

Blubbering, just because someone had done her the courtesy of making up a bed for her, and found something clean for her to put on.

She put on the shirt. It smelled like a laundry detergent that her mother had used. Tears streamed down her face.

A knock sounded on the door. That was the final blow. A polite knock, that taken-for-granted human courtesy she'd completely missed ever since they had abducted her. After months of having the door fly open, and rough hands seize her to drag her out into blinding light, to blows, pain, humiliation, insults. Restraints. The sting of the needle. She tried to make some coherent sound come out of her throat.

The knock sounded again. *Tap-tap-tap.*

"Come in," she forced out.

Miles poked in his head. "Are you—oh, God. I'll come back later."

"No!" she blurted out, and had to cover her mouth with both hands again, to keep more words from flying out. "Don't go," she added, from behind the tightly pressed fingers. *Stop crying. Stop, stop, stop.*

He sidled in, staying close to the door. Poised for a quick escape. He held a plastic shopping bag in one hand, and a fragrant, steaming plate of food in the other. Her nose identified meat, vegetables, rice.

She wiped her face, gave him a shaky smile. "You made the bed?"

He looked wary. "Hope you don't mind that I came in while you were in the shower. I figured it was safe while the water was running. I would have beat hell out of here if I'd heard it switch off."

"But where's the chocolate for my pillow?"

He honored her lame attempt at a joke with a sexy flash of white teeth. Her heart bumped in her chest. "Next time," he said. "I'm a little short on housekeeping supplies today. Sorry."

"Thanks for the shirt, too," she offered.

"You can thank Connor for that. He keeps a change of clothes stowed in his vehicle. Always prepared. Those Mc-Cloud dudes."

Miles had showered, too. His hair was combed straight back off his square forehead. So handsome. He smelled like the same shampoo she had used. He wore a clean shirt. Flannel, gray and blue plaid. Half buttoned, untucked. A wedge of his amazing chest showing.

"You cleaned up," she said, inanely. Conscious of how bare she was beneath the oversized shirt. Like she'd always been in that filmy white dress she wore in her fantasy trips to the Citadel.

"Yeah." His Adam's apple bobbed. "We were both filthy."

"Yes," she agreed.

It felt like they were conducting a conversation on another level, and these words were a thin front for the real conversation.

"I came upstairs to bring you these." He held up a plastic shopping bag and the plate of food. "Aaro picked up some stuff for you. And they cooked some food downstairs. I figured I should bring you up a plate. Unless you'd rather go down and eat with the rest of us."

The last thing she could face was the idea of a table full of guys watching her eat. But having her meal brought up to her made her feel like a cowering invalid. She played for time by checking out the shopping bag, which was full of clothing. Three shoeboxes, too.

"Aaro had to guess on the sizes, so he got three," he said.

To her starving artist mentality, that seemed like reckless extravagance. "Thanks," she said. "I'll pay for them as soon as I—"

"Don't worry about it, for God's sake. Oh, yeah, and Aaro picked up a burner phone for you. I went ahead and charged it up. Programmed all our numbers into it. Not that you need mine."

She stared at the little red and black telephone as if she'd never seen one before. She couldn't even imagine what she might use it for, right now, but what a sweet thought. They were treating her like a real human being. With normal needs and impulses.

What an amazing, mind-boggling concept. It moved her.

"So, you want to eat up here?" Miles prompted. "Or downstairs?"

She pressed her hand to her mouth to quell the trembling. "I don't think I can face dinner downstairs yet."

"Okay, then, I'll just leave you this plate, then—"

"No," she blurted.

A quick, questioning frown twitched his brows down. "No what?"

"Don't go," she said, baldly.

His mouth settled into a tight, cautious line. She felt that tingling awareness. Pressure, slowly building. "Lara?" he said softly. "What?"

"I just need . . ." The words trailed off. So stupid, so inadequate. Thick and heavy. Clumsy as big rocks in her mouth. She couldn't express how badly she needed to know if he felt it, too.

"I dreamed about you," she announced, her voice husky. "When I was in that place. I dreamed about you for months."

He cleared his throat. "Me, too."

"Were they, um . . . the same dreams?" she asked.

His big shoulders lifted. "I guess we'd have to compare them, point for point."

She took a deep breath. "Do you have any interest in doing that?"

When she finally dared to look up, there was a red stain across his cheekbones. "I'd be embarrassed," he said, huskily. "I thought I was alone, in the privacy of my own head. Who the fuck knew."

Relief flooded through her. So she wasn't alone in this aspect of the weirdness. "So it wasn't just me. When we . . . you know."

He shook his head slowly. "Nope."

She could finally breathe again. "Okay. So. If a tree falls in your head, and someone is there to hear it, does it make a sound?"

His brows drew together. "Don't get mysterious on me, Lara."

"I'm not," she said. "Just answer the question. Was it real?"

He pondered that for a moment. "Yes. It was pretty damn real for me."

"Okay. Good. Me, too." She was so relieved, she teetered on the edge of tears again. "Hold me, then."

Suddenly he was there, steadying her. "Lie down," he

scolded. "Calm down, for God's sake." He nudged her until she lay on the bed, shoving the comforter down.

"Would you lie down with me?" She couldn't believe this was her. Begging. Shameless.

He froze in place, and swallowed several times. "My pants are filthy. I'd mess up the sheets."

"So take them off," she said, rashly.

The flush burned into his cheeks deepened. "I don't think that's a good idea."

"I think it's a great idea," she said. "And so did you, all those nights, when I came to you. You didn't seem to mind."

His face tightened. "Not fair. I didn't know it wasn't a dream."

"I wasn't complaining," she whispered. "Not in the least."

His breath was coming harder, rasping in his chest. His erection was quite notably back. She noticed it. He noticed her noticing it.

He gestured at his crotch. "Yeah. This is exactly why it's not such a good idea. I don't trust my self-control right now, for a whole bunch of complicated reasons that don't have anything to do with you, so don't take it personally—"

"If you don't want me, just say so," she said. "Don't come up with a bunch of lame excuses."

"That's not it!" he said, savagely. "My dick's been hard since the moment I saw you. I've been rock-hard for you ever since you sneaked into my head. Don't manipulate me. You're gorgeous, and you know it."

It was sweet of him to say so, considering her bedraggled state, but she let it pass. "And? This is a problem exactly why?"

"I just pulled you out of a dungeon! You're bruised, hungry, exhausted. You don't need me on top of you, hammering away at you with my combat hard-on! No matter what crazy erotic scenarios we dreamed up together. I will not do that to you. It's not right!"

The thought of wrapping herself around that gorgeous

creature and his combat hard-on made her body hum. "Let me decide what I can handle," she said. "I'm not as fragile as I look."

"You're in no condition to decide. It would be taking advantage of you, and I won't . . . oh, sweet holy Jesus, Lara. Not fucking fair."

She yanked the shirt off over her head, and tossed it to the floor. She shook her damp, cool mane of hair back over her shoulders. "I don't know what's fair," she said. "I don't care. I just want what I want."

His eyes were hot as he stared at her naked body, but still he stubbornly shook his head. "I might hurt you," he said, hoarsely. "You've been hurt enough."

"You never hurt me in our dreams."

"That's because they were just dreams," he said, with unexpected savagery. "Don't expect reality to be like your dreams. You'll be in for a real let-down!"

"I don't think so." Her gaze slid slowly down over his body. She grabbed his hand, tugged it until he stumbled closer to the bed, and then laid her hand gently on the bulge of his crotch. "Is this for me?"

He flinched away, but she held him fast. "Huh?"

"This." She squeezed him, making him gasp. "Is it for me? Or is it just a non-specific hormonal glitch? Just a random mistake of nature?"

He pulled in a rasping breath. "For you," he said. "Just you."

She'd always had an uncanny ear for lies, even before she'd been flooded with a psi-enhancing drug. He was utterly sincere. Thank God.

"If it's mine, give it to me," she said. "I've been close to dead for months. Buried in the dark. Please, Miles. Make me feel alive again."

13

Miles hissed an obscenity between his teeth. He must look like an eggplant, his face was so hot. Squeezed between her emotionally manipulative come-on and his own dick-throbbing lust.

The part of him that knew right from wrong, and actually gave a shit about right and wrong, was getting ever smaller and farther away. *Weee*, it was action figure-sized now, with a whining little mosquito voice that had no authority, nattering preachy self-important shit about timing, responsibility. And essential, basic practical stuff. Like latex.

"I don't have any condoms," he blurted.

She just stared at him, blinking. Like she'd forgotten such an issue even existed. Who could blame her, what she'd been through.

"I came to bust you out of jail, Lara," he said. "Not to get laid."

"Oh. Well. I, um . . . I don't have any diseases, if that's what you're wondering. I haven't had a boyfriend in a while, so I—"

"That's not the issue." He had to struggle not to stare at her naked body. "Neither do I. They tested me up the wazoo when I was in the hospital a few months ago. I'm clean. That's not the point."

She shrugged her hair forward, as if afflicted by a spasm of shyness. "I wouldn't get pregnant."

"How do you figure? Been keeping your calender up to date in your prison? You're totally on top of it?" He was almost yelling, which was stupid and wrong, but she was the one herding him toward a cliff.

She shook her head. "My cycle stopped months ago."

He cut off the rant he'd been winding up to, mouth open, and tried in vain to process that. "Come again?"

"You have to eat a certain amount of food to make that happen," she said. "And the stress, the drugs, the dark, whatever it was, it pretty much killed my appetite. So, ah, I'm not fertile right now."

"They starved you?" His voice was getting louder. He was whipping himself into a frenzy.

"Not exactly," she said, gently. "There was food. But it sucked. And I was tense, and miserable. So not much of it would go in."

Miles clapped his hands over his ears. "Jesus, Lara. This is messing with my head."

"Forget about your head." She snagged the waistband of his jeans with her forefinger, dragging him in a drunken stumble, right up next to the bed. "I'm not asking you to use your head."

Her scent intensified into a humid cloud. He wanted to wallow in it. The shampoo, which would have made him nauseous only half a day ago, mixed with the scent of her skin, her hair, transforming into something intoxicating, verdant, full of hot yearning. He dragged in greedy lungfuls of it. Dick throbbing with each thud of his heart.

He didn't even remember reaching out, before he was touching her. First her face, as she tilted it back with the abandon of a kitten being petted. His fingers slid into that thick fall of damp, silken hair. She shivered as he lifted it, stroking pale, soft skin, the fine muscles over her ribs, the curve of her spine. Delicate, feminine. Fragile.

Fragile. She was fragile, damn it, and he was big and thick and helpless, jacked up with raw animal hunger. He'd fuck it up, be clumsy with her, and she'd regret it. And he'd have to throw himself under a bus out of sheer embarrassment.

He pulled his hands away, but she snagged them, pulled them toward her and placed them on her breasts.

He shook, but his hands went on without him, already exploring, stroking, cupping, hefting the velvet soft weight of her tits, the pert, puckered dark nipples. Tickling his palms, filling his hands.

Her head dropped back, eyes closed. He was so lost in the perfect sensation of her tits, he didn't even register the tugging on the buttons of his jeans until they were sliding down his hips.

His cock sprang free. *Thwang*, in her face.

She stared at it, and then reached out with a soft sigh, gripping and petting him with her soft hands. A sound came out of him like air wheezing from a pricked balloon. "Lara."

He was embarrassed by his cock, which was engorged and beet red. Blatantly willing and ready to serve, belying his protests. Locked into full-out battering ram mode. "You, ah, don't have to deal with that."

"Mmm." She gripped him, stroking. "You're beautiful. And so big. Like the dreams. I thought it was just my extravagant imagination."

"I told you this was a bad idea," he said, his voice strangled.

"Shhh." She leaned forward, as if she were about to kiss his cock.

His muscles tightened in protest, and he grabbed her, held her still. Not that the idea didn't make him practically explode, but, Jesus, not tonight. "No," he said.

She covered his hands, stroking them. "Don't you like it?"

"Fuck, yes, but not now. It's not the right vibe. I have to treat you like blown glass."

"I'm not fragile!"

"I don't care," he said. "It's that way, or we stop."

Her radiant smile dazzled him, until what he had said sank in. What a chump he was. Committing himself like that. So snookered.

He breathed down his jagged nerves, stroking her arms, and a multitude of bruises came into focus. He bent to take a closer look. She shivered, her body going rigid.

"Those are finger marks," he said.

"I got jerked around a lot," she said. "They'll fade soon."

His jeans were snarled around his knees, so he kicked them off, and knelt on the bed. Held up her arm, cataloging every bruise.

He started kissing the ones at her wrist. She let out a jerky sigh as he lifted it higher, pressing his lips against every mark he found.

He was not going to give in to the urgency. He was taking it easy, slow. Steely self-control. Padlocks and chains.

He kept the kisses gentle, dragging, dreamy. The more bruises he kissed, the more he found. This was going to take a while, which was fine. He didn't have the least concern about his dick going south. In fact, it might not soften again in this lifetime. Certainly not while her skin was pressed against his lips. The glow of contact made his whole body thrum, like a pulsing drumbeat.

Lara was shivering violently, and he'd only made it up to her elbow. He raised his head. "You cold?"

She shook her head. "No. What are you doing to me?"

"My job," he said, bending to the task again.

She laughed, but he stopped short when he got a look at the underside of her breast. Bruises, from clawing fingers. Her ribs were shadowed with blue, green, splotches of yellow. New bruises on top of old ones, on top of still older ones. "Jesus, Lara," he whispered.

"It's okay," she assured him. "I'm not feeling it. Your kisses are magic. I am feeling no pain. Really."

God, how he wished they were magic. He bent down and went at them with the same total, single-minded concentration he would employ if kisses really did have healing power. Caressing her with hands and mouth, no pressure, just petting and tonguing every inch of her.

He rolled her onto the side, to get a good look at the—oh, Christ. Her back, too, her flanks, her ass, her thighs. Everywhere.

He straightened up, found her eyes squeezed shut. Her face was wet with tears. "I should stop," he told her. "Now's not the time."

She yanked him down, fiercely. "Wrong," she said.

He held himself carefully off her body, afraid of crushing her, and blurted out the burning question that there was just no delicate way to ask. "Were you sexually abused in there?"

She shook her head, to his immense relief. "No. That was just Anabel, being a hag. She was the worst of them. She got angry when I hid from her. Behind your shield. In the Citadel."

He let out a startled laugh. "That was what you called it?"

"Why? Does it sound strange to you?"

He propped himself on his elbow, settling his hand into the curve of her waist. "Citadel sounds so massive and important. A fortress on a mountaintop. My shield's just, you know. Encryption. To protect data."

"It *was* massive and important," she insisted. "It protected me."

"I'm glad it was good for something." He bent to kiss her breast again. Lara curled up around his body, clutching his head. Her fingers wound into his hair, trapping him. He could cheerfully nuzzle those rose-petal-soft, perfect tits for the rest of time, rubbing those tight, puckered nipples against his cheek, his lips. Swirling his tongue around them, a hot, liquid, suckling pull, feeling her arch against him, trembling, like she was trying to give him more of herself, tightening, like she was going to . . . oh, *God* . . .

Like light, blazing out of her chest, blinding him, blessing him.

Her orgasm was long and drawn out. Her body shuddered and hitched. He held her as tightly as he dared, amazed and humbled.

"Wow," he whispered. "I never made a girl come just from playing with her tits, I mean. Except, um . . ."

"In our dreams?" She laughed. "Yeah, I remember that one. We're still in the same dream. Let's just keep dreaming."

"Sounds good," he said, fervently.

The rays of afternoon light had gotten longer and yellower, slanting in the side blinds. They painted her pale body with stripes that accentuated every graceful dip and curve. His chest clutched with nervous excitement as he let his hand stroke over her belly, and drift lower. Tangling in the dark, silky puff of her pubes.

She dragged in a hitching gasp of air, and opened her legs for him, inviting him to get on with it, but he had no intention of rushing. He just petted with his fingertips. She hid her hot face against his shoulder, moving her hips against his hand.

When it felt right, he teased his finger inside, found her slick seam. The scent of her made him crazy, but he reined it in. Time enough later to mount up and ride off into the sunset.

His world narrowed down to that intimate contact, that tender slit, the tightly furled folds inside. His mind was clean of everything but the secret details of her body. He memorized her, marveling at her perfection. Poetry made flesh. Shades of pink shading into crimson, a glowing, shining contrast with dark hair, pale thighs.

He had so many shifting memories of touching her, tasting her, fucking her, in their shared dreams. Hard and juicy and unchecked. Front, back, sideways, all ways, there had been no limits in their erotic dream world, but somehow, this careful, anxious petting was more raw and momentous than all those scorching episodes combined.

She grabbed his shoulders and tried to tug him down on top of her. "You've teased me enough," she said. "I'm out of my mind."

He held his weight off. He outweighed her two to one or more, right now, although he fully intended to improve that ratio, soon. But he poised himself so that he didn't pin her down, and reached down again, to heaven's gate, teasing his fingertip inside . . .

She heaved, pressed herself up against him with a moan.

Hot, wet, slick. Plush and tight. Incredibly tight. He had to force it deeper. Just his finger. Oh, man. This was not like the dreams at all. In those, they'd been perfectly matched, like a key to a lock.

"Lara," he said gently. "You're so small. Are you a virgin?"

"No," she said, breathlessly. "Don't stop. Please."

"But it'll hurt you." He kept his voice gentle, though it came out through clenched teeth.

"No! Seriously? What would hurt me would be you chickening out on me, leaving me high and dry! Don't do that. Don't you dare!"

"Calm down," he soothed. "The madder you get, the more you clench around my finger. Your muscles are really contracted. Relax."

Her bark of laughter sounded bitter. "Oh, wow." Her voice shook. "That's a wee bit of a tall order for me right now."

"Get inside," he said, on impulse.

She looked dubious. "Huh?"

"You know. Inside the Citadel. Like you did in the woods."

Her eyelids fluttered. "I . . . I don't know if I . . . that was a life or death kind of thing." She wiggled, clutching her pussy muscles deliciously tight around his finger. "I'm, ah, distracted. You know?"

"I know," he rasped, and caressed her breast with his mouth again, sucking as he thrust his finger deeper inside. Twisting, thrusting, slick and slow. "Try," he urged.

It took a while, but he put every second to good use. The stripes of light that had painted their bodies slid on up the wall as he petted, nuzzling, caressing her slick opening. She clutched him, her thighs clamped around his hand, shaking with strain. Her fingernails dug into his shoulder. He waited, listening in the silence . . .

And there she was. A light, blazing on inside him. Her radiant presence. He didn't see the images, because his eyes were too busy with the visual stimuli coming from her physical body, and he couldn't be bothered to look inside at a waking dream. But the inner contact felt as great as it always did. That glow. So close. So intimate.

The words scrolled, on the screen in his head. happy now?

getting there, he replied. i go 4 this. u inside. makes me hot.

She vibrated with laughter. ur hot already. like a kiln.

He wound his hand full of her hair, and forced her to lift her face away from his chest.

She was smiling, eyes lit up. Crazy beautiful.

He kissed her. Ravenously, like it was life or death, and that inner place where they were linked went off like fireworks blasting. Color, heat, noise, and movement, like a dancing, singing flash mob. She made a shocked sound and kissed him back. Opening to him.

She tasted so good. His tongue in her mouth, hers in his, dancing, melding. She squirmed against his hand, which was slippery with lube, softening against the onslaught of that devouring kiss.

They came up gasping for air a time or two, but dove back into the kiss as soon as they replenished their oxygen stores. After a few breathless, desperate minutes of that, he was seriously in danger of losing control and coming all over her. She worked herself against his hand, desperate jerking thrusts. His hand shone, wet and hot. He thrust two fingers in, following the trembling, the gasps, the heat. Urgency built in both of them. He drove her like he was driving for his own release.

And off they went, straight into it. Oh, *fuck*, yeah.

Her pleasure throbbed through his mind and body, echoing. Lighting up his head, his chest, his cock.

He lifted his head, at great length. Rolling her up on top of him, so that she was sprawled over his body.

"That's more like it," he said. Trying not to feel smug.

She was glowing pink, dewy with sweat. Eyes dazzled and dilated. "I never knew it could feel like that. Not even from the dreams."

"We've barely even started," he said.

They gazed at each other, for seconds that ticked slowly into minutes, but time ran differently now, and the silences were not empty. They were eloquent, charged with poignant meaning.

She shifted, so she could stroke his stiff, longsuffering cockhead which had been trapped between them. Beet purple, shiny with precome that had left a gleaming slick on her pale skin.

He helped her position herself, because she seemed awkward and unsure of herself. He draped her legs where they needed to be, adjusted her knees. Lifted her up to the perfect angle, so he could slide his cockhead tenderly against those slippery folds.

No hurry, he told himself, grimly. No fucking hurry in the world. With lots of wiggling and squirming, he wedged himself a little deeper. So hot and slick. She sank down, and he slid slowly, inexorably inside her . . . into total fucking heaven on earth.

Now it was a brand new challenge. It had been hard enough not to come when it was just his finger in that tight clutching hole, but now, oh God, it felt like his entire self being bathed in scalding perfection.

She arched, forcing him deeper. Hugging and squeezing his whole length. A little deeper, another shove and sigh and delicious squirm, and he was all inside.

He held his breath, shaking on the edge. So good.

The deed was done, right or wrong, and he was not sorry. He felt defiant. After all she'd been through, she actually trusted him with her body. It was a fucking miracle, and he was not, by God, going to fumble it by coming too soon. No, and no, and *no*.

Her hair had almost dried. Undulating dark locks draped over both of them, a ticklish, caressing cloud. She gazed down, with that soft, dazzled look that made his chest ache and his throat twist and his eyes sting, but now was no time to get weepy, for fuck's sake.

He had to make damn sure she did not regret this.

The world flipped. He'd rolled her over onto her back, was pushing her down into the mattress. "Is this OK? Am I squishing you?" he demanded. "Scaring you?"

She slid her hands up and around, to clutch at the thick muscles bunched in his back. "I love it," she said, slowly and clearly.

They stared into each other's eyes as he established the rhythm. Their bodies were so attuned, every movement was a caressing call and response, each slow, rhythmic plunge and slide. Each individual stroke felt so achingly perfect, she couldn't imagine anything sweeter, until the next one, and the next.

She abandoned herself to the sway, the surge, the rocking blissful perfection. After some time, the pace quickened, but she could not tell who was driving it, whether it was her urgency or his that swept them helplessly along.

He made a rough sound, and pressed his face against her shoulder. "Shit," he ground out. "I'm sorry."

"For what?" She nuzzled his hair, inhaling his scent hungrily.

"For this." He drove inside her, deep and hard, jarring against her hips. "I'm sorry. I'm not going to be able to control . . . oh, *fuck* . . ."

His voice broke, gave way to pants. Her own gasps were a rhythmic counterpoint. The pace grew frenzied, his strokes deeper. Such sweet relief, to have her mind razed clear, steamrolled by giddy excitement, mounting tension, by each hot lick of pleasure, by each heavy jolt of his body against hers.

She was opening, like a flower. Amazed that there was so much still inside. It had been locked down, hidden away, but now it was sprawling open, air and light flooding in. She lifted herself to meet every stroke, clawing to get closer. Pleasure swelled, crested . . . tipping her over and into the deep, throbbing darkness.

She floated back to consciousness, pinned beneath him. His chest still heaved. He'd hidden his face against the pillow. His damp shoulders shook. She hugged him. Tears leaked out of her eyes. Feeling all of it, so keenly. The helplessness, the hugeness.

He lifted himself out and off her body, and spun around to sit on the edge of the bed. Facing away from her.

"Miles?" she whispered, sitting up.

His hand jerked up, an imperative gesture that choked off the question she'd been trying to frame.

She touched his shoulder. He flinched. "Don't."

She curled in on herself, startled. "Sorry," she whispered.

"No," he said. "I'm the one who's sorry."

"Are you okay?"

"No." He got up, strode over to the dresser, displaying the amazing muscles of his back, ass, hips. He grabbed the knife and fork, and attacked the steak, carving it into chunks. "I can't believe myself. I pull you out of a stinking hole where they've been starving you to death, and end up fucking you before I even feed you. What a prince."

That made her smile. "It's not your fault."

"The hell it isn't." His eyes snagged on her naked body, and his penis swelled. He gestured at it, bobbing before him. "See? My priorities are perfectly straight, even now." He walked over to the bed, brandishing the plate and fork. "Eat, Lara."

She held up her hand. "I'm not sure how much I can—"

"Eat." The bed rocked and swayed as he knelt.

She stared into his narrowed eyes, and sighed. He'd throw a fit if she defied him. She took the fork, which held an overlarge chunk of steak, nibbled off a bit. The grilled meat was delicious, but too rich to endure. "I'm only going to be able to eat a few bites," she warned him. "I'm not doing this to bug you, I promise. I've just got to take it slow."

"Two more," he said, his voice steely.

She accepted another bite. Managed a third, a small one. He scooped up some rice. "Carbs." His tone dared her to argue with him.

A few bites of rice, a few rounds of sautéed zuccini, and she was done. He slapped the nearly untouched plate down onto the bedside table, disgusted. "Jesus, Lara. You hardly touched it. You need food."

"Leave it. I'll try again later, I promise," she assured him. "Have you eaten anything yourself?"

He looked shocked at the idea. "Fuck, no! I brought the first steak Davy cooked up here to you." He frowned at the plate. "And then forgot all about it while nailing you to the bed."

"Stop scolding yourself," she told him. "You must be ravenous. Go downstairs, for God's sake. Get something to eat!"

"Need a shower," he muttered, and stalked into the bathroom.

Lara pressed her hand against the inert lump of food that sat there in her bewildered stomach as the shower began to hiss.

She'd messed it up. Come on too strong. She was going to freak him out. Scare him off. He was so tense and twitchy. Too bad he hadn't invited her into the shower, but enough, already. She'd been more forward with him than she'd ever been in her life. Granted, they had their red hot dream history, but dreams were not something one could build expectations upon. She had to give him space.

Hard to do, when she wanted to cling to him like a kudzu vine.

He came out a minute later in a cloud of steam, and jerked on his jeans without looking at her. He found his shirt hidden beneath a fold of the comforter. He shrugged it on, buttoned it.

"You're angry?" she asked.

"At myself, not you. Get some rest." The door swung shut behind him with a decisive click.

She tried, she really did, but the meltdown happened anyway. At least she was alone with it this time, under the covers. Hidden.

Seducing him had seemed like such a good idea. So perfect, to latch onto something exciting and beautiful. Something to cling to while the rest of the world went to shit.

But she was laying too much on him. He'd given her protection with his mind. He'd risked his life to save her miserable ass. Now she expected him to lift the darkness in her soul, too? Already? With sex?

Good luck with that, airhead. Sex happened, and maybe it was good, or great, even transcendent, but afterward, there you were, in the bathroom, cleaning up the mess. Still alone, and staring into the mirror at the same screwed-up, ambivalent person you'd been before.

Pain cramped her inside. She missed their magic connection, craved it like a crack addict, but she would not give in to the temptation to crawl back inside that guy's mind just because she could.

Just because it felt so damned good in there.

That wasn't a good enough reason. She lectured herself in the harshest possible terms. It would be childish, rude. Creepy, even.

It was time to grow the fuck up, and leave his mind *alone*.

14

The low murmur in the kitchen subsided into ominous silence when Miles walked into the room. Their ranks had grown while he'd been closeted upstairs with Lara. Kev McCloud had arrived, and Val with him, Tam's super-spy lover, and the father of her baby.

They all watched as Miles grabbed himself a plate from the stack on the counter and pulled the heels of the loaf of Italian bread out of the paper bag, heels being all that were left. He scraped the dregs out of the rice pot. Snagged the last smallish steak, its juices congealed on the bloody serving plate. He tossed the final shreds of vegetables that clung to the sides of the skillet over the meager heap of rice, surprised at how hungry he was. He'd gotten out of the habit of food.

He sat down at a stool at the kitchen bar, since all the places at the kitchen table were taken, and attacked the small plateful of food.

Everyone was staring. He ignored them, concentrating on getting fuel into himself. He had an uneasy sensation that he was in for an ass-kicking. He was bracing for it. Fueling for it.

To their credit, they waited until he mopped up the last

bits of steak and grains of rice with the last lonely chunk of bread. Trying not to look around pathetically for more.

Sean made the opening gambit. "So. How was it?"

Miles counted slowly down from ten before daring to raise his eyes from the plate. "What the fuck is that supposed to mean?"

"It means, don't insult our intelligence," Connor said.

"I don't know what you—"

"Oh, shut up." Sean's voice was thick with disgust. "You come down to eat an hour and a half after we cook dinner. That's your second shower, less than two hours after the first, you dirty, dirty boy. And when you put on Connor's shirt before you went upstairs, it wasn't off by two button-holes, dick-for-brains. Wake up, already. Can't you at least try to cover your own ass? You're embarrassing me."

Miles looked down at the shirt, appalled. "Aw, fuck."

"But the biggest clue is that guilty, dog-on-the-furniture look in your eyes," Connor said. "If we took you outside and all took turns kicking the shit out of you, would it make you feel better?"

Miles considered his various responses in the split second that followed, among which was killing every guy in the room. A tall order, considering who they were. It would be quicker and more streamlined to just kill himself. Throw himself into the chasm that should be opening up in front of his feet right . . . about . . . *now*. Please, God.

But the chasm didn't materialize, so he muscled himself past it.

"Fuck off, all of you," he muttered.

"I can't believe this," Aaro said. "You extracted her from that fucking snake-pit, and for what? To be your bed toy?"

"No! I do not have to justify myself to any of you!"

"No, you do not seem to feel that need anymore," Sean said.

"I know it's been hard on all of you, lately, not having

your errand boy at the ready to jump and fetch and carry," Miles said.

The silence that followed was flat and cold.

"Nobody expects anything from you anymore," Davy announced. "At this point, we know better."

"Cut out the guilt trip," Miles said. "I'm doing the best I can."

"Oh, I just bet you did, loverboy," Aaro said, his voice taunting. "I bet you gave her your all. What, was the dungeon thing a turn-on?"

He didn't even remember moving. Just landing with a crash, sprawled on the detritus of plates, food, silverware, paper goods. Pinned flat to the table by four very big guys.

He'd lunged across the table for Aaro's throat. Without thought or hesitation, or even the faintest, most remote hint of ingrained socialization making a play to stop him. Like, what the *fuck?*

So much for his unshakable calm, his emotional distance. It had gotten all burned up in the past hour, writhing in bed with Lara Kirk.

Aaro sat just out of reach, eyeing Miles over the rim of his coffee cup. He grabbed a paper plate, cut a big, gooey slice of German chocolate cake from a white bakery box and stuck a plastic fork into it. "Bring the chick some dessert. She needs the calories, now that servicing you sexually has just become part of her job description."

Miles convulsed against the eight ruthless hands that shoved him down against the table again. "You're a fine one to talk," he retorted. "I don't remember you holding back with Nina."

"I hadn't just rescued Nina from months of incarceration in a fucking black pit of hell," Aaro shot back.

"Calm down, both of you." It was Kev.

Something about Kev's voice always mellowed everybody down a notch. Some magic glitch of his personality.

Miles had always envied the guy that trick. It would come in handy, with all the hotheads in his life.

"You did good, today," Kev went on. "Nobody's questioning that—"

"I just did," Aaro snarled.

"Shut up," Kev said calmly. "I'm talking about the extraction. You improvised the whole damn thing, on the fly. Blew everybody's minds. That was good work."

"You don't need to stroke my ego," he muttered. "I'm not an idiot."

"Could have fooled us," Connor muttered, but he and the other guys cautiously loosened their grip on him and allowed him to stand. He brushed splotches of food from his shirt.

"Totally aside from the opinions flying around about how you spent the last two hours, we need more info to proceed," Kev went on. "Because, despite what you seem to think, we do actually give a shit about you. And we still want to help. So what's your plan?"

Miles stared at the mess he'd made on the table, abashed at Kev's words. "I don't have a plan," he admitted. "I pulled her out, but she's not safe. There's nowhere on earth she could be safe from that guy. You saw what he can do. I have no idea what to do with her."

Davy's voice was quiet but clear in the silence that followed.

"Keep her," he said.

Miles stared at him. Davy took a pull on his beer and stared back, straight on and unapologetic. "You know you want to," he said.

Miles opened his mouth, and closed it before something stupid and inane could fall out. His brain was wiped clean.

Seconds passed. Sean started to nod, enthusiastically. "Yeah, that works. That girl is not the fuck buddy type, my friend. That's the only way to make it right. Otherwise, you're just an opportunistic dickhead."

"Shut up, Sean," Davy said. "You'll scare him."

Miles just stood there, like an idiot, a buzz running through his body. A subtle electrical current, tingling. Like fear, but brighter.

"That's Neanderthal, Davy," he said.

Davy grunted, untroubled by that assessment.

"She's a grown woman," Miles said. "She might have plans. She might not want to be kept."

"Who asked her?" Davy said.

Miles blinked. Whoa. That was a level of self-confidence to which he could scarcely dream to aspire. "It's not as easy as that."

"I never meant to imply that it's easy," Davy replied. "It's not easy at all. It's a total mind-twisting clusterfuck, trying to figure a woman out. But what the fuck else do you have to do with your life? You've got all those brains coming out of your ears. Use them for something useful. Blow her mind. Be irresistible. So it's hard. Big fucking deal."

"Do the hard thing?" Miles said.

A smile flashed over all the McCloud brothers' faces, to hear their crazy father's classic maxim coming out of Miles' mouth.

"She's not stupid," Con said. "And she does need you."

"True," Val chimed in, in his mellifluous, accented voice. "This can be helpful. And a woman's mind can be changed, even if it is made up against you. It has been done. I am proof. I still live."

True enough, considering that the guy was brave enough to get cozy with Tam. That took serious gonads, in Miles' book.

"Yeah, dude. Use your assets." Sean was picking up steam, eyes aglow. "You made one hell of a first impression. The rescue from the black pit, ka-pow! Giving her your shirt, ah. The bare-chest gambit. Packing gallantry, self-sacrifice, six-pack abs, and sexual magnetism all into the same hot package." He paused, delicately. "All depends, however, upon how things went in the past two hours up in the master bedroom. Which brings me back to my original question. How was it?"

Miles stared at the guy, from under lowered brows. "Ask that question again, and I will break all the bones in your face."

Sean lifted his beer bottle with a snort of delighted laughter. "Yes," he crowed. "Just the answer I was fishing for."

"Slow down. I just met her four hours ago," Miles reminded them.

Davy's eyebrow quirked. "She won't forget those hours soon."

Damned if that wasn't the God's own truth.

"So she's nervous," Connor said. "So she has doubts. Put them to rest. After years of Cindy purgatory, you can finally put all that turbocharged mojo in the service of something worthwhile. Halleluia."

Miles looked around at the shuttered faces of the men in the kitchen. "Who's on guard duty? I'll take a turn."

"We're covered," Davy said. "Go back upstairs."

He looked around. "You're all tired, too. I can—"

"It's going to take a hell of a lot to make up for what happened to that girl," Davy cut in.

Miles didn't really want to know where Davy was going with it, but the guy was waiting. "Meaning?" he prompted.

"So stop fucking around and get to it." Davy's voice cracked like a whip.

Miles got moving, but stopped at the foot of the stairs and turned back to scoop up the slice of cake Aaro had cut, ignoring the muffled cracks of laughter and muttering. He ran up those stairs like he had jet-propelled shoes. Davy's directive had torn the door in his head wide open, to consciously think and feel what had been simmering underground, hidden and smothered.

Keep her. You know you want to.

The words rang in his head, like a gong.

It was true, of course. It wouldn't have moved him like

that if it hadn't been. He wanted her. But no one knew better than he how hard it was to keep a woman. How mysterious the whole process was. How insanely hard it was to make it stick. Women slipped through his fingers, despite his good intentions, his best efforts. Who knew why?

But this was a new game, new rules, new stakes.

He opened the door without knocking.

Lara jerked up onto her elbows, heart pounding, when the door opened. Miles walked in, holding a plate with a big piece of cake.

"Oh," she said, weakly. "You."

"Yeah." He turned, and flicked the lever on the knob lock.

She sat up as he walked toward her, glad she'd put the shirt back on. She felt emotionally raw, and terribly shy. Her unaccustomed boldness was all gone, as if it had never been, and she missed it.

The light had shifted, a lot less of it came through the blinds, but there was plenty to examine him by. The look on his face was different.

Harder. Calmer. But it made her feel cautious, flustered.

His eyes just rested on her, like he could just stay there, looking, for hours, and not twitch or blink.

"You're, um, still upset?" she asked, cautiously.

He shook his head. "I brought you some cake."

"Thank you," she whispered.

He set it on the bedside table, finding room beside the remains of her meal, then matter-of-factly unbuttoned his shirt, his jeans. He tossed his clothes away. Erect, but he didn't seem the least bit embarrassed about it this time. He lifted the comforter, jerked his chin for her to scoot over and make room for him.

She did so, bemused. This was certainly a different vibe. Not that she minded. On the contrary, her heart rate spiked.

He reached for her. She almost cried out, it felt so wonderful, to be held against that hard, scorching hot, solid body. His erection pressed her leg. His arms slid under the shirt. Stroking her butt, pressing the small of her back so her whole length was plastered to his.

A blush of oh-my-God-he's-actually-touching-me thrills overwhelmed her, a shivery ripple over her astonished skin, like a whole body orgasm all by itself. If she pressed her thighs together, she'd come.

So don't. Just breathe. Don't flip out. Don't be the needy, crazy, broken girl. Though, after her time in the rat hole, she'd forgotten what normal felt like. If she ever had a clue.

She couldn't pretend to be normal, so she wouldn't bother to try. She'd just cling to him, shivering, and ride those waves of emotion. Just keep existing, and feeling it. Second by second.

They lay facing each other, eyes inches apart. He pried her hand off the thick muscles of his bicep. He gazed at it a moment, then kissed her skinned knuckles.

The gesture unraveled her. She dissolved, hiding her wet face against his shoulder until she had the nerve to look him in the eye.

His face was thoughtful as he smoothed back the hair that was stuck to her wet cheek. "Get inside," he suggested.

She laughed. "Of your mind? Really? I thought you were tired of having me in there. 'Twiddling with your shit,' I think was how you put it. Wasn't that why you went to the trouble of rescuing me?"

"Nah," he said, frowning. "Not at all. God, did I say that?"

"Pretty much. On the computer, remember? We could probably find an archive with transcripts, the way your brain is organized."

He grunted. "What an asshole. Sorry. A lot of smart-ass bullshit comes out of my mouth. Terrible character trait. Pay no attention."

"Hah," she muttered. "Right."

"Truth is," he went on. "I didn't mind having you in there. Apart from the small matter of thinking that I was going crazy, it was kind of fun. And those sex dreams, man. They were excellent."

Her gaze fell, face heating. She stared at his collarbone, the hollow at the base of his throat. "They weren't dreams," she said.

"Right," he mumured. "Whatever you say. I loved that thing you wore. What was it, a white negligee?"

She choked on her laughter. "Um, no. It was more like a—"

A wedding dress. She bit the words off just in time.

He nudged her. "Like what?" he prompted.

"An old-fashioned ball gown," she hedged. "A vintage prom dress."

"Huh." He sounded dubious. "Whatever it was, it made me hot. Barefoot, hair hanging down. Mmm. I thought I'd created my own ultimate sexual fantasy, so I could just go for it, you know? Sorry about the cave man vibe. If I'd known I was interfacing with an actual person, I'd have been more . . . fuck, I don't know. Polite, maybe? Restrained."

She shook with silent laughter again. "I liked how you were."

That lazy grin transformed his lean face. "And then, you start typing messages to me," he whispered. "My head just about popped."

"Sorry I made you think you were crazy," she said.

He shrugged. "I was used to it by then. Talking to you was great. Kinky, but fun. I was lonely, too. The last few months have been a weird time for me."

"Tell me about it," she whispered.

The smile vanished. "Sorry. Didn't mean to—"

"Don't apologize," she said, swiftly. "I would still be in the rat hole if not for you. You can say anything you want to me. Don't guard your words. I can take anything you say. I won't break. Got it?"

"Okay, okay, calm down." He kissed her knuckles again, methodically pressing his caressing lips to each one.

"There's one thing I still don't get, though," she added.

He rolled his eyes. "Just one? You're doing better than me."

"Stop," she scolded. "I mean, the Citadel. How do I get into it when Greaves can't? It makes no sense. He's so strong. You felt him. And I'm just me. I'm not even a telepath."

Miles tugged the comforter up to cover her bare shoulders. "Nina had a theory about that."

"Nina who?" she asked.

"Nina Christie," he said. "Remember her?"

She shot bolt upright in the bed. "Nina Christie? You know Nina Christie? How do you know her? Oh, I love Nina!"

Miles rolled onto his back and folded his arms behind his head, displaying the muscles in his arms, shoulders, and chest to amazing advantage. "Of course I know Nina. She started this whole thing. When your mom got away from Rudd . . ." He paused, delicately. "You knew about her death in the fire being faked, right?"

She willed her jaw not to shake. "Yes. And dying anyway, a few months ago. Anabel and Hu told me. Greaves confirmed it. I was hoping it wasn't true." She tried not to hope he would tell her it wasn't true. She tried so hard, she didn't even dare to look at him.

He squeezed her hand. "I'm sorry," he said. "But it is true."

She nodded, exhaling slowly. So. Moving on. "And Nina?"

"Your mom had escaped. She'd been trying to blackmail Rudd. Rudd was one of Greaves' stooges. Your mom had created a new formula of psi-max. A binary dose. If you don't get the B, the A dose kills you after a few days. She hid the B dose, and tried to get Rudd to take the A, so she'd have leverage to make him let you go. But he didn't take it. They injected her instead, and she'd already sent the B dose away."

"I see," she said, although she didn't, not yet. "And Nina?"

"Your mom chased Nina down in New York," Miles went on. "By then she was dying. She only had hours left. She'd lost her English, from the brain damage. She injected one of the last A doses into Nina, and left a recording on Nina's phone, with instructions on where to find the B doses. Begging her to save you. She died that same day."

Lara drew her knees up to her chest, and hid her face against them. Miles sat up crosslegged beside her, stroking her back with long, soothing, gentle strokes. They did not speak for a long time.

"I missed her so much," she said, voice choked. "She was alive the whole time. And now she's not, again. It's like a cruel joke."

"She put everything into saving you," Miles said. "She loved you. It was all she cared about. Getting you out."

She lifted her face, wiping it defiantly. "Injecting Nina with a dangerous drug? That doesn't sound like the mother I remember."

Miles looked uncomfortable. "That move was iffy, but I'm not inclined to judge. She was desperate. She knew she was dying. She had to pass the torch, and Nina was her last hope."

Lara shook her head, trying to shake the image away from herself. "So did Nina get the B-dose in time?"

"She did. I was there. In Colorado, at this big fundraising bash held by Greaves. Lots of blood and drama. It was . . . well, special."

She smiled at him. "A talent for understatement is another of your defining character traits. You have to tell me the whole story some time. The story behind the laconic understatement, I mean."

He snorted. "This shit is so way out there, it desperately needs understatement or no one will believe it at all. But anyhow. We've been looking for you ever since. Me, Nina. And Aaro, Nina's fiancé."

She sniffed the tears back. "Well. You found me. Lucky you."

"Yeah, lucky me," he repeated softly. He stroked her cheek, the point of her jaw. His finger was rough and thickened, but his touch was so delicate, like being stroked by a feather. "Here you are. In flesh and blood. Amazing." His arms slid around her, tightening. Pulling her against his bare, hot chest. It felt so good.

"Thanks for looking for me," she said.

His body tensed. "Lara. Please. Stop thanking me."

"I thought there was no one left who cared about looking for me." She squirmed in his arms until she was facing him. "I thought I'd just die in there. I was hoping it wouldn't take too much longer."

"Matilda Bennet kept looking. She never gave up on you."

She was so pleased to hear the name, she didn't register his tone. "Oh, Matilda? She was so good to my father. I have to thank her for . . ."

Her voice trailed off, as the look on his face sank in. "Oh, shit. Oh, shit, no. Don't . . . don't."

"I'm sorry," he said quietly.

"They got her, too?"

"A few days ago. Home intruder, they say. Threw her down the stairs."

She squeezed her eyes shut and tried not to see it in her head, but she had a very powerfully developed capacity to visualize, and it did its thing without her permission or consent. Oh, God. Matilda.

"You should have left me in there," she said. "This is terrible. Everyone who tried to help me has died badly."

"Not me." He leaned his forehead against hers.

Her eyes opened, in spite of herself, and she stared into

his intense dark eyes. She cleared her throat. "It's just a matter of time."

"I'm hard to kill," he said.

The contact of his forehead against hers was as intimate as a kiss, but she didn't dare give into the sweetness of it, or she'd melt into a weepy puddle again. She leaned back, biting her shaking lip. "You said Nina had a theory," she said. "As to how I get through your wall."

"Yeah. Nina was the one who introduced me to the concept of mind shields, on that very special night at Spruce Ridge. Her shield's like a smoke and mirrors setup, and Aaro's is like a bank vault. She said, pick an analog that works for you. So, hopeless tech nerd that I am, I picked an encrypted, password-protected computer."

That was a lot to take in, so her mind latched onto the trivial bits first. "Nerd?" She looked him up and down, the deep, weathered tan, the battered hands, the sinewy, ripped muscles. "You?"

"Me," he said. "Total geekitude. To the core of my being."

"That is such bullshit." She put her hand on his chest, catching her breath at the solid heat, the throb of his heart. "Tech geeks don't tend to be heartthrob gorgeous."

His grin flashed. "Right. With this nose."

"Yes," she said, forcefully. "With that nose."

"Whatever. As I was saying, I picked a password. And I put your name in it."

She was startled and moved. "Me? You put me in your password? Why me?"

"You were on my mind," he said simply. "I used all the usual tricks, of mixing up numbers and symbols. But essentially, yeah. You."

"But . . . but how did you ever know about me at all?"

"Nina already knew you'd been abducted. Aaro contacted me to do some research about your mom. I found pictures of you at your father's house." He hesitated, and added gently, "I was the one who found him."

"Oh," she whispered.

"I'm so sorry," he said.

She shook her head, lifting her hands. Silently begging him to leave it alone. Which he was smart and sensitive enough to do.

He waited a few minutes, and went on. "Anyhow, to get back to what I was saying. I couldn't stop thinking about you after that."

"So that's why I can get through the wall?" she said. "Because I'm in your computer password?"

His big shoulders lifted and dropped. "You got a better explanation?"

She shook her head. All out of brilliant ideas.

"You've been my only social contact for weeks now," he said.

"*That's* what you call social contact?"

That earned her a flashing grin. "I was hiding up in the mountains until yesterday because I couldn't bear to be with people. I got pretty messed up in Spruce Ridge. Rudd, the guy who locked your mother up, he was heavy into psi-max. It gave him coercive power, and he used it like a billy club. He bludgeoned me with it, basically. I spent time in a coma. Brain swelling, the whole deal."

"Oh, God, Miles. I'm sorry."

"I wasn't trolling for sympathy. Just filling you in. Anyhow, afterward, it was bad. Lot of pain, and the sensory input was disproportionate. Like, the filters in my brain got messed up. Everything bugged me. Smells, light, sound, radiation from computers and cell phones, smog. There were drugs I could have taken, but they sucked. So I ran off. I was out in the woods camping when you started visiting."

"Social contact," she murmured.

"Yeah, very social." He pulled her back down on top of him, and kissed her. A gentle, questioning kiss.

But she wasn't done questioning him yet. "Do you still have the sensory overload problem?"

His eyes went thoughtful, narrow. "Not exactly," he said, slowly. "I did until a few hours ago. My senses are as intense as they ever were, but when you started visiting my head, I started keeping my shit together without the meltdowns or the stress flashbacks. And now, after today . . ." His voice trailed off for a long moment. "It's weird."

"What's weird?" she burst out. "Besides absolutely everything?"

"That it doesn't bug me anymore," he said. "Once I hooked up with you, I got extra bandwidth. I grew into it. It fits me now. You know how when you hit puberty, suddenly your legs are too long or your arms, or . . ." He stopped, looked her over. "No, never mind. Not you. I bet you've always been perfectly proportioned. Since babyhood."

She swatted that away. "So you're inexplicably cured, then?"

"Who said anything about inexplicable? I just explained it."

"When?" She shook her head, frustrated. "What cured it?"

"You did," he said.

"Me?" She squinted, uncomprehending. "*What?*"

"You fixed it," he said. "You cured me. Pulled me together, somehow. When I'm with you . . . hell, I don't know. It's like, the better to see you with, my dear, the better to smell you with, you know?"

She snorted, helplessly. "Oh, come on. Give me a break!"

"No. Totally. You're the one who gave me a break. I don't know how else to describe it." He lifted a handful of her hair, pressed his nose to it, inhaled with obvious gusto. "Mmm. I feel better. Thanks."

"Ah . . . you're welcome."

For some reason, his admission scared her. She felt so small and lost. The thought of having had such a powerful effect on him, with no idea how or why, unnerved her. Like she'd suddenly found herself with a loaded gun in her hands. Vast, unexpected power, and she had no idea where it came from, or what to do with it.

"No pressure," he said, sensing her unease. "It's just a feeling. But it's a really good one. So don't sweat it."

"Um. Yeah." Right. Just a feeling, her ass. It was a feeling with a million complicated implications. And dangers.

"You go to art school in San Francisco, right?" he asked.

She shook her head. She was so far distant from that previous Lara Kirk, it was hard to remember who she'd been. "I don't know," she said. "I did before they took me. But the things I did then, the things I thought were so important . . . they all seem so small, now."

"So if all this was magically resolved, and Greaves disappeared from the face of the earth, you wouldn't go back to art school? You were getting pretty famous, from what I could tell."

She laughed at that. "No, that's just promo spin from the website. I was maybe on track to make a decent living, but I wasn't famous. And I wouldn't want to live in a city now. The one thing I dreamed about, besides you of course, was being someplace beautiful in the mountains. Big towering trees. A waterfall. I went there in my mind, every day. If I could do anything, I'd go find myself a waterfall and just sit there, listen to the water rushing for a few centuries. And then we'd see."

He gave her a smile, the amazing one that made the deep groove carve itself sexily into his cheek, that flash of gorgeous white teeth.

"How about you?" she asked. "Vital stats?"

"I grew up in Endicott Falls," he said. "Not far from Seattle. You'd like it. It has good falls, as the name indicates. The Gorge does, too. Toward Portland, Old Highway 30. I could show you lots of great falls. We could do a tour. You can listen to them all. One after the other."

She smiled her appreciation of the lovely, impractical thought. It was only the sweetest, most lovely thing anyone had ever suggested to her. In fact, it made her want to burst into tears again. She distracted herself by rushing into another question. "Where do you live now?"

"I don't have a place right now. I've been in limbo. Not that I'm a deadbeat living out of my car, or anything," he hastened to add. "I make good money when I put my mind to it. I'm just in a state of transition."

"I know that state," she said.

"My friends have been bugging me for years to buy my own place. I've been holding off, until I figure out what I want."

"And have you figured it out yet?"

He took his time with his reply, shifting her so she was basically sitting on his lap. Feeling the heat of his unflagging erection, stiff against her bare bottom. "Yeah," he said. "I'm starting to get a clue."

She had a fleeting sensation that she might be walking into some sort of a trap, but she just kept going with it. "What, then? What clue?"

He nuzzled her neck, and the soft caress of his warm breath made her shiver and press closer to him. "It has to be in the mountains," he said. "With some good climbing nearby. I might have to design it myself, because I want something really specific."

She stared at his hands, which were clasped around her waist, beneath her breasts. His forearms were sinewy, the hair lying flat and shiny crosswise across the ropy muscles and bulging veins and tendons, so dark against the white tee shirt. "Specific how?"

"Huge trees," he said, almost dreamily. "Big, old growth forest. Cedars, spruces, silver pine. With ferns and trillium and starflowers and rock lilies. A mountain stream nearby. With a waterfall."

She caught her breath, and blushed. "Ah . . ."

"Not too close to the city, but not too far, either," he went on. "Lots of space in the house. Living quarters downstairs, huge deck, fabulous view, fireplace. Windows everywhere. A big man-cave dug into the back, where I can do all my tech geek stuff and have a big nasty tangle of circuits and wires and shit. And upstairs, a huge loft. Vaulted ceilings, skylights, space. For the artist studio."

"Oh," she said, weakly. "Uh, wow."

"An outbuilding, maybe, for the metalworking stuff," he went on. "And a kiln out back. For the ceramic pieces."

"You know my work?"

"Every last piece in your online website," he said. "I've never been much for visual art. I specialize in sound. But your stuff really does something to me. I never get tired of looking at it. The ceramics were my favorites. *Persephone's Pride*, I loved that one. *Pandora's Box* was amazing, too. I was bummed that somebody had already bought those, or I would have gotten them for myself. My very first art investment."

She was startled, and touched. "Wow. Thanks."

He shrugged. "None necessary. You did all the work."

"I thought I knew about the nature of evil, back when I made those pieces," she said.

"And now?"

She shook her head. "I didn't know shit."

"So make new versions," he said. "I'll commission them from you."

She shook with silent emotion, to high and fine a vibration to be laughter. "They wouldn't be pretty," she warned.

"I'm not scared," he said.

She looked him in the eye. "No, you aren't, are you? I've never met anybody as fearless as you."

He looked uncomfortable. "We all have our strong points and our weak points," he said.

"Miles," she said. "Listen to me. You're a sweet guy. Amazing. Brave, special, gorgeous. Heroic. You saved my life already, multiple times, if you count the mind shield. It's more than I ever dreamed anyone would ever do for me. You've done your part. Thank you."

"I already told you not to thank—"

"I'm not finished!" she snapped, frustrated. "I have a huge shadow hanging over my life. I blight everyone that I touch—"

"Not me," he said. "You did the opposite to me, and I—"

"Huge shadow, got that? You should run in the opposite direction. Run! Don't walk."

He was silent, his face thoughtful. He shook his head. "I'm not going to do that, Lara. How can I do that when you keep pulling me back in? You've been pulling me from the beginning. I can't walk away from you, let alone run. I can't pry myself away with a fucking crowbar!"

"I'm sorry," she whispered. "I can't seem to stop."

He frowned. "Stop what?"

She flapped her hands. "Coming on to you. Clinging. Pleading for attention. Sneaking inside your head. Begging you to fuck me."

"I'm not complaining," he said. "I liked it. Even when I thought I was psycho. I like it even more, now. You don't have to beg."

She hid her face in her hands. "Oh, God. Will I be responsible for you getting killed, too? And all your friends too, most likely?"

"Those guys are as tough as they come," he said. "And as far as that shadow goes, it's hanging over my life, too. Same damn shadow. I wouldn't get away from it by running. And you make me strong."

Indefinable emotion blazed through her, making her heart twist and ache. So hot and sweet and painful. "I'm glad I have that effect on somebody," she whispered. "I don't feel strong at all."

"But you are. You're a survivor. You're incredible."

She shook her head violently. She couldn't bear to give in

to this, to him, and then have it torn away from her, but that was the way it was destined to go. She could feel it. No way to stop that machine.

"I have no idea what my future holds, Miles," she said. "All I know is that it's probably not going to be pretty."

"I know one thing your future holds," he said.

She shook her hair back. "Yeah? And what is that?"

"Me," he said, and pushed her down onto the bed.

15

Mine.

He'd never felt it like that. Beyond emotion. It rose up from the depths of his being. She felt it in his kiss, the way he handled her, covered her, held her. Tight, jealous. She wasn't slipping away from him. He wasn't falling for any bullshit about danger or blight or shadows. Let them just try to mess with her.

Let them try. Bring them on. He would fuck them up so bad.

She felt good beneath him. Strong and pliant, legs wound around his waist. That sweet mouth pressed to his, gasping for breath. Twining and pressing up against his weight. His hands were all over her, shoving the shirt up so her breasts pressed his chest. He cupped her ass, slid his hand down to stroke her thatch. He petted the length of her tender slit with his finger, up and down.

"You washed off all your lube," he observed.

She blinked up at him, straining for little panting breaths. "Huh? Oh, ah . . . yeah. I didn't know we would . . . that you would want to—"

"No problem." He slid down her body, folded her legs out wide. "There's more where that came from."

He heard, vaguely, the frantic words. Felt the fingers tangling into his hair, pulling desperately, but he was in the grip of a huge, muscular impulse. *Mine.* The moment he tasted her sweet salty lube against his tongue, it multiplied, exponentially. So slippery hot and succulent, all her sweet tender pink inside bits. He wallowed in her quintessential femaleness. Could not get enough of it, not ever. *More.*

She still yanked on his hair, but she wasn't trying to pull him away from herself, and she was making those sounds, trembling and jerking, lifting herself against his sliding, thrusting tongue. He explored every delicate detail of her pussy with his tongue, all spread out and shining, flowerlike gradations of pink and rose and scarlet, whenever he managed to move his mouth far enough away to focus on it visually. That soft-focus flush of arousal fogged his brain to madness. And her clit, taut against his tongue. He trilled it, suckled it. Yum.

He'd always liked going down, had thought it was juicy and sexy and fun, but he'd never had his mind blown by it like this. She was so fucking beautiful, every detail of her. He licked and laved and suckled voraciously at her until she came, and came . . . and still, he stayed, mouth pressed to her juicy slit, wallowing in bliss while she jerked and sobbed through the shuddering waves of pleasure. Every shining little pulse, throbbing straight through his own body.

And she hadn't even done her mind thing. She wasn't even inside.

She was more than wet enough at that point, for anything he might have dreamed up, but he was having such a great time where he was, lapping up yummy girl juice, he just kept at it, following her sounds, her sighs, the quivers against his delving tongue, until he brought her off again.

He shifted, wiping his mouth and crawled up the bed to poise himself over her, folding her legs up high. She was so graceful, so pretty. Every part of her. Her smiling lips, her soft, dazed eyes. Open and willing and trusting. Her hands on his chest. Pulling him.

Wow. She made the word, but no sound came out.

"Glad you like it," he said. "I'm going to be doing a whole lot of that. You're so small. Delicate. You'll need lots of licking."

"I'm not delicate," she said.

"Then I'll just have to come up with some other excuse to spend hours with my head between your legs. Lose the shirt."

He helped her tug the shirt up, and pulled her up, too, piling pillows behind her until she was halfway upright.

"Watch us," he said.

Her gaze darted down, to his hugely enthusiastic cock, beet red with eagerness to get down to business. "Okay," she murmured.

He wrapped her hands around his cock, and covered them with his own. They played with it together, leisurely strokes of his cockhead, up and down her slit. Sliding inside, but not too much, just a teasing push, and then up again, to swirl over and around her clit, like a tongue licking. Up, down, around, little wet sounds in the silence. Until he was shiny and hot with her lube, until she was squirming, trying to maneuver herself so she could force him deeper inside.

He held her firm. "Get inside me first," he told her.

She laughed, her cheeks hot pink. "That sounds kinky. It's hard, when you're, ah . . ." She gestured down at his cock. He slid it a little bit deeper, and pushed, until he encountered resistance.

"In," he said again. "You might as well get used to doing it when I make love to you."

"Oh, really?" Her giggles were breathless, jerky. "Why is that?"

"I like you in there," he said. "Like a Chinese box. You, inside. Me, inside. Makes my balls practically explode."

"That state seems to come pretty naturally to you."

"Just do it." His voice was rough. "I need it."

She closed her eyes, pulling her soft lower lip between her teeth, and concentrated.

He hung onto his self-control and kept petting her, nudging himself deeper inside. Twist, swirl, and stroke. Twist, swirl, and stroke. She whimpered, squirming for more, but he held back, waiting.

"Concentrate," he whispered.

"I'm trying, but you're making it harder," she complained.

"Technically speaking, you're the one making it harder," he said. "That's your job. I'm trying to make it softer."

"Oh stop it, smart-ass." She wiggled, gasping, and then—

Ah. It lit up, that sensation inside, a shining glow in the Lara place. Every time, she did it quicker. It made his cock swell and his balls ache, and his throat twist up. His chest felt hot.

"Yeah," he muttered, hoarsely. "Do that. Stay there. Right there."

She placed her hands on his chest, like she was bracing herself, and the words scrolled on the screen inside.

ur different this time. ur vibe. its changed.

He circled her clit with his thumb, pushing deeper. ?? he replied.

all commanding whoa

that a problem 4 u? Another slow swirl, twist . . . and a deeper thrust made her gasp.

dont know yet.

tell me when u do know. He bore down and drove deep inside.

They cried out, together at the slick, plush caress of her perfect body. His cock, hugged, squeezed, and loved by every quivering muscle inside her. He pressed the mouth of her womb. Stroking, swiveling, pulsing. Finding the inner places that lit up. The mind connection intensified his awareness, making his pleasure hers.

He set a slow, surging rhythm. They clutched each other, breathless, staring down at the point of contact, where his thick flushed shaft slid inside, and then dragged slowly out, gleaming wet and caressed by her soft folds. Surging, thrusting.

"Look at you," she whispered. "Master of all that you survey."

He kissed her hungrily, tangling tongues before he lifted his head. "That sounds arrogant and hateful and entitled. Am I that bad?"

"God, no," she said. "Not bad. Amazing, rather. I want you. If I didn't want you, we'd have a big problem, but as it is, go ahead, feel as entitled and arrogant as you want. Oh, my God . . ."

She arched, head flung back, softly sobbing as another throbbing wave enveloped her. The most awesome sensation, the clenching pulses squeezing, petting him. He almost came with her, but teetered back from the brink. No way. Not yet.

Long and slow. Orgasms for hours. He had a point to make, a precedent to set. "The vibe seems to work for you," he said. "As long as my arrogant entitlement makes you come, I can work with that."

"I shouldn't encourage you," she whispered. "It's dangerous."

"Too late," he told her.

And it was. Their hands twined, locked on either side of her head into clasped fists. His hips drove against hers. So hot, so tight, so wet. Her mouth open to him, her tongue, so sweet, darting, twining. She was strong, for being so narrow and slender. Lithe and flexible. Meeting him, holding him. The rhythm got wilder, pounding desperately.

Their mutual explosion blasted them to oblivion.

So much for the orgasms for hours. The point he had wanted to make. His arrogant entitlement, too. When he got the use of his brain back, he was as humble as they came. Wrecked. A pile of steaming, smoking parts. He rolled off her, flopped onto his back so she could breathe. Stared at the ceiling until he got the strength and courage to turn and gaze at her face. Nervously. Hopefully.

She looked dewy and soft. Her eyes were endlessly deep and lovely. A mystery he would never plumb, but he could die happy trying.

"You okay?" he asked. "Did I, uh . . ."

She shook her head, with that secret smile. She formed the word *no*, with her mouth, shook her head. Blew him a little kiss.

That radiant, luminous smile scared him to death. All that "mine" bullshit. No longer an issue. Probably never had been.

He was hers. After all his arrogant posturing. All hers.

He stared at her, the fear setting in. Like a drumroll rising, now that the urgent thrum of sex no longer overlaid it. And he thought he'd had problems before, walking the tightrope of all his tedious problems. Brain damage, mortal danger, pissed-off friends, psycho monsters.

Now he got to field it all while holding his naked beating heart out in front of him, in his hand. *Uh, excuse me . . . I think this is yours.*

Yeah. Sweet.

Better than food, better than air. It felt so good, pressed to his hot skin, his arms wrapped around her.

She wanted to bathe in his life energy. Taste his salt flavor, lick him, stroke him. Eat him up. She was high on him. Craving more.

So wrong. So poorly timed. She had no business inflicting her shipwrecked self upon him now. He deserved someone whole and functional, not a broken, gasping, grasping thing. Clinging like a shred of seaweed. Feeding off his strength.

He propped himself up onto his elbow, stretching out his other arm, making his back ripple and flex in the most breathtaking way, but he was unselfconscious about it. He grabbed the cake from the bedside table. He gave her a menacing look. "Food."

"What is it with you and food?" she complained. "I promise, I'll eat everything in good time! Lighten up!"

"No." He forked up an intimidating bite of chocolate cake with an oozing glob of coconut caramel goop draped on top, and waved it in her face with a threatening air.

She took the fork, carefully cut the bite into two pieces, and ate one of them. Sugar shock almost made her dizzy. "Sweet," she gasped.

He held out another forkful.

"Wait a minute." She took the fork from him, and pointed it sternly in his direction. "We take turns. It's a huge piece."

He narrowed his eyes, but she waited stubbornly, fork in hand.

He finally accepted the bite. "Wow," he said. "Sugar orgasm."

He gave her the next bite. She gave him one, and so it went until the chunk of pastry was reduced to crumbs and smears of caramel.

And by then, the hunger on his face made a yearning open inside her, hot and wanton. She set down the plate on the bedside table, and held out her arms. A disorienting spin, and *oof*, she was flat on her back, with Miles all over her, his deep kisses faintly flavored with caramel. But he pulled himself off, turning away.

She sat up, bereft. "What's wrong?"

He shook his head. "You need rest."

"But I like it."

He held up his hand, a warding gesture. "Saying no,

being sensible, cooling it down, all that is up to me, evidently. I get that you're not going to do it. But don't mess with me when I try."

"But it's fun to mess with you. And I haven't had fun in months."

"No." He ran an assessing eye over her body. "We'll discuss more fun after you've finished that meal, slept ten hours, and then eaten another meal."

"That's harsh," she commented.

"Yeah, brutal." He swung his legs over the side of the bed, groping for his jeans. "Gotta get this thing into my pants and put a padlock on it." He buttoned the fly, and groped in his pocket for a smartphone. "Mind if I make a quick call?"

That was such an odd request, she was taken aback. "Uh, sure."

"I need to distract myself." He lifted the comforter, tossed it up over her naked body. "Cover your chest. The view melts my brain, and I'm going to need my brains to make this call."

"Who are you calling?" she asked.

He shot her a dour look. "My mother."

That startled a peal of laughter out of her. "You're kidding. Now?"

"Don't think I'm one of those guys," he said, defensive. "It's just that I haven't spoken to her in weeks. Not since I lit out camping. She's out of her mind with worry, or so they tell me, and I felt really bad about it, but I just couldn't talk to her. Not in the shape I was in."

"Then why now?"

He frowned. "I don't know. I guess because, for whatever reason, now I can. And if I can, then I damn well should. I promise, I'll make it short. I just have to catch the impulse, before I lose my nerve."

"Go on, then," she urged. "Want me to leave? For privacy?"

He looked shocked at the idea. "Hell, no! This is your

room. Stay right where you are. Don't even move. Unless it's to eat." He picked at the keyboard, and turned, giving her a perfect opportunity to admire the muscles in his back. The astonishingly perfect shape of his ass.

"Hey," he said, his voice uncertain. "Mom? . . . yeah, it's me . . . oh, God, Mom, please, don't." There was a long pause, then he spoke again. "I know. I'm sorry. Sean told me he talked to you, and that you . . . yeah. I was busy . . . yeah, I know. No, it's not an excuse. There was this girl in trouble, and I . . . yeah, that's what I said. A girl . . ." He shot a grin over his shoulder at her. "Her name is Lara. She's an artist. Yeah . . . it was tricky. Of course I was careful." He listened patiently for a moment, and she could see, though his face was turned away, that he was grinning. "Yes, she's a nice girl . . . yeah, pretty, too." His gaze darted to her. "Beautiful, actually. Sure, first chance I get . . . don't know yet, Mom. Things are dicey, and I have to . . . yeah, but . . ." He held the phone away from his ear, frowning. "Yes, she is, but she's just gotten out of a bad situation, and now is not the time to ask her to . . . no, Mom! Not a chance!"

Lara could hear the shrill, tinny lecture from across the room.

He turned, gave her a dismayed look.

Lara felt her lips twitch. "She wants to talk to me?"

"You don't have to, for God's sake," he said. "Don't sweat it."

"What's her name?" Lara asked.

"Helen Davenport," he said.

"Is she nice?" she asked.

He looked puzzled. "Of course she's nice. She's my mom."

Lara held out her hand, on impulse. "I haven't heard a nice woman's voice in months," she said. "Give me that phone."

Miles handed it to her without a word.

She held it to her ear, marveling at how familiar and unfamiliar the heavy little device felt in her hand. "This is Lara. Mrs. Davenport?"

"Lara?" The older woman's voice was distorted with tears. "Hello. I'm sorry to put you on the spot like this, honey."

"That's okay," she said.

"I just can't seem to stop crying. I'm so emotional right now. It's been so long since I heard his voice, you see."

"Of course," she said. "I've been doing a lot of that myself today."

Helen Davenport forced brightness into her tone. "So. Miles tells me you're an artist."

"Yes, that's right," she said. "A sculptor."

"That's wonderful! How creative of you. And you go to art school?"

"Not lately," she said. "I was in some really bad trouble. But Miles saved me."

"Did he, now?" The woman's voice sharpened.

"Yes, he did. He was incredibly brave," Lara told her. "And so smart. He was amazing. You should be very proud."

"Oh, I am. I am." The woman's voice dissolved again.

"Oh, please. That is enough of that shit," Miles snapped, twitching the phone out of her hand. He held it to his ear. "Me again, Mom . . . no way! You cannot talk to her anymore . . . as soon as I know what's going on. Hanging up now, Mom. I love you. Hanging up, okay? Yes . . of course I'll call again. Yeah. Love you, too. Give Dad a hug. Yeah . . . hanging up for real, Mom. Yeah. Bye."

His hand dropped. He blew out a long breath, and sat down heavily onto the bed. "Wow," he said. "That was intense."

"Pretty much," she agreed.

He set the phone down on the bedside table. "Thanks," he said.

She shook her head, tried to smile. Mostly failing.

"She can't wait to meet you," he added. "She's going to love you. My dad, too."

That did it. Too much cheerful normalcy on an empty stomach.

"My mother would have loved you, too." Her voice cracked.

Miles' gaze whipped over to her, alarmed. She looked down at her lap. Her face was shaking. About to melt right off.

"Uh, Lara?" he said, warily. "Are you okay?"

"And my dad," she said. "He was such a snob about all the guys I dated. None of them were smart enough for him. But if he'd ever met you, I don't think he would have been able to think of a single thing to complain about. Not after what you did for me."

"Lara," he said. "I'm sorry. I didn't mean to—"

"But you'll never meet him. Or her. They're gone. There's nobody left to pass judgment on the men I sleep with. No impossible parental standard to live up to. It's so simple for me, from now on."

"Aw, shit." He scooted to sit next to her, touching her shoulder.

She flinched away. "I'm the one who's sorry. Somebody put a blow torch to my life, and it's not your fault, but there's nothing left that's normal for me anymore. A phone call like that one, for instance. Never again. And I'm so fucking jealous of you. And that's so unfair." Her voice was shaking to pieces. She stopped, breathed, tried to still it. "You've done so much for me. I'm such a bitch to feel this way."

"No, you're not!" he said. "Just feel the way you feel."

"That's very generous of you." She hated the words the instant they flew out of her mouth. Hated herself for saying them. She was on her feet, running toward the bathroom. Miles called out behind her, but she slammed the door on him. Sank onto the floor, hiding the shaking, agonized grimace her face had become against her knees.

So ashamed. She'd tried not to let the ugliness into herself, but she was steeped in it. Stained by it. She was toxic, bitter, ruined. She shouldn't inflict that on anyone. Particularly not someone like him.

The bathroom door opened. It had not occurred to her to lock it. It had been so long since she'd had any sense of autonomy about when doors opened or closed. Or maybe she'd been hoping to be followed.

He crouched down beside her on the cold bathroom tiles, and then sat next to her, crosslegged. Put his warm hand on her shoulder.

"I'm sorry," she whispered. "I set you up for that. I told you not to treat me like I was broken. You took me at my word."

"I should have known better," he said. "I was just thinking about myself."

"And your mom," she said, sniffing hard. "You were thinking about your mom, and that's great. I applaud that. Really, I do. It's just hitting me all at once. My parents. I tried not to think about what happened to them, but . . ." She shook her head. "He was so afraid of pain. My dad. Even a headache made him panic. He was afraid of a lot of things. You'd never know it to look at him. He was this confident, successful professor, handsome, smart, popular. But underneath, he was scared. Anxious. To think of him going through that . . ." She pounded her fists on the hard tiles, as hard as she could. Bruising her knuckles, but she didn't care. The pain helped, in a weird way.

Miles caught her fists in his, and stilled them. "He was brave that day," he said. "He was a goddamn superman that day, in my book."

She dared for a moment to look up at his face. "Why do you say that? How could you know that?"

Miles was silent. Considering his words carefully. Nervous about touching off a full-out nervous breakdown from the crazy girl.

"I knew that he'd gotten a letter from your mother, giving him certain information," he said slowly. "Matilda told me about it. It had a rendezvous point, a date, to meet up and save you. When I found him, I also found a ticket to Denver to the rendezvous point. He'd planned to go. They hurt him, and killed him, but afterward, the bad guys still didn't know about the letter, or the date, or the rendezvous point. They didn't know about them because he did not tell them, Lara."

She just looked at him, openmouthed. "Oh."

He lifted both of her clenched fists to his lips, and kissed one, then the other. "Love makes you strong," he said.

She came apart. Was a total shaking mess for a long while.

He pulled her into his lap and held her in his strong arms until the storm passed through and left her soft and limp.

It was chilly. When he felt her shiver, he muscled her onto her feet, set the shower running, and shucked his jeans.

He guided her into the stream of hot water, and joined her in there. They stared at each other, hands twined, as the water poured down over them and steam fogged the glass. It was like floating in a bubble, a magic place outside time and space.

He was so gentle. He had water tangled in his long, thick eyelashes, dripping from the ends of his long, shaggy locks. Naked emotion blazed from his eyes. She put her hands on his chest, blocking the rushing pattern of water racing down his chest, down his treasure trail, flowing around the turgid cock. Wow.

On impulse, she seized his thick, veined shaft, stroking it. He gasped, shuddering, and abruptly she was desperate for more. She wanted him to feel as vulnerable as she felt.

She put her arms around his neck, lifted her leg to curl it around his thigh, pressing his cock against her sensitive folds. "Hold me."

He frowned, shaking his head. "Lara, I—"

"Hold me, goddamnit! I need this! I *need* you!"

He muttered something obscene under his breath, but he cupped her ass and lifted her to that perfect height where she could take him inside. Wide open, pressed to the wet, tile wall, her knees draped over the crook of his arms. She was still wet from the last time, so he entered her in one deep, smooth lunge. She clutched his shoulders, sobbing at the perfection of that thick club caressing her inside. Her tears mixed with the water from above, sluicing them down.

It was so good to cling to him, to give herself up. She didn't have to do a thing but hang on, be caressed by his strong arms, his big body, the deep aching slide and shove of his cock. Each slow stroke was a shimmering glide of pleasure, turning her liquid, molten and soft.

This time, he didn't have to ask. He looked at her, and she knew exactly what to do. It was almost automatic, shaking loose, dancing through the barrier until she was inside, in that safe, beautiful place. It was lit up, blindingly bright and wonderful, and she could hardly tell what was inside, what was out, what was analogous, what was real.

It was the sweetest, realest thing she'd ever felt, his powerful body thudding into hers. So raw, so hot, so incredibly right.

He came, pouring himself into her, and she followed along, in a sweet shivering rush of utter surrender.

Neither of them could bear to break the panting clinch. She could have stayed locked together with him in the pounding water forever.

16

Miles set her gently down on her wobbly feet. He was too abashed to look her in the face. She made his eyes ache, she was so beautiful. Those thick, twisting wet cables of dark hair, clinging to her shoulders, eyelashes wet and tangled.

He reached for the bottle of shower gel, just to have something to do, and got to work on her, caressing her with the slippery suds. He could do this for the rest of time, particularly when he slid his hand between her legs. Soaping, rinsing, delving, until she sighed and squirmed, clenching tight around his fingers. He loved those soft silky tender bits, hidden in her wet thatch. His cock was already thickening. Even after all their inappropriate excesses.

He toweled her off when they stepped out, and scooped her into his arms, carrying her back into the bedroom. Too light. She had to eat. He wasn't going to stop bullying her about it. Probably ever.

He tucked her in, lifting her wet hair, squeezing the towel around it again and again before spreading it out onto the pillow. He wanted to know everything about her, every moment she'd ever lived. To punish everyone who'd ever injured her. He was enthralled. Utterly fucked up.

He tucked the comforter up under her chin, and used the towel to dry himself. Dragged on the jeans, again, and the shirt, which he did not even bother to button, since who the fuck was he fooling, anyway. "Try to rest," he said. "I'm going to see what's happening downstairs."

She gave him that shy smile that revealed nothing. He wondered if she knew how he felt. That she had the keys to the Citadel. And he loved having her in there. As much as it freaked him out.

But then, he'd never claimed to have any damn sense.

He ran down the stairs. The kitchen was deserted, dishes washed. Aaro was out near the car, talking into his cell. Davy sat out on the huge deck, reassembling one of his guns.

Miles walked out onto the deck. The cold wind chilled his wet hair, whipped the unbuttoned shirt back from his bare chest. Davy's eyes flicked over him, registering it.

Miles met his eyes, straight on. Fuck it. He'd done what he had done, and he wasn't apologizing. They could all just kiss his ass.

Davy's eyes narrowed. "So?" he said.

"I'm keeping her," Miles said.

Davy's face froze, for a long moment. Then he turned, looked away, as if he were admiring the view. But Miles knew the guy well enough to know that he was trying not to grin.

The grin won. "Ah," he said. "Well, then. Good luck with that."

"I'm sure I'll need it."

Davy slid the reassembled pistol into the side holster inside his jeans. "Come on inside," he said.

"Why?"

"Because the beer's in the fridge, and this calls for a toast."

Miles followed the other guy inside. "Alcohol? Now?

What about, 'lack of vigilance will get you killed,' and all that?"

"Bite your tongue, punk. Don't you quote Eamon Mc-Cloud to me after rolling around in bed with your woman for two hours."

The guy had a point, Miles conceded, as he watched Davy pop open two bottles of amber ale. They clinked bottles, drank.

His augmented senses were now able to embrace the flavors of whatever he put into his mouth, rather than being overwhelmed by them. The beer went down, sharp and salty and excellent.

Aaro walked in, scowling. "Drinking, now, too? Loser."

"Shut it, and have one," Davy suggested calmly.

Aaro accepted the beer that Davy handed to him. "Just talked to Nina," he said. "She and Edie and Tam will be here tomorrow. I told them to wait, let her get a night's sleep." He looked at Miles, eyes slitted. "If that's gonna happen."

Miles stared back. "I'm glad they're coming," he said evenly. "Lara will be happy to see Nina. She needs her people."

"She has you, doesn't she?" Aaro said. "She has you all over her."

Miles smiled, lifted his bottle in a silent toast, and drank. A mass of intricate sensory information started to crunch in his mind.

Fuck this. He couldn't just drink a damn beer, like a normal guy. The micro-analysis happened automatically. He felt every increment of the changes the sugar and alcohol made inside his body. Changing his perceptions, relaxing his muscles, lowering his defenses.

His enjoyment of the beer drained instantly away, like a plug had been pulled. What the fuck was he doing, beer in hand, like a normal guy chilling after work? Who the fuck had given him permission to relax? He could not degrade his capacity to protect her.

He stared at the sweating bottle in his hand. The Mc-Clouds were tougher than boot leather, all four of them, and so was Aaro, but they were no match for Greaves. That was definitely proven. It was a hard fact to swallow, but there it was, in his face.

It was up to him. It was all on him. *I'm keeping her.* Was he, now? What manic shit-for-brains actually dared to say something like that? What had felt like steely confidence now rang in his ears like swaggering arrogance. Keep her, would he? Keep her where, in a pumpkin shell? He had fuck-all to fight Greaves with, other than a good mind shield, and a gun. The gun was useless against an opponent like that. His other assets were all defensive in nature.

Unless he counted his brain. Which was currently flash-fried.

Until he took out Greaves, he couldn't keep her. Alive, maybe, but not living. What did she have to look forward to? Living on the run, eating crap strip-mall food, sleeping on lumpy, sagging beds in cheap hotels and rentals, tense and terrified, looking over her shoulder every second, jumping at every sound? No work, no art, no friends or family or children—or life. No ripening, no hope for the future, no peace. Just him, trotting along beside her like a hopeful hound dog, happy to be needed.

Until she started to hate him for it.

He'd find a way for her to be free. He had to. Just not free of him.

He set the bottle down on the kitchen counter with a decisive thud, all impulse to drink it gone, and answered the question in Davy's eyes. "Lack of vigilance will get you killed," he said.

Davy nodded sagely. "Whatever."

"I can help keep guard," Miles said. "Where are you guys posted?"

"Go guard her," Davy said. "Do your mind-shield thing.

That's the best way to be vigilant right now, since none of us can do it."

That made sense, though he had to be suspicious of his reasoning, being how there was nothing on earth he wanted to do more than wrap himself around that girl's naked body.

Crazy. As completely fucked up as he had been, he'd suddenly found this vast geyser of sexual energy. He'd always had a lusty appetite for sex whenever he could get it, and granted, it had been a while since Cindy had gone on the fateful tour with the rock star and subsequently dumped him. He'd been celibate for over a year now.

But the feelings assaulting him were so far removed for his mournful adolescent pining for Cindy, he needed a whole new unit of measure for it.

Maybe it was the dreams. Her visits to his brain, all those weeks in the mountains. She'd imprinted on his brain somehow, and now he was helplessly programmed to nail her every chance he got. Out-of-control, like the rest of his life. It was like living in a fucking centrifuge.

He didn't knock, not wanting to wake her if she slept. She was such a slight bump underneath the fluffy white comforter. He tried to close the door without making a sound, but the door latch clicked, and she exploded into movement, sitting bolt upright.

He froze. The cover flew back. Her hair was wildly tangled over her face, her eyes wide and staring. She was staring at him, but did not see him. Her heart raced. He could hear it, stuttering in a desperate skip-hop.

Stress flashback, maybe, or a nightmare. He was afraid to move, for fear of scaring her. Something flickered in her eyes. She blinked.

"You okay?" he ventured.

She hid her face in her hands and shook her head, violently.

He still hesitated to approach the bed. "Bad dream?"

She shook her head again. "Tripping," she whispered. "I took off the moment I started to drift off to sleep. Got sucked right down into the vortex."

"Vortex," he repeated, letting his silence be the prompt.

She nodded. "When I trip. That's how it feels. Like I'm being sucked down into another dimension. Oh, God. Is this going to happen to me now, all the time, at random? Am I going to start seeing alternate realities while I'm in line at the grocery store? I might need to be locked back up in a cell after all."

"No!" His voice was savage, as if the force of his declaration could make it so. "No, that's not going to be your life."

She just shook her head back and forth.

He ached to sit down next to her, take her in his arms, but he'd had enough stress flashbacks to know that she probably wouldn't be able to stand the contact. "You're shaking," he said. "What did you see?"

She shuddered. "My two favorites, you might say. Or anti-favorites. I saw these visions almost every time they injected me. Now I'm seeing them even when they don't. Disaster and doom."

Dread mounted in his belly, but he didn't want her to be all alone with it. "What did you see?"

"The first one is like a recurring nightmare," she said slowly. "I see a park, but it's overgrown, and the people in it look listless, vacant. Sometimes a man is collapsed on the sidewalk, and two people are sitting on the park bench next to him, staring into nowhere. They don't even seem to see him. People are lying on the grass, and it's not clear if they're dead or alive. Garbage is blowing everywhere. Then I see a woman, staring out the window, and behind her a baby in a crib is screaming, but she doesn't hear him. I have no idea what it all means."

He shivered, too. "Creepy," he commented.

"Oh, yeah. And I saw the bomb one, too, like always. The Tokyo train station. A terrorist attack. Four hundred and sev-

enty-eight people dead. Every time I saw that, I begged Hu
and Anabel to do something about it, but they ignored me."

"That's awful," he said quietly.

She looked up at him, lip caught tight and bloodless between her teeth. "Did it happen? The bomb?"

"I haven't heard about it," he said. "I've been in the
mountains, but I think someone would have mentioned a
disaster as big as that. Let me do a search." He crouched
down, pulled the laptop and router out of the bag that one of
his friends had pulled from his vehicle and left outside the
bedroom door. He ran a check for bombs, terrorists, Tokyo.

Nothing relevant or current jumped out. He shook his
head.

The look of dawning excitement on her face scared him,
in some obscure way. "What's today's date, Miles?" Her
voice was shaking.

He glanced at the computer and told her.

"Oh, my God," she whispered. "It hasn't happened yet. I
remember, in one of the trips, I saw the digital clock. It happened on the seventh. At afternoon rush hour."

"That's tomorrow," he said. The clenching sense of dread
grew.

"But it's a day later there! It's morning, nine hours later,
but tomorrow! Miles, if it hasn't happened yet, then I can
stop it! I can call someone about the bomb before it goes
off!"

"Yeah, but call who? Tell them what?"

Her eyes were feverishly bright. "The police! It's a big
green rucksack, packed full of explosives, left in the luggage
compartment of a commuter train that's coming into Tokyo
Station at five in the afternoon. But there's still time. Oh,
God, Miles."

She grabbed the burner phone that Aaro had bought for
her, and stared at it, helplessly, like she was trying to remember how it worked.

He couldn't say no, but he felt the doom, like a distant drumbeat.

"Who are you going to call?" he said. "The police? Do you speak Japanese?"

Her excitement shifted to anxiety. "No. I speak some European languages, but no Asian ones. Do you?"

He shook his head.

"There will be someone there who speaks English," she said.

"They'll want you to explain your source," he said. "It's going to be a hard sell. Even without the language barrier."

"I have to tell someone!"

He lifted his hands. "Just as you say," he said quietly. "I'm not saying you shouldn't. I'm just saying it's not going to be easy, and you're not in a good position to make them believe you."

She hunched over, pressing her fists to her mouth, thinking furiously with her eyes squeezed shut. "Wait. I know a guy," she said. "We were in high school together, in New York. He's an art director for an online magazine in Seattle, but he grew up in Kyoto. He can call for me. He'll help me sell it to them."

"You know his phone number?" he asked. "You're going to call him, right now? It's midnight."

"Yes." She started to punch in a number.

He watched, with dread building in his body. Any way he looked at it, this call was a bad idea security wise, for so many compelling reasons, he didn't even want to start listing them. But it was an untraceable burner phone, and they were sure to be gone from here tomorrow. Sooner rather than later, if he had his way.

He could not discourage her from making this call. It was an immediate way for her to turn some of the badness into good. To make some sense of the madness, the pain she'd been through. To strike a blow for righteousness, the light. He couldn't take that away from her.

And yet, for some reason, it was scaring the shit out of him.

"Hey, Keiko? . . . it's Lara . . . yes, I know. I know . . . yeah, not yet, but I will. I can't tell you now. I was in trouble, but I'm okay. But I have to tell . . . no, really, Keiko. Listen to me. I have to ask you to do something for me. You need to call the police in Tokyo. There's going to be a bomb in the main train station. It's coming in on a commuter train that arrives at five P.M. That's when it will go off today, if someone doesn't stop it. Could you call the . . . no, I'm sorry, I can't, but . . . it doesn't matter how I know. All that matters is that I *do* know! . . . I'm talking hundreds of people, Keiko! . . . yes! Tell them it's an anonymous tip . . . do I seem like a person who plays practical jokes? . . . Just do this for me, and I swear, I'll . . . thank you. Yes, I'll take all the blame if it . . . yes. Yes. Thank you . . . and I—"

"Lara," Miles broke in.

"Just a sec, Keiko," she murmured, looking up. "What?"

"Tell him to leave town, after he makes the call," Miles said. "Tell him to lay low. Just in case."

Lara stared at him, eyes huge with dawning realization. "Oh. God. You mean, you think he'll be in danger?"

"Just tell him, Lara."

"Ah, Keiko. My friend here was just suggesting that you leave town for a while, after you call," she faltered. "I'm really sorry, but it might be dangerous for you. I don't mean to mess up your life, but—"

There was a burst of voluble talking on the other end of the line. Lara just listened, her hand over her mouth. "Yes, I know," she whispered. "Sorry. Yes. Thanks. I will, I promise. As soon as I can."

She let the phone drop. "He'll make the call. He thinks I'm nuts, but he'll do it, just in case I'm not. Good old Keiko."

Yeah. Keiko, whose cell phone number she still knew by

heart, even after six months in solitary confinement. "Good old Keiko," he echoed. "So. Was he your boyfriend?"

That startled a smile onto her face. "I'm talking about terrorist bombs, and you want to know about my ex-boyfriends?"

Miles shrugged. "Call me shallow."

She convulsed. For an awful moment, he thought she was sobbing. Then he realized it was silent laughter. "Right," she choked out. "You, shallow. If you must know, yes. He was my boyfriend. For a little while." She dropped her hands, eyes demurely fixed on the comforter in front of her. "It fizzled out. But we stayed friends."

"Fizzled?" He stared at her, his mind blank. It just was not a word he could associate in any way with the naked woman curled up on that bed. Her gorgeous eyes, her perfect tits, her swirling cape of hair, her slender legs. She was perfect. Everything about her pulled him like a tractor beam. Her smell scrambled his brain at twenty paces.

"Fizzled how?" he demanded.

She waved, vaguely. "It happens," she said. "If I knew how it happened, maybe it wouldn't happen to me so fast."

"I don't get how any man wouldn't kill to be with you."

With that gut-clenching hindsight that so often afflicted him, the words stuck him as stalker creepy. But he couldn't take them back.

He clamped down on the urge to backpedal, and just waited, teeth clenched, for the fallout.

Her eyes skittered shyly away. "I, um . . . don't usually inspire such violent throes of emotion in men."

"Get used to it," he said.

This time she did meet his eyes. The silence between them was charged, buzzing with meaning. He was attuned to her every breath. Her scent fogged his brain. Yanked him toward her.

He walked to the bed, and stood, staring down at her. She cleared her throat, eyes darting down over his body.

"Keiko is gay," she said. "He came out senior year. He's with this new guy now. Franz. A dancer. A Norse god type. Full of muscles."

Miles let out a slow breath. "Ah. I see."

"Just, you know. To give you a little context. For the fizzling."

"Thanks. I appreciate that. It was tying my brain in knots," he told her. She clearly was trying not to smile, so he ventured to continue. "Great. I wish them all the best. Go, Keiko and Franz. Tear it up, boys."

She snorted into her hands again. "I can't believe I'm laughing right now," she whispered.

"I love it," he said. "I love it when you laugh."

She gave him a look that made a lump swell into his throat. "Thank you. For loving that. I really . . . it means a lot to me."

Then he was really in danger of starting to cry, which was so very not on his agenda for the evening, so he did the hard thing. Which was to smash a hammer down onto the tender moment before it fucked him up.

"You might have put Keiko in a tight place," he said. "The police are going to be real focused on him. Even from across the ocean."

The smile faded, and he mourned it, sharply. "I know," she said. "I'm sorry about that. I'll try to—"

"No, you won't," he said. "You aren't doing jack shit right now. You're running for your life. You can't help him."

She flattened her lips to a bloodless line. "I know. I'm sorry to do this to Keiko. But hundreds of people will survive who might have died."

"If there actually is a bomb," he said, hating himself for it.

Her eyes flashed. "You think I'm lying?"

"Never," he said hastily. "I think you've been locked in a hole for six months and forcibly injected with shitloads of a very powerful drug. That's what I think."

"Ah," she said. "So. I'm crazy, then."

"No, Lara." He sat down on the bed. "I think that you're fucking amazing. You put me to shame. It's incredible to me that you're focusing on helping a bunch of strangers in a train station, after what you've been through. I am a pathetic, self-absorbed, jerk-off dickhead compared to you. All I ever think about is poor little me."

"It's not such a big deal." She sounded like she was trying to convince herself. "All they have to do is look for the bag. If there's no bomb, all they've lost is some time. It's an inconvenience. A stupid bummer of a bomb scare. Worth the risk. Totally worth it."

"As you command." He lifted his hand to her lips. "You save the world, and I'll be your body servant and lady's maid while you do it."

"Oh, stop it," she said, crabbily. "I don't like being manipulated."

He kissed her knuckles, one by one. "How about worshipped?"

She snatched her hand away, and swatted him on the chest with it. He caught her hand, by reflex, and held it there, over his heart.

Her pulse stuttered, raced. His chest felt so hot, with her hand flattened over it. Hot and soft, like something was turning in there, stretching. Unfurling.

The buzz of hot awareness built and built. So close to just seizing her, just letting that hot prod of lust spur him on and bear her down onto the bed. He was slavering to spread her open, tease another lake of hot, slippery lube out of her sweet flower of a pussy before mounting up for a hard, juicy ride into explosive oblivion. And she was so there with him. He saw it, felt it, smelled it. Lips rosy and parted, nipples tight and peaked, eyes dilated, glowing. Oh. *Yes.*

He clenched his jaw, and broke eye contact. Three hard, athletic bouts of sex were way more than enough for the girl who just got rescued from the pits of hell.

The abandoned plate of food on the bedstand caught his

eye, and he lunged for it. "It's been a couple hours," he said. "How about you ingest your next shot of calories?"

She looked at the plate, doubtfully. "I'll try the rice and veggies," she conceded. "The meat's too rich for me right now."

"Whatever. As long as it's something."

He watched every bite go down, and felt himself fed. When that was all gone, he let himself be persuaded to polish off the steak, which she insisted she could not eat. He tried to be nonchalant about the erection as he peeled off his clothes and slid in next to her, tucking the comforter up to her chin.

He switched the light off, and pitch darkness thudded down onto them, pressing in on all sides, charged with menace. All at once, he remembered that she'd been confined in the dark. Thoughtless asshole.

"Oh, shit, Lara, I'm sorry," he said, groping for the lamp. "We can leave the light on, if you—"

"It's fine," she whispered, pulling him back down. "With you, it's fine. You're all the light I need."

His heart thumped, and his eyes fogged. He wrapped her in his arms, amazed. She was so sweet, so soft. And paradoxically strong.

He wound around her, settling her cheek against his chest, wrapping her leg around his.

She slid her hand timidly down over his belly until she encountered his stiff cock, in its perennial slick of precome jutting toward his navel, ferociously unappeased. She petted it, with appreciative fingers. "You can rest like that?"

"Better learn how," he said, ruefully. "Or I'm not going to get much sleep for, oh, say, the rest of time?"

"Wow." Her fingers curled around, squeezing.

He pried her hand away. "Don't. I'm making this huge effort not to be a pig, and you are not helping."

"You are the farthest thing in the world from a pig."

"Hah," he muttered. "How innocent you are." He dragged

her hand away from the danger zone, and flattened it against his chest, pinned beneath his own. "Sleep."

"I'm afraid to," she admitted, after a pause. "I'll get sucked into the vortex again. I'll start tripping, and he'll find me out there."

He mulled over the implications of that for a while, and remembered Davy's suggestion. An elegant and eminently desirable solution. "Get inside," he told her. "Sleep inside."

She propped herself up onto her elbow. "You think?"

"Why not? Is that any weirder than all the rest of it?"

"But what about you?"

He thought about it. "I'll stay awake."

"No!" she protested. "You have to rest, too. And it should still work, even in your sleep. You kept me safe for weeks when I hid in the Citadel, and you were asleep then, right?"

"Yeah, but I don't like letting go of conscious control," he said. "That feels wrong to me, with that guy out there gunning for you."

"You have to let go sometime," she said. "You'll crash if you don't. You kept Anabel out of your wall when you were fast asleep. Every time. Your shield never goes down."

"Okay," he said, dubiously. "We can give it a go. If you want."

She petted his chest hair, a slow, seductive caress. "The only question is, can I sleep if I'm inside the Citadel?"

"Why couldn't you?" he demanded.

She paused delicately. "Well. My associations with the Citadel are extremely, shall we say, erotically charged. Every time I went there, the Lord of the Citadel appeared, swept me off my feet—"

"And right onto your back. Yup. I know. I was there."

"It was amazing," she assured him. "I hated when the drug wore off and I got dragged back. The dance, to get through the wall, it felt like foreplay. The whole thing just shone with sex. It was the one good thing I had to cling to. It's what kept me alive."

"Oh, come on," he mumbled, abashed.

"Seriously. I'm not exaggerating," she said. "That's how it was for me. I never thought I had such a creative sexual imagination. Now I know that, in fact, I don't. At all. That was your imagination, not mine."

"Um . . ." His face was hot, in the darkness. "Sorry."

"Stop apologizing. What I'm saying is, if I go inside the Citadel, I can't answer for the consequences."

He stared up into the darkness, a big, stupid grin tugging at his cheeks. "Are you threatening me?" he asked, wondering.

She draped herself across his chest. Even in the pitch dark, he could swear he saw that subtle Mona Lisa smile on her face.

"Are you scared?" she asked.

"Shitless," he said bluntly.

She cupped his cheek. Kissed him.

It was like his heart burst in his chest, and the light of the flash-pop startled them both, but only for a moment. Then the kiss yanked them deep into itself, wild and sweet and tempest-tossed, each launching a tender, frantic assault upon the other to taste more, feel more, know more. He wanted to crawl inside her soul, drink light, heat, life from her soft mouth, and oh God. He had . . . to . . . *stop*.

He dragged himself away, gasping for breath. "No." Lust and frustration made his voice harsh.

She went stiff, tried to pull away, but he locked his arm around her. "No," he said. "You stay right here. In my arms, in my mind. I don't care if it turns you on. Be turned on. Just get some sleep, someplace safe. And do not tease me. I've had enough."

"Or else what?" she said, peevishly. "Mr. Masterful."

He laughed. "Tell you what. We get you fed up, healed up, we find someplace safe, solve your problems, and then, I will offer myself up as a sex slave. Okay? Whatever, wherever, whenever you want. Until then, I'm concentrating on keeping you alive, and getting enough sleep is part of that enterprise. You get me?"

She was silent for a moment. "I want it in writing."

"Huh?"

"The sex slave bit," she said. "In writing."

He was grinning so hard now, his cheeks actually ached. "I'll get it notarized for you," he promised. "Inside. Now."

She shifted, snuggling closer, and draped her slender leg between his. He sensed her fierce concentration in the stillness—and ah, yes, there she was. The sweet bright glow, in the Lara place, flicking on.

The incredible intimacy of the contact sent a fresh surge of lust surging through him. He hauled himself back. By brute force.

It took a long time for her to drop off, but eventually, he felt the change as her breathing slowed, steadied. The quality of Lara light changed, from a bright focused point to a glowing, diffuse cloud.

That glow was so beautiful. It felt almost like being happy. Or at least, it felt like one tiny, perfect fragment of happiness. A sweet, perfect oasis, surrounded on all sides by a blasted wasteland of terror and danger.

He spent hours staring up into the darkness, hot-eyed. Slowly stroking the silken coils of her hair that lay on his chest. Challenging the monsters in the darkness, as he listened to her breathe. Slow, steady.

Celebrating each single individual breath as a personal victory.

17

*T*he sun was hot against her skin. The grass she lay in was soft, fragrant, tickling her cheek, rustling in the wind. This meadow was one of her favorite places in the Citadel, which was full of shifting rooms, realms, landscapes. The weather constantly changed according to the mercurial moods of its gorgeous, brooding inhabitant.

For whom she waited, breathlessly.

He appeared out of the trees that bounded the clearing. Tall and strong, dark hair blowing back from his face in the wind. Dark eyes, ardent and glowing with purpose. Fixed on her. Focused utterly on her.

He moved toward her as she rose from her nest of crushed grass and flowers. The white dress fluttered in the wind, flattening against her legs, revealing every detail of her body.

A blatant offering, and he wasted no time taking her up on it. He seized her, urgent, wordless. Jerked the bodice of the dress down to bare her breasts. She struggled to free her elbows from the sleeves, but he kept her trapped, wiggling against his hard body as he kissed her, his hands moving eagerly over bare skin, thin fabric, making her shiver and sigh.

His tongue moved in her mouth, probing and questing. She

was still struggling to free her arms when he dragged up her skirt, and made a growling sound in the back of his throat when he found her naked beneath. He slid his hand between her legs, stroking tenderly to bring forth her slick lube. She'd been soft, wet. Aching for him before he even appeared.

She fought her arms free, and abandoned herself to his kiss, to his skillful hand, the heat of his erection pressing her belly.

She sank to her knees, groping at the opening of his pants. Hungry to hold and lick and play with his hot, thick cock. It sprang out, swollen, jutting red and thick from its nest of hair. She clutched at the broad stiff shaft with both hands, stroking from root to tip, wetting her hands with saliva. Swirling her tongue around and around, tonguing that broad, velvety smooth cockhead. Lapping and lashing with joyful enthusiasm.

He guided her head to take him deeper, and she slowed down and drew him inside; long, swirling strokes that left his cock gleaming, shiny, the thick veins snaking around, blazing an angry red. He withdrew with a harsh groan, prying away her clutching hands, and turned her, pushing her around, pushing until she stumbled down into the thick grass, on her hands and knees, skirt flung up over her back. Arching back to meet him.

He waited, sliding his cock tenderly around, a teasing dip and swirling push, a slow slide down the length of her slit, petting each slick, shivering fold and crevice, bathing himself in her lube. Circling, stroking, so careful and deliberate, so sure of himself. Teasing, circling, swirling.

Driving her mad. She shoved back against him, demanding more.

Finally, he slid inside. It was slow, deliberate, delicious. His thick cock plumbing her depths, swiveling, pressing over every hot spot. Remolding her body with each delicious dip and stir, swirl and thrust—

She woke up in the dark, disoriented. Convulsing. Throbbing pleasure, as she clamped jealously around—

Him. Oh, God, him. Miles' naked body was plastered to

her backside. His cock was thrust deep inside her from behind.

She was so startled, she cried out. Miles woke up, and let out a sharp gasp. "Oh, God. Lara, I—"

"Please," she gasped out.

He started to withdraw. "I'm sorry. I swear, I didn't mean to—"

"No!" She shoved herself back so that his erection slid heavily inside her once again. "Don't you leave me! Don't you dare!"

He was frozen, confused for a second, then he made a wordless sound in the back of his throat, rolled her onto her belly and jerked her up into the same hands and knees position she'd had in the dream.

He thrust. She was primed for it, bracing herself as his body thudded against her, stroking himself voluptuously over that bright sweet place deep inside, and it glowed, swelling to ripeness—

A profound explosion of heat, light, color, in her depths.

He let go along with her, emptying himself, and collapsed on top of her. Aftershocks jolted through them both.

After a minute, Miles rolled onto his side, taking her with him. He didn't leave her body. In fact, he was still hard. He pressed his hand low on her belly, to keep them tightly joined. His breath still came fast.

"I don't know how that happened," he said. "I was fast asleep. I know it sounds like a raft of total bullshit, but I swear to God—"

"I warned you," she said.

He laughed. The vibration shivered through her, where their bodies were joined. "I don't know how to control it," he said. "Not in the dream, anyway. I feel so weird about it."

"About what? What's to control?"

He hesitated. "The vibe," he said. "That arrogant lord of the manor thing that I've got going. Ripping off your

clothes, throwing you on the ground, fucking you from behind. Our dream sex is always like that. I don't even know
myself like that."

"I know you," she said. "And that wasn't fucking. Not in
the dream, and not out of it. I know the difference."

"Hmmph." He sounded unconvinced.

She twisted around, as if she were looking at him, in spite
of the darkness. "Did you feel me come?" she asked.

His answer was slow in coming. "Ah, yeah."

"Yeah," she repeated, with emphasis. "You pleased me."

"Well," he said. "Good. Thank God. At least, that."

"No," she said. "Get it straight. The way you acted? Your
vibe? That's not arrogance. That's the vibe of a man who is
absolutely sure of his welcome. Who trusts his lover. And
knows that she wants him."

Tension still sang in the darkness.

"That's great," he said, after a moment. "For the dreams,
anyway. Where do you go in real life to buy that kind of confidence?"

She found his hand in the darkness, pulled it to her cheek.
Kissed his palm. "You don't," she said. "Because I'm giving
it to you. For free."

She could actually feel his smile lighting up the Citadel,
warming her from the inside. His penis jerked inside her,
sliding deeper.

"God," he muttered. "What a turn-on. Don't get me
started."

"You know I can't stop," she said again. "Explain something to me, Miles. Is it possible that you don't know how totally smoking hot you are?"

He snorted. "Oh, come on. You don't have to say stuff
like—"

"Shut up," she snapped. "And that's completely apart
from the sexy superpowers, and the blazing heroics. I'm
talking, you know, just basic, superficial, droolworthy hubba
hubba."

He was silent, but his hand slid up, cupping her breast, caressing and delicately squeezing her. "Thanks for saying that," he said carefully.

It was clear that he didn't believe a word of it.

Lara shifted, breaking the contact, but only to clamber up on top of him, straddling him. She leaned over, flicked on the light, lifted the cover, draping it over her shoulders against the chill, and gripped his cock, commanding him with her eyes. "Inside," she said. "Now."

He laughed, but held his cock obligingly up, nudging inside her. He arched, with a sharp hiss of pleasure as she slid down onto him.

"Oh. God," he gasped, and then held her still, his big hands clamped hard on her hips. "You must be sore. I'm not moving. Not one muscle. Got that? Are we clear?"

She placed her hands on his chest, letting her dangling hair stroke and tickle him. "I just want you inside me."

"Fine," he said. "I'll put it anywhere you want it, and keep it there as long as you like. But I'm not moving."

She smiled, and he caught his breath, his eyes dazzled. "You're so beautiful like that," he said. "That cover over you. A goddess's mantle. I can't believe you're here with me. On me."

"Believe it," she said. "I need for us both to believe it, because that's exactly how I feel about you. I still don't believe you're real."

He cupped her breasts, hefting them tenderly. Every point of contact was a sweet blushing glow of pleasure, a sweet kiss, a benediction. "I was with this woman, Cindy, for years, and I . . ." His eyes narrowed, doubtful. "Maybe this is inappropriate. Do you mind if I talk about her while I'm, you know, inside of you?"

"I like it when we talk," she said. "It's one of the many things that's even better than the dream sex in the Citadel."

"Oh, really?" His eyes lit with curiosity. "How's that?"

"You never talked in the dreams," she said. "You were always very, um . . . well, focused and purposeful, you might say. But go on. You can say anything to me. You were saying, about this Cindy?"

His grin flashed. "So, yeah. Cindy is the sister of Connor's wife, Erin. I carried a torch for her for years. Ever since college. Then we finally got together, and I thought I'd died and gone to heaven. Until she started cheating on me. Repeatedly. For years."

"Oh." She winced. "That's so awful. I'm sorry."

"She'd cry, and be so sorry, and say she really loved me, and she'd never do it again, yada yada, and then, boom. Again." He shook his head, lost in thought. "I spent all this time agonizing about why I just wasn't enough for her. Hard as I tried. Drove me flipping nuts."

She petted his chest, quietly waiting.

"I finally realized, it was like a joke, or a puzzle with no solution. She would only want me for real if I stopped wanting her. And it did no good to pretend. It didn't count if I faked it. She could tell, somehow."

She nodded. "I'm familiar with the dynamic."

"Anyhow, I don't think it had much to do with me," he said. "It was all about her. How she felt about herself. She hated herself. She had no respect for herself. No amount of love could make up for that."

Lara shivered. "Bad," she whispered. Anabel flashed through her mind, the woman's self-loathing. Along with Lara's own, after all her endless hours locked in the dark with herself, her fears and monsters. "I'm sorry for her. And for you."

"I wasn't asking for pity," he said. "I'm just thinking out loud. I can finally see it for what it is, with you to compare it to. It's so different with you. Even after what you went through, you're so, I don't know. Dignified. Regal. A goddess."

She stirred, uncomfortable. "Please. Now you're overdoing it."

"Really," he said. "It's not just the sex, even though that

totally blows my mind. It's so different to be with someone who knows her worth. That's the only kind of woman who can make a man sure of his welcome. It's in you, Lara. And it's so sexy it fucking kills me."

She dropped kisses upon the taut muscles of his pecs. "Don't build me up into something I'm not," she pleaded. "I'm feeling small right now. Not very worthy. Don't ask me to be a goddess."

"Too late," he said, his hands spanning her waist. He stared at her body, his eyes bright with fascination. "You're regal, and selfless, and brave. And that's apart from being smart, and artistically talented. And did I say anything about gorgeous? Did I mention that?"

"Please." It was her turn, to be uncomfortable. It scared her. A nervous, superstitious fear that if he created this lofty story about her in his mind, he would be disappointed in the stark truth of Lara Kirk. She'd pondered that stark truth for many dark, lonely hours, and it wasn't pretty. She didn't want to even accept it. Let alone share it.

"Like your sculpture. *Persephone's Pride*," he said. "You peer inside the hole in the vase to see her, but even trapped in the dark, she's dignified. She stands so straight. Like a knife blade, with the one ray of light falling on her face. I love that one. She's a princess, and nothing can change that. No wonder Hades totally lost his shit for her."

She pulled the comforter tighter around herself. "Don't invoke her," she said. "Remember. She had to go back to him."

He sat up suddenly, catching her in his arms. "You're not going back to him. I'll see to it."

She let herself be hugged tight against his warmth, trying to be comforted. "Thanks for the sentiment," she said.

"No, really," he said, more forcefully. "I'll die first."

The words made her heart freeze. "Don't," she said, thinly. "I really, really don't want you to die. So please, don't even say it. Don't put that thought out there. Please. Don't."

"I'll do my best," he assured her. "I promise."

As promises went, it was a damn good one. It rang with heartfelt sincerity. And she had seen his best, with her own eyes. His best kicked ass. It was superb. Superhuman, even. But that did not calm her fears.

Not after having seen Thaddeus Greaves' worst.

She wasn't ready to be this brave, to care this much, but she didn't have a choice. She hid her face against his chest, squeezed her legs aound his waist. Sought out the bright safety of the Citadel, in a deft flicker of mental maneuvering. In a moment, she was in.

The safest place in the universe, for everything but her heart.

Oh, God. This was bad. She didn't fear death anymore, after the rat hole. She didn't fear solitude, or hunger, or pain, or even madness. She'd come so close to being free of caring about anything. She'd had nothing on earth left to lose, except for her own body. Everyone she cared about, gone. Nothing left to fear.

And hey, presto, out of nowhere, she had just acquired a whole new set of things to be terrified of losing.

And wasn't that just fucking perfect.

Greaves paused by the window, struggling for patience. Crushing the man's mind in a temper would yield him nothing, but he was so angry. He reminded himself of the results of his anger at Geoff. He'd lost control, and look how that had turned out. Disaster.

Easy does it. Don't kill the goose.

"Tell me about his speech patterns," he said to Hu. "I'm still astonished you didn't have the audio in her cell. I can't imagine what possessed you to turn it off. Start at the beginning."

He turned to meet Hu's dim, bloodshot eyes. The man drooped like a wilted flower, head slack on his chest. A judicious zap of coercion jolted the man's spine, straightening it with a jerk.

Hu whimpered. His battered face was almost unrecognizable. His broken arm hung useless, his hand hugely swollen and empurpled.

"Jason," Greaves said gently, "sharpen up. Again, from the top. And perhaps I will let you have some painkillers."

"Yes. Ah . . . the tire blew. In the mountains," Hu faltered. "I stopped to change it. That must have been when he got into the trunk of my car, but I just don't understand how I didn't feel it, or hear him, or something. He was huge. Enormous, six seven at least—"

"Just under six five, according to the video from Kirk's cell," Greaves corrected. "Do not exaggerate. It is unhelpful."

"Ah, no, sir. And he said . . . he said—"

"What was his accent?" Greaves prompted. "East coast, Midwest, Northwest? California? New York? Southern? Foreign?" He'd tried to hear the attacker's speech in Hu's stored memories, but Hu's brain was not wired particularly well to retain aural impressions.

"I didn't notice any accent at all, so I'm guessing West Coast."

"Guessing," Greaves said. "I did not hire you to guess, Jason."

"Sir, I'm sorry. I—"

"So at the car park, he grabbed you and put the gun to your head. And then?"

Hu stumbled and stuttered once again through his pathetic litany of failure, defeat, and betrayal. Whimpering cravenly while the attacker had slashed all the tires in the garage and gutted the security center. As if he had not had a single opportunity to raise the alarm.

Worthless, gutless, ball-less turd.

But he listened carefully, for the umpteenth time, trolling for that one fragment of information that might yield some new avenue of inquiry. He had reamed the man's brain telepathically three times, now. The smallest detail that Hu was too stupid to see as salient could be the key to everything.

"He was so strong," Hu whimpered, tears bubbling in his nose.

It was painful to watch. Greaves walked to the sideboard for a cup of coffee, upping the volume on a newscast that played on the computer monitor, so as not to hear the man's wet, phlegmy gasps for breath.

A map of Oregon was on the screen. He stared at it, mentally superimposing all the roads and byways the thieves might have taken.

How had they gotten past his telepathic sentinels? He'd posted people on every exit from all the roads they might have taken. His range was enormous, but even he had to narrow them down to within a five-mile radius before he could telepathically sweep with any effectiveness.

". . . in her psi-max visions." Hu's voice, somewhat steadier.

"Excuse me?" He looked at Hu.

Hu was staring at the newscast. "The terrorist attack," he said. "In Tokyo. Lara must have called them and told them about the bomb. She was always on me and Anabel about that. Begging us to tip them off."

Greaves shook his head angrily. "Call who?" he snarled. "What the hell are you talking about?"

Hu jerked his chin toward the screen. "The bomb. At the train station in Tokyo. They found it just in time. Lara kept seeing it in her visions. It would have taken out a big chunk of the central Tokyo train station."

". . . an anonymous tip," said the attractive Asian female newscaster. "This tip led to the recovery of a duffel bag of explosives on a commuter train, which was discovered at two this afternoon. There is no information yet as to who is responsible for the bomb, and the investigation is ongoing.

An amazing story, with hundreds if not thousands of lives saved—"

Greaves muted the audio and turned back to Hu. "You mean to tell me that you and Anabel knew about a terrorist plot to blow up the Tokyo train station, and you did *nothing?*"

Hu looked confused. "But, ah . . . well, at first, we didn't know if she was having true visions, or . . . and with the secrecy we need to maintain for you, we just assumed—"

"Two gifted, highly trained minds put together, and you could not eke out enough creativity between you to come up with a way to discreetly, safely notify the authorities in Tokyo about this bomb?"

Hu's mouth worked frantically. "Ah . . . ah—"

"Don't." Greaves held up his hand. "There's nothing to say. You don't care about my mission. You don't care about the health and well-being of the people in the world around you. You are self-interested, thick and heartless. And you do not belong on my staff."

Hu sagged, panting in short, ragged breaths, which Greaves, with his heightened senses, could not fail to smell from across the room. The wretched man lifted his eyes. Awareness of his impending death was clearly written there. Greaves did not even need telepathy to read it.

Luckily, as he did not have the stomach for it.

"Sir," Hu said, his voice weary, but clear. "Please, just tell me. The attacker said he'd changed the info in the database. The suxamethonium. For my wife's surgery. Please. Do you have any news about her?"

"You mean, is she dead from malignant hyperthermia, as your ogre threatened? No. The ogre was bluffing, Jason. He evidently has a kinder heart and more scruples than you do. Willing to let hundreds die in a pointless explosion, for the love of God."

Hu sagged in relief. Tears trickled down his face. "Is she . . . did they—"

"Remove the tumor? Certainly. She's still in intensive care. Doing well, all things considered, from what I was told. Asking for you, poor woman. Oh, good God, Hu, don't start crying again."

"Thank you, sir," Hu said, brokenly.

"Don't," Greaves snapped. "Your ogre might have been bluffing, but I do not, Hu. Since this woman is clearly the only thing you care about, there is only one appropriate punishment for you."

Hu started shaking his head. "No," he said, wagging it back and forth as if he could not stop. "No, no, no. Please don't hurt her."

"Don't worry, Hu." Greaves smiled. "You'll be there to greet her."

"But I . . ." Hu's voice broke off, as he fought for breath.

But there was no more breath. Greaves had caught him on the exhale, and would not allow his diaphragm to descend.

But it took many tedious, long minutes to asphyxiate, and such a lengthy period of twitching was unpleasant right before lunch. So he applied a telekinetic clamp onto the man's heart, too, squeezing vessels shut, stilling the pump. He felt the man's organs with his psi senses, fighting to continue their functions, and tightened his grip.

Hu's face contorted with agony. He fell from the chair, lay sprawled on the floor. The twitches slowed, stilled.

Greaves walked over and stared down, sickened. He nudged at the man's face with the toe of his shoe. Hu's staring eyes were spotted with broken blood vessels. Greaves could feel no vibration, no trace of mental activity. No hiss of labored breath, no thud of a heartbeat.

He hit the mute button on the computer to stop the female newscaster's yapping, and hit the intercom on his wrist. "Levine."

"Yes, sir?" she replied.

"Who do we have on the Tokyo police department?"

"I will look that up for you, sir."

"Be quick about it." Stupid bitch. All that enhancement, and she couldn't even keep their bribe roster straight in her head.

She was efficient in her information retrieval, fortunately for her, considering his state of mind. In less than a minute, she was back.

"Sir? We have a Lieutenant Tanada in Tokyo."

"Get him on the phone. Immediately."

"Right away, sir."

He put some distance between himself and Hu, and the unpleasant odors seeping into the room as the dead man's bowels relaxed. "And send a cleaning crew in here, too."

"Of course, sir."

Greaves sipped his coffee, more to mask that unpleasant smell than from a desire for coffee. He mused upon his own behavior. He tried to be stern and uncompromising with himself, as well as his staff, to hold himself to the same high standard, and he had to admit that it had been rather spiteful, tormenting Hu with threats to his wife right before executing him. Perhaps he would let the woman live after all. After having probed her mind, for the sake of security. If she was clean.

But he had been sorely proven. Saving the ungrateful world from its own worst self was thankless work, and he could expect no reward other than the personal awareness of a job well done.

For God's sake. With the effort he made, and the stress he faced, he was entitled to a little tantrum now and then.

18

"Shut up, asshole."

John Esposito spat the words over his shoulder as he negotiated the hairpin turn on the mountain road. He rubbed the sore spot on his knee. He wasn't usually so bad tempered on a job, but Franz, the target's asshole boyfriend, had put up an unexpectedly good fight, and John was feeling it, being no spring chicken. Franzie boy had gotten in a vicious kick to the knee during their brief tussle. Of course, Franz was no match for John, who was unmoved by pain while in combat. He felt it, but did not give a shit, not while he was working.

Afterward was a different matter. He gave a shit now, after two hours sitting in a car, driving up here from Seattle with that crybaby piece of shit trussed in the back, blubbering through his gag.

It was going to be very tough on Franzie boy if the directions he'd finally coughed up about Keiko's hidey-hole were incorrect. Stakes were high on this one. Pay was great, if things happened very fast. His client needed conclusion by mid-afternoon. If things didn't work out, pay dropped to zero. With the added implicit threat of a bullet to the head, of course. Live by the sword, die by the sword, and who gave a fuck.

But today would not be his day. Today was the day for frisky Franzie, with his fucking Tae Kwon Do roundhouse. Sobbing pussy sonofabitch. And here was the place. Conveniently isolated. Not much of a hideout, considering that it was Keiko's boss's vacation property, and that he'd blabbed his location to the big-mouthed pussy boyfriend.

John pulled on his mask, negotiated the long driveway, and parked. An attractive lodge-style mountain retreat, huge windows with views of the mountains. He did not see video-cameras. He got out of the Jeep, deciding to stick with plan A, using the mask just in case.

He heard not a peep. Just the wind in the trees. Keiko was cowering in the house, peeking out a window. No idea what to do.

John jerked on heavy-duty rubber gloves. He pulled the back open, hauled out the duct-taped Franz, dumped him onto the concrete. He wrenched the tape off the man's mouth, and pried out the slimy little ball, sticking it back into his pocket for later.

Franz gulped for air. John grabbed him by the scruff of the neck, and pressed a gun to the nape of his neck. "Call him," he commanded.

"Huh? Who?" Franz was purple, disoriented from lack of oxygen.

"Call Keiko, shit-for-brains. Now." John grabbed the guy's balls, and squeezed. Hard enough to repay the kick to the knee.

Franz shrieked and complied, calling out his boyfriend's name.

It took Keiko about twenty seconds to come to the door. John smiled at the sight. No problem here. Asian pretty boy, long shining hair, rolling eyes, girlish hands. Clutching a kitchen knife. Oh, please.

"What have you done to him?" Keiko's voice was shrill, shaking.

"Nothing yet." John strode toward him. "Give me time."

Keiko actually did attempt to use the knife, making a few amateurish slashes, but a smooth parry, grab, torque, and the weapon flew to the ground, bouncing. John sprayed the guy briskly with knock-out juice, held Keiko still until it took, and dragged him inside.

It took some muscle and creativity to set the scene. First Keiko had to be firmly bound into a chair, hand and foot. The chair was placed strategically in front of the big beam, from which hung a wrought iron medieval-style chandelier. Very handy, that.

John hung up the silken noose, and went about the business of persuading Franz to stand up straight on the stool, and put his head into it, which he was understandably reluctant to do. A few feints at cutting off Keiko's ears got him moving, and eventually, there he was, jaybird naked, clothes sliced off. Gagged and duct-taped.

Just in time for Keiko to wake up and start freaking out.

John didn't really have to do all that much to Franzie to get results. It was clear that Keiko would tell him anything, but sadly for Franzie, he did not seem to have much to tell. Just that Lara Kirk had called late last night, after being missing for months, and had begged him to call the Tokyo police department and tip them off about a bomb set to blow, which he had subsequently done. The number was on his smartphone. That was all he knew. He repeated himself frantically.

John located the smartphone in question. Indeed, there was the number. And no, Keiko did not know her location. John made very sure of that. To Franzie's great cost.

It was clear, based on his experience with interrogation, that Keiko was telling the truth. No more info would be forthcoming.

Clean-up time.

John set to it, meticulously careful to see that the appropriate fingerprints and genetic material were deposited on the right items. Keiko's boss was in for a shock. Handy, that there were no neighbors to hear the screaming, or the gunshot.

He cleaned and put away the kitchen knife Keiko had dropped, moving carefully and deliberately. Every move thought through, like a game of chess. His trademark was "no mistakes." He scrubbed and exfoliated himself before every job, wore latex, shaved his head and body. Never left even the faintest trace of himself behind.

He seeded Keiko's car with a few extreme S&M magazines, as he had done in Keiko's apartment. He left also a small laptop, bought used and reconfigured, with rough gay porn sites bookmarked on it. To explain the bruises, the ligature marks.

Once the work was done, he called the contact.

"What have you got?" she demanded.

"A cell phone number," he said.

"That's all? We needed an address! We have a time crunch here!"

"She didn't give him an address when she called," John said. "With your contacts, you can find the location with the number more quickly than I can. I did what I was told to do, and I expect to be paid."

"Give me the number," the woman grumbled. "Have the phone couriered to the Portland address. Immediately."

"Agreed." John rattled off the phone number.

"What's the status of Keiko Yamada?" the woman asked.

"Dead," John said. "He was playing nasty S&M games with his boyfriend. Sexual asphyxiation game gone tragically wrong. He shot himself, out of guilt and remorse. True love, and all. Poignant."

"Hmmph." The woman's snort was heavy with disapproval. "Sounds news-mongering to me. I would have preferred a simple missing-person case."

"You wanted info, not just a simple hit," John said, through his teeth. "I fished for it. That's messy, and the mess has to be accounted for. It doesn't just disappear."

The bitch hemmed and hawed, but finally gave him the transfer number before breaking the connection.

That quantity of money transferred into his bank account had a salutory effect on his aching knee. In fact, the pain vanished.

He got a rush of energy from it, so much so, he was sorry he'd already dispatched poor Keiko and Franz. Usually, John preferred to conduct celebratory fun and games with women.

But he could be flexible.

Sun streamed through the blinds when Miles opened his eyes.

He was disoriented. Hardly knew who the hell he was, waking up in a soft, warm bed, in a bright room, no pain in his head, no tension in his body. And a silken soft fragrant angel in his arms.

Wow. It was real. *She* was real. Holy fuck. It blew his mind.

She rolled to face him, eyes fluttering open. Her gaze seemed both bold and shy. It gave a sweet, bright rush to all his senses, a sudden sense of opening deep inside himself. Like arms thrown wide.

Joy pulsed through his body, and suddenly they were wrapped in each other's arms, clutching, knotted. Kissing madly.

The kiss was revving into something inevitable, but he dragged himself back from the brink and grabbed his phone from the bedside table to check the time. "Holy shit," he said. "It's after two thirty."

She jerked up. "Wow. Really? We slept, what, fourteen hours?"

"You needed it," he said. "I'm just surprised at myself. I haven't slept more than a couple hours at a stretch for months. Are you still, ah . . ." He put his attention to that part of his mind that he'd begun to think of as hers, not his own. Their secret point of contact.

Ahhh, yes. He basked in that bright glow. A constant source of pleasure. Maybe that was what had zapped his headache. The Lara Kirk mind meld. Good medicine.

She smiled at him, sat up, letting the comforter fall. Ah, man. Not fair.

still inside appeared on his inner screen. no worries.

He laughed, in delight, and responded the same way. awesome. works even in deep REM sleep. just stay there now its safer

love 2. u dont have 2 tell me 2X

dont ever leave, he invited.

tempting, she replied.

whos tempting who? 4 the love of god put on ur shirt

She laughed at him. Her low, husky laugh was so sexy. It took all his self-control not to just roll over on top of her and mount up.

But the day was more than half gone, they were in mortal danger, there were decisions to be made, actions to be taken. To say nothing of a houseful of twitchy, judgmental people downstairs, twiddling their thumbs, looking at their watches.

It was past three by the time they were both decent. Lara insisted that she felt well enough to come downstairs, but her face was rosy as she followed him down the stairs and into the kitchen.

She looked awesome in the teal-blue pile sweatshirt and jeans, and purple high-top kicks that Aaro had gotten for her. Hair still damp, face pink. Lips, too. So pretty.

Aaro was in the kitchen, his habitual disapproving scowl carved into his face. Sean looked Lara over, glanced side-wise at Miles, and nodded. "Looking good," he said. "She's got color. Breakfast?"

"Please," Miles said, fervently.

He was stonily ignored by all, but a parade of food appeared anyhow. Fluffy scrambled eggs, sausage, home-fried rosemary potatoes, toasted English muffins, fresh orange juice, coffee. Sean set a place for Lara at the table, and was deferential and charming with his gigolo/major domo routine, serving her food, urging her to eat.

No one urged Miles, or brought him a plate or fork. Sean left the loaded serving plates on the table and fussed exclusively over Lara, letting Miles slink into the kitchen to scrounge for his own dishes and flatwear. Still in the doghouse. He was lucky they didn't make him lie under the table and beg her for scraps. But he wasn't inclined to get his feelings hurt today. He was floating, like he was attached to a hot air balloon. The balloon was that soft Lara glow in his head.

The other guys were filing on by made-up errands, intent on checking out Lara, watching her eat. She got down more food than she had the night before, plus a whole glass of orange juice. Progress.

Miles turned to his own refueling, loading up his plate with eggs. Protein, lay it on him. Fried potatoes, glory halleluia. He guzzled orange juice, wallowing in the citrusy, liquid-sugar orgasm. Drank one sip of coffee, and put the cup right down, instantly concluding that his adrenal glands did not need their asses kicked any further by caffeine.

Food had never tasted so fucking good.

He didn't start slowing down until after his third plate. He'd polished off all the eggs, all the potatoes, and was eyeing the last English muffin on the plate when he noticed six pairs of eyes, all staring at him. Including Lara's. She was trying not to smile.

"What?" he demanded. "Never seen a guy eat before?"

Connor cleared his throat. "Not like that."

The faint, far-off sound made him leap into the air. The other men jumped to attention in reaction to him. Guns appeared in all hands as Miles lunged for the window, twitching back the curtain. He'd left his Glock upstairs, and was cursing himself for a sloppy brainless fool until he caught a flashing glimpse of the vehicle through the distant trees.

Air rushed back into his lungs. "Tam's car," he said. "She's driving. Nina's in the front, Edie's in back."

"You heard the car from here? And saw it?" Aaro peered out the window, disgruntled. "I can barely see it, let alone identify it as Tam's."

Miles was weak kneed with relief. So it wasn't going to be mortal combat right after breakfast. Give him time, for the love of God. Time to find a place to keep her safe before engaging with that prick again.

"Nina? You said Nina's here?" Lara's voice broke in on his reverie.

"Coming up the driveway now," he told her.

Before he could say a word, Lara was out the door, pelting across the meadow in front of the house toward the big curve of the driveway. Out in the open, under a huge, threatening sky, where anyone could see her, snatch her, put her in the crosshairs of their fucking sniper rifle. He bolted after, irrational panic clutching him.

Tam's car came around the bend and braked. The passenger side flew open, and Nina sprang out and sprinted toward Lara.

They came together in a tight, shaking hug.

Tam and Edie climbed out, stopping at a discreet distance. Miles waited, too. They were crying, for God's sake. He'd wait until they'd slogged through it. At least this sob fest was one that he didn't have to navigate. But they took their goddamned sweet time, babbling and weeping. He tried not to listen in with his souped-up hearing.

It was really hard not to listen when you *could*.

After an inappropriately long time, he started to fidget and twitch. Jesus, out in the open, exposed on all sides. Of course, they were backed up by several tough guys with guns who had all filed out to watch the floor show, but that meant nothing. There was no reason the cathartic, girly sob-fest could not take place indoors on a comfy couch.

"Uh, Lara? Nina?" he ventured. "Could we, like, take it inside?"

The women ignored him. "Thanks for looking for me," Lara was whispering soggily. "Thanks for sending Miles."

Nina lifted her eyes, fixed them on Miles. "I didn't send him, honey. I would've, if I could, but I can't take credit for that. He did that on his own. All of it. With no help from us."

Miles clearly heard the acerbic tang of reproof in her voice.

"Ladies?" he said again, plaintively. "Can we take this in-side? Please? I could use some cover. This is making me ner-vous."

"I just bet it is." Nina let go of Lara and strode toward him with purpose. "I have just two things to say to you, Miles Davenport."

Miles took a wary step backward. "Uh, let's hear them."

"They're both non-verbal." She reached out, gave him a fierce, tight, shaking hug. Then just as abruptly, she stepped back, hauled off and whacked him hard in the face, *smack*. A bruising open-hand.

"Fuck!" He reeled back. "Jesus, Nina! What was that about?"

Lara ran toward them. "Nina? What the hell are you doing?"

"I am so pissed at him!" Nina's voice vibrated with fury. "Well and good that he saved you, but he is an opportunistic son of a *bitch* for seducing you right after!" She turned on Miles, cherry red with anger. "You might have waited! Even a few days would have been less indecent, for God's sake! But I imagine your dick wanted what it wanted, right? You thought you had the right? You saved her, so you get to fuck her? Was that how it was? You *dickhead!*"

Miles pressed his hand to his stinging cheek, and opened

his mouth to say he knew absolutely not what, but Lara broke in, leaping in front of him. A human shield.

"Do not hit him!" she yelled. "Not ever, Nina! You hear me?"

Nina pressed her fist to her shaking mouth. Her eyes were wet. "He shouldn't have done that! He shouldn't even have *looked* at you!"

"It wasn't up to him! I jumped on him with all four feet! He had no choice!"

Tam snorted, giving Miles a mocking once-over. "Awww, poor little Miles. Forced, were you? Did she have to tie you down?"

"Fuck off, Tam," he growled, licking blood off his lip, which Nina's lusty blow had smashed against his tooth.

"If I were wrecked and broken, you might have a point, but I'm not!" Lara raged on. "Do you get it? They did not wreck me!"

Nina cupped Lara's face. "Okay," she crooned. "Okay, okay, I believe you. Good for you, sweetheart." And they melted into a sobbing embrace once again. Miles was blessedly forgotten. Thank God.

Not by Tam, though. She sauntered toward Miles, giving him one of her X-ray stares, the ones where she read every fear and doubt and fatal fault line. She then turned the same stare onto Lara, who met it squarely, over Nina's shoulder. After a minute, Tam nodded, having come to one of her inscrutable conclusions.

"Leave them alone, Nina," she said. "Look at her eyes, her color. She's all right. He's doing his duty." Miles flinched as she smacked the same reddened cheek Nina had slapped. "It's about time, big boy. Glad to see you finally misbehaving like a man." She punctuated her statement by swatting his ass, very hard.

"Hey!" Miles backed away. "Public service announcement. Next person who slaps me, I slap back. Girl or no girl." He glanced at Lara. "Except for you," he amended.

"You can slap me any time you want. Thanks for sticking up for me."

Her eyes swept down as a subtle smile quivered on her lips. "Least I could do. You were such a good sport about being tied down."

Miles gaped, and turned his gaze wildly upon the other women. "Uh, that was a joke," he told them hastily. "You get that, right?"

That cracked them all up.

He suffered through the snickering and chortling as they walked back to the house, but his discomfort melted away like magic when Lara grabbed his hand, a defiant, possessive gesture. Her slender hand was cool, her narrow fingers closing around his, jealously tight.

Staking her claim. He liked it. Let them mock and scold and slap and kick him around like a fucking soccer ball.

When she touched him like that, he could feel no pain.

19

Lara rocked in Nina's tight embrace and groped in her pocket for a tissue. It did something strange to her, seeing Nina after all these years. She'd worshipped the older girl as a child. And though they weren't blood relatives, Nina was the only person left with whom she shared actual memories of her mother. It made Mother feel closer, somehow. More real. It had been such a sad, remote feeling, being the last repository of memories for a person. Like being lost in space.

Problem was, this warm fuzzy stuff melted her to mush. Nobody seemed to judge her for it, but still. She quelled another wave of emotion. "I can't believe how different you look." She stared at the bright, fitted sweater Nina wore. "I always thought you were pretty, but you wore baggy dark clothes, so I never knew you had a hot figure, too."

"Oh, well. Aaro insists." Nina darted a smile at her guy, Aaro, who sat on the couch near them. He was tongue-tied and uncomfortable, but clearly unwilling to be more than a few feet from his lady. Even if she was hugging the sobbing girl. Tough-guy Kryptonite.

Miles was seated on the other side of her, twitching with

discomfort and embarrassment, but whenever he made a move to go, she grabbed his hand and yanked him right back down. *Nope. Plant your ass right here, buddy. Do not move it one inch.* Everyone needed to get the non-verbal cue that she had not gone to rack and ruin, she was not a poor, broken girl that Miles had taken advantage of in her moment of weakness. Hell, no. None of his fierce friends would dare to slap or scold him if she was clutching his hand in a white-knuckled death grip.

So there, everyone. Take that. She hung on. He was all hers.

Hours had gone by since Nina, Tam, and Edie had arrived. Big platters of deli sandwiches had appeared on the table at one point, and Miles had nagged and poked and prodded until she'd successfully gotten around half of a turkey and swiss, and another glass of juice.

The room was packed. It was an overwhelming number of people, after months of solitude with only occasional vicious attacks from Hu and Anabel to break the monotony, and she and Miles were the main attraction. But damn, out of nowhere, a group of smart, brave strangers had saved her and borne her up. How crazy and improbable was that.

She would endure their focused attention if it killed her. She fished for the tissue again.

"You okay?" Miles leaned in close.

She nodded. "Need more tissues," she muttered.

"I'll go and look for—"

"No!" She yanked him back. "Don't go anywhere. Sorry to be clingy, but just . . . just stay put. I'd rather just leak."

"Uh, okay." He sank back down, lifted her hand to his lips, kissed it. Eight people in the room took notice, and exchanged meaningful glances. The stunning redhead with the tight bun and the skintight black clothes, the one they called Tam, clapped her hands briskly.

"Time for one of Edie's drawings," she announced. "We

need to speed things up. Do you know about Edie's drawings?"

Lara looked up at Edie, who had been introduced as Kev's wife. She was tall and slim, with a long, loose, dark braid and a gentle smile. Very pretty, in an understated way. "Know what?"

"I have this ability," Edie explained. "Maybe a tiny bit like yours. When I draw, I see things about the people I'm drawing for. Sometimes they can be useful. It's not a precision instrument, but it can help."

"It only happens when you draw?" Lara asked.

Edie nodded. "It only runs on that channel."

Lara sighed. "I wish I could pick a channel. When it comes on me, it's more like an epileptic seizure."

"We can probably help you with that," Nina said. "We've been working on blocking techniques, control issues. Me, Aaro, Edie. We'll help you out. We'll work on it together."

She tried to smile, but her smile felt weighted down. She had a hard time imagining what kind of conscious control could keep her from tripping when the pull started to suck her down into the vortex.

"Thanks, I guess," she said, faintly.

"Of course, when it comes to shields, nobody beats Super-Miles," Aaro said, sourly. "The magical boy that no bullet can kill."

Edie serenely ignored him. "So? Can I draw for you, Lara?"

Lara stared for a moment, blankly. Still unaccustomed to the idea of her wishes being considered. She stammered a little. "Ah . . . sure."

Edie still hesitated. "Sometimes it's scary."

Lara just looked at her. Edie broke eye contact, her face reddening. "Um, sorry. Forget I said that. Stupid of me."

"It's okay," Lara said quietly. "Go ahead."

A hush came over the room as Edie started to draw. It was

quiet enough to hear the scratch of the pencil on paper. Everyone seemed afraid to breathe. Clearly, they all took Edie's ability very seriously.

Kev, Edie's husband, the scarred twin of the one they called Sean, came over and sat next to his wife. Val, too, came over, sliding his arms around Tam, from behind. Nina grabbed Aaro's hand.

Lara glanced at Miles. Her gaze stuck on him. Those beautiful, soulful dark eyes, so charged with emotion. His gorgeous, battered face.

He held out his arms to her, and she moved into them with such a feeling of magnetic inevitability, it made her heart shake.

She huddled there, folded up tight, her head beneath his chin. Blocking everything out but his warmth, his scent, his heartbeat.

Sometime later, she sensed the breathless tension in the room resolve. She looked up. Edie stared down at her sketchbook with a puzzled frown. Kev pondered it, too, over her shoulder, his mouth grim. Neither of them seemed to like what they saw.

Gee. Why was she not surprised.

The others were clustering around, peering at the sketch with various expressions of perplexity.

Lara held out her hand. Edie passed the sketchbook over.

It was a sharp icicle-in-the-belly feeling, to see something from inside her head externalized. She'd witnessed this scene over and over. It was as disturbing rendered on paper as it had been in her head.

It was a freeze-frame from the worst vignette in her weird sleepwalker vision. The woman in the pink shirt staring out the window, hair uncombed, mouth slack, eyes vacant, while behind her, the toddler wailed desperately in her crib.

Superimposed over the woman's head was another drawing, an odd, ball-shaped thing with tiny tentacle-like protuberances all over it, like an illustration in a biology book. She had no clue what it could be.

She looked up into their expectant faces, and cleared her throat, trying to make her voice loud enough for all of them to hear.

"This is a scene from one of my recurring visions," she said. She glanced at Miles. "I had it last night, along with the Tokyo bomb one, remember? It starts in a city park, and things seem normal, but it's too quiet, and the grass is too long, and deer are grazing in the park. And people are just sitting there, or lying on the ground. Maybe alive, maybe dead. Then I see . . . her." She indicated the woman in the sketch. "But I don't know about that thing that's drawn on top."

"It looks like a virus," Kev said. "I'll identify it, if I can."

"Another terrorist attack, maybe?" Miles offered. "With biological weapons?"

"Could be," she said, reluctantly. What a horrible thought.

"Another? What do you mean, another?" Con's voice was sharp. "You mean there was one already?"

"One she stopped," Miles said. "Tokyo. Last night."

"Oh, yeah," Nina's eyes widened. "We heard on the radio when we were driving here from Portland that they evacuated the main train station in downtown Tokyo, and the bomb squad found enough explosives on a train to blow up . . ." Her voice trailed off, as she looked into Lara's eyes. "Wait," she said. "You mean, that was you? The anonymous tip?"

"Yeah," Miles said. "She got a Japanese friend to call for her."

"Keiko, this guy I hung out with in high school," she explained, suddenly on the defensive. "He has no connection to my life in San Francisco. He lives in Seattle. I figured, why would Greaves or anyone make the connection? A bomb in Tokyo, and me? Why?"

She looked around at the faces of the men in the room.

The sense of growing dread in the air. No one would meet her eyes.

"She had to call," Miles said, more forcefully. "The bomb was going to go off in a matter of hours. There was no time to lose."

God, how she loved him. Never more than in that moment. Their clasped fingers tightened.

"I'm not saying she should not have called," Davy said. "I'm saying you should have told us. And we should have ground the fucking phone into powder and hauled ass out of here. Last night."

"Why would this high school friend in Seattle calling with an anonymous tip pop up on Greaves' radar?" Miles protested.

"Don't even ask. Did he at least understand what he was messing with?" Davy's voice was uncompromising. "Did you warn him?"

"We told him to leave town," Lara said, pressing her hand against the flutter in her belly. "I'm sorry. I was just thinking about the four hundred and seventy-three people who would have been blown to bits. Body parts everywhere. I've seen it so many times. I wanted to stop it. I'm sorry I didn't tell you guys, but I would have done anything."

"Of course you would," Edie said gently. "And so would any of us. And you did save them." She leaned forward, tapping the sketchpad. "Maybe this is another one of the things you can actually change. That's what always tormented me about my ability, that it seemed like I could never change the outcomes. But you did, Lara! This is great news! This is a big victory! Chalk one up for the good guys!"

Lara was deeply suspicious of the impulse to see any ray of hope in this mess. Letting herself be happy seemed like a trap.

She smiled at the woman anyway, appreciating the encouraging thought. "I don't have any hard data for this one, though," she said. "With Tokyo, I had a time, a place. I saw the bomb, the date clock. With this one, all I have is random images of strangers in a park, and a picture of an unidentified virus. And a sense that it's very bad. Even worse than the Tokyo bomb."

"In any case, we need to get out of here," Connor said. "Let's settle on someplace for her to be. We talked about it last night, while you guys were resting. The most fortified places are Tam and Val's place up in Cray's Cove, or Stone Island, with Seth and Raine. We figured we'd drive up with—"

"No," Miles said.

His flat negation silenced the room. As if he had said something shocking.

"Ah . . . Miles?" Nina said carefully. "You do know that Lara needs a safe place to recuperate from—"

"I know damn well what she needs," Miles said. "But these places are not safe. All the physical security in the world won't stop Greaves when he comes down. And he will come down. He'll figure out who I am, if he hasn't already, and he'll finger all of you." He turned to Val and Tam. "You've got Irina and Rachel up at the Cove. You wouldn't be able to protect them if he came after us there. Don't give him any reason to do that. Really. Trust me on this."

Tam's face looked like a marble statue. Val's mouth was flat.

"Same with Stone Island," Miles pressed grimly on. "The security there is useless for our purposes. Who's there, Seth and Raine, their security staff, plus Jesse, and the twins, who are, what, eighteen months old? Same problem. All of you guys with kids, you're already too exposed. He'll be looking at everyone I've ever had social or professional dealings with, and you guys are smeared all over my life."

"Excuse us for that," Aaro muttered.

"Don't be a snotty bitch," Miles said sharply. "That's not what I meant. I appreciate the help you've given me already, and you know it."

"What you're saying is that we can't help you?" Kev asked slowly. "You're saying that you and Lara are better off alone?"

Miles grimaced. "Fuck," he muttered. "I don't mean to sound like an arrogant asshole. We wouldn't have made it out without your help this far. But look at the facts. These people are all enhanced. Nina and Aaro and Edie are the only ones of you all with any practical experience at all in blocking invasive telepathy, and Greaves would smash them like bugs. You felt him, Aaro. You know it's true."

Aaro stared back, stonefaced. Unable to deny it, but too angry and proud to say that Miles was right.

"You can't help us now," Miles went on. "None of you can. You can't even know where we run. It's come to that."

Lara could feel the anger and resistance vibrating in the air. She broke the silence, pulling out the cell. "I've got to call Keiko."

"For Christ's sake!" Miles flared. "Have you been listening?"

"Yes," she said. "The upshot is, we run like hell to someplace no one on earth knows about. Isn't that the plan?"

Miles shrugged. "Such as it is."

"I have to know Keiko is okay first, and I might as well call from this place, since I appear to have already burned it for us. Right?"

A tense silence followed.

"She has a point, at that," Davy said heavily. "Call, then. We all want to know. But hurry. We need to get out of here."

Lara got the number wrong twice, with her shaking, rubbery finger. The phone buzzed and buzzed. Then a recorded voice, telling her the client was unavailable, and to try later.

She met Miles' eyes. Shook her head. The dread got heavier.

"I'll call the magazine he works for," she said. "Can you find the number for me on your smartphone? It's *Beat Street Style* magazine."

Miles' finger tapped, teasing the number out of the database. He held up the display for her to see. She tapped it in, and waited.

"Beat Street Style," answered a young, male voice.

"Hi. I'm looking for Keiko Yamada," she said. "Is he there?"

"Um . . . um, no. I'm sorry, but he's not here right . . . oh, God." The guy's voice wobbled. "I can't do this, Kim. You do it."

The phone rattled, clunked, as someone dropped the headset, and a couple seconds later, a woman spoke, in an overloud, professional tone. "Hi, this is Kim of Beat Street Style! Can I help you?"

"I was looking for Keiko," Lara repeated. "Is he—"

"He's not here right now! May I take your number?"

Lara tried to speak, but her voice cracked, blocked. She coughed. "Please," she forced out. "Please, just tell me. Is he okay?"

The woman hesitated. "Are you the press?"

Fear ballooned, dark and sickening. "No. Just a friend."

The woman's voice went up in pitch, quivering. "I'm sorry to tell you this, then. He's not okay. He's dead. Both of them. Him and his boyfriend, Franz. Bill went up . . . he found them, and they were . . ."

The voice continued, but Lara no longer heard her words.

Cold swallowed her up. She had been an idiot, an asshole.

The phone bounced on her feet. Her fantasy bubble had popped, and now she was naked in the cold. Outside the Citadel. The connection between her and Miles had broken. She hadn't done it consciously.

People all around her, their mouths moving, but she was a million miles away. Keiko was dead. Franz, too. She'd killed them both, as if she'd mowed them down with a car, or pushed them off a cliff.

Just like she was going to kill all these people in the room with her, who were trying so hard to help her. All their kids, orphaned at best. If Greaves didn't decide to punish their kids, too.

And Miles. He was talking, shaking her, his dark eyes full of love and concern. She could not hear his voice over the roar in her ears. He was so beautiful and gentle and brave. She was deflating, the world disintegrating as the vortex sucked her down . . .

Keiko on the ground, the contents of his head spattered out in a broad red and pink fan, over a beige and brown patterned rug. Franz, naked, in a noose. Mouth taped, eyes bulging.

Miles lay on the ground, someplace colorless and gray and barren. Eyes empty, face white and stiff in death. Blood trickled from his nose and mouth, and pooled behind his head.

She recoiled with such violence, she jolted back into her body. She was on the floor, wedged between the couch and the coffee table.

". . . the hell is going on? Did she faint? Is she conscious?"

". . . Christ, we need a doctor, this shit's way over our heads—"

"Keiko's dead," she said. "And Franz, his boyfriend. Both killed."

The room fell dead silent.

"I murdered them with that telephone call," she said. "Just like I'll murder all of you if I stay anywhere near you." She looked at Miles. "You, too." She shoved his encircling arms away from herself. "Don't touch me. The more you touch me, the truer it gets."

"What?" Miles yelled. "What are you talking about? What's true?"

"That I'll kill you," she repeated. "You'll die because of me. Oh, God." She lurched up onto her knees. "Where's the bathroom? Quick!"

"There's a utility bathroom off the kitchen," Aaro offered.

"Lara!" Miles shouted after her. "Hey!"

She bolted, the high-tops squeaking on the kitchen tiles,

and made it just in time. She lost the sandwich, the coffee, the orange juice. Up it all came. The violent heaves felt like being torn to pieces.

When the retching was over, Miles tried to help her up, but she swatted his hands away, rinsing her face in the big utility sink. She grimly did the cleanup herself, wiping down and spraying the toilet.

She caught a fleeting glimpse of herself in the small mirror over the sink when she straightened up from that task, and looked away fast. Frightening. Those red, wet eyes, staring out of her white face.

She splashed with cold water again. Fighting for air. The feeling was unbearable. Writhing on the floor, begging for death—unbearable.

"Lara." Miles was still in the door. No shoving or snarling rudeness would dislodge him. "Get back inside my shield, please. You're safer when you—"

"No." She whirled on him. "I can't. It's not safe, Miles. It's not just about me. It's about Keiko and Franz, and all your friends, and their kids! And you, too! You're going to die, if you keep trying to help me. I've seen it. Understand? In a vision. I have *seen* it."

"No, I'm not going to," he said. "Trust me, Lara."

Despair sank deeper, looking at his stubborn face. He was so convinced that he was doing the right thing. Blindly following his own heroic instincts, even though they would drive him right into his grave.

She refused to let that happen. "Get away from me, Miles."

His gaze did not flicker. "Too late for that, Lara. Dream on."

"It's not a dream. It's reality. I saw you dead! Do you get it?"

"You saw Tokyo, too. Doesn't have to happen."

"I paid a price for that! I sacrificed Keiko and Franz for Tokyo! Who do I sacrifice next? Your friends? Their children? Your mom?"

His mouth tightened. "We'll find a way, Lara."

"Get away from me. Run!" She flapped her hands at him. "Your friends, too! I'm poison, I'm toxic! I'll kill you! Can't you see it?"

"You're just having a freak-out," he said. "Stop. It's stupid."

Oh *fuck*, it was the vortex pulling her from underneath. She fought it, with all her energy. She just did not want to see anything her personal oracle might show her right now.

She was the vortex, she herself. She saw it, with horrible clarity. How anyone near would be sucked inevitably to their doom.

Pain jolted her. Knees, thighs, spine, jarring her teeth. She'd fallen to her knees. Miles was down there with her instantly, trying to hold her, but she fought him off furiously. "Don't. Just don't. Please."

"It's not you!" he insisted. "You're not the one who's toxic. You're clean, Lara. Your heart is pure." He pinned her flailing arms. "You're not the one who killed Keiko and Franz, and you're not going to kill me. I won't let you. I'm tough. So get inside. *Now*."

An odd quality reverberated in his voice that shocked her into doing exactly what he asked, as if he'd pushed some button while she wasn't looking. It happened before she could stop it, her mental dance.

Suddenly, she was through the wall. Behind his shield.

good u stay there damnit

She could not bring herself to reply, but oh, God, it felt so good.

And it was so wrong. How had he bullied her into this? She was stupid and weak and selfish, and still she sagged there against him, in a state of empty, dumb relief. Staring blankly at the plastic buckets and pails, the shelves of cleaning supplies, the washer, and dryer.

His arms clamped around her. He smelled so good. He embodied everything she knew she could never have. Or even try to have.

People were talking from the bathroom door, making suggestions, lecturing, scolding. Miles said something sharp, and swung the door shut. The loud *thunk* sent mops and brooms toppling around their heads like tumbling toothpicks.

Miles shoved broom handles away and held her against his chest. Inside his mind, too. The embrace was warm, full of welcome. But she couldn't take comfort with that vision burned into her mind's eye.

The vision of his face, staring up from the bottom of the vortex, with dead, staring eyes.

"How far now?" Greaves demanded.

Silva, in the front passenger's seat, had the self-preservation not to indicate how childish that question was, even telepathically. In fact, the man and woman in the car with him were both breathlessly careful with their thoughts. All three had been in the room on the day that Chrisholm had been chastised.

"Fifteen more minutes to the address where the phone signal originated. If the phone is still located there, of course. You should be in range in about—"

"I can calculate my own fucking range, Silva. I have a grasp of basic arithmetic."

"Of course, sir."

Greaves stared at the mountainous forest flashing by from the tinted window, vaguely noticing the pain in the palms of his hands. He turned them over. Half-moons, from his carefully buffed and filed fingernails. The crescents turned red as he watched. Blood welling.

He was literally trembling with eagerness, to sink his claws into Lara Kirk and her rescuer. Her shield was like a beacon of hope. The only ray he'd had since those first, early years after Geoff went into the coma. Before he realized that the boy really, truly would not come out.

His people had compiled extensive files for Lara Kirk

and her parents, friends, lovers, acquaintences. There was no figure in those files who corresponded in any way to the physical description or profile of the mysterious figure who had rescued her. The man was clearly enhanced with psimax or something comparable, and had astonishing physical characteristics, as well as combat skills that suggested military training. He must be gifted with long range telepathy to have communicated with Lara Kirk from outside the complex.

Most importantly, he had to have a compelling reason to help her.

That was the part that perplexed him the most. Lara was alone in the world, family gone, no husband or siblings, not even a casual lover, as far as his sources could tell. And the list of human beings on the planet capable of what Lara's rescuer had done was very short. Cross-reference it with anyone who might have even a passing interest in or connection to Lara Kirk, and he came up blank.

Unless, of course, there was a new rival factor operating out there that he knew nothing about as of yet, and they wanted Lara's unique abilities for themselves. That was a hypothesis that made sense to him.

In any case, he would soon know the truth.

He reached out, his mind a soft, wide net that extended miles in every direction. It was easier to sweep like this if he'd already tasted the flavor of a mind before. He homed in on familiar signatures much faster. The minds that he had touched thirty-six hours ago had all been very distinctive. All five of them shone very brightly.

Perhaps that was why he picked them up from so far outside his usual five- to six-mile range. Three of them he had tasted the morning before. The unshielded ones. Male, adult, intelligent, aggressive. Lara's shooter, and his cohorts. They shared a bond that puzzled him, until it clicked into place. Genetic similarities. Brothers, or cousins.

Odd. That did not fit his hypothesis. Family connections

suggested a more emotional reason for the rescue, but who? Why?

He scanned for Lara, but felt nothing. Other signatures surrounded his three. He sensed the fourth one, the shielded one that had been on yesterday's attack team. Silva and Levine were in his car, and Biehl, Mehalis, and Wilcox were in the other. Miranda's telepathic abilities were on a level with Anabel's, and Silva, besides his knack for coercion, had a specialized ability almost as precise as Greaves' own—to cause telekinetic damage on a microvascular level. He could constrict a person's blood vessel, provoking a fatal heart attack. He was the ideal assassin. Greaves had trained him personally.

"Drive faster," he said.

"Sir, I'm already going eighty-five, and—"

"Shut up!" He closed his eyes to savor the contact. Almost close enough to read their thoughts.

He could hardly wait to tear them apart.

20

Something was coming down. Something bad.

Even closed in the bathroom, locked in one of those apocalyptic hugs with Lara, Miles felt the change in the energy outside the door. His neck, his balls. Tingling in a nasty way.

He knocked aside the tangle of broom handles. "Let's see what's going on out there."

There was a knot of agitated people around the bar when he emerged. He pushed closer.

Davy was doubled over, his head resting on the bar, holding his temples. His eyes were squeezed shut. "Oh, shit," he gasped. "Bad."

Davy being stoic almost to the point of insanity, that sight scared the living shit out of Miles. "What's going on? A headache?"

Davy slowly lifted his head. His face was gray, contracted. "We didn't leave soon enough," he croaked. "He's here."

"Yeah." Sean's face was pinched, "I'm feeling it, too."

"And me," Connor said, grimly. "Asshole. Squeezing us."

Miles looked around at the people in the room. Davy dragged in a sobbing breath, clutching his head.

They were all here in answer to his call. He had dragged them into this, assuming as always that these exceptional people could handle anything thrown at them. But nobody could handle this crazy shit.

"Got a sense of what direction he's coming from?" he asked.

Davy lifted a hand, wagged his finger "no."

"Just pain," Sean muttered. Sweat shone on his forehead.

Miles turned to address the room. "We'll split up, and take all the vehicles. Nina and Aaro each drive one, with your shields up. I take Lara, and go south, Nina, you turn right and take Hauser Road north, Aaro, cut across the pasture and offroad until you get to the other side of the valley, and go east. Kev, you and Edie get your car out, too. Everyone. No vehicle can stay here for them to trace."

Val slapped Miles' back, and held out two sets of keys. "I brought my motorcycle. It is in the back of our van. You might need it, no? Take the van."

Miles pulled out his own keys and handed them over. "Thanks, man."

He grabbed the bag by the couch that had the computer, the router, the smartphone, and slung it over Lara's shoulder. He helped Aaro lead the staggering Davy out the door. He was slumped, eyes half closed, blood streaming from his nose.

Once they'd heaved Davy into Connor's vehicle, he muscled Lara into the van. Tam's car, Nina at the wheel, was already barreling down the driveway at top speed. Connor's vehicle, Aaro driving, tore straight across the pasture, due east. Tam and Val followed Aaro in Miles' pickup, peeling off in another direction. Kev and Edie followed them.

He made haste, wheels spinning madly in the gravel before they found purchase and propelled the vehicle, heaving and bouncing along the driveway and onto the road, south-bound. Which is when he realized he'd left the goddamn gun upstairs, too. Christ. In mortal danger, with the woman he loved, and he was stark fucking naked. Unarmed.

"Miles." Lara's voice was hollow. "Your friends won't make it in time. The shape Davy's in."

The dead tone to her voice scared the shit out of him. "They might," he insisted. "Those guys are bad-ass. You would not believe what they have pulled off in the—"

"It has nothing to do with toughness, or smarts," she said. "He's too close. He'll track them down. And he'll kill them."

"Fuck," Miles muttered under his breath. "Fuck, Lara! So what do you want me to do?"

"It's something I have to do, Miles," she said. "Not you."

He realized what she intended, and fear stabbed deep. "No, Lara," he said. "Don't. Don't do this. Don't you fuck-ing *dare*."

"Listen carefully. I'm leaving the Citadel. If I offer my-self up to him as bait, he'll follow me, and the others will have a chance."

"Don't! Stop, just a second, and let's—"

"When you've gone a ways, stop the car, and leave me. Just run. He'll never find you, not with your shield."

"No! Fuck, no! I'm not leaving you!"

"It's the only way." She looked at him, with terrible, quiet purpose in her eyes that drove him absolutely bugfuck. "Thanks for everything."

"Wait! Wait just a second! You can't just—"

"Goodbye," she whispered. Words appeared on his inner screen.

i love u

And the bright place in his head went dark.

He howled, swerved madly to avoid a fencepost, fish-tailed on the gravel in his panic. "Goddamnit, Lara!"

But she was already past hearing him. Her eyes were

wide, staring at nothing, hands to her temples. She gasped for breath.

Miles took a sharp curve on screaming tires, yelling obscenities as her convulsions started.

"Stop the car!" Greaves barked. "Turn. Go back!"

Silva braked abruptly. "But the others are—"

"I don't care about the others!" He squeezed his eyes shut, lunging for her. She shone in the mist like a pearl. He lunged for her, again, with desperate, slavering eagerness.

And he had her. He wound himself around her, psychically immobilizing her. Exulting. "Lara Kirk is south of us. Turn!"

But it took too long for Silva to do the maneuvers on the narrow road. Halfway through, Greaves lifted the vehicle and its inhabitants two feet off the ground, spun it a hundred and eighty degrees, and let it drop with a teeth-rattling thud to the roadway. "Drive!" he snarled. "Tell the others to follow!"

Silva obeyed. The other car would lose the scent of the other men without Greaves' guidance. They weren't close enough for Wilcox's hunter talent to lock onto a target. But Lara Kirk and her rescuer were more tempting. And considering the state in which the mysterious ogre had left his staff the last time he visited, six people might by no means be too many to deal with the man.

Miles veered around the hairpin, fishtailing on loose gravel, perilously close to the sheer edge. A dry streambed on the hillside that fed into a big culvert under the road caught his eye. Further on, a logging road switchbacked sharply uphill once again, in the opposite direction.

It wasn't a plan so much as desperate impulse. He braked

on the curve, leaped out. Hauled out Val's precious Ducati, and shoved the gleaming machine into the huge culvert, along with the dirt, the gravel, the drifts of dead brown scrub oak leaves and pine needles. He tossed his computer bag in, too. Back to the van. Lara was gasping for breath. She had slid down, crumpled half on and half off the passenger seat.

He revved the engine, whipped it around the sharp turn on two wheels, and bounced and rattled up onto the logging road, lurching and tipping and swaying on the deep ruts.

Lara was terribly silent. Her body swayed with the centrifugal force, hitting the gearshift, then the door. Limp and flopping.

Where to stop was an arbitrary decision, based mostly on the fact that he could not listen to that silence for another second without exploding. He jerked the vehicle to a stop. Raced around, and extracted Lara's rigid, shaking body. She was still breathing, but her eyes were wide, dilated to vast black pools.

He couldn't feel her, couldn't find her.

He loaded her onto his shoulder, and took off through the trees. Not that there was any point in running while Greaves had a telelpathic fix on her. The first flat, grassy place he found, he let Lara's body slide down, and laid her gently on the ground.

She stared up at the sky, breath shallow, heart racing. Her body trembled, as if she were lifting a weight that was too heavy for her.

He slapped her cheeks. "Lara! Goddamnit, Lara! Do you hear me? Get back inside! You can't do this to me!"

Fucking duh. Could, too. The world did what it wanted. It knocked people around with no regard for their feelings or wishes.

Still, he shook her. Bellowed and pleaded. Bawled into his hands, like a child. Hit the ground until his hands bled. He was so fucking furious, he was having a tantrum, slapping at the tree branches.

Jesus, just let him do this for her. Let him go and do the mortal combat with that evil motherfucker on her behalf. Let him be the one to get trashed, for God's sake. He'd been totaled already, so what the fuck, why not? What else was he good for? Throw him out into the ring, let him freak out, crush everything that came his way. Mayhem Miles.

He'd do anything, if she'd just open her eyes and come back.

He held her in his arms, his face wet. He would follow her, but where was she? How the fuck did she get to that place in her head? She was the active one, the seasoned psychic traveler who made the wild flights into the otherworld. He just huddled inside his shield.

Unless . . . he didn't.

Bone weakening fear thrilled through him at that thought.

If he opened his shield. If he even could at this point. If he went out into the dark, naked as a newborn in that other dimension where his logical brain could not guide him. Could he find her?

It scared him to death. He'd tried so hard to block all that stuff out, hold it away from himself. The whole concept of psi offended his logical ideas of the way the world ought to be, so he hid from it, like a kid hiding under the covers with a flashlight.

But Greaves was coming. And Lara was dying.

He could hear them already, with his enhanced senses. The vehicle on the road below was slowing on the hairpin turn to come up the hill. The engine hummed and labored as it climbed. Two cars.

Worst case scenario, it killed him. No biggie. His life was worth nothing anyway if he didn't try.

Blood trickled out of Lara's nose, splitting into twin rivulets.

He called up his parents' faces in his mind, and he offered a silent plea for forgiveness for being so distant. For not saying goodbye.

He wiped away tears and snot with his sleeve. Grabbed Lara's cold hand, with his own grubby, bloody one. Tried to open the shield.

It wasn't wired to open from the inside. All his efforts had been aimed at automating the mechanism, making it stay shut without having to think about it. He had put no effort at all into automating a reverse process. Each time he tried, he froze, and choked.

Not until he held the image of Lara's beautiful face in his mind did he make any progress. Those shining eyes, the soft, shy smile. Her hand on his chest. Pressing his heart. Their lovemaking.

And he got it. The softness. Opening.

It was slow, awkward. Gears grinding, sparks flying, the shriek of metal against protesting metal, big wheels rolling, big bolts retracting.

Darkness swirled in, chilling him. Filling him. An infinity of . . . he had no way to frame it, other than darkness. Other-ness.

He moved through it like a swimmer in a dream, reaching out. Casting a huge net, like he did when he was fishing for ideas, but he was fishing for her. He was a flare in the darkness, a beacon fire.

Lara. Lara. Lara.

It didn't take long. He was bound to her. They were like a rubber band stretched out, poised to snap back together.

He sensed her presence, and her struggle. She was wrapped in a strangling, consuming darkness, like shadowy spider-silk. Fighting it.

He gathered his energy into a ball, and hurled it like a bolt of blinding light, straight at that amorphous thing that was clamped around Lara. Surprise jolted it loose . . .

Get back inside, now now now, he wanted to scream, but he had no voice, no interface. He wanted to bellow his frustration but he had no throat, no body.

And suddenly, like a light flashing on, she was inside. His

shield snapped shut like a clam instinctively against the attack from outside.

Energy battered against his shield. He hunched over her, panting, with deep, rasping breaths. Stinking with fear sweat.

He opened his eyes. She was looking up at him.

wt the hell were u doing? goddamn it why didnt u run?

if u have 2 ask, he snapped back. cmon lets go

Cant move im done pls go without me run run run

fine then give up if you want 2 watch me die tnx 4 caring

go! fuck off!

no

Her body shuddered and arched as she suddenly dragged in a breath, like she'd been underwater. "Goddamn you, Miles," she croaked.

"You're welcome," he said. "Move."

He made a move to pick her up. That roused her right away.

She pulled out of his grasp, and followed along in a staggering run, with much stumbling and a terrifying amount of noise. Periodically Miles stopped, held her tight against him, listening around the racket of her panting breaths, and her thudding heart for Greaves and his team.

His perceptions kept spreading, wider and wider. He didn't feel any limits to them. He was amped up to the max. Information organized itself into a topographical grid, with his attackers as bright moving points of energy. No self-doubt. No stressing about making some dumb-ass mistake and paying with Lara's life. No time to play out the worst-case scenarios. He was in the zone. Everything was channeled into the algorithm that crunched data and churned out an array of continually shifting strategies. Taking their opponents out, doubling back down to the road, and hauling ass while Greaves still assumed they were on foot, that was their best bet, at this precise second.

He dragged Lara into a grove of young trees, pushing her

down into the wild rose bushes. "You stay there," he said. "And stay inside the shield. Got me?"

Her eyes looked haunted. "Where are you going?"

"To clear a path," he said.

She gave him a short nod. b careful

He moved silently down the hill. Maybe his shield had a component like Nina's. They didn't seem to sense him at all, but he could clearly feel the closest three opponents, moving steadily uphill. All enhanced up the wazoo, but in distinctly different ways. One was a telepath. Miles had enough experience with telepaths to recognize the vibe. The guy—somehow, he knew it was a guy—was scanning for Miles' thought waves, but his probes just slid over his shield like it was oiled.

The other guy, a little further downhill and moving fast in Lara's direction, was using a different part of his brain, a more animal part. Sniffing, feeling with instincts, using his brain stem. More like the cougar Miles had met up at the Forks than his fellow goon.

One more was farther down the hill. Coercion. Then there was Greaves himself, plus two more, near where the vehicles had stopped.

Greaves was the brightest spot on that topographical grid. A red, toxic throb of energy, battering Miles' shield like hurricane wind.

Yesterday, he might have hesitated to use deadly force. Seeing Lara on the ground with blood running from her nose had burned that hesitation right out of him. Those evil scumsucking motherfuckers had hurt her, and now they were going to die.

He pulled out his blade, and moved in on them.

"Sir? Sir, are you all right?"

"Get your hands off me!" Greaves' blast of telekinetic energy flung Silva six meters through the air. He thudded to the ground, stunned.

Greaves put his hand on the door handle, dragging himself to his feet. The other hand touched the stream of blood that had burst in his nose, around his eyes, and probably on his sclera, as well, leaving what was sure to be unsightly red spotches in the whites of his eyes.

The sneaky little bitch! She had led him into a trap and suckerpunched him! He was so angry, he almost squeezed Silva's hiccupping lungs closed, but that would be wasteful.

Levine stood in the clearing, frozen still, eyes wide. Afraid to speak or move. God, was it always to be his fate to be surrounded by cowards who shit themselves at the faintest whiff of difficulty?

If she did not move or say something in five seconds, he would kill her, too, and never count the cost. Five, four, three—

"A tissue, sir?" She dug in her purse, handed him a packet.

He plucked one out, pressed it sullenly to his bleeding nose.

Lara Kirk and her ogre were on foot. No way could they be outside his range. Which meant Kirk's shield was fully as strong and impervious as Geoff's, and that she could lower it and raise it at will.

Greaves did a telepathic check of his enhanced commandos, all drawn from his own elite security squad, the ones who traveled with himself and Geoff at all times. None of them had engaged yet.

He gestured impatiently toward Silva. "Get him up. Get out there and help look for those two. Both of you."

Miranda's eyelids fluttered, and her gaze dropped to her houndstooth pencil skirt, the sheer black hose, the costly four-inch heels. Vain, useless bitch. "Me, sir?"

"Of course, you," he said, pitiless. "Both of you. There's a lot of ground to cover."

Silva struggled to his feet. He wore dress shoes, and his Armani suit was somewhat the worse for wear, with mud on his knees and chest. He and Miranda headed into the forest with gingerly steps.

Greaves tried again to scan for Lara Kirk. The flat silence felt like Carol's punishing silence. Like Geoff's . . .

Like Geoff's. Of course it did. Of course.

He composed himself to stillness, and brought the crazy-making quality of Geoff's silence clearly to his mind. The heaviness of it, the feeling of constant rebuke. His son's silence was a mirror, highlighting his father's sins, flaws, crimes.

It was painful to dwell upon, but he kept grimly at it, until something like Geoff's shield began to shimmer on the edge of his consciousness. Almost there . . . and he lost it again.

He tried again, making his mind soft . . .

Yes! He'd felt it. Not exactly like Geoff, but similar, and he—

Sir? It was Miranda, pinging him telepathically. *There's a—*

I AM CONCENTRATING! He punched the sharply articulated thought back at her, together with a punishing stab of mental energy that was liable to affect her sleep and digestion for days. Stupid cow.

I know, sir, but this is SERIOUS please come

He gave in to the inevitable, following the beacon of Miranda's mental signature. He reached out to monitor the rest of his staff . . .

And found nothing.

He came upon Miranda. She pointed, her face white and stiff.

Mehalis hung from the bough of a spruce tree, from a noose fashioned from the duct tape he had carried on his belt. His arms and feet were taped together. His face looked startled, eyes bulging.

Ten meters away, Biehl too hung, by his feet. Blood dripped copiously from his slashed throat. Greaves walked past Biehl's dangling body. Twenty yards further downhill, he found Wilcox. Also hanging, suspended, from plasticuffs which held his hands together over a tree bough, three feet off the ground. His neck dangled at a strange angle.

Lara Kirk did not kill those men. All the yoga in the world would not render a hundred and ten pound girl powerful enough to hoist those men into the trees. This was her ogre's work. Her brawny champion.

A loud rustling and snapping of twigs indicated that Miranda and Silva were joining him. Greaves closed his eyes, scanning for Lara Kirk, using that faint, elusive anti-signature, so like and yet unlike Geoff's.

He heard the faint, faraway rev of a motor. A motorcycle. So they had a hidden vehicle down on the road. They would have a ten-minute lead by the time they got back down to the road to give chase.

So. This round went to them. Again.

Greaves turned, and started walking back toward the car.

Silva and Miranda hastened to follow. "Sir, what do we do now? Do we—"

"Cut them down," he said. "Load them up. There are body bags in the car. Get to it."

Silva and Miranda looked at each other, shocked. "Ah, sir . . . Mehalis was the one with telekinesis, for the heavy lifting. Do you suppose that you could, ah . . ."

"No," he snarled. "I am not a stevedore. Go get those body bags, and hurry, unless you want to fill one of them yourself."

They scurried through the forest to collect the body bags.

The silence mocked him like a smirk, broken only by the *plop*, *plop* of blood, dripping from the dead man's hair.

lara! haul ass! he's coming!

Lara jolted out of her startled contemplation of the last hanging corpse, and struggled onward. His sharpness jolted

her into a shaky trot. Her rubbery knees and ankles kept giving out on her, making her stumble and slip.

4 the lv of Christ pls less noise change course 20
degrees 2 ur right and fcking HURRY

She didn't reply, just pushed on. Tears streamed from her
eyes. She wasn't quite sure why. She had no point of contact
with whatever feeling had provoked them. She was numb.

A strong arm clamped her from behind. Sticky with
blood, to the elbow. She squeaked with terror before she recognized him.

The world swooped, breath whooshed out of her lungs,
and they slipped, slid, tumbled together down the last steep
slope—and came up short, battered and coughing in the ditch
at the roadside among drifts of knapweed and pine needles.
Miles was up, hauling his computer bag and the motorcycle
from the dark maw of the culvert before Lara even got up
onto her hands and knees.

He yanked her to her feet and hoisted the vehicle onto the
roadway, draping the computer bag over her back.

"You hold this." He shoved an assault rifle into her hands.
"Move!"

His voice stung like a flail. She swung her leg over the
seat, clutched the heavy weapon against her belly, trying to
hang on as the bike surged into motion.

Wind battered her face. She pressed it between his shoulder blades. His shirt blew open, flapping, wrapping itself
around her forearms. Wet with blood. Thick and viscous,
flapping her wrists.

She squeezed her eyes shut. Saw hanging bodies, staring
eyes, dripping blood. She dug deeper, trying to find that
place in her mind where she felt safe, inside the Citadel.
She'd been comforting herself for months in that safe haven,
and it had never failed her yet.

But it was different now. The warmth had all bled out of it.

It was the dead of winter in there.

21

He'd declared war.

Miles pondered that with the small part of his mind that was not co-opted by the churning machine. He had thought it was a shield, but now he realized that it was much more than that. The minute he'd opened a door and fired a shot outward, a huge waiting engine had roared into life. The Citadel was not a static wall, not a fortress to huddle inside.

It was a big, nasty, evil motherfucking war machine.

With that war machine's engine humming, he could let go of scruples and doubts and all his usual monkey-mind bullshit, and just do the job. Going after Greaves' commando freaks, taking them all out with his knife, for instance. The person he'd been before would not have been able to coolly slash a guy's carotid artery, hang him by his feet to bleed out like a slaughtered pig, and continue on his way. To kill again.

He didn't even know the guy who had done that. Lara didn't think she knew him either. He could feel it in her trembling arms against his belly. He could still feel her inside his shield, but it wasn't the usual happy glow. There was tension, frozen uncertainty.

She was afraid of him now.

It had been sort of like that back when he started using the shield, but in a smaller way. People had complained about his coldness, his distance. It was that phenomenon, taken to its natural, inevitable conclusion. The possibility of becoming a stone-cold monster didn't register so much as a blip on his emotional sensors right now.

No, he was just fine with it. All his energy was dedicated to the tasks of keeping Lara safe, and grinding that dickhead Greaves and his lackeys into pink slime. Chill, steely purpose. Nothing else.

He headed into the maze of orchards that opened up in the valley, following random impulse, since he had no other compass. He ached to get onto the biggest, fastest road he could find and just fly, but they had no helmets, he was soaked in blood, and Lara was clutching an assault rifle to her bosom. Plus, he wasn't sure if Greaves' reach extended into the net of videocameras that were thick on the ground in all populated places. Their passing would be recorded dozens, if not hundreds of times in any town they went through, and if anyone on earth could find a way to smoothly commandeer all these electronic eyes, it was Greaves.

The orchard grid gave way to foothills again. A sign leading up a mountainside indicated that it led to Herald Lake, twelve miles up into the mountains. Remote, high altitude. He needed a place to park Lara, warm her up, let her rest. A place to do some thinking, plotting. Or rather, to let his new war machine do it for him, since it was far and away better at the task than he, Miles, had ever been.

The road became a sharp uphill grade of rough, rutted gravel that Val's fancy-ass bike was most definitely not built for, but it labored gamely on. There were houses on the road. He used the extension of his senses that he had employed in the recent fight in the forest, slowing down near each dwelling and sending his perceptions outward to gather information, organize it on a spatial grid, feeling for bright points that indicated people. The first house was currently inhabited. The second had no bright points, but it looked inhabited, and had a sense of fresh energy. Someone had left the place recently and meant to return soon. Some were derelict, with no human energy at all, but that was no good either, if he wanted to forage for food, clothes for Lara, maybe even a hot shower and some sleep. He needed a middle ground.

More torturous climbing. Lara vibrated against his back, violent, convulsive shudders as her body sought to warm itself. Night was coming on. If she went into shock from exposure, he was so fucked. It was surprising she had not already done so. She was as tough as nails.

Still, he laid on the gas.

The lake itself came into view. Smallish, shallow, surrounded by waving marsh grasses and encircled by a dragon's spine of dead white skeleton trees peeking up through the younger green conifers. There was a rough road around it, and some small cabins.

One caught his eye. He slowed down, pulled in close.

It was small, simple, a roughly built A-frame. It had exactly the vibe he was looking for. No vehicles outside, but the house looked intact and well kept, not abandoned for more than a couple of months, based on the drifts of pine needles that had blown up against the door.

The McCloud Crowd's training in lock-picking came in handy, with the emergency pick set in his bag, a Christmas gift from Sean years ago. He defeated the knob lock and the padlock both in less than three minutes. This was the first time he'd tried to pick a lock with his new, enhanced senses. A whole different experience. He could sense the inner mechanism now, the guts of the lock, shifting pins and tumblers.

Inside, the air was stale. There was a small living room with a fireplace, a tiny kitchen, and a bathroom in the back.

A bedroom was upstairs, in the loft. Electricity that functioned. A gas stove, and a propane tank, all good. He went looking for blankets.

He wrapped her up in a tattered wool army blanket, like an olive-green burrito. Plopped her on the couch, and fished for the burner phone Aaro had gotten him. He punched in Sean's number, let it ring.

Sean picked up instantly. "Yeah?"

"It's me," he said.

"Yo. Glad to hear your voice."

"You guys okay?" Miles asked.

"Not exactly." Sean's voice was flat. "We stopped in Salem. Davy's being prepped for emergency surgery. Cerebral aneurism."

Sub-zero cold pierced his flatlined calm. "Fuck me," he whispered.

"Pretty much. They put him in an artificial coma. We'll see how it goes. He's a tough bastard."

Miles' mind was blank. He wished he could think of something encouraging to say, but he didn't have any access to the part of his brain that might be up to a task that emotionally complex.

"How about everyone else?" he finally said.

"Fine. He only put the squeeze on Connor and Davy and me. Connor and I both have bitching headaches. Val and Tam took off to collect their kids from Sveti and Zia. I have never seen Tam that pale."

"You guys should get checked out," Miles said. "I've had this kind of brain damage, so trust me on this. You're in the hospital already, so get some testing right away on your—"

"Yeah, whatever," Sean said curtly. "We're on it."

"Right." Miles swallowed, his hand fisting, opening, fisting again. "How about Margot? She holding up okay?"

"She's on her way down now, with Jeannie and Erin and Kevvie. They left the little ones with Lily and Bruno in Portland. Should be here in about an hour." Sean hesitated. "Did you engage with him?"

"Yeah," Miles said. "It was no fun. But we're alive."

"Wow. Intense. Oh, hey, there's one of Davy's surgeons. Gotta go."

"Okay. Later, dude. Good luck."

He thumbed it closed, slipped the thing into his pocket. "Davy has an aneurism," he told her. "They're operating now."

Her eyes closed. "Oh, God," she whispered. "I'm so sorry."

"Yeah," he muttered.

Appalled silence spread. She stared up from beneath the shadowy cowl of the blanket, shivering and blue-lipped. Clutching it beneath her chin with a scratchy, muddy hand. Her dark, fathomless eyes seemed to stare straight into his brain.

Anger flared inside him. She shrank back.

"What?" he snarled. "What's with the look?"

Her gaze flicked down. She shook her head, mutely.

"You look like you think I'm going to hit you," he said.

She wouldn't look up. "That's how angry you seem."

Stating it out loud seemed to roll a rock off it. It roared up, inflamed and huge and horrible.

"Yeah, I'm fucking angry." His voice cut through the darkness. "What you did? Jesus, Lara. Throwing yourself in front of him like that? What the *fuck* were you thinking?"

"That too many people have already died trying to protect me," she said. "My parents, Matilda, Keiko, and Franz. I didn't want Nina and all your friends to die, too. And you. You, more than anyone! You were supposed to leave me and run, Miles!"

"Right. Like I'm going to do that, in this lifetime. In this universe."

She pulled her knees up and wiggled her arms out of the green wool to hug them to her chest. "Cold," she whispered.

He leaned to turn on the lamp next to the couch. To his surprise, it flicked on, a sickly, flickering, yellow glow. "I'll try and get some heat going in here."

"No. I mean you," she said. "Inside, outside. Even in the Citadel. It's never been like that in there before. It scares me."

His teeth ground. "Yeah, well. Slaughtering people does a real number on the warm fuzzy vibes. So does having my girlfriend offer herself up like a sacrificial goat to a psycho maniac. Real mood-killer."

"Don't be sarcastic!"

He snorted. "That's like asking me not to breathe."

"Then hold your breath!" she said flatly.

He stared at her, fighting for control. Teeth grinding. "If you don't like me this way, avoid forcing me into situations where I have to kill large numbers of people to protect you."

"Stop it!" She covered her face with her hands. "I can't stand it!"

"I am what I am. If it sucks, take some goddamn responsibility for what you've made with your own hands."

"Me? You think I'm responsible?" Her eyes widened, outraged.

"Yes, you! This passive human sacrifice schtick pisses me off! It's not enough to just waft around looking wounded and ethereal! Fight, goddamnit! For your life, your future! Strike a blow, get off your ass!"

The blanket fell as she jolted up. "That's not fair. I am grateful that you protected me, but you are being a dickhead!"

"Can you promise not to do that again? Or will you just rip my guts out again, anytime you like, no warning?" he yelled back. "How can I trust you? What can we have together under those conditions?"

"I don't know," she retorted. "Probably not much."

A glass-framed poster on the opposite wall suddenly fell to the floor. The crash of broken glass jarred them both.

"So that's your position," he spat out. "You'll just throw yourself in front of a bus, no warning for me, no collaboration, no working together to find a solution—"

"There was no time! You know I'm right. You're just throwing a childish tantrum! You can't fault me for what I did."

"Yeah? Watch me, Lara. Memorize it. This is me, faulting you."

The lightbulb in the lamp popped, bulb exploding in a high pitched, tinkling shower all over the lamp stand, the floor.

"What the fuck is going on?" Miles growled.

Lara put her hands over her ears. "Ouch," she hissed. "Stop that."

He was bewildered. "Stop what?"

"That thing you did, in my head."

"I didn't do anything except yell at you. And I was justified."

She gave him a long, level look. "Uh uh. It hurt. I've been yelled at plenty, and it didn't ever feel like that, even when Anabel did it. That's coercion, Miles. Like Greaves. Don't do it to me again. Ever."

"So now I'm like Greaves? That is such *bullshit!*"

Crack. The long mirror that hung on the door that led to the kitchen cracked down the middle. A triangle of mirror glass tumbled out of the frame, fell to the floor, shattering into four smaller pieces.

"Oh, for God's sake. Would you please stop it?" she snapped. "It's immature, and it's stressing me out."

"What the fuck are you talking about?" he roared. "I didn't!"

She gestured at the lamp, the picture, the mirror. "Bad enough that we're breaking and entering. Do you have to trash the place, too?"

"But I didn't . . . that wasn't . . ." His voice trailed off. He stared at the remaining shards of mirror. He was reflected in it, distorted, broken, jagged. "I can't do that stuff," he said. "Any of it. You're wrong."

She sighed. "Refusing to face reality wastes a lot of vital energy," she said wearily. "Not to preach, or anything. Try to calm down."

Calm down, his hairy ass. He backed away, breathing hard, and stared at her slender form, silhouetted against the last of the fading light sifting through the trees outside. And even now, underneath his distress was the pounding drumbeat of his awareness of her body, her scent, her sex. So slim and straight. Strong.

He wanted to shove her down onto the couch, rip off the muddy clothes. Pin her into the cushions beneath his weight and go at her like a rutting wild animal. He wanted to plunder and pillage and possess all her secret girl parts, with hands and tongue and cock, until she'd forgotten how pissed she was at him. Or was too exhausted to care.

But his anger was draining away, leaving sickening dread behind. His back hit the fireplace mantel. "I'll just, ah . . . go do something useful with myself," he said. "Before I fuck up again."

"Miles, please," she called, but he stumbled into the kitchen.

There were no words for how horrified he was. He had to concentrate to steady himself. Light worked, check. Hot water heater turned on, check. He had to scrounge for clothing for her. Some food. See if there was propane in the tank to power the range. Procure some wood for a fire. That was the plan. Warm her. Feed her. Try not to hurt her, or scare her to death.

He was mortified. Coercion? Like Rudd, like Greaves. He felt like an evil spirit had possessed his body and slugged her in the face. It was exactly that bad. Hurting an innocent, injured girl, half his size. Holy fucking shit.

He started rummaging in the shelves over the stove, behind some dusty blue gingham curtains. They yielded a can of turkey vegetable stew and a box half full of stale crackers. Now for a can opener. Some rattling in drawers with his grimy, shaking hands found him one, but when he pulled the drawer, he accidentally ripped it out of the credenza, scattering its contents over the floor with a rattling crash.

He crouched down and started picking up utensils and flatware, and stopped, staring at a rubber-handled vegetable peeler with a rusty blade. Wondering, with a sick sort of dread, if he really could . . .

Aw, fuck it. He had to know. He concentrated, imagined the thing moving. Charged the image with energy. Jolted it, poked it, pushed it.

Nothing. At first he was relieved, but unease still tugged down on his guts like a load of dirty ice.

He thought about how it had felt, to pry open the shield. He perched on that weird inner balancing point . . . and tried it again.

It took a few minutes, but when he managed to keep it open longer than a split second, he looked at the peeler . . . pushed . . .

It trembled, jerked. Slid across the floor. Picking up speed. *Whack*, it smacked into the china closet on the far end of the kitchen.

Huh. He let the shield snap shut again. Well. That sucked.

So he was now dangerous to himself and others in lots of new and fascinating ways. Whoop-de-fucking-do.

It was coercion that scared him the most. He was afraid even to think about it. Afraid he might accidentally activate it.

All he could do was hope that Lara was wrong. There was no way of proving if he had it or not without inflicting it on someone, and that he would not do, now or ever. Coercion struck him as innately evil.

Not that Aaro was evil. But Aaro was . . . well, he was just Aaro.

So he'd let the ability sit there, unused. With luck, it would atrophy. Shrivel up and just blow away. Please, God.

He picked up the rest of the silverware the old fashioned way. Fitted the warped drawer back into the credenza, and turned his attention to the stove. He sensed a blockage in the gas line. He let his perceptions sink into the workings of the machine. Opened the valve, following the gas through the hose with his senses . . . yeah, there was the place.

He opened the shield, applied pressure, turned on the sparking mechanism. Still nothing. He gave it a little tap—

Whoosh, flames roared up, outsized. Miles leaped back just in time. The blue gingham curtains caught fire.

He stared at them, dumbstruck. Holy *fuck*.

"God, Miles!" Lara shoved him out of the way, yanked the blazing curtains down, and threw them into the sink. She turned the water on. The fabric hissed, steamed.

She turned to him, white faced. "Are you trying to blow us up?"

He shook his head, and coughed, to unblock his frozen throat. "I'm sorry," he croaked. It was all that would come out.

"Oh, shit." Lara grabbed him by the arm, and hauled him over next to the sink. "You are such a mess. Come here."

She grabbed both his hands, still dark with mud and dried blood, and placed them under the flow of numbingly cold water.

It flowed over his forearms, pinkish, muddy, swirling over the charred blue-checked fabric. He stared at it, hypnotized by the caressing strokes of her hands. She grabbed dish soap and got into it, sudsing him up to the elbows. Making his blood-stiffened sleeves soggy.

It felt awesome. It felt sexual.

Blood kept rinsing down, until the basin, now blocked by the burned cloth, was more than half full with pinkish water.

"It doesn't wash off," he said.

She made a disapproving sound. "Yes, it does," she said tartly. "It's not innocent blood."

"Blood is blood," he said.

"You're being self-indulgent." She plucked the fabric out of the sink so it could drain. Water gurgled through the pipes.

"I don't know what's happening to me," he said.

She kept hold of his cold, wet hands, squeezing them. "Growing pains," she said. "You'll get used to this, the way you got used to the rest of it."

"But you felt what I did to you," he said. "I couldn't control it. I didn't even feel myself do it. It's not safe. I'm not safe. I should stay away from you—"

"Bullshit," she said crisply. "I'd be dead in ten minutes without you. Sorry to be a clingy burden, but it's true."

"I could hurt you," he said. "I could—"

"But you won't. You could also snap my neck, or smother me, probably one-handed, or shoot me, for that matter. Easily. But you won't. And I know that you won't, so it's not a problem. Understand?"

His chest was still heaving. "I don't want you to trust me," he said. "Not when I don't trust myself."

"Too late," she said. "I trust you anyway. Deal with it." She grabbed a hand towel from an oven handle, and proceeded to dry his arms with it. Long, gentle, soothing strokes.

The cloth was still blood-smeared when she was done, but his hands looked better than before. She clasped them both in hers, and brought them to her lips, kissing one—

He jerked them away. "Please, Lara. Don't."

"I'll warm up some of that soup," she said gently. "Why don't you go and chill out for a little while? Rest."

Now she was trying to take care of him. His spasm of laughter turned into a cough. "I'll go get some firewood."

"Take it easy," she called as he headed out into the back.

He found some wood, but it needed splitting. He found an ax in a lean-to out back, and a big chopping block.

It was a blessed relief, to unload some of his jittery nervous energy by whacking the living shit out of something, but the movement got his emotions running, and each blow became a phantom death blow to Greaves, and it did a number on his shield. He didn't even have to do the balancing act. His shield yawned open as the ax descended, and he silently shouted, from the depths of his being—

And stared, appalled, at the massive chopping block, thigh high and wider than it was tall, rolling on the ground, riven in two pieces.

Pine needles tumbled like rain around him, pattering softly.

The kitchen door opened. He didn't turn. Not wanting to see the reproach radiating from her slender silhouette in the doorway.

dude. seriously?

He shook his head. He had nothing to say for himself.

try a little harder with the psychic scream i dont think they heard u in Salt Lake City

That jolted a laugh from his chest, which turned to a sob. He was grateful for the darkness as he leaned on the ax handle.

Melting down into a total fucking basket case.

22

She was going to die today, Anabel reflected, as she stared at Greaves' moving mouth. Probably badly. But who cared. She had come to expect pain, humiliation. It was her normal state of being.

Maybe death would roll that crushing weight off her. All those shadows, the darkness that clung, ooze that stuck and crept, and—

"Concentrate, Anabel!" Greaves' voice was a whip-crack. She gasped at the coercive sting. Her head still hurt from when Lara's pet ogre had slammed it, but the medics who tended the turnip—that disgusting, corpse-like thing that Greaves hauled with him everywhere—had pumped her full of antibiotics and pronounced her fit for the meeting. A throbbing concussion and a bullet through the meat of her thigh was no excuse to miss a session of ass-reaming.

Greaves had left the doors that opened onto the terrace open, the frigid November wind swirling in. A reminder of the conclusion of the last conference. Which of them would float into the air and go speeding out into the great emptiness tonight? Let it be her. It wouldn't be a bad way to go. First it would be like flying, which she'd always longed to do. And after, boom. Nothing more. It would all just . . . *stop*.

Flying, with the wind in her hair. Like Lara did. Why couldn't she have been a clairvoyant, and go on these dreamy trips? Why did she have to be a goddamn telepath, doomed to see all the garbage in peoples' minds? Steaming filth. Trash dumps. She was sick of it. She had enough filth of her own.

". . . data-gathering network, using the facial-recognition software?" Greaves was addressing the room at large. "What is the status of that project?"

Silva piped up. "At this point, we have live footage available twenty-four/seven from security cams at every major tranportation hub on the West Coast, and we're expanding every day. Airports, bus and train stations, and rental car places. The facial recognition gives us warning with no more than a few seconds of delay."

Silva sounded subtly pleased with himself. Always a mistake.

"This is useless if she stays on back roads and small towns," Greaves observed. "Or if she gets a car at a smaller rental outlet."

Silva looked crestfallen. "Ah, yes. We're extending our network, but we have to outsource to cover that kind of—"

"Yes, yes. So the bots are constantly sifting this massive quantity of footage at all times for Lara Kirk's face. Very good. As soon as we identify our man, we'll do the same for him. For now, let's move on. Pay attention to your monitors, please."

Images flickered on the computer screen that each of them had in front of them. Anabel focused on hers with some difficulty.

Footage from Lara Kirk's cell. Again. For the umpteenth time, they watched the masked man burst in, with Hu clamped against his body. Lara cowered in the corner, half-naked.

"I still cannot believe there's no audio," Greaves said sourly.

"Sir, there was nothing to hear," Anabel protested. "She was alone, and unless she talked to herself—"

"Shut up," Greaves snapped. "Pay attention."

The crouching figure swiveled, glancing up briefly at the camera. He turned back to Lara, and whipped off his mask, revealing a snarled mop of long dark hair, dangling past his collar. But not his face.

"Look at Lara's face," Greaves said suddenly. "Stop, and go back two seconds."

Silva ran the footage back, and they watched the masked ogre peer at the camera, turn, whip off the mask. This time, they watched the stunned look on Lara's face.

But not terror. There was a flash of hope. Certainly recognition.

"She knew him," Greaves said slowly. "She was happy to see him."

"Surprised, too," Anabel said.

"Yes," Silva said. "She wasn't expecting to be rescued. She didn't respond quickly. He had to force her to move."

"Yes, Silva. This implies that she was not communicating with him telepathically. So who *was* communicationg with him? Hmm?"

Fear gripped them all. Anabel braced herself for the probe. Greaves was fast, and good, but oh *fuck*, ouch, she was still sore and bruised from the headache and from yesterday's telepathic reaming.

He moved swiftly down the line and jabbed them all, even the medics. They'd been summoned to this meeting, too, all but one left to constantly attend the turnip. To guard it, no doubt, since it was not permitted to die. She felt almost sorry for the loathsome thing.

The door opened, and that smirking whore Miranda Levine burst in. Her face was perfectly composed, but even on the sad downslide from her last dose of psi-max, Anabel could sense the woman clamping down on her own excitement, playing it cool. Posturing bitch.

"I heard from our contact at the forensics lab," she said. "They had a hit. The prints from the gun he used to shoot Bixby match up to a Miles Davenport, last known address, Sandy, Oregon."

"No!" Anabel jerked upright. "It can't be Miles Davenport!"

Greaves regarded her impassively. "Why not?"

"I know that guy! And he was there, that night at Spruce Ridge! The fundraiser, remember? He was the one who attacked me and tied me up, the one who attacked Alex Aaro and destroyed Rudd's architectural model! He ended up in a coma after his talk with Rudd. It couldn't have been him, sir. I probed that guy! I couldn't get through his shield, but he wasn't enhanced, or I would have felt it. He was just a big beefcake with a good security system!"

"So you wrote him off?" Greaves said softly.

"No! The guy who took Lara was loaded up with psi! I never forget a signature. I would have known if I had ever come across—"

"Unless his signature had changed," Greaves said.

"Signatures don't change!"

"Do not raise your voice in my presence," he said.

Anabel shrieked as something clutched and cramped in her groin, as if she were being clawed there.

The sensation eased after a few horrible moments. She sagged onto the table, trying not to sob.

"Have you composed yourself?" Greaves asked. "Can we proceed? Are you prepared to act like a professional?"

Straightening up in her chair put painful pressure on her aching nether parts. "Yes, sir," she croaked.

"Good. As I was saying. You wouldn't recognize his signature if it had changed. By your own account, after you encountered him he was attacked by Rudd, and almost killed with psychic energy. It's very possible that he woke from his coma with a very different psi profile."

"Do you know of other cases like that?" Silva asked.

"Yes," Greaves said. "Me."

The wind banged the glass doors loudly as they stared at him.

"That's how my powers were unleashed, years ago," he explained. "In my youth, I was subjected to prolonged psychic pressure very similar to what Rudd did to Davenport. It took months for my brain to heal, but when it did, my profile had, in fact, changed. Radically." He looked around, a sardonic smile curling his lips. "You all take psi-max tabs. But I could give you permanent psi like mine, if you're willing. The price is screaming agony, followed by constant, crushing head pain, disorientation, and depression. Followed by years of chronic headaches, stress flashbacks, and the occasional psychotic break. All this in exchage for enormous power. Is there a hardy soul among you? No?" He snorted. "Why am I not surprised?" He tapped his pen on the tabletop. "Miles Davenport paid that price, but Rudd didn't even know he was creating a psychic monster. As far as he knew, he was just beating up the smaller kid in the playground, like the thug that he was. This man intrigues me. I want him taken alive."

Eyes shifted and flickered around the table.

Greaves laughed. "Afraid?" A needle-jab of coercion made everyone at the table jump, or wince. "I invested untold millions in you people. Anything you might have to fear from Miles Davenport is nothing compared to what you have to fear from me."

He turned to Miranda again. "Tell us about Miles Davenport."

Miranda slid a pin drive into her console, and shared the file with them. "He grew up in Endicott Falls. His parents still live—"

"Send someone up there right away."

"Already done, sir. Expert in computer engineering and acoustic physics. He specializes in writing algorithms that filter sound. His tax returns indicate that this work pays very well. He's been associated with Alex Aaro's security consultancy lately, though he hasn't worked with him since before the Spruce Ridge incident. He also freelances with other security firms, principally SafeGuard, a company run by the McCloud brothers. Davy, Connor and Sean."

Anabel's burning eyes couldn't focus on the mass of documents that Miranda had dug up that scrolled rapidly on her screen, but her gaze snagged on a photo of a dark-haired, laughing girl, scantily clad, with Miles Davenport's arm around her shoulders. He was grinning, looking happy. The girl was pretty, but she looked like a barfly.

He was a good-looking son of a bitch, in his own craggy, hawkish way. Well endowed, too. She'd checked at Spruce Ridge. Impressive.

She tuned back into Miranda's droning litany. ". . . sound engineer, too, for a number of blues and rock bands since his college days, and he's been romantically involved for several years with this woman, the one in the red halter dress. Cynthia Riggs, a musician. She, however, has been linked with several different men in the past several years. She's the sister-in-law of Connor McCloud, one of the owners of SafeGuard. Davenport lived with Riggs for several years in an apartment on Capitol Hill, but he moved out over a year ago. Interestingly enough, sir, when I cross-referenced the McClouds' names with the emergency room admissions in a three-hundred-mile radius, Davy McCloud's name popped up in Salem. He was admitted to the hospital just a few hours ago. An aneurism, it would seem. They're prepping him for emergency surgery as we speak. Here are pictures of the McClouds, Aaro, his girlfriend Nina Christie, also at Spruce Ridge, and she—"

"I met Ms. Christie personally that night, Miranda."

"Ah. Yes, of course, sir. The name Val Janos also came up, in relation to the McClouds. He is the owner of the van we found parked in the woods. This is him, and his wife, Tam Steele, and their daughters."

They watched the photo gallery slide by. The McClouds, their families, their associates, Christie, Aaro. Greaves nodded, smiling.

"Excellent," he said. "Good work, Miranda."

Miranda preened like a cat being petted. "I also found that Davenport owns a piece of property up in the Cascades. Sixty acres and a derelict shack. Here it is, on a satellite map."

Greaves' eyes went speculative. He began to rub his chin. They waited, silently, well trained. Letting him finish his thought.

He turned to Anabel. "Levine and Rickman, you will go to Salem. We must start a dialogue with Kirk and Davenport, and the McCloud family at the hospital will be our contact point. You must get close enough to read them, and everyone who associates with them."

"And our plans for Phase Three?" Silva asked. "The ceremony in Blaine—"

"Continues as planned," he assured Silva. "We will inaugurate the community center day after tomorrow, and bestow their real gift in secret on that same day. Have all of you seen Maura for your vaccines?"

Everyone nodded.

"Good. As for Davenport . . . this cabin gives me an idea," he said. "This man is a formidable opponent, and needs to be taken very seriously. I want a pre-emptive strike, to discredit any attempt Davenport might make to accuse me, particularly now, right on the eve of our last testing phase. I want his reputation destroyed and his life smashed before he has a chance to come up for air. I was thinking of having him fingered for Matilda Bennett, but now I have a better idea. More juicy, more shocking, with the added advantage of accounting for Lara Kirk's long disappearance. Send a team to this cabin. I'm thinking, shackles bolted into the wall, a box of packaged food, a mattress on the floor, some bottles of water, scattered garbage, a chemical toilet.

We have all the genetic material from her cell that we need, I trust. Hairs from her comb, bedding from the cell. Objects that she's touched. Do you have samples of her blood? Be creative."

"Oh, sir!" Miranda's eyes batted, sucking up without shame. "That's brilliant! I took the sheet from the house where they stayed, so we can use that! They very definitely had sex on it."

Greaves frowned. "Poor girl. Putting her right to work for her keep, I see. Fragile as she is. It's a disgrace."

"Yes, of course," Miranda backpedaled hastily. "Terrible."

"Davenport has been out of circulation for several months. He's been depressed, injured and brain damaged, and that supports our story," he mused. "Take the bodies of the men he killed this afternoon, and bury them behind his cabin. Keep them in the body bags, so the police can find his prints on the duct tape he bound them with. We can say that these were men I hired to look for Lara Kirk myself. I am such an admiring patron of her artwork, I decided to help in the search. My men found her at this cabin, and contacted me. After which I never heard from them again. What do you think?" He looked around, bright eyed. "Does it hold water? Is it good?"

"Oh, yes, sir."

"Excellent, sir. Perfect." Fawning murmurs swept the room.

Anabel could not bring herself to say anything. Her throat felt like a tube of concrete.

Silva piped up. "He has the McClouds and his other associates to serve as alibis, and to testify about the rescue from the facility at Kolita Springs," he reminded them.

"An excellent observation, Silva, but I think that once their children start to die of inexplicable organ failure, they may rethink their story on what happened at Kolita Springs," Greaves said. "They do not strike me as stupid people."

Silva subsided, and Greaves clapped his hands briskly. "Make it happen, people. Set the bots to sift for Davenport's face, in addition to Lara's, Miranda. Silva, bring me the latest statistical analyses of the prison populations. I haven't looked them over properly yet."

"Right away, sir."

Anabel approached Greaves. "Sir," she said. "A request."

"Now is not a good time to ask for favors, Anabel." Greaves did not look up from the sheaf of documents that he was flipping through.

"I just want to go on record as saying I'm ready to pay the price."

Greaves frowned up at her. "What price?" he snapped. "Are you still concussed, Anabel? You're not making sense."

"No, sir." Her jaw throbbed from clamping her teeth. "I'm talking about the old-fashioned technique for releasing latent psi. The kind they used on you. I don't care how much it hurts. I'm willing to do it."

"Are you indeed?" Greaves was expressionless.

"I'm not afraid of pain," Anabel said.

"Hmmph." Greaves' blue eyes narrowed, speculative.

Anabel shuddered as she tried to relax into the sudden telepathic probe. He flung open door after door, peering into her darkness. Each stab of inquiry jogged loose memories that hurt, like being shocked with electricity. But she was stronger now. She could take it.

Finally, the probe withdrew. Anabel waited, bruised and shaken.

"No," Greaves said. "I think not."

Anabel stared at him blankly. "But . . . but, sir, I—"

"You don't have the right character," Greaves said. "Too much damage at an early age. That bad business in your preadolescence, the confinement, the sexual abuse, brrr. Terrible. Such a shame, with your amazing potential. Parts of your brain function are suppressed, other parts are overcompensating, there are chemical imbalances of all kinds, a general state of imbalance and chaos. You're a mess, Anabel. If I stressed you that hard, you'd almost certainly go mad. Or die."

"But I'm not afraid of pain," she said. "Or death."

"You should be," he said, with what looked almost like sympathy. "That's part of the problem. Can you imagine, if I were to give tremendous, irrevocable psychic abilities to someone, and then find that person had gone insane? It would be so irresponsible."

Anabel kept shaking her head. "But I . . but I'm not—"

"A wise person knows her limitations. To be honest, if I had been the one screening you before you first dosed, I would never have chosen to enhance you at all. Too unstable, too many issues. But there it is, so let's just make the best of it. With the psi-max, you're a very strong telepath, and your other psi talent was entertaining, too, as I recall. The sexual magnetism. You seem to have lost interest in it. I haven't seen your beautiful glow for quite some time."

"Haven't been in the mood lately," she said, woodenly.

"Just so. Can't say as I blame you. Oh, wait." His eyes widened. "I just had a thought. You are the perfect choice to head up the team that will prepare Davenport's cabin! The chains, the shackles! It's ideal, see? Use your own personal experience! This is a perfect opportunity for you to take your disadvantage and turn it into an advantage!"

Anabel stared, blank and baffled. "Sir?"

"Don't you see?" he encouraged. "Who better than you can make the scenario of Lara's imprisonment and sexual slavery watertight and convincing for the forensics experts and the psychologists? After this, anything Lara Kirk might say in Davenport's defense will sound like the results of brainwashing. We will have killed so many birds with one stone. It has to happen fast, though, because I want to tip the police off first thing tomorrow. Before daybreak, understand? So get to it."

"Yes, sir." Her voice was hollow.

"Oh, why the long face?" He patted her back. "It might help you, doing a sort of re-enactment. Lance the boil, eh? It's worth a try!"

She cleared her throat. "Of course, sir."

"No time to waste. Be careful to leave no signs of yourselves. All evidence must point to him. And now, if you will excuse me."

He walked away. She was already forgotten.

She stood like a statue, as the wind swirled in through the open doors, bringing with it the icy threat of snow.

Margot McCloud ran her fingers through the springy mop of red ringlets on her daughter's head. "You sure you don't want to go back to the hotel?" she asked gently. "Auntie Erin's heading back with Kevvie. She's got movies, and she's going to order some pizza."

Jeannie shook her head. Her mother recognized the look on her daughter's face. When Davy got that expression, it meant there was no longer any point in arguing. "I'm staying here, with you," Jeannie said. "I want to know what the doctors say about Daddy."

"Okay," Margot said. "But it'll be a long wait. Hours and hours."

"I'm waiting with you. I don't care how long."

She squeezed Jeannie's shoulders, trying to fake the tower-of-strength act. Tough, when her stomach was in free fall. How often she complained about Davy's stubbornness, his stoicism, his set-in-stone opinions and principles. Never fully conscious of how heavily she leaned on the massive, solid rock that was her husband's out-sized personality.

Not until Fate threatened to rip it away did she realize how he defined her world. He was her bedrock. Without him she would fall. With two kids in her arms, and no idea how far down there was to go.

It was unthinkable to lose Davy, and likewise unthinkable

to imagine him comatose, reduced. Davy's defining characteristic was his colossal strength and endurance. But it happened every day, at random, to all kinds of people. It could just as easily happen to him. To them. A car accident, a heart attack, whatever.

She tried to exhale, but her chest had shrunk since she got Sean's call, and found out they were prepping Davy for brain surgery. Cerebral damage inflicted from a psychic attack, from some maniac who was messing with Miles and his new mystery girlfriend. She hadn't actually been listening to the strange tale at that point. Her mind hadn't really gotten past the words "brain surgery."

It was still stuck, banging on that closed door, but too afraid to imagine what was on the other side. Her Davy, hurt. Or changed.

She fought it down. If Jeannie had consented to the pizza and movies at the hotel, she could have sat there alone and blubbered all she liked with no one but her brothers-in-law to see. But with Jeannie there, she had to be tough. It was what Davy would expect. At least little Jamie was in Portland with Lily and Bruno, and Liv had taken Maddy, Erin's youngest, to Lily and Bruno, too, along with her own little Eamon. It was comforting for everyone, to huddle together. She missed her little Jamie, though. Stoic, too, in his own way. Like his daddy.

Kevvie and Jeannie had both put their feet down about coming. They had the McCloud strength of character, in spades.

Erin walked over, after a whispered conversation with Connor in the hospital corridor. Connor grabbed her, pulled her back, and kissed her hard. Margot looked away, horrified by the stab of envy and fear the sight of that caress gave her.

Please, please, Davy, be okay. I haven't had you long enough. Jeannie and Jamie haven't had you long enough. Nowhere near.

Erin walked over. "So? Jeannie coming back with us? Kevvie's brought along the first two Harry Potter movies."

Margot shook her head. "She'll wait with me."

Jeannie's thin, strong arm wound around her mother's waist, and squeezed. Which made a fog of tears spring up. She sniffed them sternly back. *Do the hard thing, goddamnit.*

Erin put her hand on Margot's shoulder. "He'll be okay," she said quietly. "He's tough."

Margot didn't trust herself to reply. Sean came in, his arm flung over his nephew's shoulders. Kevvie, who looked just like Connor, his father. Long and lean, heavy mane of dirty-blond hair, pale green eyes.

Erin gathered up her bag and her son, kissed them all, and took off for the hotel. Sean sat down beside them, ruffling Jeannie's hair, and slumped, unusually silent for him.

"How's your head?" she asked. "Did you guys schedule MRIs?"

"First, we get through this surgery," Sean said. "That gives us time to think of a way to phrase it. How would we explain it to the staff? Excuse us, but would you mind just doing a brain scan on the two of us, because we feel like it, you know, to pass the time while you operate on our brother's brain? Or is it better to say, do it because we both just got psychically hammered from afar by an evil scumbag with magical powers? We'd end up sedated in the psych ward."

"I don't think you should wait." Margot's voice shook. "Don't risk it. I don't care what the people here think. I promised Liv I'd bug you guys about it, and you're both being assholes and ignoring me."

"Shhh," Sean soothed. "We're fine, other than the mother of all headaches. Got any more of that ibuprofen on you?"

"Sure." Margot dug into her purse, shook a couple pills out into Sean's hand, which stayed extended until she shook out another two. "You should eat something with that big a dose," she said.

Sean tossed the pills into his mouth and swallowed them dry. "Kev will bring us something," he said. "He and Edie and Nina and Aaro went out to grab a bite. Kev's all worried about Edie getting stressed out in her delicate condition. Can't blame him, really. I would be."

"You need to drink water with those pills," Jeannie lectured her uncle. "You'll choke. Here, I have my water bottle." She pulled out her little black and pink Barbie flask, and shook it, frowning. "I'll go fill it at the drinking fountain out there. Be right back."

"Don't go out of my sight!" Margot shouted after her.

"Just to the drinking fountain. It's right there." Jeannie scampered around the corner. Connor was right there, talking with one of the nurses, and Jeannie was directly in his line of sight, so she tried not to be a nervous freak about it. Jeannie came back into the waiting room a few seconds later, and plumped down on the couch between them, offering the bottle to her uncle.

He accepted it with a kiss, and it was while he was squeezing and wrestling and knuckling her head until she giggled and wiggled that Margot noticed the sticky note. It was from a prescription pad that advertised some antibiotic or other, stuck right in the middle of Jeannie's dark blue tunic sweater.

That was odd. It wasn't a place where a sticky note might normally end up on a person by mistake, like a sleeve. No, it was smack dab between her little girl's shoulder blades.

Chill apprehension condensed into fear, and froze as she plucked it off. Nothing was written on the front. She turned it to the adhesive side. Her heart stopped beating. Scrawled in ink, the note read

cute kid
she's next

"Sean," she said.

He looked up, catching her tone with his danger antennae, highly developed in all McCloud men. His eyes zapped to the note. Margot silently indicated with her shaking hand, where it had been stuck to Jeannie's back, and held it up for him to read.

Sean's face, already pale, went ashen.

His eyes met Margot's, and lit up with that hot, fierce war glow she'd seen in Davy's eyes many times. A hard comfort, but still a comfort. Thank God for the tough, strong family she had found.

"Connor," he called.

Connor's antennae were sensitive, too. He looked over, swiftly closed his conversation with the nurse, and strode over so purposefully one would barely notice his limp.

Sean held up the note. "On Jeannie," he mouthed.

"Mama? What is it?" Jeannie had caught the vibe, and was looking around, eyes wide with alarm.

"Nothing, baby," she said.

"Nothing, my foot!" Jeannie's light green McCloud eyes narrowed.

"When?" Connor asked.

"Just now," Margot replied. "When she went to the drinking fountain."

Sean paced out into the corridor, scanning up and down.

Connor put his hand on Jeannie's shoulder. "Honey, when you went to the drinking fountain, did anybody touch you?"

Jeannie frowned in concentration. "Yeah, someone did brush by me when I was filling the bottle. But when I looked over there was just a bunch of doctors walking away. They had the white coats, and those green pajamas. I didn't know which one it was."

"Man, woman?"

"I saw both in the hall." Her voice was small.

Sean came back into the waiting room. He held another note. "This was on the drinking fountain," he said.

It was from the same prescription pad, message on the back, as before.

then comes the boy in 317

Jeannie wiggled around until she could see it, too. "That's our room at the hotel! How do they know our room? Isn't it a secret?"

"It's supposed to be," Margot said. "Keep your voice down, baby."

"What name did you check in under?" Connor asked, pulling out his phone.

"Erin checked in for us. She used the new credit card and ID, the one you told her to use."

Connor cursed under his breath. He punched the phone, waited. "Hey," he said. "Come back here right now, babe. Don't go to the hotel . . . yeah, I'll tell you when you're here. Hurry. Yeah . . . I love you."

Sean was on his phone, too, presumably calling Kev and the others. "Yo, dudes. Drop everything, get back here. We've got a situation. Very bad. Yeah. Okay. Hurry."

He closed the call. They moved closer together, huddling around Jeannie. A human wall. Staring at every person walking by, sitting, working. Everyone they saw, a potential enemy with deadly secret weapons.

"God, I hate this shit," Sean murmured, under his breath.

"We have to move the kids," Connor said. "Or have someone else move them. Bruno and Lily. Nick, Seth. Petrie would help."

"To someplace we don't know," Margot said. "If they're reading us."

Sean winced. "We have to block them," he said. "We can do something like what Miles suggested, in the car. We thought about breakfast, to fake out the telepaths waiting on the road. Pick something vivid and fixate on it."

Margot almost laughed. Yeah, right. Like, her husband under the knife, his brain opened up. That was all she needed to foil a telepath.

"I'm all set with my image," she said grimly.

"We need our own psychic goon squad," Sean said.

"I tell you what we need," Connor said. "We need Miles."

23

eat yr soup

The command typed itself out onto the screen in her mind.

Lara looked up from the saltine cracker she was contemplating. Miles was not looking at her. He had not spoken to her at all since their fight, other than curt directives; take a shower, put your clothes in the washer, put these on, hurry up. No smile, or touch. Or eye contact.

She pressed her hand against the knot in her belly. The shower had relaxed her a little, but she still saw those hanging bodies and distorted faces, blood dripping. Keiko and Franz, too. Her vision of Miles, a pool of blood behind his head. Greaves' crushing stranglehold. If she'd had any digestive enzymes in her system, they were long gone by now.

cant, she replied.

He looked at her. An icy look that unexpectedly stabbed into her head like a needle. The cracker shattered in her hand and the table rattled as she lurched to her feet, hands to her throbbing temples.

"Oh, ouch. Jesus, Miles," she gasped. "That *hurts*."

"Oh, fuck." Miles shoved the dishes out of the way and

sagged forward, knocking his forehead against the table. "Fuck, fuck, *fuck!*"

She tried to breathe. The sharp pain was slowly beginning to recede. "Miles," she said, somewhat shakily. "You cannot do that to me."

"I know." His voice was muffled.

She waited for him to get a hold of himself. After a few seconds, he sat up, shoved his snarled hair back, and met her eyes.

"We're running for our lives," he said. "You've been starving for months already. What am I supposed to do if you collapse? Where do I take you, Lara? What do I tell them? Help me out, here!"

"I'm not going to collapse," she said. "I'm strong."

He gave her a grim look, red eyed and exhausted. "I noticed, but you'll be stronger if you eat. Just try. Do it for me. *Please.*"

She swallowed back the protests. This was not worth a fight, with all the other things they had to fight about.

ok fine

She spooned some broth into her mouth, made her throat relax enough to swallow it. Miles watched the first few bites travel from bowl to mouth, and got up, rummaging in the small utility closet beside the stove while she slowly finished the soup.

He came out with a dustpan and broom, and a plastic bag, and headed into the front room. She heard the clink of broken glass as he cleaned up the mess he'd made earlier. He paraded through the kitchen with his bag full of shards, still sweaty from his exertions with the ax. So gorgeous, even with his face a taut mask of misery and tension.

"I'll build a fire," he said.

"No, don't," she said hastily. "I'll do it."

He frowned. "I'm not a pyro, if that's what you're thinking. The gas tube had a block. I just gave it a tap with my mind, and I overdid it. That's all that happened."

"Even so, I'll handle the fire," she assured him. "Take a shower."

"So you think whatever I am is at least as weird as pyrokinesis?"

"Actually, I'm not worried about it," she said. "I've got so many things to worry about, your new psychic stuff doesn't even register. I'm more concerned about your attitude. And your manners."

His grin flashed, which emboldened her to give him a playful push. "Go on, take a shower," she urged. "The water should be hot again by now, and you are filthy. I can't even bear to look at you. Are there any clothes here that fit you?"

He looked wry. "Not really. The guy who leaves clothes here is a foot shorter than me, and a lot bigger in the gut. But the sweatpants have a drawstring. They'll cover my junk."

When he was in the bathroom, she finally let air into her lungs. So much of her time with him was spent in that rapt, breathless state, it was amazing she could oxygenate her brain enough to stay conscious.

He'd brought in lots of wood, so she got busy with the fire. The glow of little dancing flames soothed her. A fresh, cleansing image to wipe the others away. Flames were good for that. She needed the warmth, dressed only in the oversized men's T-shirt he'd found for her.

Too many images, floating around inside her mind. Her ability to visualize had saved her sanity in the rat hole, particularly when they turned off the lights. She could close her eyes and go to places she'd been, actually seeing images in the space in front of her closed eyes like a movie projector. Maybe that put her a few notches closer to crazy, but it was a fair trade—and a double-edged sword, too. Because she had no way of forgetting bad images. They did not fade with time.

But she stared at the crackling flames and let herself be soothed.

Reality was better than stored images, even when it was

scary. Just like Miles was better in the flesh than as the Lord of the Citadel. Prickly, sarcastic, and bossy though he was, he was the goddamned star in her darkness. She would trot around after him for as long as he would tolerate it.

His comment about her human-sacrifice schtick made her cringe. Wafting around, looking wounded and ethereal. Ouch.

Not that she'd had any other choice today. But still. It made her feel ashamed. It wasn't how she wanted him to see her. She wanted to be strong for him. To protect him as he protected her.

He emerged from the back bedroom, his arms full of blankets and pillows. He folded the blanket he'd wrapped her in earlier, and laid it on the couch. He was naked to the waist, jaw shadowed with stubble. Hanging low on his hips was a pair of hugely baggy sweatpants that did not reach his ankles, or even come close. He crouched down, laid a sleeping bag on the ground in front of the couch.

The implications of that gesture were not good.

"What are you doing?" she demanded.

"Got to sleep somewhere," he said.

"There's room on the couch," she said. "If we take off the back cushions, it's as wide as a single bed. Wide enough for both, if we're friendly."

"Friendly?" He looked up. "You know exactly what will happen if I lie down next to you."

"Duh," she said. "It's only the one thing on earth that could possibly make me feel better right now."

He looked down at his hands, flexing them convulsively, and gestured at himself. "You want this? Random whacks of coercion, the uncontrolled telekinesis, the shitty manners, the bad attitude? You want all that in your bed? In your body?"

"Yes," she said, unhesitating.

He looked away, into the fire. "I saw the look on your face, after that fight in the forest," he said. "The necks I broke, the throats I slit. The blood on my hands. It skeeved you out."

"It was a shock," she admitted. "But those people were coming after us. You did what you had to do. I just didn't expect you to do it so, um . . . expertly. But I don't fault you for that."

He tried not to smile. "Generous of you."

"That's not what I meant," she said, impatiently. "I didn't expect the theatrics. Hanging them in the trees. What was that about?"

"I was sending him a message," Miles said. "That was how I phrased it. You fuck with her, you go through me. And good luck with that."

She nudged the fire with a stick. "Thank you for being my champion," she said quietly. "Again."

"You don't have to thank me. You certainly don't have to fuck me. Not when I scare you and hurt you and piss you off."

"I did my share of that today, too," she admitted. "I'm sorry."

He contemplated her in the firelight for a long, thoughtful moment. "Me, too," he said, cautiously.

"I want you," she said.

"I get that," he replied. "I want you, too. All the time. But maybe we should chill for a while. With this weird psi bullshit coming down, I don't know what I would be like, if I—"

"You'd be good," she said. "You always are."

He made a frustrated sound. "I don't even know who I am right now."

"I do," she said softly. "Come here and let me remind you."

They gazed at each other. The fire crackled. Miles shook himself. "Man, you are the ultimate temptress," he muttered.

That made her shake with helpless giggles. Her? Hah. It was fun, though, to play the seductive siren. It straightened her spine. Made her chin go up and her tits stick out. All good things. Life affirming.

He scooped up the sleeping bag and flung it over the back of the couch. Progress. At some point, her smile had turned into a big, out-of-control grin, which was not an expression she was accustomed to feeling on her own face. He was smiling back and, oh, that gorgeous flash of white teeth, those sexy grooves in his cheeks.

"You're the tempting one, in those crazy pants," she said.

He laughed. "These? I almost opted to come out stark naked instead of wearing these. Didn't know quite how you'd take that."

"I would have been fine with it," she said demurely. "But the pants do have their own quirky charm. What do they say to me? Hmm . . . a story out of the Arabian Nights, maybe?"

He shook his head, still grinning. "You're reaching, Lara. You creative types. Talk about accentuating the positive."

"We might as well," she said.

He stood up. "The Arabian Nights, hmm? What was that princess's name, the one who enslaved the sultan with her stories?"

"Scheherazade," Lara said. "But the sultan was a deranged, pathologically insecure headcase who murdered his brides the morning after the wedding night so they wouldn't cheat on him."

"Ouch," Miles murmured. "Okay, so let's make up our own story. One where the brave, enterprising Scheherazade takes control of her destiny, and gets away from the asshole sultan once and for all."

"She's rescued by the king of the forty thieves," Lara said. "He sweeps her off on his black Arabian stallion, and they gallop through the desert on secret paths known only to the nomad tribes."

"Wow. King of thieves, huh? So I'm an outlaw, now?"

"You're pretty out there," she murmured. "But I go for that."

"Good." Miles' eyes were very bright. "So now that I have the sultan's prize in my grasp, what do I do with her?"

She stood up and threw her hair back. "The question you should be asking yourself is, what will she do with you?" She laid her hand gently on his bare chest.

His eyes were hot with anticipation. "Will she tell me a story?" he asked. "It gets lonely and boring out here in the desert with just my bags of plundered gold and gems for company."

She shook her head, tracing the curves and cuts of his muscular chest with her fingertips. "No way. She's got something less cerebral in mind. More direct." Her hands slid lower, under his waistband.

His breath got jerky and uneven. "I'm on it," he said. "Princess."

She shoved the baggy sweatpants down over his hips, caressing every perfect, taut dip and swell of the lean contours of his hips and ass. Caressing, slow, stroking, kneading.

She sank to her knees, and took him in her mouth. Quite the enterprise, all things considered. There was a lot of him to take.

No more talking of any kind was possible for some time thereafter. He'd objected to this move the night before, but he wasn't objecting now, judging from the way his hands shook, fisted into her hair. His whole body vibrated, and so did she, as she finally got it. The whole point of oral sex, which had eluded her thus far.

It was entirely different when her body and soul were on fire, shaken by her lover's beauty and courage and valor, his toe-curling, irresistible hotness. She couldn't get enough of his thick, marvelous cock, which had become the most desirable object on earth. She stroked and licked, sliding her tongue, her hands over him, feeling the quick, heavy throb of his heart against her tongue, inhaling his warm man musk mixed with shower soap. She laved his cockhead, licking up tantalizing drops of salty precome. He arched and groaned.

The world narrowed to the rasp of his breath, the wet sounds of her mouth, the crackle of the fire. Her own gasps for breath, between the swirling, the lapping, the stroking. She cupped his heavy balls, curling her fingers around them tenderly.

Energy rushed through her body, bright and cleansing. The feeling rose up from inside, spontaneous as a spring. This impulse to seduce him, minister to him, please him. And master him. He was so strong, but right now, he was helpless to her. It made her giddy.

She could have gone on forever, but he finally pulled her head away, with a ragged, pleading sound. "Don't make me come," he said.

She wiped her mouth, stroking the silken hair on his thighs. "Why not? There's plenty more where that comes from."

"I want to come inside you," he said.

"So do that later. We're not going anywhere tonight, right?"

He gripped her under the arms, hauled her onto her feet with an effortless jerk. "Not later. Now."

Um, wow. So much for mastering him. Just a teasing echo of his coercive power reverberated through his words. Fiercely controlled.

He cupped her face in his hands, stroking her jaw with his thumbs. The delicate rasp of his callused fingers made her shiver.

"I snatched you from the evil sultan, fair and square." He wound his fingers into her hair, stretching out her throat for him to nuzzle and kiss. "I'll decide where to put it, and when. I want you under me, your hair spread out, your body wide open. My cock, buried in your pussy, shiny with your lube. And I want to look into your eyes when we come."

She covered his hands with hers. "Take whatever you want. It's already yours." She almost lost her nerve, then blurted, "I'm yours."

Miles blew out an explosive breath. "Mine," he repeated.

She hoped it wasn't too much. Too needy, desperate. The strangling kudzu vine. *His*. Forever, always. Please, let him want it, too.

He kissed her with ferocious intensity. The coldness she'd lamented in the Citadel was gone. She was bathed in heat and light. Charged with energy. They nourished each other with tender, clinging kisses, a tender confusion of helpless giving and greedy taking. She felt like a full-blown flower, sticky and sweet for him, so lost in the kiss, she hadn't noticed him picking her up until she was bouncing against the couch. The sheet he'd thrown over the couch was chilly. He lifted his mouth away to spread her legs, high and wide. That fierce look in his eyes made her shiver and sigh. He grabbed her hands, and pressed them against her muff. "Touch yourself," he commanded. "Show me how wet you are."

She had to close her eyes, against his rapt contemplation of her splayed thighs, but she'd said "his," and she'd said "anything."

She reached down, opening herself. His hands stroked her inner thighs, spreading her wider. His breath was hot against her tender inner lips, and he groaned, when he saw how she was gleaming wet. She slid her fingers inside herself. Withdrew them, slick and hot. An offering, a plea. *For God's sake, just do it.*

He drew her fingers into his mouth, and the greedy, wet suction of his mouth around her fingers shocked her into an orgasm.

Astonishing. Long and sweet and lovely and unexpected, melting her into a bright shimmer of emotion. When she finally opened her eyes, he was looming over her, motionless. Gazing at her hungrily.

"Wow," he whispered. "Fingers. Who knew."

She tried to speak, but couldn't. She nodded instead.

"I have to lick you now," he said. "Or I think I'll die."

He seemed to expect an answer, but words were not forth-coming. All she could manage was a breathless murmur, an-other nod.

"Hold yourself open again," he said. "I love the way it looks. So pink and shiny and soft."

She did so, crying out at the intense sensation when he put his mouth to her. His hands clamped over her thighs, holding her wide, and he played her with his tongue, first a light promise, a caress of breath and cheek, oblique and del-icate, and then teasing kisses and licks, running his tongue tenderly along every groove and fold, suckling her clit, then plunging deep. Lapping her up.

The last climax had been like a rainstorm, but the next one was a thunderclap. Or a string of thunderclaps, actually, jolting her into a new bright place, soft and shining and un-known.

Some time later, he shifted his body, arching over her. She lifted herself with a moan of delight as he nudged and prodded into place, and caught her breath at the perfection of his slow entrance.

He stirred her up, inside her body, inside her mind. Bathing himself with her slick balm.

He ground to a halt. She gazed up into his eyes, clutching his shoulders. "What?"

He shook his head, eyes shut. "I'm so wound up."

She pulled him close, clenching herself around the thick hot club of his cock. "I love how you are," she said. "I love how you want me. How much you care. Give it to me. All of it."

"Look at me," he demanded. "The whole time."

Her eyes were wet with tears. "Yes."

That was the end of words. She just clutched him, hung on, gasping for breath, as the rhythm grew desperate, hard, frenzied.

Their eyes locked, all the way up to the mutual explosion.

* * *

The log shifting in the fire roused Miles. He stirred, reluctantly ungluing them where sweat and sex had stuck them together. His breath hissed between his teeth at her pussy's tight, pleading farewell clutch around his cock.

He stirred the fire, put on another log. Disappeared into the kitchen, and came back a moment later with a cup of water.

"Drink," he said.

She smiled at him with her eyes over the rim of the cup.

Miles drank the rest as she sank back onto the couch, staring at her reclining body, and stroking her breast, the dip of her waist. Then down, between her legs, toying with her drenched folds.

"Good thing we put down the sheet," he said. "Yum. Wet."

"Yes." She was abruptly self-conscious about it. "I should wash."

His hand got bolder, slipping inside her. "I'll wash you," he said. "I love groping your pussy. Makes me crazy."

She laughed. "Right. I know just how you wash me. It would defeat the purpose of washing. You'd make me wetter than before."

"So? What's your point?" He slid two fingers deeper in her slippery hole. "So we defeat the purpose. Over and over. Let's defeat the crap out of it. Let's drive the little bastard right into the ground."

She lifted herself to him, laughter rippling through her. She felt so open, yielding. He leaned over her, his clever fingers teasing her into another swelling crest of pleasure.

It broke, and washed over her in long, pulsing, rippling waves.

He climbed onto the couch and lay alongside her, clasping her in a tight, shaking hug that melted her to tears.

He looked alarmed. "Did I hurt you? Did I do something to you with my mind?"

"No. I'm great," she assured him. "It just feels good. I feel so much better. I could almost eat."

"Really?" He jerked upright. "Let's do it! Come on."

"What's the hurry?" He clambered off her body, and she was sorry she'd said it. She missed his heat, the contact.

"Don't want to miss this opportunity. Let me see if there's more food." He flipped on the light in the kitchen and washed his hands.

She watched from the couch, enjoying the spectacle of a stunning naked man reaching up to rummage through cupboards for sustenance for her. Didn't get any better than that. It didn't even matter if it all imploded on her. What mattered was this moment. Perfect, precious, and hers. She would live it completely, and no one would ever be able to take it from her. No matter what happened.

She wiped the tears away just in time, as Miles came out of the kitchen, two steaming cups in one hand, a wax paper package of crackers in the other. "Instant cocoa and stale graham crackers are the best I could do." He sounded displeased with his offerings. "Nothing but sugar and starch. Tomorrow we've got to get you some better quality sustenance."

"This is great," she assured him.

He watched her wash down a bite of the graham cracker with a sip of hot, chocolate-flavored water. "This is the first time you've independently asked for food," he said. "I feel like throwing a party."

"Don't make me self-conscious about it," she grumbled.

He rolled his eyes, but his smile was so beautiful and happy, she got down an entire second cracker, then a third, to please him.

Miles drained his cup and opened his arms. She climbed onto his lap, sighing with contentment at the contact with his hot body.

They cuddled, her head on his shoulder, her hair trailing down his back, listening to the fire crackle for a long time.

"You should get some sleep," Miles said.

"And you?"

"Going to fire up the computer, do some poking around," he said. "You might as well rest while I do it."

She lifted her head. "What now, Miles?"

He let out a careful sigh. "I've been trying to come up with a plan," he said. "We can't stay here. We can't stay anywhere for a while, at least not nearby. Tomorrow, we buy food, clothes. We stay on the back roads, we get a new vehicle. We road trip, and stay clear of him. And as soon as we can organize it, we accuse him."

She nodded. "Sounds good."

"Let me get my phone," he said, sliding her off his lap. "I have to check on Davy."

He punched in the number, waited. "Hey, Sean," he said into the phone. "So? News?"

Lara felt the tension grip him. Her skin still felt the warmth from the fire. But the temperature dropped in the Citadel.

She waited, her belly tight with dread.

"Understood." Miles closed the call, his face like stone, and stared into the fire. Lara waited as long as she could, but after a few seconds, she was ready to tear out her hair.

"What?" she demanded. "How is Davy? Is he okay?"

He dragged in a deep breath. "He's stable," he said. "Still in the coma. They think the surgery went okay, but they won't know for sure until he wakes up."

"Okay," she faltered. "Well, good. So what, then? What is it?"

"Greaves," Miles said. "He found them. He has them pinned. He threatened their kids."

It was happening already. Her beautiful fantasy bubble popped, and icy reality rushed in, sickening and queasy.

Lara wrapped her arms around herself, shuddering. "How . . . ?"

"They figured out who I was," he said. "Maybe Anabel

recognized me. Maybe it was the gun I left at the house, maybe my fingerprints, on the gun, the steering wheel. They left a note, stuck to Jeannie's back. They threatened Connor's boy Kevvie, too."

"Oh, God," she whispered.

"It's a message to me. Arrogant shithead that I am. I sent a message to Greaves in the woods, and this is the answer." He buried his face in his hands. "At least he didn't slit Jeannie's throat. Not yet, anyway. But he will, because he can. It's a promise."

Lara put her hand on his shoulder. Her throat burned. It just kept happening, worse every time. Her shit luck, spreading to everyone she touched. She was a walking black hole. It couldn't go on.

"I'm the one he wants," she said.

Miles' head whipped up, eyes blazing, and just the faintest snap of coercion flicked across her consciousness, making her wince.

"Don't. Even. Start." His voice was a low rasp of menace.

Lara threw her arms wide. "What else am I supposed to do? Let him kill your friends, their kids? I can't allow that!"

"Neither can I," he said.

"So tell me, then!" she yelled. "What can we do?"

"Not we," he said. "Me, Lara. Just me. I'm hog tied when I'm with you. I hate to do this to you, but you're going to have to run alone, to someplace I don't know. It's the only way I can swing this."

"No, Miles. Don't—"

"And when you're gone, I go after this guy. And I kill him."

24

Miles desperately needed some rest, but it wasn't happening. Too much junk in his system. Raw fear, to think of one of Greaves' goons being close enough to little red-mop-headed Jeannie to slap a note on her back. Close enough to his good little buddy Kevvie to ferret out the number of his hotel room. That opened a hole in his belly that no amount of teeth-grinding concentration could plug.

At least Lara had finally dropped off, after a protracted and emotional argument, which neither of them had definitively won yet. He kept checking obsessively for that bright diffuse glow in his mind that indicated she was there, inside the shield. Everytime he felt it, it gave him a rush of relief. So he reached all the time.

She was safe for now, until she got her next heroic notion. Then all bets were off. But he couldn't think about that, or he'd just get pissed again.

He needed to get back to that cold place he'd been after the battle in the woods, where instant, ice-cold decisions were made for him by the war machine's super-processor, and doing the hard thing came naturally. It was the only way to face Greaves, and not give a fuck that he had little to no chance of surviving the encounter. And no chance at all of surviving it with his future with Lara intact.

That was gone now. He had to cut it off. Let it go.

He worked on that, in his head. Throwing switches, laying tracks. Cold, sharp and purposeful.

There was no point in lying here, staring at the coals. He got up, stirred the fire, put on more wood. Broke down the rifle for transport, wrapping the separate pieces in a yellowed newspaper he'd found in the closet. Transferred their wet clothes from the washer to the dryer. He found an old receipt from a hardware store, and scrawled a note on it.

To owners: Sorry for breaking in. Was in trouble (not my fault). Slept one night, used shower, washer, stove, fireplace. Took a few pieces of clothing, used some bedding and some firewood. Apologies for the picture frame, mirror and broken chopping block. Grateful for the shelter. Hope the enclosed covers damages and rent. If I make it through this, I'll contact you and make sure we're square.

Best wishes, your uninvited guest.

He folded the receipt into an origami swan, tucked fifteen hundred bucks into the folds under the wing, and left it in the middle of the kitchen table. He wished he could leave more money, but he needed the cash for Lara.

Then he tucked the blankets up over Lara's pale shoulder, sat naked on the floor in front of the fire with his computer and router, and dove into the Internet's store of lore about Thaddeus Greaves.

A lot of the stuff he had memorized from his previous searches, when he'd begun investigating her disappearance. He knew by heart the inspiring tale of Greaves' humble beginnings as a private first class in the army, his years in the secret task forces running dangerous missions for his country, blah blah. Big-ass hero. After his years of military service, he had parlayed his smarts into business, and proceeded to make a vast fortune without apparent effort.

Now his money made itself, thick and fast, and he had a whole staff of people dedicated to growing it, so Greaves was free to focus on philanthropy. What a great guy. He supported medical research, the arts, education reform, literacy, scientific research, space travel. He was heavily invested in green energy projects. A passionate advocate for climate-change research and innovation.

Then he ran across something more recent. A press release, dated three days ago. Greaves had funded a community center for his hometown, Blaine, Oregon. In fact, he had a house there. Miles had compiled a list of the man's residences some time ago, and the Blaine house had been included in the lifestyles-of-the-rich-and-famous article to show the contrast between his newer lavish mansions and the relatively modest home on the shores of Blaine Lake that he'd bought for his family before he became filthy rich. Still a damn nice house.

The community center was a huge gift, worth tens of millions to the town of Blaine. There was an assisted living facility for elders, a day care and preschool to help children and working families, a sports and arts center for youths, a modern art museum, a theater and concert hall, even a cinema. A shopping district with a pedestrian mall, a town square, a fountain and a park, all in the interests of creating what Greaves considered to be the heart of a functioning community, spaces where people could stroll, socialize, plan concerts, picnic, throw a stick for their dogs. The community was appropriately grateful, and was having a big, fawning event day after tomorrow in which they were dedicating a statue to the guy. Jesus wept. The love was raining down.

At some point, he became aware that the light in the Lara

place was glowing brighter. He turned. She was propped up on her elbow.

"Find out anything interesting?" she asked.

"He's going to be in Blaine day after tomorrow—a ribbon-cutting ceremony for the huge pile of money he just shat all over the place," he said. "Dedicating a statue of himself. Getting his ass kissed."

And taking a bullet to the head from the H&K G-36 that Miles had picked up in the woods today. He refrained from mentioning that item on the agenda for Greaves' busy day. That would take a stroke of luck. He did not want to shoot into a crowd. Greaves' house would be best.

"You're going to go there," she said.

It wasn't a question, so he didn't answer it. "He's a real prince of a guy," he said. "Wants to save the world."

She sat up, let the blanket fall. Her nipples were taut and puckered and dark, her flesh covered with goosebumps. So gorgeous.

"He said something like that to me, too," she said. "While holding me in a telekinetic vise-grip. He said he wanted to save the world. Make the world a better place."

"Wow. What did you say?"

"I laughed at him," she said. "It pissed him off."

"No shit," he said drily. "So I can imagine. Jesus, Lara, what is it with you? Do you have a death wish?"

Her eyes narrowed, but her cheeks went hot with anger. "Not when I have something to live for."

Miles chewed on that for a long moment, and snapped the laptop shut. "That's how you feel?"

"Yes," she said.

He rose up , staring at her intently. "That's nice," he said. "I'm glad you put some value on your own life. That's a comfort to me."

She shrank back. "Don't be cold and sarcastic," she said.

"Can't help that right now," he said. Cold was how he had to be right now, to do this job. She'd just have to deal with it.

He lifted the blanket that covered her. Lara shivered at the rush of cool air, and brushed her hair out of her eyes, perplexed. "What's this?"

"This is me, making sure of my welcome," he said. "Am I welcome even if I'm cold and sarcastic? You said you were mine. Did you mean it? Or was it just pillow talk to make me hard?"

She jerked up onto her elbows, frowning thoughtfully. Then she lay deliberately back down again, scooting over to make room for him.

"No," she said. "It was absolutely true."

He gestured at her slender legs. "Then open up for me."

Her eyes dilated, her heart rate spiked. A subtle glow heated her cheeks, her chest, though her eyes were wary. "Don't play games."

He shrugged. "Don't make me wait."

She slowly opened her legs, and lifted her arms to him, beckoning. "Welcoming enough for you?" she asked.

"We're getting there." He shifted onto the couch between her parted legs, positioning himself, and leaning over so that his cock rested on her mound, pointing up toward her belly. "Touch my cock."

She clasped him. Squeezed him, slowly gripping, sliding, staring into his eyes as she did so.

He covered her hands with his own, slowly dragged them off his cock with a tight, milking pull, and shoved her legs wider, parting her pussy lips. She gasped, as he thrust into her tight, slick depths.

He grabbed her hands, pinning them on either side of her head as he worked himself slowly inside and out. A juicy, swiveling slide and grind and push. Rhythmic and lazy.

"Do you trust me?" he asked, surging deep.

She clenched around him. "I want you," she said.

"That's nice." He thrust again, harder. "Not what I asked, though."

"How can I trust you in this mood? You're angry at me."

"Yeah," he said. "I'm angry. Do you trust me anyway?"

"Why are you acting like this?" she demanded.

"Because it's how I feel," he said. "I'm in no mood to fake."

She struggled to free her hands. "What do you want from me?"

"A straight answer. Do you trust me? Yes or no."

She sobbed for breath, lifting herself to meet him. He had no clue where he was going with this inexplicable power game, but the dark mood had him in its grip. He wanted her surrender.

He kissed the arch of her trembling throat, feeling the delicate play of bone and muscle and tendon beneath his teeth, licking, sucking. Biting. Dragging his teeth, a delicate, teasing scrape as his hips pumped and rocked. There were tears trickling in front of her ears. He kissed them away, savored their salt. They were his, too.

He worked himself inside her with all his skill, making sure he was sliding his cock right over that spot deep inside, that glowed red hot for him. Driving her closer to her climax—then drawing back.

"Do you trust me?" he asked again.

Her body did. It was a hot liquid kiss around his cock, with every deep stroke. But he could feel the rest of her still holding back.

"Open your eyes," he said sharply. "Tell me."

She obeyed him. Tears spilled from the corners of her eyes.

"Yes," she said, her voice trembling. "Yes, I do trust you."

Maybe it was the words that brought her off, maybe it was something that he did with his body. He didn't know or care, just held himself motionless while she came and came, her pussy throbbing and clenching around his cock. His mouth fastened over hers, his heart pressed against her heart. Drinking in his reward.

He waited until her eyes fluttered open again, and spoke, his voice hard and clear. "Promise me you won't do the human sacrifice thing again," he said. "Promise me you'll get on that bus and disappear."

She opened her eyes, tears streaming. She jerked at her trapped hand, still pinned to the pillow. "Let me wipe my face," she said.

"Swear it." He was squeezing her fingers too tightly. He loosened his grip, but he didn't let go.

"Miles—"

"Do it, Lara." He didn't do the coercive mind jab, but both of them felt it there, snarling and lunging at the chain.

She bit her lip till the color fled, and shook her head. "I can't."

Lara stared into his furious face, unnerved. His eyes burned.

"You can't," he repeated.

She shook her head. Her voice was frozen in her throat.

"Are you fucking kidding me?" he said.

She shook her head again. "I can't say that to you. I have no idea what's going to happen, what we'll encounter, what choices I'll have to make. I won't make a promise that I don't know I can keep. Especially not to you."

"You're telling me you're just going to—"

"No!" she protested. "I'm not telling you any such thing! I'm just not making irresponsible promises. I don't follow orders well, so don't get all alpha on me. And stop pinning my hands. You're being a controlling bastard. And that *hurts*."

He let go of her hands. She flexed her aching fingers.

"Don't try to manipulate me with sex, ever again," she added tartly. "That's a dirty trick, and totally unfair."

"Why not? It doesn't work on you anyway. It makes you

come, but your precious integrity is intact. So why not go wild with the kinky power plays? It's just a fucking parlor game for you."

"Stop trying to intimidate me. You're being ugly. And I hate it."

They stared at each other, bodies still locked together.

"You know my ex, Cindy?" he said. "She may have been a selfish, lying slut and a lightweight piece of fluff, but damn, I could always count on her to do what was in her own best interest. I never had to worry about acts of suicidal heroism from her."

"You're a fine one to talk," she retorted. "You're being irrational. I have no plans of doing anything crazy, or—"

"Stop. I don't want to hear it. You won't promise. End of story. Nothing you could say can make that easier for me to swallow."

She reached up, stroking his stubbled cheek, and dared to speak anyway. "I won't do anything stupid. I promise that," she told him gently. "And you can always trust me to tell you the truth."

"Oh. That'll be a big comfort when you're dead," he snarled.

She heaved, shoving at his unyielding weight. It was like pushing on a steel girder. "Get off me. You are pissing me off."

Her wiggling underscored that fact that their bodies were still joined. He was deep inside her, as thick and throbbing as ever.

He noticed her gaze, and glanced down, with a harsh laugh.

"Yeah. I'm still hard. Bummer, that. I should have come when you did, but no. I was too busy jerking you around, being a controlling bastard."

Her hands flattened against his chest. Conflicting feelings trapped her voice in her throat, but he read her face. His eyes went cold.

"No, I would not do that," he said. "Since you're evidently wondering. I would not force you, ever." He withdrew instantly, and stood up. Cold rushed in where his hot body had been, racking her with shudders. "I'm not that much of a controlling bastard. Jesus, Lara. I thought you said you trusted me."

"It's true." Her teeth were chattering. "I do. Even now."

"What good is that if I can't trust you back?"

With that parting shot, he stalked off into the kitchen, and then the bathroom, slamming the door. Leaving her wrecked.

She sagged back onto the couch, shuddering with sobs. When he took away his sustaining energy, she was only two feet tall, helpless and terrified. He'd gotten in her head, made himself her pillar of strength. Without him, she would become that pile of smoking rubble that all those months in the rat hole had actually made of her.

She'd thought that the way she felt now was a miraculous healing, but she couldn't take credit for any of it. She'd just been leaning on his strength.

Now he was taking it away. Jettisoning her into outer space so that he could run off and perform his own act of goddamn suicidal heroism without any interference from her. Leaving her naked, destroyed, alone.

So unfair. It made her fucking *furious*.

She got up and stomped naked through the kitchen. Wrenched open the bathroom door.

Miles had just stepped out of the shower. He stood there in a cloud of steam, towel in hand. Drops of water trailed seductively over the taut, angular contours of his powerful body. His cock, still half hard, rose to greet her.

"You bastard," she said. "I am so angry at you."

Miles tossed the towel away, pushing heavy, dripping hair back off his forehead. "I know just how you feel."

"No, you don't!" she raged. "You arrogant son of a bitch.

You weren't locked in a hole and mindfucked for months on end. You don't know *shit!*"

His eyebrow twitched up. "Feeling sorry for ourselves, are we?"

"Shut up!" she yelled at him. "Just shut up!"

"I tried," he said. "You followed me in here, Lara. You're the one who wanted more."

"I came in here to kick your arrogant ass! Who do you think you are, having a tantrum on me, when you're the one who's riding off on the kamikaze mission? And you have the nerve to give me attitude?"

"Yeah," he said. "I'm nothing but nerve. One big raw nerve."

His move was so swift. She gasped, and then she was pinned between the chilly tiles of the bathroom wall and his hot, wet body. Straddling him, legs over his elbows. Wide open.

"If you want to say no, say it right now," he said. "Loud."

She swatted his chest. "Goddamn you, Miles!"

"That wasn't a no." He thrust his cock slowly inside her. Withdrew, slow and deliberate, and shoved in once again, deep and hard. "You shouldn't have come in here. Now you just deal with me."

He blocked whatever response she might have made by kissing her. She wrapped herself around him and kissed him back.

Furiously. Clinging to his neck, fingers dug into the thick muscles of his shoulders. Tears streamed from her eyes, and she didn't care. She wanted his heat, his light. She never wanted to let him go, never wanted those deep, slick strokes inside her body to end.

But nothing lasted forever. The explosion obliterated her.

They stayed locked together, glued. Muscles shaking, for many long, silent minutes. She sensed that the fragile bubble of perfect intimacy would pop the minute that reality intruded again.

Miles was the first to move. He glanced up at the small bathroom window. "Sky's lighter," he said. "It's almost dawn. Let's get moving."

He withdrew from her body, setting her gently on her feet, and reached to turn on the shower.

"Miles," she whispered, and switched to the head texting. are we ok?

He switched the water off again and leaned against the shower booth. He did not turn to look at her. "Just because I came?" he said out loud. "No. But we can't wait to thrash out our issues. We don't have the luxury. Can't put off the farewell fuck."

She flinched back, covered her face. "Oh, God."

He switched the water on again, testing until it got hot. "Get in," he said. "If both of us stay quiet, we can't say anything unbearable."

She was surprised when he stepped in after her.

She tried turning to face him, but he turned her back, filled his hands with soap, and caressed her all over. His strong hands were magic, transmitting a tingling heat. Letting his hands say what words could not. She turned her face to the water, let it rinse away her tears.

But the water went cold, and that moment of grace ended, too.

He switched the water off. She clung to him, as the chilly water dripped around them, and hid her face against his chest.

"I'll get on that bus," she said, her voice choked. "I'll disappear, like you said. But not because you commanded me to, got that? It's because I love you. And I trust you. And I believe in you. Okay?"

He was startled into silence for a long moment. Water plopped from the showerhead, hollow and loud in the stillness. "Okay," he said softly, kissing her forehead. "Thank you."

She pulled away without looking at him. Once dried and

out in the kitchen, Miles fished in the dryer for the clothes they'd washed. The mud had washed out, but the bloodstains had set. He yanked his stained shirt and jeans on without comment.

Lara got dressed swiftly, and groomed her wet snarls of hair with a comb she'd found in the bathroom. She helped Miles fold bedding, sweep up crumbs, wash and dry cups, pans. Silent busywork. He came down from the bedroom with a couple of oversized men's sweatshirts. Hers was a faded navy blue hoodie, with Lewis & Clark College stenciled on it. She swam in it. The hem hit her at mid-thigh, but it stayed put if she zipped it up and pulled the drawstring on the hood tight.

He tossed the sheet they'd used into the washing machine.

"Should we leave a note?" she asked. "To tell them we—"

"Done," he said.

"Should we maybe leave some money for—"

"Covered. Braid your hair. Lots of wind on that bike. Gonna call Sean." He fished out his phone, turned it on, and she waited, transfixed, while it connected.

"Hey," he said. "So? . . . okay. Yeah, will do."

He met her eyes. "Nothing new," he said. "No new contact. Davy's still out for the count. Let's get moving. We need to rent you a car."

"I can't rent a car," she reminded him. "I don't have a license, Miles. No ID at all. Nothing on earth but what you've given me."

Miles looked like he was grinding his teeth. "That sucks," he said. "I'll have to arrange for an ID and a debit card to be waiting for you somewhere. Without knowing where it is myself."

The reasoning behind that struck fear into her soul.

Miles herded her out the door. Time to abandon their oasis.

The dawn motorcycle ride was like a fever dream. She held the canvas bag that held the disassembled rifle between her legs, the computer bag swinging and bouncing on her back, barely managing to clutch Miles' waist. The air was cold, and intensely sweet. Outlines were so sharp, colors so deep, light so dazzling, shadows densely black. The gray of the sky was vast and ominous. Wind slashed icily at her face and ears. Miles' long hair whipped back, stinging her, but she still leaned closer to smell his skin. He stared straight ahead, as laser-focused in this, as he was in everything, whether it was saving her life or driving her crazy with his body.

The Citadel was wintry. Ice-bound. Protection, as always, but no comfort. She tried to be a grown-up about that. To keep her fears pressed down deep inside.

They felt like a pot about to boil over.

25

Petrie pushed the doorbell again, cursing as he shoved his fingers through his hair. It was a nervous habit that encouraged the hair to stand straight up, like he'd stuck his finger in a light socket.

Ambivalent didn't even begin to describe the way he felt about the phone call that had dragged him here. Ever since he'd met this crowd—an event marked by the bullet he'd taken in his lung at the Jersey mob boss's house—he'd been marveling at the grand style of messes these people got into. They had a talent for it.

Kind of like he did himself. Like attracts like.

But this episode was so far outside the bounds of normal, he was strongly considering jumping into his car and driving away, without a word of explanation or apology. Just cutting ties. He got into enough trouble on his own. This shit he did not need.

He liked these people. He enjoyed hanging out with them. They were smart, interesting, an amazing resource. The kind of people he'd like to knock back a few beers with when things were good, and have at his back when things got weird.

But not this weird. Telelpaths? Brain-crushing psychic monsters who burst people's blood vessels from a distance? Seriously?

He would have turned tail a while ago but for the off chance of catching a glimpse of the Snow Queen, a.k.a., the remote, sylph-like and inexplicably hostile Svetlana. The Mc-Cloud Crowd's maiden princess in the lofty tower. The chick disdained him utterly, and did not hesitate to snub him when she deigned to acknowledge his existence at all. He was such a goddamn masochist.

"*Chi e'?*" The door opened, and a wild-eyed Zia Rosa, Bruno's more-or-less batty Italian great-aunt, stared at him, wild-eyed and suspicious. Her jet-black helmet of bouffant curls was wildly askew. "What you doin' here, Sam?"

"Sean called me," he explained, making his voice low and soothing. "He asked me to come here and help drive some of the kids to a safe house. He didn't say anything to you about that?"

"I don' know what he say to who, I don' understand nothing," the woman complained. Her voice was snappish, but her hands were trembling. "*Non si capisce niente.* Crazy sonzabitches, threatening little children. What kinda crazy sonzabitches would hurt a little kid?"

Petrie kept his mouth shut. In his line of work, to his great misfortune, he'd run across many crazy sonzabitches who hurt little kids. Even some who actually got off on it. He tried not to dwell on them. That stuff took years off your life.

Zia Rosa stepped back and finally let him in. The place was a madhouse. The kids had absorbed the freak-out vibe, and were running around like mad things, screaming in shrill, ear-splitting voices. In the space of eight seconds, he identified Tonio and Lena, Lily and Bruno's twins, racing madly after Jamie, Davy's little boy, and Maddy, Connor's little daughter. Stubborn little Eamon, Sean's boy, was stumbling along behind on his chubby legs, roaring in outrage at being left in the dust.

Petrie waited for the procession to go by, and turned to Zia Rosa again. "So? What do you need me to do? Where are we going?"

"Shhhh!" Zia Rosa shushed him, her dark eyes darting anxiously from left to right. "We can't talk about it. They got mind readers!"

Petrie let out a slow, measured breath. "Mrs. Ranieri, we have to know where we're going in order to get there," he said patiently.

"They'll tell us when we're moving," Zia said. "When we're sure we're not being followed. Don't say nothin'!"

Lily came in, with tiny Marco draped over her shoulder. "Oh, Sam. Thanks for coming. Bruno said you'd drive Jeannie and Kevvie. Kev and Edie will take Eamon and Maddy, I'll take Zia, Marco and Lena, and Sveti and Bruno will take Jamie and Tonio. We just have to wait for Kev and Edie to get here with the kids. Get yourself some coffee, there's a fresh pot in the kitchen. I'm going to try and get Marco down so I can pack, so make yourself at home."

She hurried off, and he wandered into the kitchen, relieved that they'd assigned him the biggest kids. Jeannie and Kevvie were smart, reasonable, young human beings. He could deal with them just fine. Infants or toddlers would have provoked instant catastrophic brain melt.

Not that he should make light of brain melt, considering what had happened to Davy. He looked around Bruno and Lily's kitchen, thickly cluttered with baby and toddler paraphernalia. He picked out a mug, poured some brew and sipped, wondering what had really happened to Davy's brain. If the guy just happened to have an aneurism randomly, like anyone could have, and the arguably paranoid and volatile minds in the McCloud Crowd, Miles foremost among them, had blown up that disaster into something that it wasn't.

Something that it could not possibly be.

He sipped coffee, listened to the constant kiddie shrieking in the far part of the house, glad it wasn't his problem. He could hear Lily in the adjoining room, Bruno's office, humming a lullaby to little Marco. But her singing was higher and faster and jerkier than a lullaby should be, and Marco was feeling it. He fussed and squeaked.

When he finally calmed down, Lily deposited him and hurried off to do what she could in her narrow naptime window. His coffee finished, he rinsed the cup and walked into Bruno's studio.

The room was crowded with toy designs. Wild, colorful stuff was scattered and hanging everywhere. Heaps of paperwork lay all over the desks and shelves. Bruno ran a toy business, and Kev McCloud was one of the main designers. Marco's bassinet dominated the room. A hanging mobile that featured what appeared to be strands of DNA fashioned out of colored beads dangled over his head.

Petrie edged closer, peeking into the bassinet. Marco was finally starting to plump up properly, get the dimples and the chubby wrist folds. He'd lost the shriveled preemie look. His round cheeks quivered rhythmically, sucking constantly on his binkie as he slept.

Cute. Petrie enjoyed kids—in small, calibrated doses. His sister's kids, for instance, were great. But he was uncomfortable with them on a visceral level. Their vulnerability scared the shit out of him, knowing as he did just how shitty the world could be if the fickle wheel of fortune turned and dumped them down, down, down. So many dangers. Kid killers, school shootings, bullies, pedophiles, child traffickers, heroin and meth, drunk drivers, and date rape. Jesus wept.

You couldn't pay him enough to risk it.

His niece and nephew and little Marco and the rest of the McCloud Crowd's spawn all had better odds than most, but still. You never knew when the telepathic mind-melters were going to come along and mess you up.

The door opened, and Sveti barreled in. She jolted back

when she saw him. "What are you doing to him?" Her voice was shaky.

He lifted his hands. "Ah . . . nothing? I wasn't going to skewer him and barbecue him. I was just watching him sleep."

She hurried over to the crib and peered in, making sure he hadn't started the barbecuing process. "Since when have you been interested in babies?"

"I like babies just fine," he said.

Satisfied that Marco was intact, she put some distance between them, in the usual pose she tended to strike with him. Hands on hips, tilted gold-brown eyes flashing. Looking extremely fine in her fitted black-ribbed sweater that hugged her small but very curvy frame. Hair swirling down, long and shiny and touchable. And those tight skinny jeans, wow. He longed for the back view, but was certain he'd get an eyeful of it, as soon as she minced off in a huff. He could probably start the countdown to that ass twitching huff any minute now.

"What's eating you?" It was suicide to ask, but hey. He'd always been kind of dumb that way.

Sure enough, she looked outraged. "Someone threatened my little friends," she said. "Is that not enough for you, as an explanation?"

He shrugged. "Yeah, I guess."

"Excuse me," she murmured. "Please, move. Lily asked me to pack Marco's diaper bag. No, move the other way, please."

She shoved him out of her way, and proceeded to start packing a big, quilted bag with baby stuff. In went the portable changing table, diaper cream, wipes, spit-up rags. She was fiercely ignoring him.

"So you think this threat is real?" he asked.

Her gaze whipped around. "You think that it is not? Why?"

That was a trick question if he'd ever heard one, but he just opted for blunt honesty. "I think it sounds nuts," he said.

Sveti let her glossy hair swing forward to hide her eyes as she counted out a handful of colorful onesies and tiny wool socks. "I have experience in things that are nuts," she said. "As nuts as this, perhaps worse. If Tam and the McClouds say that this thing happened, it did happen. I trust them. And I trust Miles, too."

That needled him. "Miles? Really? You saw how he was at the wedding," he said. "The guy's on the verge of a psychotic break."

"He is still my friend, and I trust him," she said stubbornly.

Petrie wondered, not for the first time, if Sveti had a thing for Miles. Unrequited, of course, since the guy was perennially hung up on Cindy. Cindy herself had struck him as being in no way worthy of Miles' devotion, but there was no accounting for tastes. "He's got his hands full," he said. "Hot and heavy with the new girlfriend that he just rescued from the black hole of Calcutta. Hell of a place to pick up chicks. Not much of an advertisement for his good judgment."

Sveti gave him a reproachful look. "I would not make jokes," she said. "It is not her fault, what happened to her. And I know how it is to be in a hole for months. It is not a matter for joking."

Bring out the big guns, why didn't she. She counted out a double handful of tiny disposable diapers, and packed them into the bag, so certain that her guilt darts had hit their mark, she didn't even need to look up. But she hadn't seemed upset about Miles hooking up with the girl from the black hole. She hadn't batted an eye, in fact. Hmm.

Sveti could one-up almost anybody with her hands tied when it came to hard-luck stories. Kidnapped by a mafia *Vor* at the age of twelve, sent off to have her organs harvested in retaliation against her cop father. The father was subsequently murdered, and she was rescued at the eleventh hour by the McCloud Crowd, just as the bad guys were about to cut her heart out, but her mother had become mentally imbalanced from the tragedy and committed suicide some years after.

He figured that was what gave her the remote, tragic air. And her iron-clad moral upper hand. Hell, she was entitled to it.

But her hostility to him was still a mystery. She pushed him a little harder than she strictly needed to, to roll out the cart stowed beneath the bassinet to get out Q-tips, Tylenol drops, teething gel.

"What's your problem with me, Sveti?" he demanded.

She waited just a little bit too long before she bounced it back to him. "Problem? What problem? I don't have a problem."

"Yes, you do," he said. "You think I'm scum. I know I made a bad first impression, but—"

"Horrible," she said. "Tormenting Zia with pictures of dead people. You were disgusting. Opportunistic."

"Yeah, horrible," he agreed. "It's called 'doing my job.' It's not a very pretty job sometimes. So forgive me, already."

She gazed at him, her mouth a little open. Her eyes looked scared. Almost trapped. She smelled like some flower he half-recognized, a honey-sweet, succulent smell. Her cheeks had a blush of pink. And her skin was fine-grained, flawless. Somehow, he'd moved closer to her, without meaning to. There was a tiny nipple jut under the sweater. Like they'd just . . . gone hard.

God knows, he had. Like, when she walked in.

He cleared his throat. "You hate my guts."

She sniffed. "Certainly not. I do not put so much energy into thinking about you, Petrie."

"Wow. You cut me to the bone, Sveti." He took a step closer, which had the effect of backing her right up to the wall. Bassinet on one side, desk on the other. Nowhere to run.

"Hold still," he said softly. "You have something in your hair."

It was a cheap, transparent ploy. He'd wanted to touch her hair for a couple of years now. But she didn't call him on it. Just flinched away slightly when his fingers made contact with that miraculous stuff. Satin smooth, flashes of red in the brown. So warm. Almost like putting his fingers in a creamy, silken liquid. It made his cock ache.

Miles' jibe at the wedding flashed through his mind, and he looked at Sveti's pupils. Dilated. Vast velvet pools of black. Her face, so pink. *All those capillaries, expanding just for you.*

He hadn't checked the heart rate yet, but he was going to make a stab at it. Her lips were moving, like she was trying to speak, but nothing was coming out. "What?" he prompted.

She shook her head. She looked almost on the verge of tears. "I forgot my English," she whispered.

"That's okay," he said. "It'll come to you. But there's something I need to know. Something Miles said. I was wondering if it was true."

He eased in a little closer, inhaling that scent, for as long a breath as his lungs would expand. She wore tiny jewels in her pink earlobes.

Her eyelashes fluttered, nervously. "What did Miles say?"

He insinuated himself deeper into that soft cloud of perfumed warmth that clung to her, savoring the shocked stillness, the dazzled look in her eyes.

And then it was happening. He hadn't made a move. It was a kiss that had been forming underground for years, and now it had burst up out of the dark, ready to rock. No slick lead-in, no careful buildup, no crafty seduction. He just went at her, fierce and dominating, kissing her like he was already fucking her. He didn't remember deciding to stick his hand up under her sweater, cupping her tit, teasing her tight nipple through the filmy fabric of her bra. There was no calculation, no weighing if it might be too much, no wondering what he might get away with. His conscious mind had not been invited to this party.

She arched against him, clutching his shoulders. Totally into it.

Holy fuck. He'd started out just trying to make a point. Now he was pinning her to the wall so she straddled his erection. Her fingernails dug into his neck, her fingers gripped his hair, and her tongue twined with his. Her mouth was so sweet. So were those sounds she made. Her legs clenched him, her cheeks a hot crimson.

He could feel her racing heart, with his face pressed to her tits. Her sweater was shoved up high, puckered nipples poking through the cups of her sheer bra as he nuzzled and kissed—

She arched, making a shocked, low wailing sound. Coming.

He felt it against his cock, right through their clothes.

Oh, *yes*. Oh, sweet.

He held her afterwards, his nose still buried between her tits. Nuzzling the soft curves, the jut of her nipple, waiting for the echoes to fade. Wow. This was going to be hotter than he'd ever dreamed. And he'd dreamed it very, very hot. For years, now.

He lifted his mouth. Her eyes were closed. Two glittering tears quivered on her lower eyelashes. They detached, and flashed down.

She licked her trembling lips. Her eyes fluttered open, looking down, to the side, anywhere but at him. "Put me down, please."

His grip tightened possessively. He rubbed his cheek against the tender swell of her tit. So very unwilling to do as she asked. "We could take this somewhere, and finish it," he suggested. Hell, anyplace would do for him. A bathroom, a basement. A broom closet.

"It already is finished," she said. "Please, Petrie."

Irrational anger kindled in him. He stared at her, his face stony.

"Call me Sam," he said.

She licked her lips again, leaving a sheen of moisture that made his cock jump. "Please, Sam," she said.

He set her down on her feet, and she backed away, hastily rearranging her sweater, her hair, her face. "I . . . I don't know what happened," she faltered. "I—"

"I could explain it to you sometime," he said. "Over dinner."

She shook her head. "No, no. Things are so strange now, and I—"

"Later, then. When the weirdness is fixed. Dinner, with me?"

She backed away, lips trembling. "I can't."

"You're seeing someone else?" he asked.

She shook her head, wiping her eyes with the back of her hands.

"Then why?" Frustration sharpened his voice.

"I can't," she said. "I just can't be with you."

A swift lunge, and he had her in his grasp again. He bent her back, off balance, so she had to cling or fall. Her mouth was so soft.

He had to keep it busy. Better that she kiss him again than tell him to piss off. That was a much better use for her mouth.

The door opened, and Lily let out a squeak. "Oh, my God. I'm so sorry." She snapped the door shut again.

But the moment was killed. Sveti freed herself, wiping her mouth, running her hands over her cheeks like she could wipe that blush away.

"You want me," he said harshly.

Her face tightened. "Don't, Sam."

"Why?" He was fighting not to yell. "Just tell me, already! What is your fucking problem?"

Sveti yanked the door open and ran away. Marco woke

up, and began to squall. Lily came back in, pale and nervous, to pick Marco up out of his crib, shooting him sidelong glances.

Petrie's cell phone started to buzz. He went out into the kitchen to answer it. Sveti by now was nowhere to be seen. The display on his phone indicated that it was Barlow, probably calling to scold him again about how Miles Davenport wasn't answering his phone.

"Petrie here," he said.

"We've got to bring him in, Sam," Barlow said. "He's been keeping someone sequestered in his cabin in the woods. We have reason to think that he's been holding Lara Kirk there."

Petrie gaped for a moment, speechless. "That's not possible."

"No? Why would you say that, Sam? Do you know something about this guy? Something you're not telling me?"

"I know Miles Davenport," Petrie said. "Seven months ago, when she disappeared, he didn't know that Lara Kirk even existed."

"We'll see how he explains his cabin, then. We've been there since six A.M. Windows boarded over, mattress on the floor, cum-stained sheet, long, dark hairs on a wool blanket. A leg shackle, with blood on it. Food wrappings, MREs, protein bars, a chemical toilet. A little hellhole, Sam. And then there's the grave, in the back. Three men, throats slit, bled out, duct tape. The criminologists are working it over. It doesn't look good for your boy. And you know what? It doesn't look too great for you, either. This whole thing is going to suck for you."

"How did you find the place?"

"We were tipped off. Thaddeus Greaves had paid a team to investigate. They'd tracked her down to that cabin in the woods. They contacted their employer, and then he didn't hear anything more from them. That was yesterday. So he called us. They're the ones who are in the grave, Sam. Your boy's a killer. Among other things."

"It's not possible," Petrie said again. "It's a set-up."

Barlow was silent for a long moment. "Don't protect him," he said heavily. "This is going to mess you up, Sam. It's a career killer."

"I'm not protecting him," Petrie said, teeth gritted. He glanced over through the kitchen entrance, and saw Lily in the doorway, holding a suitcase and knapsack. The kids were gathered by the front door. He glimpsed Bruno, Kev, Edie. They were mobilizing.

"Where are you?" he asked.

"I'm outside the motel where he stayed, Pine Manor. It's on Cleary. He never checked out."

"I'll be there in fifteen," he said, and hung up.

He walked into the living room. Bruno and Kev were both looking suspicious and hostile. They'd probably heard about the hot tryst with the Snow Queen, and violently disapproved.

Good. It was time for all of them to start getting used to the idea.

"I'm sorry, but I can't help you today after all," he said.

"Why?" Sveti's voice rang out. She came walking out, bundled up in a thick, black down jacket, hair tucked under a hat. "It's your job calling you, no? More important than anything else?"

This was not the time or place for that charged conversation, so he shined it on. "I need Miles' number. His new one," he said to Kev.

"Yeah?" The man's voice was truculent. "And why is that?"

"Because I'm about to completely screw myself and my career by letting him know he's about to be charged with kidnapping, rape, and murder. And I need to go talk to the guy who's got the case. I have to tell him exactly what's going on with Greaves. All of it. I don't think anybody has anything to lose, at this point."

Kev and Bruno exchanged glances. Kev nodded, pulling out his phone. He read off the number. Petrie plugged it in.

"I'll take my car, with Kevvie and Jeannie," Sveti announced.

Bruno looked displeased. "I wanted two adults in each car, at least one of them armed."

"Edie can drive, and I'll be the one who's armed," Sveti said.

Petrie whipped his gaze around, startled. "You? Armed?"

"Of course. Tam taught me." She lifted the side of her sweater, and showed him the pistol tucked into the little holster snugged inside the waistband of her jeans. It had not been there during the kiss. He was sure of it. He'd had his hands all over that girl.

Whoa. He shook his head and pointed himself out the door.

He spent the seventeen minutes it took to speed to Barlow's location wondering how to phrase this crazy story in such a way that Barlow wouldn't call the psychologists and tell them he'd snapped. It was going to be a challenge, to gloss over the weird stuff when the omissions left gaping, improbable holes.

Barlow's sedan wasn't in the hotel parking lot, and he didn't see it on the first pass around the block, either. He was just about to call again when he finally glimpsed it parked in an alley behind the hotel. It was raining. He could see Barlow in the front seat.

He tapped the horn, thinking he'd suggest the nearby Dunkin' Donuts, or any other warm, dry place to talk this out over coffee.

Barlow didn't move. Petrie jerked up the parking brake and got out, turning his collar up against the damp wind, the sideways raindrops. Barlow's window was open, the rain blowing right in.

Barlow's total stillness sank in.

An icy claw tightened deep inside him. His feet slowed, but he did not allow himself to stop. He kept walking, bracing himself. By the time he peered through the window, he knew what he would see.

And knowing didn't help.

Barlow's eyes were wide open, frozen in surprise. His shirt had a vivid splotch of red. A gunshot wound, straight to the heart.

26

Lara was stiff with cold when they finally cruised into a medium-sized town. They drove up and down the downtown streets, as if he was looking for something specific.

He pulled to a halt in a parking lot outside a fifties-era brick factory building with a faded sign that read, "St. Vincent's Thrift Store."

"Clothes," Miles said, in answer to her silent question. "Hope you don't mind used. Too many cameras in the Walmarts and the BiMarts and the Targets. I don't know how far their ability to mine data reaches, and I don't want to test it. But this place won't have security vidcams."

"Used is fine," she said. "I like thrift shops."

"Good. Pick out some stuff, fast. I'll make some calls, set up the ID and credit cards. Then we'll grab a bite and get you to the station."

His brisk tone felt distant. "I want to stay with you," she said, instantly wishing she had kept her trap shut.

He gave her his implacable look. He didn't even have to say it.

The store itself was big and drafty, smelling faintly of

mildew and old shoes. A grizzled old man sat behind an ancient cash register near the door. He appeared to be dozing.

Miles trailed protectively close behind her as she wound her way through the tables of miscellaneous junk, ceramics, old appliances, junk jewelry, shoes, dishes, glassware, furniture. At the racks of clothing she eyeballed the sizes, picked out two pairs of faded jeans that looked about right, a button-down of slate-blue cotton, a couple of long-sleeved tees. Miles plucked a big, wool army coat, olive drab, and tossed it on top of her pile. It looked huge for her, but warm. There was another one there, even larger, and he grabbed that one too, presumably for himself. Muttering on his phone all the while.

". . . goddamnit, how many times do I have to go through this? You're dealing with fucking telepaths, Seth. All the rules change when they . . . yeah, well, look what they did to Davy! He's already fingered Davy's and Connor's families, do you want him to go after Jesse and Chris and Mattie and Raine, too? . . . we've been through that, and we can't. I appreciate the offer. Pick a town at random and send the . . . yeah, to a big chain hotel and—fuck, no! Don't tell me where it is! I can't know! Jesus, Seth, keep your finger on the page!"

Miles noticed her listening and gestured sharply, frowning, toward the racks of clothes. She turned her eyes to the hanging shirts, picked out a forest green pile sweatshirt.

". . . debit card and a credit card, too. You sure there's no way you can score a passport for her? It would be great if she could leave the country . . . yeah, well, work on it, then. Work on it fast . . . hey, don't get twitchy on me, man. I'm having a hard enough time as it is."

She kept her ears perked up as she circled the racks, flipping through totally irrelevant used vintage dresses—and then she saw it. She caught her breath, and lost the thread of Miles' phone conversation.

It was the dress. The exact dress that she had worn in the Citadel. The dress he had torn off her, or thrown the skirt up, countless times, in countless erotic episodes. Ivory white, low cut, with a satin underskirt, a gathered chiffon overskirt, a ruched chiffon sash. Right down to the rosettes that trimmed the bodice, though one was ripped loose, dangling from a single thread. Swatches of white chiffon for straps over the arms. It made her toes curl.

She peered at the size. One size smaller than what she used to wear in her former life. Which was about right, or even a little large, in her current state. Maybe it was a discarded bridesmaid gown. In perfect condition, other than a little yellowing on the satin lining inside of the bodice, and what looked like a coffee stain on the skirt.

Her heart was thudding as if she'd seen a ghost. She wanted to think of it as a hopeful omen, but she was afraid to. It was so frivolous. Mortal danger, death on every side, innocent children threatened, and here she was swooning over a dress? Time to grow up.

She was embarrassed to show it to Miles, or more to the point, to ask him if he would buy it for her, being as how she didn't have a cent to her name. But he would probably say something cutting, in his present, edgy mood, and she didn't want to deal with that.

She couldn't leave the dress, either.

Lara yanked it off its hanger, and peered at the price. $16. Whoop de doo. As deceptions went, it was a relatively harmless one, and she would make it up to him. If she got the chance.

She folded it up as small as it would go, which wasn't very, it being big and pouffy. She sandwiched it between the practical clothes and the big coat and circled the rack back to Miles again.

". . . don't know what else I can do at this point, so don't give me any more shit," Miles was whispering savagely. "Yeah, you think? And let them kill Jeannie and Kevvie? He would do it, Seth. Davy, too. He's one psychic finger jab away from death right now. The guy could probably do him from a car driving past the fucking hospital." Miles caught sight of her standing there in the aisle between the racks with her armful of clothes, and gestured her toward the wall. "Move over there, against the white wall," he directed. "No, a little to the left, so the light hits you. Hold on a sec," he said into his phone. "I'll take this picture for you right now, and call you right back."

Lara lay her armful of clothes onto one of the tables, and stood against the wall. He thumbed his smartphone and framed her, squinting intently through the viewfinder. "Smooth down your hair a little," he ordered her. "It's all over the place."

She did her best, unfastening her braid and finger-combing the wind-whipped tangles around her ears. She posed again.

He still didn't look happy. "Hold your head up straighter," he said, frowning. "Try not to look so scared."

"Try not to be a jerk," she suggested.

His grin flashed. He snapped the picture, gave it a long, critical once-over, then tapped the phone again.

"Let me see it," she said.

"Don't worry about it. You look beautiful." He thumbed open his call again, held it to his ear. "Yeah. Me again. Sent. Yeah, okay. I'll pass you to her." He held out his phone. "Here. Talk to my friend, Seth."

She looked at the proffered phone as if it were a snake that might bite her. "What . . . who?"

"He's helping us," he explained, impatiently. "He has information for you. Info I do not want to store in my own head, so I can't pass it on to you. He has to give it to you directly. Got it?"

She still hesitated, so he just grabbed her hand and slapped the phone into it. She held it up to her ear. It was so warm from his hand.

"Um, hello?" she said. "This is Lara."

"Hey. I'm Seth." The guy's deep voice sounded angry.

"Miles wants me to give you some coordinates, so pay attention. Buy a bus ticket for Pendleton, via Eugene, then Portland. There's one that leaves in an hour and ten, and if you miss it, you'll wait four more hours, so don't. Once you're in Pendleton, get a cab to the Hampton Inn. The front desk will be holding a package for Melissa Whelan. Got that? Melissa Whelan, that's you, now. Your wallet got left behind, so you had it couriered to your hotel. Your room for the night is paid. In the morning, you rent a car, and blow on out of there, fast. Once you're off, none of us will know where you are. Still with me?"

"Yes," she said.

"The debit card has twenty-five grand on it. When it runs out, use the credit card. I would quiz you on all this, make sure you've got it, but Miles doesn't want to contaminate his pristine brain with your data," the guy grumbled. "Fucking nuts, if you ask me."

"Couldn't agree more," she said.

"Another thing. We need a way to communicate, which is tricky, since we could be monitored by the big psycho badass. So, as per his Royal Highness's strict instructions, I opened up a new Yahoo account. Username, UHaveGot2BKidding, all words capitalized, U and B single letters, 'to' the number 2, no spaces. Password, PsiFreakBGone, no spaces, all words capped, B a single letter, and follow it with two exclamation points. You need to communicate with us, log onto that account and leave me a message in the drafts folder. Got that?"

Lara squeezed her eyes shut, pummeling her tired brain into a mode that could take in and efficiently store that kind of information. She had to visualize it written. "Um . . . I think so," she faltered.

"Not good enough," Seth barked. "Go find a goddamn pen and paper, if you're not sure!"

"I've got it, I've got it," she assured him.

"So this is the deal. I'll check that account a few times a

day. You ever need anything, money, documents, help, whatever, you let us know. Got it?"

The subtext was clear. That if she ever needed his help, it was because the worst had happened and Miles was gone. And they were helping her for his sake. In his memory.

"Yeah," she said, her voice thick. "Thanks. I really apprec—"

"Thank Miles, not me. He made it happen."

"Oh, I do. I have. Several times," she told him.

"Good," the man said. "He needs to hear it. Good luck, and be careful. Pass that crazy bastard back to me."

She did so, her throat too tight to speak, and gathered up her armful of clothes. Miles hunched over the phone again, pulling her behind him as he muttered and argued into it. He stopped a few times on the way to grab a big, multicolored knit cap, which he tossed onto her pile. Then it was a pair of somewhat wacky, battered, mirror sunglasses, big, perfectly round discs, like John Lennon specs. With the army coat and the hat, it was going to be quite the bold and edgy look. Certainly not her usual style, but she supposed that was the point.

The last thing he grabbed was a bright-blue canvas gym bag. He tossed it on the counter, turning away to finish his conversation. Lara lay her pile on top of it, and the old guy began ringing them up. Miles didn't turn to look, even when her frothy ivory dress was sprawled all over the counter and spilling halfway to the floor.

Miles pried out his wallet and handed it to her, just as the guy announced the grand total of fifty-two dollars. He had no small bills, just a thick, intimidating wad of hundreds. She handed one over.

The guy peered over his glasses. "Got anything smaller?"

"Sure don't," Lara said. "Sorry."

He grumbled, but made the change. Lara packed the stuff into the duffel. She donned the coat, which lapped down over her shoulders and almost reached her ankles. Miles shoved the hat down over her eyes, and perched the sun-glasses on her nose. She swatted his ass smartly when he dared to laugh at the resulting outfit.

Then it was down the block and across the street, to the funky little diner for a meal. They were very quiet after the waitress took their order. Miles put his hands out on the table, like he was going to reach for her hand, but his phone rang.

He pulled it out. Stared at the buzzing thing. Not answering.

"What? Who is it?" she asked, unnerved.

"I don't know," he said. "Only Aaro, Sean, Connor and Kev should have this number. This was the burner. I didn't give it to anyone else."

"Don't answer it," she said swiftly.

He shrugged. "If they know that I answer this phone, then they probably know where I am already. I might as well learn what there is to learn, rather than stay ignorant." He tapped the screen. "Yeah?"

He listened quietly, for several minutes, not looking Lara in the eye. "No shit," he muttered. "Wow. Yeah, of course. I'll come in and defend myself as soon as possible, but I can't now, because I . . . yeah, I know, but . . . I will, as soon as I can, but . . ."

He covered his face with his hand. Lara could hear the guy on the other end literally bellowing at him.

"Look, man." Miles' voice was hushed. "I appreciate the heads-up. I am so sorry about Barlow. Jesus, Sam. I'll do everything I can to make this right for you, but right now, I have to go."

He hung up the phone and immediately turned it off.

"Who was that?" she asked.

He took so long to answer, she started getting scared. She drummed her finger on the table. "Miles," she said, imitating his alpha master and commander voice. "Spit it out. Right now."

Miles dragged another item out of his bag, a nylon pouch

with long straps and clasps, still refusing to meet her eyes. "That was Sam Petrie. A cop friend of mine."

"And?" she prompted. "What's the heads-up for? Sorry about what? Defend yourself against what? What's happening?"

He rubbed his face, glancing around at all the other customers in the diner, and leaned closer. "Greaves has been busy," he said quietly. "He's set me up. I have this shack, on some land I own up in the Cascades. They staged the place to look like I'm the one who's been holding you captive. And they buried those guys I killed out back."

She blinked rapidly, trying to process it. "But that's ridiculous," she said sharply. "All I have to do is tell them the truth."

He shrugged. "Your trustworthiness as a witness will be in question if they think you were sequestered and brainwashed."

Something rose up inside her, close to hysteria. "So they'll call me crazy? They'll lock you up? They won't believe what I say about you?"

"We can't afford to worry about this right now," he said. "Let's just pretend that it never—"

"No! I'm not going to pretend! I'm on to you, Miles. You don't expect to live through this, so it's not really your problem, right? You're just blowing it off!"

He grabbed her hand, squeezed it. "Lara," he said. "Please."

His eyes were anguished. She cut off her rant, and pressed the paper napkin against her eyes.

When she was back under control, she blew her nose into the napkin and stared down at Miles' battered, scabbed brown hand, enveloping hers. His other hand held the canvas bag, and when she met his eyes, he shoved it across the table at her. "Put this in your bag. There's about thirteen grand. The debit card has twenty-five more."

She stared at it, recoiling. "I can't take that."

He gave her an incredulous look. "Fucked if you won't! Don't tell me you're going to get uptight about the stupid stuff? Now?"

"Thirty-eight thousand bucks? You call that stupid? You'll need that money yourself. That's a huge amount of money!"

He squeezed her hand again. "Lara," he said. "I have lots of money. I've socked it away all over the place, more than I know how to spend. If I can't spend it on the people I love, what the fuck good is it?"

She shook her head. So damned uncomfortable with it.

"If we get through whatever's going to happen, and it runs out, I'll just make more," he said. "Read my lips. Not. An. Issue. Got it?"

She stared down, miserably, at the canvas bag he'd shoved beneath her hand. All that it represented, and all that it threatened.

She didn't want his money. She wanted *him*. Always and forever, and this was a poor, poor trade. "I already owe you so much," she said.

He reached up, touched her face. "I just wish it were more. And I owe you just as much, you know. You saved my ass, too."

She snorted. "That is bullshit."

"It's true," he said, stubbornly. He lifted his hand to touch her face, stroking her cheek slowly and hypnotically with the side of his index finger. "But we are light years past this conversation, you and I."

She was lulled by his silken voice, the faint, rhythmic caress on her face. The unique mix of caustic irony and gentleness that was Miles. She turned her face, pressing it against his hand, like a cat.

He cupped her cheek in his palm, leaning closer. "You do know that everything I have is yours, right?" he asked, and this time, there was no irony in his voice at all. "Till the end of time. Did you get that memo, in all the excitement? Or do we need to play catch-up?"

She squeezed her wet eyes shut and shook her head.

"I'm not just talking about money. I'm talking all of it. Heart, soul, body. All my hopes for the future. The places I want to see with you, the stories we'll tell, our adventures together. The meals we'll cook, the walks, the drives. All the nights together, all the mornings. Coffee and toast, conversations and jokes. All the winters and the springs and the summers and the falls. For as long as we get. All yours, Lara."

She pressed her hand to her mouth. It burned, inside her. A sweet and awful twisting pain, that vision which could never exist.

He reached up with ritual slowness, and brushed her tears away.

"Oh, for God's sake, stop it," she forced out through trembling lips. "Don't make me cry. You're killing me."

He pulled her hand up. Pressed her knuckles to his lips, and then to his forehead. Bowing his head and hiding his own face.

She lost it for a while, but fought until she could drag in a breath without hitching and gurgling. She blew her nose into her napkin. Miles wiped his eyes on his sleeve, and gave the bag another push. "Put it in your bag," he said. "Don't leave it lying around."

She took it, still hesitating. "Did you take enough to rent a car?"

"I have plenty," he assured her gently.

The waitress arrived with their food, so they pulled themselves together. She got down more than half of the chili and cornbread, but even Miles seemed to have trouble getting around his sandwich today.

"Will you give me your phone number?" she asked.

He shook his head. "You don't need the phone to contact me," he said. "And if you can't reach me that way, then the phone will be useless in any case. Come on, your bus is leaving soon."

The station was a small one, just a few blocks away, next

to a railroad track. Miles stayed way back, careful not to watch or listen as she bought her ticket and tucked it inside her jacket.

He walked her over, and held her, breathlessly tight, arms shaking, outside the gaping door of the bus. The driver finally leaned out, frowning. "All aboard," he bawled.

She climbed on, clutching her bag. She couldn't look away from his eyes. Breaking that eye contact would rip something vital out of her.

She shouldn't have agreed to this. She saw his logic, she followed his reasoning, but only with her head. Not with her heart.

The bus lumbered away. She craned her neck back, staring at his tall, broad, graceful body, the coat blowing back like an old-fashioned greatcoat. His hair lifted in the wind. His love for her shone from his eyes. She clung to the sight of him. Every second she could look at him was a desperate gulp of air.

And she was about to dive underwater.

Tearful farewells played hell with the grinding war machine.

Miles was a mess when her bus turned the corner. Luckily for him, icy algorithms and laser sharp hyper-functioning wits were not required to buzz around on a motorcycle and look for a car rental. He was so grateful for the alternative identity the McCloud Crowd had given him on his thirtieth birthday. A costly, blatantly illegal gift. To think he'd laughed in their faces at the time. Hah. Payback.

Petrie said that they had recovered a Glock 23 revolver from a dumpster right near the car that held Barlow's body. His gun. As if he'd be stupid enough to murder a cop and then dispose of the gun in a dumpster at the scene. Then again, normal people did dumb things in the aftermath of committing violent crimes. He was a long way from normal now. Farther than he'd ever dreamed he'd get.

In any case, the impending manhunt just accelerated his agenda. He wished he could go to the McCloud Crowd, with their experience, their confidence, their ferocious expertise, like he'd been doing ever since they'd discovered each other years ago. But the time for that was past. He'd gotten them all into this fucking tarpit. He'd put their young, vulnerable families at risk. Now he had to put it right.

One fatal strike, fast and hard. As far from everyone that could be used against him as possible. Lara, the McCloud Crowd and their progeny, his parents, hell, even Cindy was probably in danger, if they'd fingered Jeannie. He'd lived with her for years, and followed her around for years before that. He hoped Erin had warned her.

He rented a car with the alternate driver's license, the matching credit card. Rain poured down. It would take hours to get to Blaine. He found some mindless rock on the radio to zone out to, and hit the road.

His thoughts kept on drifting rebelliously over to that fantasy he'd spun for Lara of their life together. The days and the nights, the winters and the summers. Jesus, he had to stop that self-indulgent shit. He wasn't coming out of this clusterfuck with his life intact. He'd be lucky to survive at all. Or not. Maximum security prison, or death row. Neither of them could be characterized as lucky. Oregon had the death penalty on the books, though they'd never used it.

Maybe they'd make a special exception for dickheads like him, who murdered cops and billionaire philanthropists.

It occurred to him that with his developing abilities, it was quite possible that no prison could hold him unless he chose to be held.

That idea did not make him any happier. Life as a fugitive. Great.

He blew out a hard, sharp breath. Time to rev up the war

machine and do the hard thing. As far as it took. Even if he had to forget who he was. Become something else entirely.

He would finish that bastard before they ran him down.

It was pissing rain and dark when Lara got to the Portland bus depot. She roused herself from her contemplation of the raindrops coursing sideways on the bus window, the streaks and blurs of colored light, to scoop up her bag. She had to change buses again. The money bag was belted around her waist, since it made her flipping nervous, carrying thirteen thousand bucks around in a tatty old gym bag, and the canvas was thick and uncomfortably scratchy against her skin.

The bus station blew her mind. It was the first time she'd had to deal with a big, crowded public place since Miles had pulled her out of the rat hole, and it was overwhelming. Intense echoing noise, the swirling crush of fast-moving people, the garish colors of the candy stands and the magazine racks, the juice and soda machines. So much blazing fluorescent light. She was grateful for the sunglasses.

Keep it together. Just act normal, just keep moving. This is what normal looks like. One little story swirling with a whole bunch of other stories. A strand in a cobweb. Normal. Normal.

She peered at her ticket, eyes watering. Her eyes were a problem. She was nearsighted, and had worn contacts way back when. A million years ago, the pre-rat hole, pre–psi-max Lara Kirk. A woman she barely remembered. They'd abducted her in the night, and she'd been without vision correction ever since. Not that it had mattered in her cell. It sure mattered now, though. Her blurry vision made her feel vulnerable and naked. Like she needed any more of that.

She had to walk all the way over to right under the monitor, take the sunglasses off and peer up, squinting for a long time to figure out the numbers, the destinations, the gates.

hey u howzitgoing popped up on her internal screen.

It literally weakened her knees. She was flooded with warmth and unreasonable joy. Edged with terror, of course.

im good everything proceeding as planned and u?

still driving. ways 2 go still. miss u

ME 2

did u eat? he demanded, predictably enough.

She laughed out loud, and the woman standing next to her to check the monitors gave her a nervous glance and edged away.

not yet still digesting the diner lunch

bullshit its been hours go eat smthng NOW

fine fine dont worry will do

NOW

dont text and drive u meathead its dangerous

hah There was a pause, and she could practically hear him snickering in her mind's ear. He went on. L8r then love u

b careful, she replied. I love u 2

always ttyl

She stayed that way, staring blindly up at the monitor for a minute or two, just reading and re-reading that virtual transcript in her head. Milking it for every little shining drop of comfort it could give her.

But it was time to move. Her second bus had been late, delayed by heavy rain, and it had been a tight connection to begin with. A trip to the bathroom, a bottle of apple juice, a bag of roasted cashews, not because she was hungry, but just because fulfilling her promise to him made her feel closer to him. And then it was time to hustle to her gate.

It was just a couple of minutes before boarding time, but evidently the bus wasn't going to be very full. There was hardly anyone waiting, just an elderly couple dozing on the bench, and a pair of teenagers wrapped around each other. The driver had not arrived yet. Maybe this bus was delayed, too. Maybe she'd get another seat to herself. She was not up for friendly chatting.

"Lara? Holy shit, babe! Is that you?"

She spun around with a squeak of alarm, and found herself face to face with a big, burly, blond guy in a long, cable knit sweater and a huge, draped, knit scarf. Bearded, with dreads and a big, toothy smile. His eyebrows and lashes were so white, they were invisible, and his face was very pink. She'd never seen him before in her life.

She backed away. "Excuse me? Who are you?"

"Oh, come on! Don't you remember the rave on the beach at Phuket? I'm not surprised if you don't remember. You were pretty fucked up that night. But I guarantee . . . you had a real good time." He leered, leaning closer. "Man, girl, you really know how to party."

She backed away further, and glanced around, her inner alarm bells shrilling. The kids were still kissing, the old couple still dozing. "No. You're mistaking me for someone else," she said very loudly. "I've never been to Phuket, and I—"

"Aw, c'mon. Gimme one for old time's sake!"

He yanked her into a tight, smothering kiss, his moist, fleshy lips smashing hers painfully against her teeth. Too tight to scream. His arms were like huge steel cables, tightening around her. She managed to twist her mouth away, opened it to yell—

He stuck his tongue in it. His tongue was big and muscular and slimy, prodding deep. She wiggled, mewled, as he picked her up and swung her playfully around and around, never letting her feet touch the floor, farther and farther from anyone who might be watching.

"Scream and you die," he whispered, and seized her wrist in a huge, damply hot hand, torquing it into a twist that zinged electric agony all the way up her arm. "Feel this? Inside your coat?" He prodded her with something cold and hard under her shirt. She'd dragged in air to scream, but it broke off into a cry of pain as he stabbed the gun barrel up under her rib. "It's aimed at your liver. Got me, bitch?"

She gasped for air, caught between the stab of the gun

barrel, the white-hot pain still flashing up her arm. Her heart pounded heavily in her ears and his voice came from far away. "Kiss me back, cunt," he growled into her ear, "or I will shoot you."

She looked into those bright, round, white-lashed eyes, glittering with excitement. His breath was sour. He was pressing an erection against her belly. Grinding it against her. His lips were shiny and wet.

"So shoot me," she said coldly. "Prick."

He laughed, raucously, as he swung her around and around again. He set her on her feet. She gasped, stiffening, at the needle sting in her neck.

Not psi-max. She knew psi-max inside out and this was not it. Just a sedative or a muscle relaxant, but the association with the needle sting was so strong, the vortex started to whirl anyway . . .

She walked through a wintery forest. Dead, sere grass was waist high, trees set sparsely. A park bench, almost hidden in the long grass. Rusted wrought iron. Weather-beaten. She looked at her feet and saw the pattern of paving stones beneath her feet. Ancient playground equipment, rusted and abandoned. Monkey bars. A broken swing set.

The boy darted ahead of her. It was her little friend, but he was younger today, maybe eight, his head as pale as a little bobbing candle flame. He was barefoot in the chill, wearing his usual ragged pajamas. He looked back to see if she was following, beckoning her urgently onward.

"What?" she called. "What do you want?"

More silent beckoning, more pleading looks. Desperate entreaty. Hurry, hurry. But to what, goddamnit? To what?

The image pixelated in her head and broke up, shocking her back to reality. Carried in the blond dreadlocked guy's arms. He cradled her against his chest, nuzzling her as if it were a lover's game. They were outside already, moving down the sidewalk. Rain hit her forehead. She tried to move, but the drug had paralyzed her body.

She heard the sucking "pop" of a big car door opening and was dumped into a big SUV that stank of leather, newness.

"Ah. There we go," a woman muttered, smugly. "Excellent."

The front door slammed shut and the car surged forward, out into traffic. A rough hand seized her chin, jerked her limp head around.

It was Anabel. "Bad girl," she crooned. "Daddy gonna be so mad."

Anabel looked terrible. Eyes white rimmed and staring, sunken shadows around them, twitching muscles in the tense mask of her face.

"It was like you said," Blond Dreadlocks remarked from the front seat. "The coercion didn't work on her. I had to come up with something else, right off the cuff." He hesitated, then prompted, "No time to plan."

"Why don't you just pull over and get out? Get yourself a cab." Anabel sounded supremely bored. "We're done here, so get lost. As soon as I tape her up, I can drive. I'll take it from here."

"Hey, why the attitude?" Dreadlocks's voice was aggrieved. "I extracted her for you, twenty-four minutes from the second the facial recog bot identified her, with no pursuit or alarm! It's fucking unbelievable!"

"Poor baby," Anabel mocked. "Had to use your atrophied little brain the old-fashioned way when your psi didn't work? That must have really hurt, Rockwell. Get out, now. Your B.O. is bugging me."

"Screw this shit," Rockwell muttered. He jerked the car to a stop.

He got out into the rain and walked away, leaving the car in a lane of traffic, door hanging wide open.

Anabel wound duct tape around Lara's arms, making agony flare in her injured wrist, taking her time even as the horns of the cars backed up behind began honking angrily.

Lara had sagged down onto the seat onto the other woman's lap, unable to stay upright.

When she was immobilized, Anabel leaned down and kissed her on the mouth. "I missed you, honey. So did the big boss. You've been a bad little girl, but he'll deal with you. And I hope he lets me watch."

Lara tried to visualize the computer so she could say something to Miles, but then the needle stung her again.

The impulse vanished, drowned in darkness.

27

yo! wtf? why r u not answering?

Miles forced the panic down. Panic would not help. He crouched in the trees, peering through the scope of the H&K G36 at Greaves' house.

Calm. Focus. He had to be ready, when his chance presented itself.

But it had been several hours since Lara's last response, and he was fucking *tense*.

If they'd left each other on a harsh note, he could have hypothesized that she was giving him the silent treatment, but Christ, they'd parted ways after exchanging what amounted to holy vows of goddamn undying love and devotion. So what the *fuck* . . . ?

She could be sleeping. Right. On a bus, as nervous and scared as she was, surrounded by strangers? Maybe all that accumulated adrenaline had crashed her, and she was snoring on the bus, mouth open. At least, the Lara light in his head was still on. But it was strange, indistinct. Different from before.

Fine, then. Asleep. It was the only possible explanation that didn't scare him shitless, so he was clinging to it.

It felt like a trap, the lack of security around the Blaine house. The place had been gated, of course, but there was no sign of an alarm system. This was a house Greaves had bought for his family twenty-five years ago. A convenient place for the guy and his entourage to park themselves before the ceremony set for the following afternoon. No massive security like Kolita Springs, or the Spruce Ridge complex, or the chateau in Bordeaux, or the country manor in England, or the South Sea island, or the sixteenth-century Tuscan villa, or the luxury high-rise penthouses in Hong Kong, Singapore, and Dubai.

Miles crept through the drenched trees, peering through the scope again. They were up and about, even at this hour. Almost five A.M., though the sky hadn't started to lighten yet. He'd identified Greaves through the window, plus four others, two men and two women. The guy's staff seemed somewhat reduced these days.

But then, Miles had killed quite a few of them himself.

He wished he had the materials to blow the place up. If he'd been able to access Aaro's cache, or the McClouds, or Tam and Val's, he could have flattened the guy, ka-boom. If wishes were horses. He was lucky he had the stolen H&K and a full magazine.

Looked like the big guy was being served breakfast. There was a breakfast nook off the back porch that overlooked the lake, but as luck would have it, Greaves was seated in a chair that was out of Miles' line of sight, behind a pillar. He saw a hand occasionally, reaching out to have coffee poured, to take a pat of butter. Minions scurried to do the guy's bidding. But to get a straight shot at Greaves, he would need a boat to row several meters out into the lake.

It was almost as if the guy knew that Miles was out there, and had positioned himself deliberately. But that was paranoid.

pls pls pls lara talk2me

Okay, stop. Last one. The transcript of unanswered messages was way too long. It would scroll for pages.

He crept up to the position that gave him a clear view through the French doors that led out onto the side porch. That room was dark, but he saw lights filtering from an open doorway, and mapped the house with his augmented senses, as he had done in the forest fight. Greaves glowed hot in the front room, a nasty throb of powerful energy. There were the two who had been with Greaves in the forest fight. A car was coming, and he crouched lower in the foliage and followed the headlights. They slowed and stopped at the gate.

He settled down, positioned his scope, crosshairs over the front door, careful not to let himself get blinded by the oncoming headlights.

It was a large SUV. It parked near the RV. It took a couple of seconds to recognize the haggard woman who got out of the driver's seat. Anabel had aged thirty years since Spruce Ridge. Dull skin, stringy hair, caved-in cheeks, shadowed, sunken eyes.

She jerked open the backseat, leaned in, and grabbed something, heaving it out with some effort, letting it flop heavily onto the ground.

That thing proved to be a person swathed in duct tape, in a long, olive drab wool army coat, a multicolored knitted cap, a tangled mop of long, wavy dark hair. Levis. Purple lace-up kicks. Oh, Jesus. *Lara*.

His artificial calm exploded from within, like it had been mined.

She swam up through the dark, lungs screaming. Wondering if she'd be better off falling back down into the thick, viscous darkness. Just ending the fight, and falling back into sleep. Endless sleep.

She would have, if it weren't for the lantern glowing in her head. She had no words in this dark place in her mind, but the closer she came to the surface, the more words, thoughts, images came back. Fear and pain, too. Throbbing in her head, her arm. Twisting in her middle.

Miles. He was her lantern, her beacon. Her star in the darkness. She wanted to call out to him, but she couldn't visualize images in this condition. She couldn't see the control room, the computer screen.

She felt numb, frozen. Mute and helpless.

She forced her eyes open. Her head hurt, like it had been whacked with a splitting maul. Arms still bound. She moved slightly, and almost screamed, though her throat was too swollen to make much sound. Oh dear *God*, that hurt.

She rolled onto her side, and raised her head.

She was in a small, blind room. It had shiny, reflective metal walls. She became gradually aware of a whirring sound. Movement, currents. A fan, pumping air. The room was filled with large, irregular shapes, wrapped in white drop cloths. Like stiff, unmoving ghosts.

The one closest to her was an elongated, irregular box, about three feet high. She fussed at it with her feet until the dropcloth was loose, and then turned, grabbing the edge with her uninjured hand. The cloth unwound, and the thing wrapped in it spun, wobbled, and fell.

She gaped, astonished. It was one of her own sculptures. *Pandora's Box*. It had been bought for a tidy sum, the very day before they came for her. She vaguely remembered celebrating in a bar with some friends that same evening. The Pandora figure stared at her sidewise, as if Lara herself had put that horrified, oh-what-the-fuck-have-I-done? look on her glazed ceramic face.

It gave her a bad moment of stomach free-fall, as if the place was a surreal antechamber to her own private, personal hell.

But that human-shaped thing in the corner. That was not hers. She'd never made anything of that size and shape.

She forced herself up, gasping at the needle jabs of agony

in her head, her wrist. Oh, ouch. Hung over from their junk, as usual.

She stumbled over to the statue, worrying it with her teeth, then with her good hand behind her back. She yanked at the bungee cords wrapped around it. The hooks came loose, the dropcloth fell.

Greaves. It was a bronze statue of the guy himself, snapping a photo and smiling. Yes, this was definitely hell.

It was the statue from her visions. She'd never seen its face, since it had always been covered by rivulets of birdshit, but she recognized the pose, the camera.

The vortex took her so fast, she didn't even try to fight.

She stood in that strange, empty town square, staring at the stained statue. A huge, forbidding black crow was perched on the hand that held the camera. It shook its wings, and regarded her sideways, with one beady, unfriendly eye. Gray skies, wind sweeping pine needles across the paving stones, but the grass was higher than the last time. An elk strode through the trees of the park as she watched. A fountain stood, bare and dry, encrusted with lichen. Behind her, on a park bench, was a man she had seen in an earlier vision. She'd seen him lying down, his head on a newspaper, as if he were sleeping.

He wasn't sleeping now. A weather-beaten skull now lay on the grayish lump of paper. Shreds of rotten clothing fluttered on his bones, his shriveled flesh. One of his legs had been detached, and various pieces were scattered around. A shoe lay not far from her foot. Bones protruded from it. Some carrion eater had gnawed upon him.

She turned away, sickened. There were other scattered lumps, chunks of bone, probably cadavers, too. She tried not to focus on them.

She looked around, shivering. She'd never seen the entire phantom town square before, only pieces of it, like a disjointed dream. But today, she did a full three-sixty, and saw a big marble building that faced one side of the square. It was weather-beaten and discolored. The doors gaped wide and hung askew on its hinges. Drifts of leaves and garbage had collected against the façade. As she watched, a rat came out of the open door and scurried into a crack in the wall.

Above the door, carved in stone, was "Greaves Museum of Modern Art."

Her neck tingled, and she whirled around, heart pounding. It was the boy, but this time he was even younger than before. Maybe five. He held a ragged teddy bear by the foot. He was terribly thin, hollow-eyed, dressed in the same ragged, filthy pajamas.

He looked so lonely and desolate in that dead place, her heart felt squeezed and crushed. "What are you doing here, all alone?"

The boy shook his head and stuck his thumb in his mouth.

"Do you have something to tell me?"

His eyes widened. He held out his hand, waving with the limp teddy bear toward the nearest bundle of what looked like dry white twigs and rotten fabric, as if to say, This isn't enough for you?

"But what am I supposed to do about it?" she wailed.

As she watched, he seemed to get smaller, going from five to maybe four. Eyes so wide and sad, sucking his thumb, hugging his bear. Like he had done his part, and she was supposed to be the grown-up now and make this all better. It was breaking her heart, it was driving her crazy. She wanted to hug him, scream at him. Save him.

Beyond the boy was an area that, some long time past, had been an upscale pedestrian mall. Beautiful wrought-iron benches, fancy art deco lampposts. An old-time shopping district. One of the faded signs, carved from wood, read BLAINE GENERAL STORE.

A loud squawk made her jump, spinning. It was the crow, still perched on the camera, but as she watched, it shook its black, ragged wings and dove right at her face. She cried out, ducked—

And fell right onto her back. Jolted back into her body

again, heart racing, dragging in air. Oh, God, she'd fallen right onto her injured wrist. It hurt so badly, she almost vomited.

She rolled onto her side, keening with pain, and tried once again to type onto the interface. This time, she could visualize.

miles?

WTF? WHERE HAVE U BEEN WHAT HAPPENED?

nabbed at portland bus depot dont know where I am now

ur in blaine, greaves' house. me 2. i saw anabel haul u in thru my scope oh baby

god im sorry I ruined everything, she typed in, appalled.

not ur fault. im the 1 who should b sorry. where r u in the house?

blind room 15 ft squ metal, like a bank vault. he keeps the sculpture collection here. Miles. my vision! it was of blaine!

He didn't reply for a moment, baffled. huh?

i saw the statue, remember the statue, covered with birdshit? it's greaves! they're dedicating it tomorrow! it's here! the vision, something horrible is going to happen here!

A brief pause, and then, horrible? really? i'll tell u whats horrible. mthrfckers abduct my girlfriend and lock her in a vault.

its here miles! greaves is going to do smthing terrible here in Blaine and it starts right HERE AND NOW

one. thing. at. a. time. Miles typed in, sternly. 1) get lara out of the vault. 2) save the rest of the fckng universe. ok?

ur not getting it, she responded desperately. this is huge

At that moment, bolts started to grind and slide in the massive door. they're coming 4 m L8r love u

me 2 listening waiting always ready yrs 4ever

Oh, man. This rush of sentimental tears was so poorly timed.

She snorted them back as the door sighed open, and Anabel and another man walked in. He was tall, well-dressed, Latino. He stared down at her, frowning in concentration, and shook his head.

"It's true," he said, disgruntled. "It's like she's not even there."

"What, Silva, you didn't believe us?" Anabel mocked. "Even Greaves couldn't get through that shield, and you thought you could crack her and show us all up? Asshole."

"Shut it," the guy snarled. "He doesn't like to be kept waiting."

They each grabbed her by an armpit, and hauled her to her feet. The pressure on her swollen wrist wrenched a shriek of agony from her throat, but they didn't seem to hear it. They hustled her out into a long corridor with a window at the end. The light from the window was a few shades lighter than true black. Dawn was breaking.

Through some double doors, into a large living room. Lavishly decorated, perfectly clean, but it had a chilly air of abandonment.

They passed out of the room and into a hall that served as a gallery of photographs. Anabel and the man that she had called Silva both stopped short as Lara jerked them back, rooted to the spot.

The photos.

The blond boy, in all his many incarnations. There he was as a twelve-year-old, smiling, the arm of a lovely blond woman flung over his shoulders. There was the little four-year-old boy she'd seen in the last vision, but here he was smiling and clean, well dressed, well fed, hair cut. A beautiful, happy little boy. Him as an eight-year-old in a baseball uniform. Him in a suit, holding a violin.

"Move it," Anabel hissed.

"Who are these people?" Lara asked.

"What do you care, bitch? Move it!" Anabel jerked on her arm, provoking another flash of nauseating pain, but she held firm. "Who are they?" she demanded. "Who's the boy?"

Silva made an impatient sound. "This is the boss's house from years ago, when his wife and son lived here. That's his son."

"Otherwise known as, 'the turnip,' " Anabel muttered.

"You know you'd die on the spot if he heard you say that, right?" Silva scolded. Anabel snorted, unimpressed.

Greaves' *son?* She was so surprised, she tripped, stumbled almost to her knees. A painful jerk got her moving forward again.

Greaves' son. The one who had led her to Miles, who conducted her to her visions, who had helped her hide from Anabel. Why . . . ?

They dragged her into a large room that opened onto a terrace that overlooked the lake. The sky was starting to lighten. Greaves stood there, arms clasped behind his back. His shock of hair glowed.

Anabel and Silva escorted her to where Greaves stood, and stepped back. Lara's eyes skittered around the room. A snarl of medical machines was behind Greaves, and in the midst of them, a skeletal figure barely made a bump under the blanket. It reminded her, horribly, of the cadavers in her visions, like bundles of dry twigs in their rotting clothing. He took up about that much space.

Greaves followed her gaze. "Yes, that's my son, Geoff," he said. "He's been in a coma for seventeen years, but I still hope for a miracle. Would you like to sit down, have some breakfast? Coffee?"

She stared at him, panting, from behind her snarled tangle of hair. Gritting her teeth against the agonizing pulse of pain in her wrist. The image of the thin, desolate little boy in her visions was as clear in her head as the room she saw before her.

Greaves laughed, softly. "Oh, yes, I remember now. You

disdain my offers of hospitality on principle. Anabel, unfasten her wrists."

Anabel stepped forward with a black-bladed knife. Lara braced herself for the pain as the woman sawed the blade through the tape, which had stretched and twisted into a tight, agonizing plastic cable.

It made her faint. Blood pressure going wonky. Her freed hand was thickly swollen, red and hot. She could barely move her fingers.

"Your hand looks terrible," Greaves said, his voice solicitous. "Anabel, I told you to deliver her unharmed. How did this happen?"

"That was Rockwell, sir, and I didn't tell him to—"

"You have a bad habit of blaming others for your mistakes," he chided. He turned back to Lara. "I apologize for their roughness."

"Don't bother to scold her," she said. "You don't take responsibility for your mistakes, either."

His smile froze for a moment, and then started to twinkle again.

"Feisty," he said, in an admiring tone. "Of course, you were before, too, but your romp with Miles Davenport seems to have put even more steel into your spine."

Hearing Miles' name in Greaves' mouth gave her a sickening thrill of fear. She stiffened against it.

"Finally, I can explain myself properly, and no one needs to get hurt," Greaves said. "It's what I've been trying to communicate all along. The last thing I want to do is hurt anyone."

"Tell that to Davy McCloud," she said.

"Ah, yes, that. That was a shame. But he survived, didn't he? And his little girl is just fine. I would never hurt a child. It was all a bluff."

"You don't consider what you did to me hurting?" Lara said, cradling her throbbing hand.

Greaves crossed his arms, his foot tapping as he thought it through. "Not at all. Most would have been broken by what you went through, but not you. It tempered you. Just look at you. Flashing eyes. Chin up. Indomitable. You are breathtaking, Lara."

Her throat tightened with revulsion. "Oh, fuck off. I've been through too much to tolerate being slimed by you."

His eyes flickered. "Moderate your anger," he said. "You're in no position to use language like that with me."

True. She resolved to keep her mouth shut. Then her gaze happened across the large, dark ceramic vase, displayed on a black marble stand against the wall, and she felt the same shock of recognition she'd had in the vault. *Hers.* The big, squat, circular vase was a moving vortex of clay, the multi-colored swirling glazes misleading the eye as if it were spinning. She had to look away quickly, before she started tripping. Part of the way up the vase was a triangular crack, seemingly natural, just below eye level of an average person, to peer inside.

Into Persephone's dungeon.

To think she'd cast that sculpture right before her own dungeon had swallowed her. Maybe she'd had a gift of prophecy even before psi-max. A small yellow light was placed above the sculpture, sending a single ray of what seemed like sunlight through a small hole, right down upon Persephone's upturned face, but she was immobilized by the stalagtites and stalagmites from above and below, pinned among them, as if she were clamped in toothy, goblin jaws.

"Oh, your sculpture. Yes. I was wondering if you would notice. I have several pieces of yours in my vault."

"I saw them," she said.

"I bought those for the Emerging Artists exhibit, at the new Greaves Museum of Modern Art, right here in Blaine. It will be inaugurated in just a few weeks. Your work is brilliant, by the way. I bought *Persephone's Pride* for the museum, but then I got attached to it myself. That bland, graceful façade, and inside, agony, tension, but also hope. The ray of light, the threads of hanging plant roots—it's amazing."

She stared, stonily. "You didn't have me kidnapped and beaten and dragged here to fawn over my sculptures."

"No, I didn't," he said.

A wave of faintness throbbed through her. Her heart beat deafeningly loud in her ears for a moment. She dragged in a sobbing breath, and thought of Miles to steady herself. "Tell me, then."

Greaves steepled his hands in a businesslike way. "All right. I told you how I wanted to save the world, didn't I?"

"Yes," she said faintly. "You said something about that."

"I meant it quite literally. I'm conducting a very ambitious project. It started years ago, when I was on a mission that involved researchers who were studying a virus. One of the effects of exposure was a decrease in aggressive behavior, a balancing of seratonin levels, a general state of increased calm and well-being. Naturally, I was intrigued by the possibilities. I funded further private research myself."

Ice gripped her belly as the images of the quiet, wind-whipped world full of skeletons played before her mind. "No," she whispered.

Greaves went on. "What we found was that the initial infection caused symptoms of a mild, viral, upper-respiratory infection, and the toxins released from cell death in the lungs had a curious effect upon the brain. Cumulative, long term, very slow, and gentle. And what it brings? Peace. Real peace. We've been testing it for years, in various forms, and the results are startling. We can revolutionize the human race biologically. Turn ourselves into the perfect species."

Lara realized she was shaking her head. She forced herself to stop. This was not a conversation. His tone was so chatty and light, and meanwhile, she was looking at the naked skull on the newspaper on the park bench, the rats scuttling out of the museum.

A message rolled across her inner screen. update? yr killing me

soon, she replied.

"You're releasing this virus today, aren't you?" she said. "At the award ceremony?"

Greaves blinked a few times. "That was quite a leap," he said. "I suppose I shouldn't be surprised, with your psi gift. Not exactly. Not at the ceremony. This is the last phase of testing, you see. We're still not releasing the airborne version, but we're releasing a waterborne strain into the town's water supply. I'm cutting the ribbon on a project that gives tens of millions to this town, but the real gift we're giving is this."

He opened a gleaming, hard-sided metal briefcase, and took out a tall, stoppered vial of clear liquid from its bed of molded foam. "I chose Blaine because I was born here. I owe so much to the place. This way, we can observe the results right here before we release the airborne version simultaneously in the big population centers all over the world. That will happen a year from now. Tell me, Lara. Have you seen my plan implemented in your visions?"

"Yes," she said quietly.

He looked expectant. "And?"

She forced air out of her tight chest. "Not good," she said. "Global apocalypse. Everyone dead."

He looked irritated. "Oh, come on. That's not possible, Lara. We've tested the toxin's effects for decades. There is no downside."

"Then something unforeseen is going to change," she said.

Greaves sighed. "Here we run into the limitations of your gift. It is imprecise, impressionistic. You can't see the big picture. You are focusing in on a statistical anomaly. Consider the effect upon war, crime, domestic violence, exploitation, cruelty of all kinds against all creatures. Even climate change, the environment. Everything. You will learn to see the big picture when you are working with me."

"With you?"

"Of course." He sounded as if he were conferring a great honor. "I need intelligent people, with your special abilities. We will vaccinate you, of course. All my people are vaccinated."

She actually started to laugh, though it sounded more like sobbing. "I can't work with you. I can't help you. I've seen it, Greaves! That statue of you in the square, covered with carrion crows and birdshit! I've seen wild animals wandering in and out of the museum. Human bones scattered around the fountain in the square."

Greaves drummed his fingers impatiently on the table. "Artistic temperaments," he muttered. "Maybe you haven't quite grasped the situation, Lara. If you are not on my team, you serve no purpose at all, and you will be composted. Both of you."

He stared intently into her face, and chuckled at what he saw. "Yes, Lara. I know he's out there, with the assault rifle that he took from Wilcox. I can sense him now. In fact, I thought he was you before you were picked up in Portland. I haven't pinpointed your frequency yet, but I'm confident I will soon. And he thinks he's so stealthy. I was careful not to get near any windows. Not that his bullets could get through my telekinetic shield, but it is so unpleasant, having your windows shattered. It ruins a nice, relaxing meal."

miles he knows ur out there he can feel u now b careful

bummer thnx where r u

lakefront room stay away pls stay away

Miles offered no response to that, which was not a good sign. Goddamn stubborn heroic types. She swallowed down a desperate sob.

"Let him skulk," Greaves went on. "We'll deal with him later. I want to talk to you first."

"There's nothing left to say," she said.

"Don't go running to meet that moment," Greaves warned. "That will be an unlucky moment for you. But leave aside unpleasant things for now. Let's talk about something more interesting. Your shield."

That took her by surprise and left her floundering. "My what?"

"Don't play dumb. Your psi shield. I have a very personal interest in the mechanism that generates your shield. It's like an invisibility cloak that masks your profile altogether. My son's shield is like that."

She looked at the still figure on the cot, its tangle of wires and tubes. Greaves watched her, intently. "Seventeen years he's hidden in there. And I've waited," Greaves said. "You must open that shield, and let me in. I want to study it. To understand it."

"So you can pry open his?"

His silence and his glittering eyes answered her.

Dread was filling her, but there was no way to stave off the inevitable. "I can't help you," she said. "I don't know how I generate it."

Greaves grabbed her chin and jerked her face around to meet his eyes. "You are lying."

She shook her head, as much as his bruising grip would allow. "No," she said. "I really don't know how it's generated. I have no clue at all." Which was, in fact, literally true.

Seconds ticked by. His gaze did not waver. It felt as if he were reading her mind, though she knew his probe could not penetrate Miles' barrier. "No," Greaves said slowly. "You are still lying. I can't read your mind, but I can read your face."

She tried again to shake her head, but his eyes were widening, elated. "My God. It's not your shield at all." His voice sounded almost delighted. "It's his! He's the one generating it. It was his all along. He's completely masking your profile!"

oh shit miles he knows about yr shield

im right outside, Miles replied.

no! go! run!

"You're communicating with him right now, aren't you?" He waggled her head with his gripping hand, painfully. "You sneaky bitch. He's swallowed you up, inside his own shield! That's amazing. I had no idea it could be done. Bring him in, immediately."

"Huh?" She stared, gaping stupidly.

"Bring him in!" he said, more sharply. "Call him, now! I want to know more about this shield!"

"I don't know what you're talking ab—"

Smack. He whacked her on the side of the jaw. She reeled, seeing stars, but unseen hands gripped her, jerked her upright. "Do not waste my time," he said. "I have a lot to accomplish today. Call him!"

She took a deep breath. Braced herself. "No," she said.

Greaves crossed his arms over his chest, regarding her steadily for a few moments. "Anabel," he said calmly. "Come here. Put your knife to her carotid artery and take her outside."

"Yes, sir."

Anabel's arm clamped around her, and the knife bit cold against her throat. The clamps of Greaves' telekinesis fastened around her body, locking her arms against her.

Anabel's breath was hot and rapid against her neck as Lara stumbled awkwardly in front of her toward the door. She messaged frantically.

he's coming after u run run run NOW

The door opened. Anabel shoved her out the door, onto the porch.

oh fuck oh lara baby

RUN!

no

"Mr. Davenport, please put down your rifle, come inside and have a civil conversation instead of lurking out there in the woods," Greaves announced, in a clear, ringing voice.

pls pls go let me go its ok, she pleaded.

"I will count down from five," Greaves said. "Five. Four. Three—"

"Stop." Miles' voice was not loud, but it carried perfectly through the still air of dawn.

He stepped out from behind the RV, and walked toward them. The breeze off the lake blew his coat back, so it billowed behind him. His hair blew back from his face. So beautiful, it hurt to look at him.

He looked calm and unafraid. He stopped, a few yards away from them, his eyes fixed on Greaves. He did not look at her.

"You can put the knife down," he said.

"I decide when the knife goes down," Greaves replied. "Silva, go see if he's still armed. I'm sure I don't have to tell you what happens if you're not perfectly compliant, Mr. Davenport."

"Of course." Miles lifted his arms, waiting patiently. Silva patted him down, while Miles and Greaves stared, measuring each other.

Miles broke the silence. "Shall we go in, have that conversation you were talking about?" His tone was casually polite, as if they were discussing the buying and selling of a car.

She literally felt energy prickle in the air as Greaves bristled silently. "Don't make suggestions or take any more initiatives," he said. "Just follow my lead. Is that clear?"

Miles shrugged. "Okay, fine. Your move."

Greaves' gaze flicked to Lara and then away, dismissing her. "Put her back in the vault, Anabel," he said. "Silva, go with them. I'll wait here with Mr. Davenport until you both return."

Finally, Miles made eye contact, and she understood why he had not done so before. The look in his eyes pulled her heart outside of her body. Which was where it had been since the night they met. Or even before that, in the Citadel.

Her heart's home. She belonged there, shielded and cherished. His, forever.

o my love, she sent.

He gave her a tiny, crooked smile that did not even try to reassure her as they wrenched her around and dragged her back into the house.

ttyl babe, he messaged. love makes u strong

28

"Anabel." Greaves' voice was edged with menace. "You're overdoing it."

Anabel wrapped another round of duct tape around Miles' wrist, and ripped it off, wrapping it tightly around the chair back. "I know this guy," she said, in her husky, ruined voice, and jolted to her feet, rocking. "I know his tricks. He's a filthy, dirty, tricky bastard."

Whap, she backhanded him on the side of the head.

"Stop!" Greaves snapped. "I want to speak to him, not beat him."

Anabel panted, eyes white-rimmed. "He deserves it. What he did. Chaining her in the dark. Fucking her on the floor. Pig. He deserves to have his parts cut off in chunks while he watches. He deserves to—"

"Stop!" Greaves' voice resonated with a massive pulse of coercion.

Anabel yelped, and dropped her duct tape and knife, clutching her temples. Whimpering.

"Go to the back of the room," he said.

She did so, shuffling. Thudded to her knees, and then

onto her face on the carpet, hard, as if she'd been kicked from behind.

"Sorry about that," Greaves said. "Anabel's very stressed. I gave her an assignment that cracked her ability to tell fantasy from reality."

"You do seem to specialize in that," Miles observed.

Greaves gave him a cold look. He managed to refrain from saying anything else sarcastic about the state of Anabel's mental health. A guy who was duct-taped to a chair should curb the snark. If possible.

He glanced over at the guy lying at the far side of the room on a cot. Shriveled, skeletal, hooked up to machines. "Who's that guy?"

"My son," Greaves said. "He's been like that for years."

"I see." It seemed politic to change the subject. "So. Telepathy. Coercion. Two things you've got going for you. Are there more?"

In answer, Miles' chair rose up into the air, twirling gently as if he hung on a rope swing. Higher, and still higher. Six feet off the ground. Then eight. The room had old-fashioned, sixteen-foot ceilings.

"Telekinesis, too," Miles said. "Cool."

Greaves gazed up, arms folded, eyes bright and expectant.

"Is this the part where I'm supposed to be all impressed and intimidated?" he asked. "Clue me in, here. I don't want to fuck this up."

Whoosh, he dropped like a stone. *Crash*, the chair legs snapped like toothpicks beneath his weight, leaving him sprawled and gasping, air knocked out of his lungs. Still taped to the splintered remnants of the chair. He tried moving his legs, his arms. Didn't seem to be broken.

He shook his legs free of the taped chunks of wood, but when he tried to get up and wiggle his bound arms loose from the detached chair back, a force shoved on his chest, pressing him back down. That pressure, plus his own weight, crushed his bound hands against the back of the chair. *Yow.* That sucked.

"I'm going to teach you some manners before we are through," Greaves said, walking slowly over to him. He stared down at Miles.

"If that's what you need to do." Miles stopped struggling. There was no point in it. It was like having an elephant sit on him.

"You didn't expect that, with your shield?" Greaves looked smug. "I can't get inside your head, but I can manipulate your body mass."

"That's great," Miles said. "Are you through? Or do you need to show me more of your junk? You've definitely got my attention."

"My other abilities are harder to classify," Greaves said. "I have a whole array of talents. And I'm sure you do, too. Time for you to show me your junk, Mr. Davenport. Go on, impress me. What have you got?"

"Not too fucking much, or I wouldn't be duct taped and flat on my back, hanging out with losers like you."

Greaves made a dismissive gesture. "Bullshit. I felt your energy when you punched me with it yesterday."

Miles shook his head, the only part of his body he could move. "I can't do that when I'm shielded," he said. "And I don't know how to control it. It was beginner's luck."

"It's a matter of training and practice."

"Yeah, most things are," Miles said. "But I'm not that interested. I don't get a thrill out of jerking people around. And unless I need to lift a refrigerator by myself, who cares about telekinesis?"

"That's just inexperience talking," Greaves scoffed. "You haven't grasped the possibilities yet. I can help you do that."

"Help me?" Miles peered up at him, perplexed. "Why on earth would you help me? What the hell do you want?"

"A couple of things. The first is just for you to join my cause, Mr. Davenport. I need people like you. I have enhanced dozens of talented people, but psi-max only goes so far. A potential like yours is one in a million. I could teach you to control and guide huge masses of people, all at once. You could be a vital part of my plan."

"Your plan," Miles said. "Yeah, I've heard about it. The one where everybody dies?"

Greaves waved that away. "Not at all! You've been listening to Lara, and she doesn't know what she's talking about. The virus doesn't have that effect. We've tested it extensively!"

"Virus? So you're a bioterrorist, then?"

"No, you idiot," Greaves snapped. "Shut up and listen. You're like me, Miles. There are just a few lingering energy blockages keeping you from your full potential. I could break through them, and set you free."

Miles gazed up at the guy, struggling for breath beneath that weight. "Free to what?" he asked. "For what?"

"To exercise your full powers," Greaves said, impatiently.

"Yes, I get that," Miles wheezed. "But to what end?"

Greaves just stared. "You're deliberately missing the point."

"Bigtime," Miles said.

Greaves sighed. "This virus has been under development for many years. The toxin that it produces is health-enhancing. It lowers aggression, raises seratonin level. In the prison populations where we aerosolized it, there were amazing turnarounds. Violent incidents dropped almost to zero over the course of just months. Cases of rape, suicide, drug use, even cigarettes and overeating went down. Even the prison staff's lives transformed. There's nothing this substance does not improve."

Miles grunted. "Sounds like heaven."

Greaves frowned. "I need people like you, Miles. I would of course administer the vaccine to you, and to a limited number of other people, of your choosing, if you would rather keep them unaltered. Though the truth is, you would not be doing them any favors by withholding this gift of peace. They remain who they are . . . just better."

Miles dragged in another painful breath. "I've been told that I'm wanted for rape, kidnapping, and murder, thanks to you."

Greaves waved his hand. "Fixable. In any case, the world will soon be very different. The rules will change, because I will be the one making them. But there is another thing that I need from you, even more urgently." He paused for dramatic effect. "My son."

Miles floundered mentally, coming up blank. "You mean *him?*" He jerked his chin in the general direction of the comatose guy.

Greaves licked his lips. "Your shield is the key. It's almost exactly like his. Let me inside to read your memories of how you built it, its inner workings, and I'll be able to understand how he generates his."

"You still won't get in," Miles said.

"Lara did," Greaves pointed out.

"That was because I created a hidden door specifically for her," Miles said. "You can be damn sure your son did not do that for you."

"Just let me in. I'll decide for myself what's relevant and what's not."

Miles groped frantically around in his head, like a rat in a maze for a way through this. All he could think of was *stall, stall, stall.*

"So what's in this for me?" he asked.

Greaves smiled. The pressure lightened on Miles' chest, allowing him to fill his lungs. He did, with big, rasping gasps of relief.

"You mean, besides power and fame, and a place on the center of the world stage? Noble and meaningful work? Mr. Davenport, open your mind. I can give you your life back. And I can give you Lara."

*   *   *

miles? update?

hey baby, Miles responded.

She burst into tears, seeing letters appear on the screen. you ok?

4 the moment. he wants me 2 help him rule zombieland. & wants me 2 give him his son back. bad scene

can u pretend?

not if I open my shield. cant lie 2 a telepath.

Despair gripped her. There was nothing to say, nothing they could do. She said the only thing that came into her mind. I love you.

I love you, too. No shortcuts, no abbreviations.

Lara huddled on the floor of the vault in the dark in a tight ball, hands around her head. It was a yoga pose that was supposed to calm her, but it didn't. Never worked in the rat hole, either, but she was stubborn. She wanted to keep talking to him, to milk every second of contact, but it was unfair to fracture his concentration.

She hated feeling helpless. She wanted to strike a blow, make a move, but even her psychic gift was a passive one. She couldn't attack, stab, throw, read, push, or bully anyone with it.

She thought of Geoff, and a half-formed idea tickled her mind, along with a shiver of fear, hope, dread. Possibility.

Geoff had helped her. He had proven to be an ally of a sort. And he wanted something from her, if she could figure out what it was. If she could just change the cards on the table. Something. Anything.

She tried all her tricks, but at long last, it was the image of Persephone's swirling vase that got her vortex going . . .

 . . . *into the otherworld, to the phantom town square. No place else to go anymore. All roads led to this ghostly deathtrap. She wandered through, trying not to look at the charnel scenes. No evidence of violence or conflict. Even cars were correctly parked in legal parking places. In one car, a corpse in the driver's seat still had a pink blouse adhered to its ribcage, and there was a . . . oh, God, no.*

Too late. She'd seen it, and she could not unsee the tiny, smaller body curled on the corpse's lap. The car seat in the back. The woman had parked the car, and then never roused herself to get out. The toddler had crawled up into the front seat into her mother's lap to die.

Lara stumbled on, hand pressed to her mouth. She wanted to run from her horror, but there was nothing to run from. Everything was dead.

The flash of movement caught her eye, that pale candle flame of a head, bobbing like a will-o'-the-wisp. "Geoff!" She sprinted after him.

She rounded the corner. Geoff stood there, waiting for her. Still in the ragged pajamas, but they were tighter on him. His skin was covered with goosebumps in the chill. He was older today, maybe seven or eight.

"I know who you are," she told him. "You're Greaves' son. You've been hiding behind your shield for seventeen years."

Geoff's eyes went big. He backed up, as if she'd threatened him.

"You have to help us," she pleaded. "You're the one who showed me this nightmare. We have to stop it, and you have to help!"

Geoff kept backing away, looking frightened. She didn't see the shift, it was so seamless, but suddenly he was younger, much younger, three maybe, the ragged pajamas hanging loosely. He held the dingy teddy bear again, thumb in mouth. Big, huge, scared eyes.

It pissed her off. "Oh, stop that shit! Don't try to manipulate me. There's no time for that! I need help, not more jerking around."

Geoff's face crumpled, as if he were about to cry.

"Grow up!" she yelled.

The angry look in his eyes said it all. He'd never had the chance.

Fair enough, true enough, but now was not the time to ask her for empathy and compassion. "What the hell do you think you're doing in there?" she yelled. "In a dream, in your head?

What the hell have you being doing for seventeen years? Sulking? What the fuck, Geoff?"

Geoff jerked back, and he was abruptly twelve again, tall, and angry. She suddenly saw the resemblance to Greaves, in his regal posture, his jaw, the way his pale eyes flashed.

"I need you!" she yelled. "We both need you. You have to help us. Make a move, strike a fucking blow! It's not enough to waft around looking wounded and ethereal. You have to get off your ass!"

Geoff's face twisted with anger. He lifted his arms and gestured sharply, as if he were flinging something invisible at her—

The blow knocked her right out of the vision, jolting her painfully back into the smothering darkness.

It occurred to her that with the light off, the fan had been turned off, too. No air was moving. The vault was airtight. She had clearly felt the change in humidity the moment she had stepped outside. Which meant she probably had fifteen feet squared of oxygen left to breathe.

She blew out a slow lungful of carbon dioxide, and curled into a ball again. All things considered, smothering to death in the vault was a better death than some of the others she could ponder.

The words rang between them.

"You can't give me Lara," Miles said. "She's not yours to give."

"She certainly was yours to take, wasn't she?" Greaves said, his voice faintly taunting. "Did you give her a choice?"

Miles felt bile rise in his throat. "That's between me and her."

"Is it?" Greaves tutted gently, under his breath. "There's no delicate way to say this—but that passionate love and devotion she feels for you? It was pharmacologically induced, Miles . . . by me. It will pass, as she detoxes. Six to eight weeks is standard, I think."

His body was rigid. "I'm not interested in talking about Lara."

"I'm not surprised, considering your past failures. We studied you, Miles. Your track record with the ladies hasn't been a crashing success so far. Consider the seductive Cynthia."

"Cindy's out of the picture," Miles said.

"Oh, don't worry, she's not interesting enough to warrant my attention. Not like Lara is. But it's your failure to hold her interest that's the issue here. I'll tell you a secret. Don't be jealous, but I was grooming Lara for myself. She's so desirable. You can hardly blame me."

"Actually, I do blame you," Miles said. "You really ingratiated yourself. Dark, starvation, beating, drugs. Talk about courtship."

Greaves ignored him. "She was medicated with a very specific psi-max formula. It primed her to bond, softened psychological boundaries, and stoked extreme sexual heat. Indulge my curiosity, Miles. Did you have sexual relations within six hours of leaving my complex?"

"None of your fucking business," Miles ground out, from behind clenched teeth.

"Just as I thought. By that point, she must have been in an agony to consummate. Poor thing. At the mercy of chemistry. You lucky dog."

Every part of him was stone cold. "I don't see the relevance of this," he said.

"I'm trying to explain that the effects of the drug won't last," Greaves explained. "Not unless the doses are repeated regularly. Or alternatively, you could make certain subtle adjustments to her using telepathic coercion. Which you're more than capable of learning with a little training from me. She would be yours forever. Picture it. It's no different than what you're doing now. You keep her in a cage, in there, right? Isn't that control, too, of a different sort? And don't you like it?"

The man's bright eyes had a cruel, lascivious sparkle to them.

Miles considered his next words for a long moment, and decided there was nothing left to lose. "I can see that worked real well with your wife and son," he said. "You're all just one big, happy family."

It was a shot in the dark, but his aim was dead on. He could tell by the temperature in the room, the mask of tension in the guy's face.

"You know nothing about my family," Greaves said, his voice dead.

"I know enough to decline couples' counseling from you," Miles said. "What was her name? Carol? Did you kill her? She died of a catastrophic stroke at the age of thirty-six, no previous symptoms. Wow, what are the odds? And then, right after, your son went into a—"

"Shut up!" Greaves shouted. "Shut your mouth!" He gestured angrily at the red-haired woman who waited nearby. "Miranda. Show him what we've organized for his family, his friends. Quickly."

The redhead scurried over, tapping feverishly on a tablet, and leaned over where Miles lay on the floor, displaying it to him.

It had a split screen. Two images. The first was Davy's hospital room. Davy lay there, looking limp and gray, tubes in his nose. Margot was beside him. Aaro leaned against the wall by the bed, glaring around the room as if challenging the air itself.

The other screen showed Miles' childhood home, from across the street, the window of a car. The rhododendrons and hydrangea bushes tossed in the blustery wind of early morning.

"I've spoken to my man in Endicott Falls," Greaves said. "He's both telepathic and telekinetic. Your folks are having breakfast. My man can walk up to your parents' house and stop your father's pacemaker halfway through his poached eggs. He's awaiting my word."

Miles tried to swallow again, but the mechanism seemed frozen.

"I want that shield, Mr. Davenport. I've tried with reason, with politeness, with bribes. I've offered you the world," Greaves' voice was petulant. "And yet we've come to this. Silva, Levine, get Lara out of the vault. And get the ax out of the toolshed. I want results. *Now.*"

Miles fought for breath for the next few minutes, still almost immobilized, but Greaves was evidently punishing him by ignoring him.

Then the doors were flung open. The pressure on him lifted. Miles rose to his feet, shaking the chunk of chair free. One sharp wrench and the splintered chair back broke into two pieces, leaving his hands separated if still taped to bulky, awkward chunks of splintered furniture. He locked eyes with Lara as Silva dragged her into the room, the point of the knife to her throat. The red-haired woman held an ax.

"Bring her over to the sculpture," Greaves directed.

As they approached, Greaves' telekinesis clamped down again, so tightly, he could barely make his lungs expand. They pulled Lara over to a black marble stand that had the huge glazed pottery vase on it, not far from him. Greaves approached them slowly. Savoring the moment.

"Put her right hand up on it," he said.

The dark guy grabbed Lara's pale, slender hand and placed it on top. Lara held her head high, and looked resolutely away from it.

"This is the last time you'll use that hand, Lara," Greaves said. "I genuinely regret that. You were so talented. Silva, do it."

Silva looked pale, his lips tight, but he took the ax that the woman proffered. Lara was evidently immobilized by Greaves as well, except for her eyes. Like Persephone. Tall and straight. Regal.

She did not deserve this shit. This was fucking unacceptable.

Silva lifted the axe. It came flashing down—

Energy flashed out of his suddenly gaping shield, to counter the laws of physics. Hundredths of seconds crawled by. The ax blade hung in the air, frozen. Inches above Lara's slender wrist.

Silva's face was a hideous grimace, morphing into shock. The red-haired woman's mouth was open too, but the sound was stretched out, distorted and unintelligible. The ax was torn out of Silva's hand. It hit the wall, bounced off, fell, leaving an ugly mark.

A flash of pain, like an explosion in his head, and . . . oh, *God* . . .

The bastard was inside.

Miles crushed in the grip of a gigantic strangling shadow octopus, tentacles choking, probing, squeezing . . . oh Christ, that *hurt* . . .

He fought back faintness. Fought for enough motor control to breathe, stay on his feet. When he managed to focus his eyes, Lara was on the ground, halfway across the room. Hand to her face, nose bleeding copiously. Greaves' invasion had hurt her, too.

The red-haired woman and Silva were backing away, very slowly and nervously. Hoping not to be noticed.

Greaves stood there, a manic grin of pure gloating delight on his face. "So strong! Amazing! It's not just a shield, it's a fortress!"

Miles clutched his temples, body rigid. *SHOW ME*. The blast of coercion was monstrous.

He didn't just obey. He was laid bare, X-rayed, dissected, eviscerated. He showed Greaves things he hadn't known he knew, things he'd never even articulated, things there were no words for, just images, analogs. Flows of braided energy, intricate webs, feeds from the energy centers in his body he'd only been faintly aware of.

Greaves was making his own citadel now, copying the information that Miles had given him with incredible speed.

"Yes," Greaves mumbled, eyes dilated, with intense concentration. "Yes, of course. That's wonderful. Absolutely brilliant."

Miles could still barely breathe, but something was happening, spaces opening up. Dark places filling with light. Cramped places loosening. The pressure was shaking something loose. Something new and big and raw. Powerful. It gave him traction, to counter that crushing energy, and . . .

push back.

Greaves let out a shocked cry and jerked, his hand going up to his head. "What . . . what the hell?" he gasped.

Miles jabbed again, with everything he had.

Greaves redoubled his own pressure, his face darkening. "You arrogant little piece of shit!" he snarled. "I was training my mind for combat when you were a baby playing with fucking alphabet blocks!"

He managed to make his vocal apparatus function. The words came out in a thick, rasping croak. "So hit me . . . Grandpa."

Greaves lifted his arms, and brought them sharply down with a roar that echoed like a thunderclap. The windows of the room exploded outward, a shattering crash. The light bulbs all exploded. The sculpture on the marble stand cracked, the entire top and part of one side tumbling to the ground with a majestic crash. Twisted stalactites from the fallen section skittered across the room. The remaining ones stuck up from the base of the inside of the sculpture like ragged teeth.

Miles kept grappling. He was losing ground. He had the raw strength, but he didn't have the agility, the practice. He was clumsy, slow, still figuring it all out. Greaves was just too fucking good.

So he fell back on the one thing he seemed to have a special knack for . . . pissing the guy off.

He spat blood from his mouth. "That's the best you can do?"

Greaves' eyes widened, and he gathered his energy for the final, fatal blow, arms lifting again. Miles braced himself—

"Geoff's awake," Lara said softly.

29

Greaves' wild-eyed gaze whipped around to her, saw her crouched near Geoff's cot. "Get away from him!" he shrieked.

Lara's body literally rose up into the air, as if she were a cat being swatted with some huge hand. She landed twelve feet across the room on her side, hard. The ceramic Persephone, knocked loose from her prison, lay a few feet away from her, snapped off at the base, but still whole. Lara grabbed her by the ankles.

Greaves was staring at his son, astonished.

Geoff's eyes were open and enormous in his shrunken face.

Lara struggled to her feet. Greaves had forgotten her. He was still immobilizing Miles, who swayed, locked in that unnatural pose, staring at her. His eyes flicked to the statuette in her hand, to Greaves, then back up to her face. His lips moved, silently. *Now.*

Greaves' mouth gaped as he moved toward his son, arms outstretched. His eyes were almost soft. "Geoff? Ah, God. Geoff."

Geoff tried to move his cracked, purplish lips, but no

sound came out. His eyes were clouded, gummy, and dimmed. He looked past his father toward Lara. His lips moved. She could see the boy Geoff staring at her, his huge blue eyes very clear as the smothering darkness closed around him. Silently mouthing a word, but she was so rattled by the double realities, she couldn't read it. She didn't understand.

"What is it, son?" Greaves moved closer. "Open your mind. I'll read it directly if you can't talk. I'll do anything you need."

She suddenly understood the word Geoff had tried to mouth.

Now.

She bolted across the room and swung the statuette, bashing the side of Greaves' head with it. He grunted, staggered.

Miles sprang up the second he jolted free of Greaves' telekinetic clinch. He grabbed the older man, and flung him higher than was humanly possible.

Greaves landed—on her broken sculpture. Skewered. One stalagmite protruded from his throat, another from his belly. His eyes were wide, infuriated, and the room trembled with red rage . . .

The feeling softened, dissipated. His eyes went empty.

Miles fell to his hands and knees, panting. Lara stared at the thing in her hand. It no longer looked like a statuette. It looked like the murder weapon that it was. Persephone's face, which had been a delicate glaze of flesh tones and pinks, was shiny and wet with blood.

It fell from her stiff hand to the ground, clattering and spinning.

Sudden movement caught her eye. Geoff was rolling off his cot. He hit the ground, landing on his back.

She hurried over to him, catching her breath when she saw the blood. It welled up, gushing from a terrible wound in his throat, and another in his wasted, concave belly. Blood streamed down the side of his head, too, shockingly red against his gray skin.

Then she realized, with a shudder of confusion, that he was not bleeding. Or rather, it was the dream Geoff that bled, the child-man, in her vision. She was staring at them both simultaneously. The wasted older man's skin was still unmarred. And yet, she knew somehow that the wounds were still fatal.

He gazed into her face, lips moving silently. She leaned down, sliding her arm beneath his shoulder. Cradling him carefully. The little boy, the skeletal man. One and the same. And both dying.

"Oh, Geoff," she whispered. "God, Geoff. I'm so sorry."

Miles knelt beside her. His eyes were haggard and shadowed.

"He melded with Greaves," she told him. "I felt it. Total fusion. He opened his shield, and his father just . . . swallowed him. The wounds . . . those are Greaves' wounds, but he has them in the dream world. I can see them. He's bleeding to death. Except that you can't see it."

Miles' hand clasped her shoulder, squeezing. "Oh, baby." His voice was rough, shaking with exhaustion.

"He woke up for me." Lara cradled him, her face wet. "Geoff. I'm so sorry. I didn't mean to hurt you."

Geoff formed a word, with bluish, flaking lips.

"What was that?" Lara bent, put her ear to his lips. Strained with every nerve to hear him.

Free. It was a faint, creaking sigh of a sound, she was not sure from what plane of existence. But she heard it.

She lifted her head, startled. He was smiling with his eyes.

As she watched, that smile evaporated, leaving his wasted body a delicate husk in her arms. The boy had faded from her mind's eye.

Lara gently laid him down. She closed his eyes and could

not speak, or move, or breathe. Just seeing that beautiful blond boy child. Her quiet friend. Her little guide. Flying free, at last.

"Rest in peace," Miles said, hoarsely.

She nodded. Miles helped her up onto her feet. She turned to him, reaching out, eyes tear-blinded. Laid her hands against his chest, just to feel how warm and solid and real he was.

It was so terribly quiet. She couldn't believe the quiet.

She wiped her eyes with her sleeve. "So, um. Now what?"

Miles covered her hands. "We call the cops. We give the beaker with whatever that organism is to the CDC. We let it all shake down however it wants to. Where's . . ." His body tightened. "Oh, fuck, no."

She twisted, alarmed, to look where he was looking. "What?"

"The beaker," he said. "It's gone." He strode over to the briefcase with the molded foam, then looked wildly around the room. "Anabel," he said. "That crazy bitch ran off with the virus. Come on!"

He grabbed her hand. She sprinted after him, knees wobbling.

They burst out the front door to see the taillights of the RV lumbering down the driveway at top speed. Slowing for the turn, but already two hundred meters away. Miles shouted obscenities, and sprinted after it, yelling.

"Idiot," came a gravelly voice from behind Lara. "That's not me. That's just the medics. The ones that took care of the turnip. Deserting the sinking ship."

Lara spun around, hand to her throat. Anabel was poised in the doorway behind her, holding the beaker up, uncorked and sloshing.

Her other hand held a gun, which was pointed at Lara's head.

Anabel's gun hand shook, but at this range, it would almost be impossible for her to miss.

"Anabel. Don't do this." Lara tried to keep her voice soothing and reasonable, but her desperation grated on her own ears. "This virus, it's not how Greaves told everyone it would be. It will cause a global—"

"Shut up." Anabel circled her, the gun just inches from her face, driving her until her back hit the wall of the house. "I know. I was there, remember? I saw your visions. I saw the statue with birdshit on its head, I saw the people stumbling around like they were lobotomized. It's perfect. It's exactly what I want. It's what they all deserve."

"Anabel, please, listen—"

"No, you listen!" Anabel whipped her head around, and fixed her reddened, sunken eyes on Miles, who was approaching, and jabbed the gun barrel beneath Lara's chin. "Not one step closer, you filthy freak."

Miles stopped, holding his hands up. "Don't. I'll be good."

"I know your tricks," she said. "You're a telekinetic, like Greaves. But I can feel it before it takes hold, and if you try to freeze me I'll pull the trigger before you can stop me. Understand, freak? I've been waiting for you, see. I've been wanting to tell you how I feel about scum like you for years. I want to give you a taste of the shit you dish out. See how much you like it."

"Sure," he said gently. "Just calm down. I won't do anything."

"You scum," Anabel quavered. The chilly gun barrel shook violently beneath Lara's chin, pressing deep. "They're all scum, though, you know that? You two aren't telepaths, so you don't know, but everyone is filthy inside. You too, you dirty whore. But this?" She jerked the beaker up high, as if making a toast. "This puts a stop to it. This is like a tidal wave of disinfectant. This is the ultimate Lysol."

"But they'll all die!" Lara protested.

"Let them! Let the babies starve in their cribs before they grow up to be filthy, too! And you, and me! Him, most of all!" She gestured with the beaker, making the liquid slosh dangerously close to the edge. "Sick pervert! Months, you had her shackled in the dark. And you *liked* it. You *pig!*"

"You've got me mixed up with somebody," Miles said.

"Shut up!" she shrieked. "You liar. Lying filth!"

The time between the echoing drumbeat of Lara's heart dilated into vast silences, like pools she could dive into, full of everything she had never wanted to know about Anabel. She gave in, fell into it.

And opened her mouth to speak. "No, Jilly," she said softly.

Jilly? What the hell?

It was true what Anabel said about his telekinesis. He wasn't smooth or quick enough to get a grip before she pulled that trigger. And the open beaker swirled and sloshed. Anabel was not paying attention to it. She was staring at Lara, her expression naked and frightened.

"What?" she said. Her voice seemed higher, softer.

"That wasn't Miles, Jilly." Lara's voice was as even and calm as if she weren't being held at gunpoint by a crazy woman. "That was Mr. Welcher. He was the one who did that to you. Not Miles."

Anabel shuddered. The gun wavered. Liquid sloshed. Anabel shook her head, violently. "No. No, you're lying."

"He's not here, Jilly," Lara said. "Put the gun down."

"Don't," Anabel snarled. "Don't try to trick me."

"I'm telling the truth. Miles isn't the bad one. Mr. Welcher was. And you're not dirty. You're not filth. That was him. Not you."

Anabel hesitated, confused, and then her expression hardened. She let out a short, ugly laugh. "Maybe not before, but

I'm filth now. Too late for me. Maybe I can chug-a-lug some of this. Clean myself up." She swished the liquid in the beaker. "Or even better, I'll just throw it on you." Anabel swung the beaker in Lara's direction.

"No!" Miles yelled, leaping forward.

Anabel snarled like a feral cat. The beaker soared up . . .

The gun went off, *bam*. The beaker froze in the air, suspended. The gun's kick had forced Anabel's arm up. Miles clamped her into immobility so she could not shoot again, but Lara was sliding down the wall, hand clamped to her wound, a streak of bright red blood smeared on the white planks behind her.

Anabel's eyes shone with fury as she fought him. She sagged, put her chin over the gun barrel—

Bam. The contents of Anabel's head fanned behind her on the white siding.

Miles didn't even watch her fall. He righted the beaker, lowered it to the floor, and dove for Lara. Shoulder, not chest, thank God. So pale.

He wrestled himself out of his coat, ripped out some of the flannel lining, pressed the wad of fabric against her wound while groping inside his coat for the smartphone hidden in the lining. An eternity of one-handed fishing before he found the thing. He switched off the recording mode, smearing the touchscreen with so much blood he could barely see the numbers on the keyboard to dial nine-one-one.

He got someone on the line, delivered details as coherently as possible. Address, ambulance, police, people shot, heavy bleeding, yada yada. He let the phone drop, forgotten, and concentrated on Lara's wound. Christ, so pale. Her lips, almost blue. But she was smiling.

"You're going to be fine," he told her.

She nodded faintly. *I love you*, she mouthed.

"Me, too." The rag was soaked. He put more pressure, wincing as she gasped.

"You killed Greaves." It was a man's voice, awestruck. "Jesus, how did you do that? How the hell did you kill that guy?"

Miles looked around. It was the big dark guy. Silva. The woman followed him out, too, the redhead. He was intensely aware of the uncorked beaker, but the two of them made no move to approach it.

"That's amazing," the redheaded woman said, her voice admiring.

"Do either one of you have medical training?" he asked.

The two glanced at each other and shook their heads.

"Then shut the fuck up and get down on the ground, hands where I can see them," he said.

"You're as powerful as he was," the woman said. "My God. You're just like him. Telekinesis, coercion . . . how did you do it?"

"I am not like him," he snarled. "Lady, what part of 'shut the fuck up' do you not understand?"

She batted her large, hazel eyes. "We could work for you," she offered hopefully. "With psi-max, we can do anything you want. Greaves controlled our supply, but if you could just get us more psi—"

"No," he snapped. "I don't have your fix, and I want nothing to do with you. You're a couple of sick ghouls who tried to chop my girlfriend's hand off. Go to jail and rot. Now get . . . the fuck . . . *down*."

They weren't moving, so he used telekinesis on both for the smackdown, as Greaves had done to Anabel. A vicious jab at the hamstring, a hard tap on the back, and *whap*, they were on their faces.

He clamped them down. Scary, how easy it was. Every time he used it, it got stronger. He could keep them flattened now with just an idle corner of his attention. And all of this souped-up power was utterly useless, for the purposes of helping Lara. Her lip was clamped between her teeth. She'd lost so much blood. "Lara," he said. "Stay with me."

Only when her eyes popped open, startled, did he realize he'd used a little jab of coercion on her, without even thinking.

Bad, but whatever worked. He was desperate. Not that a person could coerce another one into not bleeding to death. But still.

"Keep your eyes on me," he said. "Help is coming."

She nodded, and he suddenly felt that soft tickle at his consciousness, the lovely one that made sex and happiness hormones squirt directly into his brain and his bloodstream. The feeling he got when she was doing her seductive mind dance to get inside the Citadel.

He blocked it, instinctively. Shifting energy flows, forming walls, blocking holes. *No.* She could not come in, not until he knew what he had become, and how dangerous it might be for her. For them.

You're just as strong as he is. You're just like him.

Yeah. And his war machine, cool and expedient, had chosen the beaker of death to freeze telekinetically in that split-second he had to choose. Not the trigger of the gun that shot his girlfriend point-blank.

Arguably, a logical choice, considering the circumstances. But this wasn't about logic. It never had been.

He couldn't let her back into the Citadel. Where he could feel her, see her, control her, manipulate her at all times. That was one step short of confining her. Which was the beginning of the end.

That wasn't who he was. It wasn't who he would become.

You keep her in a cage, right? Isn't that control too, of a different sort? And don't you like it?

Yeah, in fact. He'd liked it fine. Greaves' words echoed in his head, making him sick inside. Even now, he was tempted to glom onto her. Hey, she was gunshot, clinging to him like a lifeline. What better time to pound on that particular nail? Shore up that bond, make it unbreakable? His forever. Swallowed up. Always his. Only his.

No. He clenched his teeth, his guts. It hurt like hell, but *no*.

She couldn't get into the Citadel.

She kept trying. She was exhausted, but aching for the comfort, the closeness, the sense of safety. To say nothing of being able to talk to him without having to use her lungs, her muscles.

But she couldn't find her way in. Maybe because she was hurt, stressed, her concentration shot. She studied his grim face, his set mouth. Heard sirens wailing faintly in the distance. "Miles," she said.

"Don't talk. You have to rest."

She touched his arm. "What happens now?"

"The EMTs are coming," Miles said. "So are the police. We'll tell them what we know. And warn them about that." He jerked his chin toward the beaker, still sitting there, gleaming in the pale gray light of morning. "They'll take it from there."

It sounded bland and normal and reasonable enough, but dread and fear built inside her anyway. "And us? Will you stay with me?"

He looked toward the ambulance coming up the drive, and the red and blue lights flashed rhythmically across his face. "You'll go to the hospital, of course. Get yourself patched up."

"And you'll stay with me there?"

"No, Lara," he said. "They're going to arrest me."

She jerked up onto her elbows, and sank back down with a cry of pain. "What the fuck are you talking about?"

"I'm a wanted man. And this mess, these bodies, it does not look good. It'll take them a while to work it out. I expect they'll lock me up in the meantime. I would, if I were them."

"But you didn't do anything wrong!" she wailed.

"Shhh," he soothed. "I know that, and you know that, but Greaves framed me for some very scary shit, and it's going to take some time to sort it out. But I will. Of course, I will. Don't worry. I'll be okay."

"Okay? In police custody? How can you say that?"

She tried again to get into the Citadel, and it hit her, all of a sudden, like a slap. The doors, the spaces she usually slipped through. They were deliberately closed. Dear God. He'd done it on purpose.

Hurt jangled loud inside her. "You locked me out," she whispered.

He would not meet her eyes. "I'm sorry."

"Sorry?" Utter betrayal threatened to engulf her completely. "You changed the password on me? Now? Of all times?"

"It's better this way. At least until we work things out."

Blue and red lights pulsed. Car doors slammed, people were shouting, running. She couldn't look away from his dark, intent gaze.

"How could you do this?" she whispered.

"With difficulty. Sometimes you've just got to do the hard thing."

She wanted to tell him exactly where he could put his hard thing, but her ability to speak had broken down. No more complex concepts or phrases. She was down to single-word epithets.

"Bastard," she whispered.

She fell backward, still staring at him as she tumbled down into that bottomless well.

30

Ten weeks later
Seattle

"You want some hot mulled cider? It's freezing out here."

The gentle voice made Lara turn from her contemplation of the whitecapped surface of Lake Washington. Davy and Margot McCloud's house on the water had an awesome view from their back porch. It soothed her to stare at the expanse of water. The sight was cooling to her hot, reddened eyes.

She tried to smile reassuringly into Nina's worried gaze, and took the hot mug, just to make her friend feel better. "I'm fine, but thanks."

"You shouldn't be out in the cold," Nina fussed. "You're delicate."

"Not anymore," she reminded her friend. "I'm all healed up. And my coat is really warm."

She was shivering, truth be told, even in the big, military wool coat. It was similar to the one Miles had bought for her at the thrift store, those many weeks ago, except that it fit somewhat better than the original. She'd bought it at a vintage store in a moment of nostalgia to replace the one soaked in the bloodbath. Fortunately, neither Nina nor any of her other friends knew of this pathetic past wardrobe detail.

"Please, come back inside?" Nina coaxed. "Aaro is fretting about you, and they're almost ready to serve dinner."

Lara turned to look at the big picture window, and waved at the array of kids peering through it, ranging in age from eleven to barely standing. They waved back, with assorted gap-toothed grins. Behind them, the room was full of adults talking, shooting surreptitious glances that slid quickly away from her. People she'd met at the safe house, their spouses, their numerous offspring, and more besides.

Nice people. Welcoming, warm, intelligent, helpful, concerned for her. But she was still having a hard time enduring crowds of any kind, even good and worthy ones. Being profoundly miserable did not help.

Davy McCloud was seated on the couch inside, just a couple of weeks out of the hospital and much better, though he still had some problems with head pain. He'd lost a good bit of his massive muscular bulk, and looked a lot more like his longer, leaner brother Connor than he did before. Connor was sitting next to him, hovering protectively. Tam and Val were there, with little Irina perched in the crook of her father's arm, playing with his long hair. Their older daughter, Rachel, was leading the other kids in some raucous game. Seth was there, the guy who had tried to courier her a new identity, accompanied by his wife, the beautiful silver-blond Raine, and their kids—older son Jesse and the toddler twins, Chris and Mattie. Kev was there with Edie, whose pregnancy was now visible to the naked eye, and Sean's wife Liv had announced that she was three months along with their second kid on that very day. Bruno and Lily Ranieri were there, with their boisterous brood. They were all so nice, with their beautiful, burgeoning families. So goddamn happy.

It was hard to swallow. She was so low, she barely bothered to scold herself for the envious, unworthy thoughts.

Screw it. Who had the energy? She hadn't wanted to

come to this soirée. She would have preferred to stay alone
in Sandy, in Aaro's forest. Huddled in the extension to Aaro
and Nina's house that they kept for guests. Taking long, solitary walks in the forest.

But Nina and Aaro had nixed that idea. They were afraid
to leave her alone in her current fragile state, though the danger was past.

She'd missed all the initial drama in her drugged haze at
the Intensive Care Unit. They had been quarantined, not that
it had mattered at the time that the doctors and nurses attending her had been helmeted and swathed. Who cared,
when you felt that bad.

When she finally came out of the fog, she started asking
for Miles. Nina, bless her soul, had been there for her,
spelled from time to time by the other McCloud woman
she'd met at the safe house, Edie. Even Tam had made a few
appearances, though she was uncomfortable with sickbed
duties, like providing ice chips or helping Lara to the bathroom.

Lara appreciated their efforts, but she wanted Miles.

Nina had been the one to explain the situation. It was just
as Miles had warned her. They had locked him up. For
weeks.

It wasn't so much the issue of the crimes for which
Greaves had framed him. Miles had hidden his smartphone
in the lining of his coat, leaving it in recording mode, so that
everything that had been said near the souped-up micro-
phone from the moment he walked up to Greaves' house had
been recorded. Greaves' assistants, Silva and Levine, had
confessed that the evidence at the cabin had been planted,
that Barlow's murder was Anabel's doing, and corroborated
Miles' claim that the three men buried on his property had
been killed in self-defense. The process of exonerating him
had been slow, but inevitable.

It was the recording itself, the profound weirdness of it,
that had raised red flags. People from various levels of state

and federal law enforcement had decided, for a time, that Miles might be a threat to national security. After that, it had been impossible for anyone to contact him. And he had refused to let her head-text. Those walls stayed bricked up. It hurt so badly, his silent, flat refusal.

But not as much as it had hurt when they finally let him go.

He hadn't come to her. Three weeks and still nothing. She was trying to face that stark fact, to process it. The second they let him go, he'd vanished. To his friends' bafflement and dismay.

At first they had made excuses for him, assuring her that he'd be back. Those assurances had eventually petered out into embarrassed silence. He'd appeared out of nowhere, saved her life, made her fall into mad and frenzied love with him, and then hauled ass, no explanation. He hadn't contacted her once. Not even to dump her formally, if that was what was happening. She just had to assume, surmise, infer.

He hadn't even needed Lara's testimony, in the end. The cops had interviewed her, of course, but they clearly considered her a head case after all her travails, and were talking to her just as a formality. So her fervent testimony on behalf of Miles' heroism was irrelevant. He wasn't thanking her for it. He wasn't speaking to her at all.

Oh, God, whatever. She was alive and free, thanks to him. And grateful for both things. Sort of. When she forced herself to be.

She hadn't been able to think about practical matters yet, like supporting herself. They'd all assured her that she didn't need to worry about it. Nina and her friends had filed a lawsuit on her behalf against Greaves' vast estate for damages, and the chances were good that they'd award her a huge chunk of money, once the legal machinery had ground through it all. Not that money could compensate her for months of soul-killing darkness, or being turned into a human oracle, or losing Mother and Dad. It was kind of hard to give a shit, actually.

Whatever. A pile of money. Fine. One less thing to worry about.

She had to stop sitting around and holding her breath, waiting, hoping. She had to start living her life again. Maybe she could run away, travel the world. Wander through Prague, trek in Nepal, sleep on a beach in Bali. Anything to distract her from that bricked up wall in her head. That stupid conditioned reflex she had, to continually reach for his mind for comfort, like Pavlov's dog. She couldn't stop throwing herself at that wall, though she was bloodied and bruised from her efforts. She needed neural reprogramming. Urgently.

The door slid open, and Liv stepped out, gorgeous and vivid in a red cashmere wrap. "Hey," she said gently. "It's so cold out here."

Lara hung on to her patience. "I'm all right. Really."

The women flanked her, and insistently escorted her back inside, into warmth, music, sounds of kids playing. Rich, appetizing cooking smells. Too much normalcy. She hardened her belly to iron, breathed through her nose, and smiled, enduring it.

They led her back to the kitchen. Many of the women were congregated there, watching Becca, another of their friends that she'd met that day, decorate a fancy chocolate cake. Becca smiled at her.

"Taste?" she offered, dipping a spoon into a chocolate glaze.

There was a commotion at the door as Lara shook her head. Someone on the porch was knocking. Margot peered through the door.

"Oh, boy. Liv, run and get Erin," she said. "Her sister's here."

Everyone got ominously quiet as Liv scurried into the other room.

Margot opened the door, and a young woman swept in on a gust of cold air. She was slender and curvy, in a pink, fur-trimmed jacket and tight jeans. She shoved down the hood and tossed out a wavy mane of shiny, perfectly styled hair. She was very pretty, similar to her older sister Erin, Connor's wife, but flashier, and with a lot more makeup.

"Hey, Cin. Great to see you," Margot said.

"Is it really?" Cindy gave the woman an overly sweet smile. "Funny, how I had to hear about this party from Kevvie. You used to invite me to your things before, but I guess it was just Miles you wanted around, right? I was just an appendage. The truth comes out."

"No, Cin," Erin said quietly. "We were always happy to have you. You weren't invited this time because we thought it might be awkward."

"Yeah? Because of . . ." Cindy's sharp gaze swept the room and fastened onto Lara. "Her." Her voice hardened.

They looked at each other. Lara's back stiffened instinctively, spine prickling up to absolute straightness.

Cindy tossed her hair. "Well, would you look at that," she said. "She looks just like me. Except too skinny. And without the grooming."

Lara was acutely conscious of her unstyled hair, her reddened eyes, her dowdy sweatshirt, the big, drab coat hanging to her ankles. She wanted to shoot back something snappy, but she felt stuck in tar.

"That's bullshit," Nina snapped. "She doesn't look a thing like you, beyond the coloring."

"Cindy," Erin said, in a warning tone. "Don't do this."

Cindy ignored her. "Doesn't have much to say, does she? That probably made it easier for him in bed. Pretending she was me."

A chorus of gasps sounded. "That's enough," Nina said sharply. "After what she'd been through, the last thing she needs is—"

"Stop, Nina." Lara stepped forward.

"Oh! Wow!" Cindy's eyes widened, in mock wonder. "She speaks. It's a miracle!"

"Yeah, I speak," Lara said. "And I did not go through hell

on earth to get kicked around by a brainless cow like you. Back off."

Tam applauded. "Yes!" she crowed. "Catfight! Bitch-slap!"

"Shut up, Tam!" Margot hissed.

Cindy ignored them all, staring intently at Lara. "He'll come back to me, you know," she said. "He always does. We belong together."

"He's free to do whatever the hell he wants," Lara said. "But I doubt that he wants you. You had your chance. You didn't even know what you had, or you would've hung onto it."

Cindy bristled. "Oh, I know him," she said. "Great body? Super hung? Total god in the sack? Gives great head? Sound familiar?"

"Stop it!" Erin sounded disgusted. "Don't be gross, Cin! You're embarrassing me." She glanced at Lara, apologetic. "I'm so sorry."

"It's okay," Lara said. "I'm the one who's sorry for her, if that's all she ever valued about him. Or all she ever noticed."

Cindy snorted. "Whatever," she said. "I didn't come here to talk to you, anyway. Where's Miles?"

There was an uncomfortable pause.

"Not here," Lara finally said, quietly.

Cindy swept a keen glance around the room, her face breaking into a slow, triumphant smile. "Oh! I see. I thought you were up in the mountain love nest together. Awesome. So he's already over the rebound bunny. That was predictable. And it makes things simpler. Because I am getting him back."

Lara shrugged. "I doubt that."

"You do that, if it makes you feel better." She darted a glance at her glaring sister, and her eyes slid away quickly. "Later, sis. Nice party. Kiss the kids for me."

Slam. The kitchen door fell to, hard enough to rattle window panes. The kitchen was deathly silent for a few moments.

"Wow," Becca murmured. "Well. That was . . . surreal."

Erin laid her hand on Lara's shoulder. "You okay?"

"I am *fine*." Lara's voice rang out, disproportionately loud, as she stared through the window at the trim hot-pink package mincing up the walkway. Swaying on her spike-heeled boots. Butt cheeks twitching saucily. Off to win Miles back. Up at the mountain love nest.

Her Miles.

Energy tingled up her back. Her hands tightened to tingling fists. That cheap, no account piece of fluff . . . with Miles? As. Fucking. If.

"Lara." Nina had that soothe-the-mental-patient tone that was beginning to grate on her nerves. "We don't want to upset you, but—"

"I am *fine!* Stop pussyfooting around me! Yes, I was moping. I admit it. I'm sorry. I'll stop, okay? The moping is finished!"

Nina's mouth hung open. "Uh . . ."

"Sorry to yell at you, but it pissed me off. To think that alley cat has the nerve to go after him, after she lied to him and cheated on him! And me? What the fuck am I doing here, sitting on my ass? Feeling sorry for myself?"

"Um . . . healing?" Edie offered gently.

"I'm healed," Lara announced. "Halleluia! Can I borrow a car from somebody?"

There was a nervous silence. "To go where?" Nina asked.

"To go drive up to this place in the mountains that you guys all evidently know about, but didn't tell me for fear of upsetting poor Lara in her delicate state," she said. "To plant the toe of my boot in that cat bitch's swishy little ass if she even tries getting near my man."

Tam's chuckle broke the stunned silence. A wad of car keys sailed up. Lara snagged them out of the air, one-handed. "Take mine," Tam said. "Cat bitch ass-kicking is a cause that I always support. Just let me get the kids' car seats out before you leave."

"Lara." Nina looked worried. "Please, don't go off on a tear. Just take it easy. You have to take things slow."

"No," Lara said. "There's times to take things slow, and there are times to make a move. He can turn me down if he wants to. I won't break. I promise. I've been through worse. Much worse. I'll be fine." She looked around, and repeated it, more forcefully. "Really. Fine."

"Of course you will," Nina said, sniffing.

A chorus of reassuring echoes followed that statement.

Lara turned to Nina. "I need to get my bag out of the trunk of your car," she said. "I need to change." She turned to Margot. "Could I borrow a needle and thread from you? And some makeup? And a blow dryer and a round brush?"

"I'll go get my sewing kit." Margot exchanged discreetly delighted glances with the other women in the room. "Use the bathroom off the master bedroom. All my stuff is there. Help yourself."

Lara closed herself in the bathroom after Margot had gotten her what she needed, and stared at her reflection. She looked so pale. Fragile. And sick to death of it.

She was done wafting around, looking wounded and ethereal. If the hell she had gone through had been good for anything, it had to have taught her that much.

She shrugged her coat off and got down to it.

The waiting was killing him. Weighing down on him, like a pile of broken rock. It was so hard to breathe.

The wind off the mountain peaks was below freezing, and burning the hell out of his ears. Miles hunched down into the collar of his coat as he paced the site he'd mapped out for the house, trying to lose himself in pondering the best angle for the big picture windows.

He'd forgotten a bunch of basic items when he loaded the camper onto the back of his pick-up to drive up here. A warm winter hat was one of them. Damn, it was cold up here. Inside and out. Body and soul, every day that he waited. It was turn-the-knife torture, knowing that Lara perceived his silence as abandonment, but every time he started to give in to the urge to go to her and drop to his knees and beg for mercy, something stony and implacable stopped him. Whispering, *wait*.

He couldn't muddy the waters now. Or he would never know if Greaves' taunt was true, or if the guy had just been blowing smoke.

The entire extended McCloud Crowd had been up to chastise him, one after the other, after they'd hacked his location. Probably it was the property purchase that had tipped them off. He certainly hadn't told anyone, not even his parents. As soon as the Special Task Force types had let him walk out of there, he'd contacted a bunch of realtors. Given them his wish list, his price range. Told them he could pay in cash.

They'd leaped to accommodate him.

It hadn't taken long to find the perfect place. But three days after he'd parked himself and the trailer here, his friends had begun to arrive. An unending procession of lectures about what a shithead he was, how sad and fragile Lara was, how she was losing weight, yada yada. Breaking his balls, breaking his heart. Tam had been the worst. It made her frantic, that he'd finally jettisoned Cindy and found a girl who was worth the effort, and now he was deliberately fucking it up.

It was impossible to explain. Yeah, he was miserable. Lara was miserable, too. But she was free. Free to make a move herself, if that was what she chose. Free to feel her feelings, whatever they might be. Not a cocktail of drugs, stress, extreme circumstances. Not a result of being locked up inside his mind. No head-texting, shield swallowing, coercion or psi sleight of hand. No dirty tricks, not even plain old guilt or gratefulness, or obligation, God forbid. None of that shit.

Just her own naked truth. One that she had to come to alone.

He looked around at the frost-encrusted mud of the building excavation he'd begun the week before. It was the wrong time of year to start building a house. He wouldn't pour the concrete for the foundation until spring. Even so, he didn't want to be anywhere but up here. This place represented all his hopes for the future.

Snowflakes blew sideways in the blustery wind, into his stinging ears. He rubbed them, and caught slight of a flash of headlights.

He peered through the trees. A green VW Beetle. Oh, God. The last person he wanted to see, on the tail end of a very long list. Cindy.

She drove up the long, winding driveway, and parked down in the churned, frozen mud next to his trailer. She was a garish pink spot of color in the drab greens, whites, browns, grays of the landscape as she picked her way up the rugged footpath that he was going to have to extensively landscape. Telekinesis might actually come in handy when it came time to manipulate massive stepstones of granite. Only if no one was looking, though. He tried to be rigorous about not using the psi, but every now and then, he cheated. Like with the Task Force types. He'd resisted the urge to the bitter end, but on week seven of the interrogations, he'd begun to delicately nudge those guys into deciding that he was not just harmless, but literally killing them with boredom.

He wished he could use his psi now. He'd pick Cindy up, waft her back to her car, and spin the Beetle in mid-air until it was pointed in the correct direction. Away from him.

But he did not do that scary, Greaves-style shit. "Hey, Cin," he said, resigned.

She'd just freshened up her lipstick, and her blinding smile was an alarming, shiny candy-apple red. "Hey there, big guy."

The flirtatious salute chilled him. She picked her way up

the footpath, ankles wobbling. It was so Cindy, to wear spike-heeled dress boots into the mountains. "How'd you find me?" he asked.

"Connor knew where you were," she said, scrambling up onto the leveled ground with some effort.

"And he told you?" Odd, that didn't sound like Connor's style.

Cindy rolled her eyes. "Are you kidding? That guy wouldn't tell me what time it was if my life depended on it. I snooped in his office when I was babysitting Kevvie and Maddy. There's a big accordian file on you."

"Wow," he said. "I'm touched."

"Yeah, don't bother trying to keep anything secret from those dudes. They are, like, scary. So anyhow. This is your new place?" She forced enthusiasm into her voice. "Sure is . . . remote."

They stared out at the view for many long moments. "Two hours and forty minutes from downtown Seattle," he said. "Not so remote."

"Oh, well. I guess that's cool. As a country place."

"Nope," he said. "Primary residence. No town place."

Cindy hugged herself, shivering as she stared up at the fluttering snowflakes. "I thought you wanted a townhouse. In Capital Hill, or Queen Anne," she said. "We've been talking about it for years."

"Yeah, well. You always had this tendency to confuse what I wanted with what you wanted."

Cindy gave him a soulful look. "I'm so sorry if I was selfish. But I've changed, Miles. Really."

Snow gusted harder. Courtesy demanded that he invite her into the trailer for a hot beverage. Courtesy be damned. Being confined in such close quarters with Cindy was beyond what he could tolerate right now. "I appreciate the apology," he said. "But I've changed, too. And you shouldn't be here."

She gave him that shimmering look that used to melt him,

back in that other lifetime. "Miles. We're good together. You've been my best friend since, like, forever."

"I know. But you killed it, Cin," he said quietly. "I've moved on. This snow is getting thicker, and it'll be dark in a couple of hours. You should head back right now. There's no place for you here."

She sniffled. "It's her, isn't it? She's the reason?"

He didn't feel like responding to that, so he stayed silent.

"You're so cold," she whispered, forlornly. "When did you get so damned cold?"

When I was forcibly mutated into a freak with deadly psi abilities. It almost made him laugh. It would be impossible to share what he'd become with someone like Cindy. She'd probably think it was cool, even sexy. Yeah, just ask Greaves. Phenomenal psychic power was way cool, until you went nuts with it. Started killing the people you loved.

"Actions have consequences," he said.

"I know," she said. "I fucked up. No forgiveness?"

"Of course I forgive you," he said, more gently. "And now you should go."

She sniffled again. "Fine. I get it." She took a step, caught the heel of her boot on a mud rut, and stumbled.

He was there in a flash, catching her elbow. He helped her down over the rough part. Stepped back when they got to the straight stretch where her car was parked. That part, he'd let her go alone. Duty done.

He called out, on impulse, as she pulled her car door open. "Cin!"

She turned, wiping a rivulet of mascara tears from beneath her eyes. "What?" she demanded, her voice soggy.

"Get some help," he said.

She stared at him. "Who do you think you are, preaching to me?"

"I'm not preaching. I just want you to be happy."

"Happy?" She laughed, a sharp, bitter sound. "Get lost, Miles. You always were a condescending bastard."

He thought about Lara. Her regal, unshakable dignity. The thought was a keen, sharp ache in his chest. "So stop letting yourself be condescended to, Cin," he said. "By anyone."

"Okay." She gave him a tight smile. "I'll start with you. Goodbye, and go fuck yourself."

"Goodbye," he replied.

He watched her car vanish into the trees. A knot inside him was loosening. Wow. He hadn't known that he cared that much.

And he really did genuinely wish her well. He wasn't forcing it or faking it. He wished her happiness, fulfillment, peace. Dignity. That wasn't too much to hope for an old friend, so he'd hope it.

From a safe distance.

That encounter had been stressful enough to warrant defrosting his ears and his fingers, so he headed into the trailer, which was not big enough for his six foot almost five inch frame. He had to hunch over like Quasimodo when he moved around the place. He turned on the space heater, put the water on, pulled out a teabag. Wondered, rather dispiritedly, if he'd better start thinking about putting fuel into his system. He'd take the time of a cup of tea to ponder his limited options.

But the snow swirled thickly, and time dilated. He forgot to drink his tea. Just sat, staring through the small, clouded window, hypnotized by snowflakes. Until the liquid was stone cold, and too bitter to drink. He caught the faint sound of another vehicle. His heart sank. What was the point of a remote mountain lair if everybody kept parading through it to whale on him?

He peered out the window. Tam's Mercedes. *Fuck*. He was still lacerated from her last punishing visit. No time to run and hide. Just please, God, let her vehicle have snow tires, so she could leave when she was done with him. The thought of being stranded in a snowstorm in a trailer with

Tam Steele for an extended period of time—well, shit. Soul-shaking dread would not be stating the matter too strongly.

Man up, dude. He struggled into the coat, hunching down to shimmy his big frame through the door. Crunched heavy boots along the frosty ruts and pine needles to greet his latest uninvited guest—

And stopped, mouth agape.

It was Lara. She wore a long, green wool coat that hit her almost at the ankles, giving her an old-fashioned, nineteenth-century look. Pale white hands peeped at the bottom of cuffed sleeves. No gloves, no hat.

Holy God. He remembered her beautiful, but not this beautiful.

He stared, openmouthed. She'd done something to her hair, loosening the fuzzy dark waves into swirly silken ringlets. And makeup. That was it. She was wearing a little makeup, and he'd never seen it on her, except in photographs.

The bottom of his world dropped out. His insides swooshed, in free-fall. He tried to say her name. His throat had thickened into cement. He coughed. "Lara," he said. "You look beautiful."

Her swift, mysterious smile did something intense and uncontrollable to his glands.

"Thank you," she said demurely. "I primped."

"You were always beautiful, but now . . . but wow."

She ran, lightfooted and swift, up the footpath in her practical lace-up climbing boots, and stopped a few feet from him. Close enough to smell. Her scent was life itself. Spring, rain, sea foam, and earth—and loam and honey and blooming flowers. And sex.

"I expected to find Cindy here," she said.

It was weirdly discordant to hear Cindy's name from her lips. Cindy inhabited a whole different layer of earthly existence. "Uh, she was," he confessed. "Been and gone. What about her?"

Her beautiful smile flashed again. "Is that so? I'm almost disappointed. To think that I wore my heavy boots up here on purpose."

He floundered for the through-line. "Boots? What purpose?"

"For the ass-kicking," Lara explained. "Cindy had wicked designs on you. I objected to them. We even had a catfight, in front of all of your friends. Shame you missed it. Ever had two girls fight over you before?"

"Ah . . . no," he said, bemused. "Can't say as I have."

"It's something to see," she told him. "Tam loved it."

"Wow." A crazy grin was starting to pull at his mouth. "You mean, like, a hair pulling, clawing, screaming kind of catfight?"

"Yup," she said. "A total bitch-slapping smackdown."

"Jesus." He blinked, bemused. "I'm surprised she didn't say anything about it."

There was a silence. Twitchy and embarrassed on his part. Sphinx-like, inscrutable calm upon hers.

"So," she said finally, taking pity on him. "How are you doing with the psi?"

He shrugged. "It's irrelevant. If I had, say, the power to heal the sick, then I might feel called upon to use it for the good of humanity, but coercion and telekinesis? Not so much. I don't get off on bullying people, and I do okay lifting and throwing stuff with my regular muscles, so I'm mothballing it. I have better things to do with myself."

Like spending the rest of my life worshipping you. His eyes moved over her, hungrily.

"Did you use the coercion when you were proving your innocence?" she asked.

He hesitated. "I didn't need it to prove my innocence," he hedged. "The recording was enough, and Levine and Silva did the rest."

"What about Levine and Silva? Did you coerce them?"

Miles sighed. "Nah. Not really. I did tell them to tell the

truth or else I'd make their eyeballs explode before the cops came, but that was just old-fashioned threatening. I didn't mind-flog them."

"Ah." She folded her arms over her chest. "And later?"

"Later," he said, heavily. "Yeah, I used it a little, later. Sorta kinda. Not a lot. The recording freaked people out. They needed some help to conclude it was just Greaves' megalomania and crazy talk. That I was just playing along with him. I didn't do any hard-core coercion, though. I just nudged them a little. You know, to drive home how totally boring and harmless I was."

"Right," she murmured. "You. Harmless." She took a step closer. Her skin glowed, luminously pale. Pearly. A forest dryad come to beguile and enthrall him. Making him thick and helpless and stupid.

He struggled to stay sharp. "You are messing with me."

"Oh, Miles," she said softly. "I have not even begun to mess with you."

He lost his whole train of thought in her luminous gaze, and had to struggle to recover it. "Should I be afraid?"

She considered that for a long moment. "It depends on what you say to me in the next few minutes."

"Oh, God." He rubbed his eyes with the heels of his hands, and when he lifted them she was still there. Still real. "Fine. Okay. Hit me."

She crossed her arms across her chest, lifted her chin. "Why did you abandon me?"

It was a blow right to the chest. He caught his breath, blurted out the first brainless thing that popped into his head. "I was incarcerated?"

She batted that away, impatient. "Don't be annoying. I mean after, and you know it. You ran away from me. You kept the Citadel closed. Why?" Her voice rang, clear and challenging. Snowflakes settled on the gleaming swirls of her hair and did not melt. One was poised on the tip of her long eyelashes. She flicked it away, waiting.

Oh, man. With all the times that he'd been forced to defend his unpopular decisions to the McCloud Crowd, he still hadn't found adequate words to explain or justify them.

But this was it. His last chance.

"I had to be sure . . ." He petered out, groping. "That it was real for you. That you weren't just, you know. Trapped in my head."

"Trapped?" Her eyes went huge with outrage. The pearly pink blush of her cheek deepened. "I was never trapped. I loved it in there! It was like paradise for me! You know that, Miles!"

"Maybe, but you were still trapped," he said, grimly. "What's it called, when you can't step outside of a place without getting ripped to pieces, Lara? It's called being trapped. You were under seige. You no longer had a choice, even if you started out by going there of your own free will. Greaves told me—"

"You made decisions about our private life based on something that *Greaves* said?"

"Hear me out! Greaves said that I kept you in a cage, and it was true. Fucking you senseless, right after what you'd just gone through? Swallowing you up inside my shield? Keeping you right where I could see you, inside my mind, snuggled up in a little box, safe and sound, and all mine? And I loved it, Lara. I fucking *loved* it."

"So did I!" she yelled.

"Of course you did!" he roared back. "You needed to feel safe! You were fucked up, traumatized!"

"Yeah, well, for the record, I'm not fucked up or traumatized any longer. I am fine! Is that clear?" Her eyes were bright, burning.

"That's great," he said. "But you have to see it, Lara. That thing we did? With the shield? That takes the scary, controlling boyfriend vibe to a whole new level. A Greaves-style level. He controlled his wife right into the grave. And his son . . . well, you saw what happened there. He killed his son, swallowing him up like that. Ate him alive."

"Yes," she said. "Yes, he did, but you wouldn't. You aren't like Greaves. You're brave and generous. And good."

He dragged in a deep breath. "Greaves said that you were . . . oh, shit, don't get mad, okay?"

"Can't promise that," she said crisply. "Go on."

Miles braced himself. "He said he'd been preparing you with drugs, breaking down psychological barriers. So that when he had sex with you, you'd bond with him instantly."

"Him?" Her mouth tightened in disgust. "Oh, Miles. That's gross."

"He said you would have bonded with anyone right after," he forged stubbornly on. "That I was the lucky dog. He said he'd show me how to coerce you into being my eager nympho sex slave forever after."

"Ah." She gave him a sidewise look. "Were you tempted?"

He just looked at her. "Don't torture me," he said, hoarsely.

"No?" Her eyes were bright with tears. "Why shouldn't I, Miles? What do you think you've been doing to me for the last several weeks?"

He shook his head. "I'm just telling you what he said."

"And you believed him?" Her voice quivered dangerously.

He shook his head. Out loud it sounded stupid, wrong. But he had still been compelled to wait. To be sure.

"I couldn't know, unless I stepped back from you," he said. "And about the Citadel, well, Jesus, Lara. After what happened to Geoff, it was clear that mind-melding is dangerous. Plus, I didn't know what was going to happen to me. Prison, death row, who knew? I didn't want you connected mind-to-mind if I was going to get fucked up. Plus, I felt like shit, because my efforts to keep you safe were a total fail."

"How can you say that?" she said angrily. "That is such bullshit!"

"You think?" He shrugged. "I put you on a bus, alone, no protection. I let you get shot, point blank."

"It wasn't your fault!" she raged. "And all this angst, all this doubt? Why couldn't you just *tell* me about it? Why not ask me? I'm not even saying mind-to-mind. The telephone would have done just as well. A fucking postcard would have been fine. Anything!"

His jaw clenched painfully. "I didn't trust myself not to put pressure on you. I would have been all over you, like a Labrador puppy. Blocking every exit, taking up all the air, hogging up all your RAM. I know myself, Lara. I just know it."

She pressed her hand to her mouth, eyes brimming. "Oh, Miles," she said, her voice strangled. "You are such a goddamn jerk."

"I know," he admitted. "I'm not anywhere near as nice a guy as you seem to think. I fight my demons, too. And I love control. I really do." He paused, blew out a shaky breath. "But not as much as I love you."

He couldn't bear to look at her after saying it. He stared out at the mountains, which were barely visible now, the vast expanse of sky was so blurred with falling snow.

"So, you think that all my feelings for you are just some chemical brew that Greaves cooked up artificially?" Her voice was small. "You think I'm some plastic doll? You push a button and she falls in love? That's all my love is to you?"

"Not at all," he said wearily. "I was just trying to let you figure out how you really felt. Without all the drama, all the weird stuff." He hesitated, then forced himself to ask, "So, uh. How do you feel?"

"Like you don't trust me," she said.

He let out trapped breath in a long exhalation and reached out, taking her hand. "Let me show you something," he said.

She let herself be led across the site. Her slender hand

was so cool. Their fingers clasped, tightening, and his heart practically leaped out of his chest.

"Where are you taking me?" she asked.

"It's a surprise," he said. "It's not far."

She let her hair swing down as she walked, shielding her face from his gaze, but every now and then, he caught a glimpse of her shy gaze, her smiling lips. Her fingers wound around his, and the pressure made every cell in his body vibrate with startled joy. They paced through the towering cathedral of trees. The shadows deepened, but there was still light in the sky as they rounded the curve of the hill.

They heard it before they saw it. An incredulous smile illuminated her face. "Oh, my God, Miles," she said. "You didn't. No way."

He gave her a crooked smile, opting not to speak, since he didn't trust his voice. He led her around the bend, to show her the reason he'd bought the property.

A mountain stream meandered down the mountain side. It had channeled itself into a mossy cleft between two dark stones, creating a natural spout that gushed down in a thick horsetail of water, about seven feet high. When that stream hit the rocks below, it splashed out and subdivided into smaller ones, creating a pyramid of waterfalls. Icy clear water swirled below into a small, deep pool, which was going to be an awesome place to cool down on a summer's day. The spray had frozen onto every twig and leaf nearby, turning the place into a crystalline facsimile of itself.

"In a while, it'll freeze," he said. "It'll be an ice sculpture, until spring. Then it will come to life again. If you're patient." He couldn't look at her, just stared at the falling water, his face hot with emotion. "So. As you can see, I had very high hopes about the quality of your love."

She took his arm and gently turned him to face her. "This is for me, then?" she asked. "For Lara, who loves waterfalls? Not a machine manipulated with chemicals, who can be had by any lucky dog who comes along? You know who I am, right? You feel me?"

"I know you." His voice was thick. "I feel you. It's all for you. Only you."

She pulled his hand up, stroked it against the impossibly soft, warm skin of her cheek. Then she unbuttoned the top button of her coat. "I feel you, too. And this feeling is specific to you. Only you."

"Yes," he said.

"You believe me?" She undid another button.

He laughed, wiping his eyes. "Yes. I believe you. I swear. What the hell are you doing with that coat? Button it up! It's freezing out here!"

"I have something to show you, too." She undid the buttons all the way down the heavy coat, and shrugged it off her shoulders, letting it drape from her elbows.

He rocked backwards, dazzled.

His dream Lara made flesh, right here, so soft and hot and real. She wore the very dress she'd worn in their dream trysts. He would not have been able to describe the garment until he saw it, but he knew it inside out, right down to the nose-tickling texture and smell of it. So soft and girlish and sexy, with those flirty puckers and swirls and flounces. The low neckline showed off her gorgous tits. An intoxicating waft of hot, honey-sweet Lara scent rose up, dizzying him. His erection, ever at half mast in her presence, swelled to two hundred percent.

"God," he said, helplessly. "Where did you find that?"

"At that thrift shop," she said. "I found it the morning that you put me on the bus. You actually bought it yourself, but you didn't notice, you were so busy talking to Seth, setting things up for me."

"It's . . . it's amazing." He reached out, touched her.

She had goosebumps from the cold. Under the filmy wisp of chiffon over her shoulder was the scar, angry red against pale skin, the cruel marks of the surgery, the stitches. His fingers brushed over it, and he wished, not for the first time, that he had the power to take all that away. Heal all the hurts with a magic wave of his hand, his love.

"I thought I'd lost the dress at the bus station. That's where they nabbed me, you see. Then Nina suggested that I try the lost and found, and lo and behold. The bag was there, with everything still in it."

He shook his head, speechless. Memorizing the details with his eyes, with his fingers. So soft, so warm. The pale globes of her tits, compressed lushly against the tight bodice. Bodacious cleavage. Yum.

She gathered up the skirt, fluffing it. Gave him a sultry glance up under her lashes that made a shiver ripple up his spine. "I'm wearing gartered hose under it and nothing else. For old time's sake."

"You're bare-assed, with garters, and hiking boots?" He was grinning like an idiot. "God. You're going to give me a stroke. Show me."

Her laughter was breathless, indistinguishable from her violent shivering "Here? In the snow?"

"Just a glimpse," he pleaded. "Go on, torment me."

His head swam, watching her hike up the filmy flounces. There was a lot of it, multiple layers of teasing froth, but she finally got it all up bundled in front of her so he could see the celestial vision; her pale, perfect legs, swathed in ribbed brown stockings up to mid-thigh, held up by the garters. And her sweet, dark, curly muff up there, yummy shadowy concave woman parts that just beckoned and pulled him.

He placed his shaking hand between her legs. Slid it up, to feel her softness, her warmth. The humid seam of her pussy, hidden in springy ringlets, just hinting at the juicy hot pink parts. He couldn't believe this was for real. Her, right here, in his grasp. Wanting him.

She clutched his shoulders for balance, her thighs clamping tight around his hand like she wanted to trap him there. Fine by him.

But she was shivering, hard. "You're cold," he said.

She shook her head. "Hot," she corrected him. "Very hot."

"We should get you someplace warm," he said, but still he teased his finger deeper, to feel her muscles clench and pulse around him.

"I'm fine right here," she said.

He withdrew his hand, sucking on his finger. Oh, God, yum. Heaven's balm. So good. "Not here," he said, resolute. "It's too cold. You'd freeze your ass off, and besides, we have to keep this dress nice."

She was laughing again, a high pitched vibration. "We do?"

"Yeah. We take it someplace dry, and wrap it in plastic and hang it up carefully. I want you to wear it on the day that you marry me."

Her teasing smile softened to a look of startled wonder.

Suddenly, they were locked in a desperate kiss, with all the explosive power of fireworks, all the melting tenderness of coming home. But the kiss had a thundering agenda of its own, as usual, and Miles had to stagger back from it, face hot. Brain fogged with lust.

"Not here," he repeated, more to himself than to her.

"Where, then?" she asked. "The trailer?"

"No. The bed's not soft or warm or clean enough for you, and I don't have anything fit for you to eat there."

"I'm not fussy," she said. "Or hungry. All I want is you."

"I'm thinking of this lodge up at the lake," he said. "I stayed there while I was buying this place, and I fantasized about having you there, in that big four-poster bed with me. Clean white sheets, patchwork quilts. An old-fashioned clawfoot tub in the bathroom, big enough for us both. A good restaurant downstairs, for after. When we're hungry."

She hid her face against his chest. "As long as you're there."

"Hell, yeah. You could not pry me away with dynamite."

As soon as he could lift his head from the tight, trembling hug, he prompted her. "So, uh. You didn't actually respond to my formal proposal of marriage."

Her laughter rang through the trees. "Come on. You just told me what you wanted me to wear. That's not a formal proposal."

He jerked her coat closed, and started to button it. "How many ways do I need to declare myself? I declared myself in the diner, too, before you got on the bus. Remember? The days and the nights? The meals and the talks, and the winters and the summers?"

"I remember," she whispered. "I thought it was all lost forever."

He bent to finish buttoning, and since he was down there already, what the hell. He dropped to his knees. Which was right where she'd had him since the moment he'd first seen her anyhow. "It's not lost. I'm offering it to you now, formally. All my tomorrows. They're all yours."

She dug in her coat pocket for a tissue, dabbing at her eyes, her nose. "Oh, get up. You'll get your knees soaked," she said. "Of course I'm yours. Of course I'll marry you. You're making me cry. Stop it."

He rose, running his hands over her slender, perfect body all the way up. She seemed so frail, so fragile, as if she'd snap, but she was anything but fragile. God, how he loved that. So sexy. So freeing.

"Just making it official," he said. "Tomorrow, let's take off. Go on a road trip, someplace warm. We could go down the coast, see the Grand Canyon. Or head down into Mexico. Do you have a passport?"

"I've been back to my place in San Francisco," she assured him. "I have all my documents again."

"Good. Let's go. Anywhere you want."

She snuffled into the tissue again. "It sounds so wonderful," she said. "I just can't quite believe it's real. My fantasy come true."

"Nah." He grabbed her hand, pulled it up to stroke over his beard stubble. "If this were a fantasy, I would have showered and shaved, and I'd be wearing a clean shirt. What you have here is nude, crude reality."

"Oh, shut up," she snapped. "You're gorgeous, and you know it."

"Let's get you someplace warm," he said again, scooping his arm around her waist.

She held him back. "One last thing you're forgetting."

He read what she wanted in her eyes. "Really? After all we've been through, all we've seen, you want to risk head-texting again?"

"Absolutely," she said. "It's not a risk. Not with you. It's wonderful, and I trust you. Besides, I'm strong. You couldn't swallow me up if you wanted to, because I wouldn't let you. You'd choke on me."

"Oh, I don't know," he murmured. "You're pretty yummy, Lara."

"Seriously." She gripped the lapels of his coat. "Please, Miles."

He stared into her searching eyes, and let his tension out in a long, quiet sigh. He rested his forehead against hers. Closed his eyes.

It wasn't automatic to tease it apart again, the braided energy flows, to open that sealed shield again. Not anymore. He couldn't do it at the first level of concentration he reached, or even the second. He had to go deeper. He was just getting some traction when she spoke up.

"You know, for a mindbending killer monster freak, you sure are a slowpoke," she murmured.

"Give me a break," he grumbled back. "I have to go in and reprogram the bastard on the spot. Write new code. Under pressure."

"So rise to the occasion, already."

"So stop distracting me." He couldn't stop grinning, shaking with laughter. "This takes concentration."

It was the laughter that did it. It kindled a glow of happiness that pulled it all together for him.

The door opened, wide and welcoming, just for her. Beckoning her in with perfect trust.

She made a soft sound of pure wonder, and *ahhh*. She was inside.

o god i missed u so much. i missed this.

me 2 yours now forever and always my love

They stood in the swirling snow, locked in that tight, swaying embrace. The deepening shadows swathed them like a dark cloak, but they were warmed from the inside. Lit up, glowing. Shining with the perfect, holy rightness of it.

With no fear at all of losing their way.

Read on for a taste of ONE WRONG MOVE,

available now!

Nina looked back. Her heart jolted up into her throat. That car was following her. It wasn't nerves, or paranoia. She'd slipped into the all-night supermarket for a few minutes to talk herself down, sip some weak coffee from the deli counter, get over the crawling sense of being stalked. It didn't seem possible. It was so very obvious that she had nothing worthwhile to steal. She made a point of that. She dressed down to the point of vanishing. She'd made it into a high art.

And yet, that car had parked somewhere and waited for her while she dawdled in the supermarket. And now, it was crawling steadily along behind her once again. A Lincoln Town Car, nondescript beige color. She noted the plate number as her nervous, fast walk quickened into a trot. She wished she hadn't drunk the nasty coffee. It roiled in her chilled guts like acid slush. She punched 911 into her cell with the useless, scolding rant blaring through her head, how she should have trusted her instincts, stayed in the store,

called the police from there, yada yada. No running back to
the supermarket now. The car was between her and it, and all
the businesses on the street were deserted this early in the
morning. Across the street were apartment complexes, lots
of shadowy lawn and shrubbery to sprint through. She'd
never get anyone's attention in time. She couldn't have picked
a worse spot to be at this hour if she tried. *Shit.* Brain-dead
idiot, thinking she could walk to work at this hour. Idiot, for
agreeing to man the hotline this early in the morning, for not
getting the car fixed in time, for not calling a cab.

The engine revved. The car was gaining on her. A squirt
of raw panic jolted her even faster, rubber-soled sandaled
feet thudding as the 911 operator squawked into her ear.
"I'm being followed by a beige Lincoln Town Car," she panted
back into the phone, and gabbled out the plate number. "I'm
on Lamson, just turned off Avenue Y—"

The car screeched to a stop right behind her, and a door
popped open. "Nina? Nina!"

What the *hell?* It was a woman's voice, thin and shaking.
Nina teetered as she twisted to look. Her breath rasped in her
chest. She thumbed the speakerphone button on. As if that
could help.

A wraith stumbled out of the backseat and onto the sidewalk. A woman, older, graying. Skeletal. Bloodshot eyes,
sunken into sallow, shadowy pits. Blood dripped from her
nose, and from a cut lip. Her clothes hung on her, and her
hair was a snarled black-and-gray mess.

The woman lurched closer. "Nina?" Her voice sounded
beseeching.

Nina skittered back, her hackles rising. A feeling was
growing, almost like recognition, but not quite. More like
dread.

"Excuse me?" she asked cautiously. "Do I know you?"

Tears streamed down over the woman's sallow, caved-in
cheeks. Words burst out of her in a language Nina did not
recognize. And she was coming forward way too fast.

Nina backed up. "How do you know my name?"

Another impassioned outburst, and Nina did not understand a goddamn word of it. She continued backing up. "Look, I don't know who you are or what you want, but stay away from me," she said. "Just keep your distance."

Thud. Her back hit the newsstand. The woman came on with unnerving swiftness. Her gibberish had a pleading tone. She grabbed Nina's phone out of her hand, and clicked at it, still babbling.

"Hey! Give me that!" Nina lunged to get her phone back. The phone dropped to the ground, spinning, as the woman grabbed her arm, snake-fast. Nina twisted, squirming to get free, but the woman's icy hand was horribly strong. Her other hand flashed out.

Nina screamed as a hypodermic needle stabbed into her forearm. It burned like a wasp's sting.

The woman let go. The syringe dropped, rolled into the gutter.

Nina's back hit the newsstand again with a jarring thud. She stared into the other woman's haggard face. Gasping for air, but she had no place to put it. Her lungs were clenched in a huge, cold fist.

Recognition finally kicked in with a shuddering prickle over her entire body. "Helga," she croaked. "Oh, God. Helga?"

The woman raised her hands, flapping them in mute apology. She bent down, and scooped up Nina's phone.

"What was—wha—why did you do that?" Nina's voice no longer felt like it came from her own body. It floated, small and tinny and disembodied. "Wha—what the fuck was in that needle?"

Books by Bestselling Author
Fern Michaels

___**The Jury**	0-8217-7878-1	$6.99US/$9.99CAN
___**Sweet Revenge**	0-8217-7879-X	$6.99US/$9.99CAN
___**Lethal Justice**	0-8217-7880-3	$6.99US/$9.99CAN
___**Free Fall**	0-8217-7881-1	$6.99US/$9.99CAN
___**Fool Me Once**	0-8217-8071-9	$7.99US/$10.99CAN
___**Vegas Rich**	0-8217-8112-X	$7.99US/$10.99CAN
___**Hide and Seek**	1-4201-0184-6	$6.99US/$9.99CAN
___**Hokus Pokus**	1-4201-0185-4	$6.99US/$9.99CAN
___**Fast Track**	1-4201-0186-2	$6.99US/$9.99CAN
___**Collateral Damage**	1-4201-0187-0	$6.99US/$9.99CAN
___**Final Justice**	1-4201-0188-9	$6.99US/$9.99CAN
___**Up Close and Personal**	0-8217-7956-7	$7.99US/$9.99CAN
___**Under the Radar**	1-4201-0683-X	$6.99US/$9.99CAN
___**Razor Sharp**	1-4201-0684-8	$7.99US/$10.99CAN
___**Yesterday**	1-4201-1494-8	$5.99US/$6.99CAN
___**Vanishing Act**	1-4201-0685-6	$7.99US/$10.99CAN
___**Sara's Song**	1-4201-1493-X	$5.99US/$6.99CAN
___**Deadly Deals**	1-4201-0686-4	$7.99US/$10.99CAN
___**Game Over**	1-4201-0687-2	$7.99US/$10.99CAN
___**Sins of Omission**	1-4201-1153-1	$7.99US/$10.99CAN
___**Sins of the Flesh**	1-4201-1154-X	$7.99US/$10.99CAN
___**Cross Roads**	1-4201-1192-2	$7.99US/$10.99CAN

Available Wherever Books Are Sold!
Check out our website at **www.kensingtonbooks.com**

Romantic Suspense from
Lisa Jackson

Absolute Fear	0-8217-7936-2	$7.99US/$9.99CAN
Afraid to Die	1-4201-1850-1	$7.99US/$9.99CAN
Almost Dead	0-8217-7579-0	$7.99US/$10.99CAN
Born to Die	1-4201-0278-8	$7.99US/$9.99CAN
Chosen to Die	1-4201-0277-X	$7.99US/$10.99CAN
Cold Blooded	1-4201-2581-8	$7.99US/$8.99CAN
Deep Freeze	0-8217-7296-1	$7.99US/$10.99CAN
Devious	1-4201-0275-3	$7.99US/$9.99CAN
Fatal Burn	0-8217-7577-4	$7.99US/$10.99CAN
Final Scream	0-8217-7712-2	$7.99US/$10.99CAN
Hot Blooded	1-4201-0678-3	$7.99US/$9.49CAN
If She Only Knew	1-4201-3241-5	$7.99US/$9.99CAN
Left to Die	1-4201-0276-1	$7.99US/$10.99CAN
Lost Souls	0-8217-7938-9	$7.99US/$10.99CAN
Malice	0-8217-7940-0	$7.99US/$10.99CAN
The Morning After	1-4201-3370-5	$7.99US/$9.99CAN
The Night Before	1-4201-3371-3	$7.99US/$9.99CAN
Ready to Die	1-4201-1851-X	$7.99US/$9.99CAN
Running Scared	1-4201-0182-X	$7.99US/$10.99CAN
See How She Dies	1-4201-2584-2	$7.99US/$8.99CAN
Shiver	0-8217-7578-2	$7.99US/$10.99CAN
Tell Me	1-4201-1854-4	$7.99US/$9.99CAN
Twice Kissed	0-8217-7944-3	$7.99US/$9.99CAN
Unspoken	1-4201-0093-9	$7.99US/$9.99CAN
Whispers	1-4201-5158-4	$7.99US/$9.99CAN
Wicked Game	1-4201-0338-5	$7.99US/$9.99CAN
Wicked Lies	1-4201-0339-3	$7.99US/$9.99CAN
Without Mercy	1-4201-0274-5	$7.99US/$10.99CAN
You Don't Want to Know	1-4201-1853-6	$7.99US/$9.99CAN

Available Wherever Books Are Sold!
Visit our website at **www.kensingtonbooks.com**